AT THE BREAKFAST TABLE, Dioneo's surviving children couldn't stop talking about something that had happened in the skies early this morning. They hadn't seen it themselves, but they had heard the story from their housekeeper. Shortly after the last of the stars had disappeared, a white streak had ripped across the sky, as if the firmament could be split like the skin of a fruit.

By the time Niccoluccio had woken, it had long since disappeared. According to the people who had seen it, it had been like a comet's tail. Comets always heralded disaster.

Dioneo's children were struggling to determine what could be worse than the pestilence. Finally, they turned to Niccoluccio.

"Is this the end of days, uncle?" the oldest boy asked. He sounded as though he were asking if there would be fruit after breakfast.

"Never believe that," Niccoluccio said.

He ate the rest of his bread in silence while his nephew at once disregarded him. He'd hardly had to think about his answer. He didn't know what other people had seen, but he knew the end of days wouldn't look like that.

TRISTAN PALMGREN

Quietus

ANGRY
ROBOT

ANGRY ROBOT
An imprint of Watkins Media Ltd

20 Fletcher Gate,
Nottingham,
NG1 2FZ
UK

angryrobotbooks.com
twitter.com/angryrobotbooks
Watcher of the skies

An Angry Robot paperback original 2018

Cover by Dominic Harman
Set in Meridien by Argh! Nottingham

Distributed in the United States by Penguin Random House, Inc., New York.

ISBN 978 0 85766 743 4
Ebook ISBN 978 0 85766 744 1

Printed in the United States of America

9 8 7 6 5 4 3 2 1

To Charlotte and Gary
For putting up with me
while I pursued my fantasies

One news came straight huddling on another
Of death and death and death.

– JOHN FORD

Oh happy posterity who will not experience such abysmal woe
and will look upon our testimony as a fable.

– PETRARCH

PART I

1

There was no such thing as a quiet place in Messina, not at this time of morning. In the evening, the hours of the bell could be heard from one end of the harbor to the other. Now, the tolls didn't reach the shore. Shouting was the only way to be heard, and that made the cacophony worse.

It was a wonder that anyone could think. Habidah doubted they did. Everywhere she stepped, someone blocked her path, or trod on her shoe. She smiled tightly and shifted aside. On another day, she would have fought through. Today, she didn't trust herself enough to speak. She wouldn't have been heard if she tried.

Messina's streets followed no plan. They ran like dirt-scuffed streams through squat houses and businesses before finally emptying out into the docks. "Stream" was no poetic exaggeration – rivulets of waste ran down their sides, following the flow of traffic. Even the locals couldn't stand the odor. Women walked with cloth pinched over their noses.

A seaborne wind brought a moment's relief. It was cold, at least by Messina's standards. Smoke from heating fires stained the sky. Gray clouds scudded across the sky, low enough to touch. Winter would arrive early this year, as it had for all of the past six.

Closer to the port, the noise blended into a chorus, less background than a battering. Fish hawkers and vegetable stands jammed traffic at every intersection. More foul smells lingered about the carcasses hanging in a butcher's shop. A trio of alewives stood outside their shop, holding aloft wooden mugs and hollering. A sloppily painted red and white pole marked a barber-surgeon's shop. Blood streamed from a shallow pit where the barber had dumped his last patient's blood. Most people stepped over it.

Habidah paused. She'd spent weeks in the city, but she was still having trouble getting used to these things. It didn't bode well for her assignment. After an angry mutter from behind, she stepped over the blood and kept walking.

Traffic pushed Habidah onward. Few people noticed her. A lone woman in a dirty kirtle, thin and probably poor, didn't have any reason to be out here except to get in the way. She wasn't the first-choice target of the hawkers, but not a single person could step through Messina without attracting some manner of attention. A bruised-eyed boy, shod in cloth that must have been quite nice once, tugged at her scarf, to tell her about an inn with nice, fresh rushes.

He must have assumed she was a traveler. On every day but today, she'd been able to pass the locals' casual inspections. She was tempted to ask what had given her away, but she already had a good idea.

It had to be her eyes. She'd seen them in the reflection of her water basin this morning. They were dry but red, like a woman fleeing home.

She could see the ocean from here: a long, flat stretch of clear blue. Wonderful weather for sailing, and one of the last before winter's storms hit the Mediterranean. People knew it. They marched to the port like an army. Another knot of them blocked her path. Someone was selling mutton pies, freshly baked.

She should have waited for the crowd to disperse. On another day, she would have. She cast her eyes about. A fat, half-feral pig lay on pillows of its own fat, giving walkers a baleful eye. The locals instinctively shied away from it. She darted beside the pig, forging her way past before it could rouse itself to bite her.

She squelched through muddy runnels, down an alley guarded by a nest of rats. She emerged away from the worst of the morning's traffic, on a street that led to two small piers. The roofs of the houses around her were fungus-like stubs, barely more than head height. The beach was too unstable to hold any but the poorest homes. The sea lapped sand only two dozen meters from the last house.

The morning's ships had all arrived at the north end of the port, far from here. Their broad, brown sails were drab against the bright sea and sky. She picked the closest of the two empty piers and walked out onto it. A half-rotted crate made a reasonable seat.

When the cold wind shifted, she could smell the galleys even from here. The oarsmen didn't have toilet facilities. If they were slaves, they weren't ever allowed away from their benches.

Two more ships stood against the far horizon, making slow progress. Very slow, in the case of the farthest ship. Only a few of its oars moved. The winds languidly pushed its sail.

Even from this distance, the noise of the crowds at the north piers carried across the water. Her audio filtering programs isolated individual voices, gave her a sense of what was being discussed. The ships, as always, had brought news of the political turmoils on the mainland. More importantly, they'd brought meat, flour, oats, and cloth. The cloth got the most attention. Flemish cloth was as drab as the ships' sails, but among the finest-feeling and most affordable on this side of the world. People nearly pushed themselves into the water to get a closer look as the crates were offloaded. The galley's finely dressed captain let the Messinans get as close they wanted, driving up excitement.

Habidah retrieved a wooden cup from her folded clothes. Next, a thermos, taking care to hide the stainless steel underneath her sleeve. This was the kind of work that ordinarily demanded coffee, but the smell of coffee would have marked her as richer than she otherwise appeared. The tea she poured now, though, was a transplanar genengineered variant, transparent and mostly odorless.

She should have been able to do without. But the tea helped remind her that she was separate from all this. As far away as if she were watching from the stars above.

She should have been out earlier, watching and waiting. She'd need to spot the signs quickly. It would be subtle at first. She swallowed. What happened today would dictate so much of what came afterward.

"You be welcome here, lady."

She turned too fast to hide the fact that she'd been startled. She'd been too focused on the crowd. A fish-smelling man stood three meters away, wide-brimmed hat clasped in his hand. His clothes were filthy, but his face was clean, even his beard. He towered above her.

In a manner she hoped was dismissive enough, she said, "Our Lord give you a good day," and turned back.

He didn't take that as enough of a hint, and sat on a stump of a mooring. "I imagined I knew all of the fisherwives who used this pier."

"Do I look much like a fisherwife?" She had no pole or basket.

"Truly? You are not married?"

She turned again, expecting a lecherous smile. But he was frowning. Concerned, she realized. She said, "I'm no prostitute, either."

He leaned back with his hands against his seat. He had no fishing pole or basket, either, though he was dressed for a long day under the sun. "There's not much else to catch out here, besides fish and men."

"Except peace and contemplation," she said, significantly. He nodded sagely, and withheld further comment. He made no sign of leaving, though.

A low groan swept through the crowd as one of the captains shook hands with a merchant. That could only mean they'd made a deal for some large portion of his unsold cargo. The

Messinan had agreed too quickly. It was common practice among merchant captains to hide rotted cloth in the back.

People continued to gather around the empty piers, waiting for the still-distant late arrivals. Heavyset porters pushed their way through the crowd. One gangly merchant fell off the pier to jeers and laughter.

One of the new arrivals struggled against the sea. Its sails were in good shape, but it still languished a kilometer from shore. Even from a distance, she sensed the crowd's impatience.

A pit formed in the center of Habidah's stomach. She'd skipped breakfast. She'd known she wouldn't be hungry for long. Her team's observation satellites had tracked the Genoan galley's meandering journey up and down the Mediterranean. It was one of several merchant galleys, all Genoan, fleeing from farther east. She knew what the ship would look like before she saw it. She'd reviewed the images every morning. There were no mysteries left. Even still, there was a difference between recording and watching the ship with her own eyes.

For a moment, even with the docks' bustle and jostle, everything seemed so still.

The fisherman said, "If you're thinking about plunging in and not coming out – there are easier ways to accomplish what you're looking for. Less painful."

She looked back at him. He thought she'd come out here to commit suicide. She bit back a sharp word. She couldn't snap at him for being concerned. Seeing the becalmed ship out there had dampened her mood and even irritability.

Besides, it was important to find out why he'd said it. It could be relevant. "Do many people come here to drown themselves?" she asked.

"Once in a great while," he admitted.

There would be many more in the next weeks and months. "Don't worry about me, sir. There are plenty of women, and men, worse off."

"I don't often see many who look as frightened as you did just then."

She ought to be feeling safer than anyone in Messina. Before she could think of anything to say to that, he asked, "May I hear your name?"

It took her a moment to remember this month's alias. "Joanna."

"Joanna…?"

"Just Joanna," she said. Another time, she would have stopped there. Today was different. She owed him something, even if only an honest answer. "That's all we decided on. Nobody is supposed to ask about the rest. I'm meant to blend into the background."

He looked back out to sea, as if what she'd said was entirely reasonable. And then back at her as it sank in. "You sound like you're a spy."

The peoples of the coast lived in fear of Muslim pirates, and for good reason. Many of the oarsmen on these galleys were probably Muslim slaves captured in raids on North Africa, and the Muslims returned the favor in kind. Habidah had lightened her naturally dark skin tone specifically for this assignment.

"I just know too much."

"Most people I find here know too little." He was trying to brush this off as a joke. He must think her a madwoman. These people had curious ideas about mental illness. If she could convince him that she was in some way blessed, then she might be able to do him a favor. She wasn't supposed to, but she couldn't help herself.

She nodded out to sea. He followed her gaze to the last ship, the one still floundering at sea. She said, "It doesn't matter if the breeze is calm out there. Good oarsmen ought to be making better progress than that."

He nodded, after a moment. It hadn't occurred to him, or probably to many of the people standing and waiting for it to arrive. Her eyesight was better than any of the locals', but the ship was near enough that, unless he was nearsighted, he should be able to see the unmoving oars, too.

She said, "That's because most of the oarsmen are dead.

16

Their bodies were thrown overboard between here and its last few ports. The captain will claim they were caught in a storm and his men drowned, but, really, he just wants to sell his cargo and move on. It's losing value every day. That's all that's important to him."

"How do you know all of this?"

"That's what they did on their last stops, too. All the way from Caffa through Byzantium and other Greek ports."

"You came on another ship?"

"No. I just saw them, that's all."

He shifted, visibly uncomfortable. He was about to leave. A minute ago, she would have welcomed that, but now her pulse beat against her temples. "The missing oarsmen died horribly," she said. She loosened her wimple and tapped her neck. "Black growths like little lentils grew on their necks and on their thighs. Then came fever and vomiting. It happened very quickly, and spread fast. Many of them went from feeling fine to dead in less than a day. Eventually, when the next oarsman vomited or seemed dizzy, his compatriots just threw him overboard."

The fisherman stared at her for a long moment. He played along with her long enough to say, "Any ship with a crew in that state would be turned away from port at once."

"*If* you spotted it in time. The dead oarsmen are gone, but you'd be able to smell it, if you were aboard. That many dying men will leave signs that can't all be thrown overboard. Some of the crew, the higher-ranking ones, and the merchants weren't tossed overboard, either. They're being taken home for burial." At least that was the idea. The galley probably wouldn't make it that far. "You can find them if you look. It won't take people long to realize something's wrong, but then it will be too late."

The locals weren't stupid. Once they realized what had happened, they would respond quickly, take all the quarantines and precautions their knowledge and capabilities allowed.

It just wouldn't be enough.

The fisherman sat silent. He looked at her as if she were a

gull who'd begun to speak. Now that she'd started talking, she couldn't make herself stop: "You need to get out of the city. Take anyone you care about with you. There are still places you could go, even on an island. Don't come back if you can avoid it."

"You should not tell anyone else this," the fisherman said. "We've seen too many false prophets and doomsayers. Nobody has patience for them. Some here might just throw you to the sea if you mistake us for gullible."

"You're right. I *shouldn't* have told you this. I know you can't believe me. But, when it starts, remember. The sooner you run, the better your chances."

She held his gaze. She hoped her eyes were still as red as they had been this morning. Every day she spent here, she felt like she'd spent it crying, but the sea air made her eyes so dry they itched.

After a moment, he *tssked*, stood, and walked back to shore.

She breathed out.

Looking back at the crowd around the docks, she supposed that shouldn't have surprised her. The Messinans were as skeptical as any people who lived by trade.

Her cheeks cooled. Her pulse stopped pounding against her ears. She couldn't let that happen again. Now, more than ever, she needed her attention focused on the docks, on the ship struggling to port. If any of her team found out–

"God keep you," she muttered at the fisherman. Messina was far from the coldest place on Earth, but she retightened her wimple.

A cluster of boys had gotten into a fight. The youngest – a crow-haired boy who couldn't be more than seven – burst out of the group, clutching a bloody nose and sobbing. The other boys gave chase. Passersby didn't pay any more attention than it took to avoid them.

The crowds were only growing thicker. So many crates and sacks had come out of the galleys already, and the porters were still unloading. Most of the cargo was already spoken for, carried to Messinan merchants who'd contracted them. That didn't stop the captains from auctioning off some goods right on the wharf. All in the interests of advertising. Some men forcing their way back through the crowd were already wearing new, dark brown cloth, or carrying bundles of fruit.

The Genoan galley had almost reached port. People must have started to notice how few of the oars were moving, but Habidah couldn't detect any disquiet from this distance. Perhaps she should have gone closer. Even after all these years on the job, that was a question she still wrestled with. Would she get a more accurate picture by infiltrating the crowd, identifying and understanding its members, or was her time better spent trying to understand the aggregate? She hated to admit that she'd let her roiling stomach resolve the question. She didn't want to be that close. Not today. Even with that fisherman, she'd nearly lost herself.

On her other assignments, she'd never been in danger of losing control like that. She wasn't here to meddle. If anyone at her university had heard what she'd just said, she would have been in mounds of trouble. Maybe sent back home.

The wind shifted, carrying more noises and odors from the northern docks, more data than she could sift through at the moment. A quick flutter of thought instructed her demiorganics to begin recording. The shift was almost imperceptible, a slight sharpening of her vision. All of her senses were now being routed through the cluster of processors nestled behind her ventral intraparietal cortex. Her demiorganics captured everything: the cold wind on her cheeks, the flutter of her scarf around her neck, the smell of saltwater and fish.

She hoped that nobody back in the Unity would notice her raw throat or the tightness of her breath.

Of course, all of the data would be sent to the amalgamates at one point or another. *They* wouldn't miss it.

They couldn't expect her to be perfectly impartial about this. They would have sent drones if they wanted impartiality. Still, they had standards.

Throughout her career, she'd been able to distance herself from her subjects as well as anyone could. This was different. This was the worst thing any tragedy could be: familiar. This city's tragedy had hardly begun, and already she'd felt like she'd lived through it all.

It was too much like what was happening back home.

A cheer ran the length of the crowd. The last galley was less than two lengths from the dock. The captain perched on the prow, holding aloft a box of pearls and perfumes, tilted to let people see. Merchants forced their way to the front of the crowd, already instructing their porters where to stand to receive the cargo.

Even with the recording going, she couldn't keep herself from muttering, "God keep us all."

2

When the precentor took his place for morning Lauds, there were still three empty seats in the church choir. Niccoluccio glanced through the open door. No hint of them in the cloister walk, either. He was the only one to look. The other brothers silently raised their seat lids. If they knew anything about what had happened, of course they could not say.

Then the precentor began reciting the Lord's Prayer, beginning the Divine Office. The empty seats dropped away from Niccoluccio's mind. It was enough of an effort to stay awake. A steady weight grew behind his eyes. He'd had difficulty finding sleep again after the nightly Vigils.

He had thought that, by now, his body should be used to rousing two hours after midnight. He had spent most of the night staring at the wood slats overlying his cell. He couldn't explain the unease that settled over him then. It felt like the shadow of a cloud crossing the moon. A chill draft carried under the door, one of the many heavy breaths of winter.

Some of the unease lingered into Lauds, but this time it was easy to explain away as exhaustion. When he was allowed to open his eyes, he surreptitiously glanced around the back of the seats, looking for any of the leftover peppercorns the other brothers chewed during Vigils to help them stay awake. There were none.

He steeled himself to push through the hymns and the psalms. By the time the precentor fell silent, he was nearly awake again. A moment of silence lingered in the choir. Niccoluccio rose to his feet with the other brothers. The novices left first. Niccoluccio waited his turn to join the procession filing out. His choir neighbor, the German monk Gerbodo, silently fell into place alongside him.

Out in the cloister's daylight, Niccoluccio almost felt better again. The cold wind was at once uncomfortable and purifying – stepping out into it was like splashing cold water on his face. Sacro Cuore's founders had meant for the cloister walk to be symbolic of Paradise. Frost fringed the grass in the center. The sunlight was beautiful, but so bright that it was impossible, even reflected in the snow, to look at for longer than an instant.

The glare hid the state of most of the buildings around him. The Sacro Cuore Charterhouse was not the place it had once been – at least, not according to the older brothers' tales. The monastery had been built to keep a watch on the Via Romea di Stade, a pilgrim's road that ran through northern Tuscany. It lent shelter to, and took donations from, travelers on their way to the Holy City. Today, with the papacy relocated to Avignon, and Rome ruled by mobs, few people traveled the old pilgrimage road. But Sacro Cuore remained.

Sacro Cuore's water clock had been replaced with a new mechanical device, but everything else just kept getting older. The infirmary's roof still sagged from the weight of last year's snow. The brothers who'd spent more than a night there said they forced themselves to feel better just to get away from the drafts.

The library had once been its own building, but, as Sacro Cuore's numbers dwindled, too many of the books had been sold to other monasteries. Now the "library" was in a cupboard in the chapter house on the east side of the cloister.

The dormitory stood to the east. Two of the monastery's dogs sunned themselves beside it. The building seemed fine from the outside, but most of the cells stood empty and dust-ridden, with rushes that hadn't been changed in years. Only the rooms still in use were cleaned. Decades ago, the monastery had housed over one hundred brothers. Now fifty-two, plus seven novices, lived inside its walls. The community of laymen who helped with fieldwork had shrunk by a similar proportion.

Niccoluccio could see the disrepair if he looked closely, but he didn't care to. With the exception of the infirmary's roof, Sacro Cuore had looked like this the day he'd arrived, twelve years ago. All the elder brothers' tales of more affluent days were just sand in his ears. He was one of the few of the younger brothers who'd come here knowing what to expect.

Niccoluccio glanced instead to the seyney house, where all the monastery's bloodletting took place. His last bloodletting had been only a month ago. The memory still made him queasy. The infirmarer nearly hadn't been able to close Niccoluccio's vein in time, and Niccoluccio had fainted watching. But he *had* felt better afterward. The other brothers had all left pale and lightheaded, but significantly less burdened by their hot blood and bad humors. After a bloodletting, the air felt cooler, food sweeter, and sleep deeper and less troubled by dreams. Even Brother Lomellini, their old goat of a prior, always breathed easier after a bloodletting.

Maybe that was what he needed to put this bad temper behind him. His stomach instinctively clenched at the thought of it. But last night's disquiet had been unlike anything he'd felt since his last bleed. It could only have come from some deep, hateful restlessness within him.

His body had been born in order to be mortified. Every year that passed in Sacro Cuore, he understood that a little better. If his body recoiled at the memory, then that was a sign that he needed to force it onward.

Most of other brothers glided towards their cells for contemplation before Prime, the next of the Divine Offices after Lauds. Niccoluccio turned away from the procession, and toward the infirmary. The infirmarer had been one of the three brothers absent from Lauds, and he might find him there.

A gentle hand on his shoulder stopped him.

Gerbodo stood beside him, his hood raised. A short, brown

23

fuzz stood out between the ring of hair that circled the rest of his head. He was overdue for another tonsuring. He gently pulled Niccoluccio back into the procession.

In the otherwise-voiceless environment of the monastery, Gerbodo had become Niccoluccio's natural companion. They spoke as often as two Carthusian brothers could – perhaps twice a week. There was no opportunity to exchange words now, though. They were too close to the other brothers.

Once again, disquiet cast its shadow. Niccoluccio frowned, but let Gerbodo lead him away. Gerbodo's lips were locked in a tight line.

Back in his cell, Niccoluccio was left alone with the library's copy of Saint Jerome's *Letters*. He paged through the book for several minutes, recalling passages from memory. He strolled to the back door, to his little garden, and sifted through the dirt. He knew better than to try meditation in this state. Instead, he dug little furrows in the soil with his fingers, tending the garden as if it were still summer.

Silence permeated the rest of his day. It was comfortable, familiar, but for once stifling rather than liberating. Words had to wait until supper, in the refectory.

The brothers of Sacro Cuore ate as a group once a week, on Sundays. On other days, like today, they were left to their own devices. Niccoluccio was returning from his evening inspection of the novices' dormitory when he spied Gerbodo taking a quick turn toward the refectory door. Gerbodo glanced once in Niccoluccio's direction, and then disappeared inside. Niccoluccio made discreet haste to follow.

The refectory was as plain inside as out: wood walls, floors littered with rushes that hadn't been changed in weeks, and endlessly chilly. Niccoluccio and Gerbodo silently dipped their hands into the *lavatorium* basin. The cold water was a bracing shock. Dirt slaked off Gerbodo's hands. Niccoluccio wondered what he'd been up to all day.

Warm gusts issued from the kitchen door. Four brothers and one novice sat at the tables nearest the kitchen, eating in silence. Niccoluccio frowned. Usually, this close to Vespers, it was much busier. Brother Stefano, an older monk balding even below his tonsure line, drifted from the kitchen. He looked expectantly at Niccoluccio and Gerbodo. Niccoluccio signed a circle in the air with his forefinger, and then tugged at his pinkie, the signs for bread and milk.

During Sunday meals, Prior Lomellini enforced the brothers' silence with a reading from scripture. Right now, the brothers had nothing but their own consciences to keep them quiet. Niccoluccio and Gerbodo sat far from the others. After a quick glance at them, Gerbodo muttered one word: "Pestilence."

"I…" It had been so long since the last time Niccoluccio had tried to speak that he needed a moment to find his voice. "I wouldn't have disturbed any brothers resting in the infirmary."

Gerbodo looked at him as though he were a particularly ignorant child. "Not sickness," he said. "*Pestilence.*"

Now it was Niccoluccio's turn to give him a strange look. He couldn't help the feeling of sinking in his stomach. It probably showed.

Gerbodo asked, "You haven't heard?"

There was very little to "hear" in the cloisters of most Carthusian monasteries. Outside of prayer and clandestine meetings like this, the brothers only spoke during their communal meetings at the chapter house. Niccoluccio had missed the last two meetings, first to take his turn in the kitchen, and then to inspect the storehouses before winter.

The other brothers had seemed more withdrawn than usual recently. He'd attributed it to the end of autumn and the lack of travelers. Gerbodo said, "You need to pay more attention to the whispers."

Brother Stefano asked, just as quietly, "And how often do you whisper?"

Niccoluccio reddened. He hadn't heard the whisper of Stefano's robes beside him. Ordinarily, such a noise never would have escaped his attention. Stefano watched them archly, like they were a pair of novices. Lines underscored the older man's eyes. After a moment, he set their bread and milk in front of them.

"This is a time to make peace with God," he said, and strode back into the kitchen.

Niccoluccio looked down, not daring to meet Gerbodo's eyes again. Gerbodo had spoken of whispers. How often did he and the other monks speak? Niccoluccio certainly had never been invited to hear them.

Gerbodo curled his fingers into claw crooks and drew them across his eyes, as if rending them. Niccoluccio hadn't seen the sign very often. It was the brothers' universal sign for trouble and disaster.

The pit in the center of his chest lingered through Vespers and the nightly Compline service. The three empty seats in the church remained unfilled. The infirmarer's seat, too, remained empty. When the last of the Divine Office ended, Niccoluccio saw several of the other brothers glance at them when they could. Gerbodo kept his gaze lowered, and wouldn't look at Niccoluccio.

Niccoluccio sat beside his wooden bed. Usually a moment's peace and meditation helped him sleep. He went through the motions, knowing it wouldn't help. All the sounds of the night impeded his concentration: the shifting and creaking of floorboards as the brothers settled in, the scrabbling of the rats who quartered with them.

He heard no whispers, or any discreet footsteps from one cell to another. Gerbodo had said that the other brothers spoke often, but it must not have been at night. By design, the slightest movements were audible to everyone in the hall.

Niccoluccio had never quite fit in among his cohort. He was too young, too ready for monastic living. The other brothers had come here later in life, after they'd chased other goals, and usually failed. He and Gerbodo had been novices together, but Gerbodo was ten years older than him.

To his father's dismay, Niccoluccio had wanted nothing other than to be a monk since he was sixteen. There had already been too much to put behind him. He'd come when he'd turned twenty-two, the youngest any Carthusian charterhouse would accept him.

He was avoiding the real problem. He knew now where last night's disquiet had originated. The peace of the monastery was always replete with noises, even now. The susurration of the wind, padding of footsteps, clearing of throats, coughing, the endless creak of the floorboards.

He may not have been a part of Gerbodo's network of chatterers, but that didn't mean he wasn't in touch with everything around him. He had been here twelve years. Every part of Sacro Cuore was more familiar than his own toes. Today and yesterday, something had been wrong. The dormitory had been quieter, as if the brothers had been afraid to leave their cells.

Niccoluccio climbed into bed fully clothed, keeping his cowl up until he'd pulled the sheet past his elbows. He hadn't counted on sleeping, but he startled awake at a sharp rapping in the cloister. It was the sacrist, beating his wooden *tabula* to call the brothers for Vigils.

He shuffled into the church in darkness. The brothers lit no candles. Prior Lomellini led the prayers by memory, his voice sharp enough to keep Niccoluccio awake all by itself. Even surrounded by shadows, Niccoluccio could see that the empty seats remained unfilled, and the infirmarer hadn't joined them.

He could detect no change in Prior Lomellini's voice, but the rest of the choir was oddly quiet. He heard no stifled yawns, no chewing of peppercorns. All the brothers, even the novices, were wide awake two hours past midnight.

Only a few minutes after the next morning's Lauds, the sacrist stood in front of the chapter house and once again beat his stick against his *tabula*. A summons to a communal meeting. Most of the other brothers had somehow contrived to be nearby the chapter house. Niccoluccio was one of the last to arrive, once again wondering how word spread.

The chapter house only had a few articles of furniture: a table with several chairs, and three rows of benches facing it. Prior Lomellini and the monastery's other office-holders – including, Niccoluccio noted, the infirmarer, Brother Rinieri, who looked exhausted – were already around the table. Niccoluccio took a seat on the rear benches.

Lomellini's gaze passed over each of them, as if to mark their faces. The brothers' tonsures, hoods, and identical rough robes deemphasized their individuality. Lomellini's eyes flickered over Niccoluccio only a moment. Niccoluccio was taller than all but a few of the brothers. Even sitting behind two rows of brothers, he had no problem seeing the front.

Lomellini stood. He had always struck Niccoluccio as disturbingly political for a monk. Niccoluccio had known no time here free of him. He had once been Niccoluccio's novice-master. Shortly after Niccoluccio had graduated from his novitiate, the old prior died and Lomellini succeeded him. Lomellini peered at the brothers cannily; not like a father judging his children, but a guard hound sizing up an intruder.

Carthusian monasteries had no abbots. Lomellini was the prior in charge of the chapter house. Unlike the abbots of the Florentine monasteries Niccoluccio visited as a child, Lomellini showed no symptoms of the privileges of his position. No wide girth, no soft and flabby cheeks or jowls. He had a prominent, horse-like nose and a sharp jaw. Wisps of gray hair floated out from under his hood. He might have been naturally balding, but his tonsure made it impossible to tell.

"The news you have heard is true," he said, abruptly. "Two of our number have been stricken by the Genoan pestilence."

The silence was, on its surface, identical to the silence that preceded it, and that which was the natural state of affairs at Sacro Cuore. Nevertheless, Niccoluccio read a hundred flickering emotions in it. He looked straight ahead, refusing to look at any brother.

Lomellini said, "A number of you have come to me in confidence and asked for leave to depart. I have many reasons to decline these requests. However, as news continues to reach us, the circumstances seem to override those reasons."

He seemed to be searching for something else to say, but couldn't find it. Two novices in the back row whispered something to each other. Lomellini did not spare any harsh looks for them, itself a sign of the gravity of the situation. A pair of brothers took that as license to do the same.

From the whisperings and from Lomellini's words later, Niccoluccio was able to piece together the news that had reached the charterhouse.

A pestilence of incredible mortality had descended upon the Italian coast. It had started only weeks ago, and already swept inland as fast as a crow in flight. Its speed made Niccoluccio feel a little better about having missed the news until now. The reports must have only reached Sacro Cuore days ago, especially since most travelers this time of year came from the north, on Christmas pilgrimages to Rome. A handful came from the south, though. Now, it seemed the travelers who'd brought the news had also carried the pestilence with them. The speed of it had plainly caught Prior Lomellini by surprise. He'd probably thought he'd had more time to prepare. Niccoluccio had never seen him falter for control of the room.

Niccoluccio tried to remain unmoved. Surely these stories were exaggerated. Yet they all agreed upon the symptoms of the disease. The stricken developed black bulbs on their legs, or neck, or in the pits underneath their arms. The growths were exquisitely painful, and, more strangely, loud. They gurgled like water circling a drain. They couldn't be popped like pustules, and the bearers would do anything to keep anyone from trying.

Brother Durante claimed to have heard from their lay stablekeeper that two out of every three men in Genoa had perished, and that no child survived in Orvieto. Pietro, a novice, called the pustules "death's tokens." He said that anyone who had them would perish within a day.

Niccoluccio remained sitting, his hands folded in his lap. The best way to weather this storm, like all storms, was to let it pass over him. He would not participate in this breach of decorum. He kept his gaze fixed on Lomellini.

The prior cleared his throat. Somehow he managed to be louder in that than anyone else in the room. The novices fell silent. "Brother Rainuccio, Brother Durante, Brother Gerbodo, I have heard your requests and am willing to give them proper public consideration."

A seat ahead, Gerbodo shifted uncomfortably. Here were Lomellini's political instincts: not only had Lomellini singled out the brothers who had come to him in private, but he held up a finger before any of them could speak: "I must caution you, however. We have no place for you to go. There are no transfers to other charterhouses available this year, and, by the judgment of our Father, they would likely be afflicted by this same pestilence.

"We must decide as a community – as a single body – how to react to this emergency. With death ravaging the coasts, we may shortly be inundated with refugees. They will need shelter and succor, the aid of Christ's body. However, they will also no doubt be bringing their affliction with them. I will not decide for you how you will face this crisis. I have called you here to ask each of you, in turn, how you will answer your calling."

Lomellini turned to the infirmarer, Brother Rinieri. Rinieri was the youngest of the chapter house's office-holders – which did not mean he was young. He answered at once. "I can do no better work elsewhere than here. Whatever will be done is God's will." He had clearly rehearsed his answer.

The sacrist was next: "God's will does not need my permission. If I shall die of the pestilence, I shall die regardless of where I am. I would rather die serving."

The precentor, the novice-master, and the almoner took their turns. Like the other senior office-holders, they'd clearly known what to expect of this meeting, and had already assembled their answer.

The cellarer, the brother in charge of the monastery's

supplies, was the last to speak. "I would like to take my leave for reasons which I have discussed in private with the prior." He cast his gaze briefly to Lomellini, and then to the floor.

Silence followed. So, Lomellini's control of the officers wasn't as complete as he wanted everyone to believe. Niccoluccio kept his gaze rigidly focused on the wall.

It was left to the almoner, the brother in charge of tending to poor visitors, to announce the obvious: the monastery's meager winter supplies couldn't cope with many additional travelers or refugees, certainly not if they were sick. He said, "We should send a messenger to the bishop to request additional financial resources."

Brother Rainuccio, one of those Lomellini had singled out earlier, stood and humbly bowed. "I would like to volunteer for that assignment."

Lomellini said, after a moment, "The pestilence travels swiftly. That duty would likely expose whoever volunteered to travel to more danger than staying. That goes without mentioning the ordinary hardships of travel during winter."

Rainuccio said, "My offer to serve stands."

Brother Rainuccio could hardly make the perilous journey alone. Niccoluccio swallowed. If he volunteered now, he would surely get chosen to go with Rainuccio.

Barring trips to the lay community a mile away, Niccoluccio hadn't set foot outside Sacro Cuore in twelve years. He'd had several opportunities. He could have transferred, traveled as a messenger to the bishop, or gone to purchase supplies. He hadn't wanted to. Until this moment.

The moment passed. Brother Arrigheto stood and said, simply, "I wish to accompany Brother Rainuccio." The monks around him tried to hide their relief. Niccoluccio breathed out. A little of the burden of the choice lifted off his shoulders.

Brother Durante, the second monk Lomellini had mentioned, stood on trembling legs. "I have a great anxiety about this pestilence," he said, and then hesitated under Lomellini's gaze. For a moment, he seemed unsure about what he'd planned to

31

say next. "However, I will serve in any capacity my superiors desire."

Then on through the brothers. Most echoed Durante, deferring their decision to Lomellini, which was as good as saying they would stay. Gerbodo was next. As he was the last of the brothers Lomellini had singled out, everyone's attention fixed on him. He said, "God's grace delivered me here, and I trust that God's grace will deliver us from pestilence. If not here, then in the kingdom of our salvation." He sounded sincere enough, but he didn't meet Lomellini's eyes. After he returned to his seat, he stared ahead at nothing, as if his thoughts had left his body.

Niccoluccio stood when his turn arrived. Not all of the brothers had, but it was only proper. As before, he needed a moment to find his voice.

He thought he'd known what he was going to say until the moment arrived. The words came before he realized he needed to say them. "If it is necessary that I die, then I will die, as we all eventually must. 'Every day we are changing, every day we are dying, and yet we fancy ourselves eternal.' As with every other worldly thing, this pestilence is the Father's will. Moreso, and more long-lasting, is this brotherhood. We are made brothers here by our shared love of Christ. I am nothing without Sacro Cuore. I will not run from it."

He only realized near the end that everyone was watching him. After a moment's hesitation, he returned to his seat. Then it was the next brother's turn to speak.

It took several minutes for the flush to leave Niccoluccio's cheeks. He felt dizzy. He couldn't remember the last time he'd spoken so long. There was more to this headiness, though, than the act of making sound.

Only the novices weren't allowed to speak. The prior spoke for them. The only way for them to leave Sacro Cuore was to give up their vows, and Lomellini clearly wasn't about to offer them the opportunity. In total, besides Rainuccio and Arrigheto, only two brothers requested leave of the charterhouse.

32

The cellarer said nothing, kept his eyes downcast, when Lomellini announced that the charterhouse could not spare supplies for travel for anyone but Rainuccio and Arrigheto. Any other brothers who wished to leave would have to do so with their own resources. In the midst of winter, that meant not leaving at all. They all lived in imitation of Christ's poverty.

Niccoluccio and the other monks followed the officers out in the reverse of the order that they'd arrived. The novices trailed everyone else. Every brother had their own chores. The others were already going their separate ways, off to their own worlds.

Niccoluccio returned to his cell and sat with folded legs. He focused on his copy of the *Letters of St Jerome*, not really reading even the passage he had quoted to the others. He had just managed to slip into a meditative trance when the sacrist began beating his *tabula* outside again.

Niccoluccio had gotten all the way to the church when he realized that no one was following him. He glanced to the mechanical clock at the edge of the cloister. It was too early for Prime. Yet the sacrist was standing outside the infirmary, still beating his wooden *tabula*. Others gathered around him.

Niccoluccio's wits needed time to catch up with him. His stomach sank as though he were falling. The sacrist was drumming a pattern of beats Niccoluccio had only heard a few times before. It was a different kind of announcement, signifying the death of a brother.

3

On the day Habidah had arrived in Messina, she'd rented a room in a quiet little wayfarer's lodge a few houses away from a church. She visited only to sleep. Thanks to genengineering, she needed only three hours' rest per day. Now that her observation had begun in earnest, she got by on one and a half, and substituted stimulants and neurochemical reprofiling for the remainder. She paid for it with a leaden weight behind her eyes.

Surrounded by so much misery, she hardly noticed, and certainly didn't complain. She needed to be about at all hours, watching, studying. Even ninety minutes could have meant the difference between returning with useful data, or nothing at all.

Her work took her through the docks and whorehouses and moored ships of dead and dying, to the parish churches and cathedral, to the homes of the wealthy merchants. She visited hospitals no longer tended by any living nurses. The hospitals had hardly been safe or sanitary before the plague, but now they were just repositories for the bodies of strangers, living or dead, discovered in the streets. She walked through the ashen remains of a whole block of slums the city authorities had burned to try to contain the plague. She'd gone to packed churches, filled with endless processions, prayers, pleas for help, and watched the plague spread seed there, too.

On the seventh day after the Genoan plague ship arrived,

her landlord had died, along with his wife and five out of his six children. Their street's priest had shipped the sixth, a nine year-old boy, dead-eyed and silent to the nearest orphanage. The priest had hardly looked at him, hadn't touched him for fear of infection. She lost track of what happened to the boy, though she knew the overpacked orphanages also festered with plague.

When she came back to her cozy little room, no one came for rent. No one told her to leave, either. No one seemed to own the house at all anymore. The church down the street still saw traffic, but it was neighbored by empty houses, abandoned or sealed and occupied only by the dead. Not only had the owners died, but so had any inheritors foolish enough to visit and survey the property.

Her daily walks took her past mass graves on the peninsula outside the city. The lots of misshapen, crow-pecked earth looked like they'd come from another plane. She tightened her scarf against the cold wind and broken gray skies, and hurried past. She was here to study the living, not the dead. But the dead were everywhere.

Everyone but the gravediggers stayed away from the graveyards. It wasn't just the smell that repelled them. Or the faces and broken, shovel-smashed limbs poking through the soil. Or even the fact of the mass graves themselves, antithetical as they were to the religious sensibilities of the people. It was the danger. Habidah had seen wild dogs wander into the graveyards to scavenge and come back hours later, pestilential and drooling bloody foam.

The most interesting thing she'd found so far had been outside Messina's cathedral, the Duomo of Santa Maria Assunta. A mob had surrounded a visiting ecclesiastic. They'd begged him to bring the relics of St Agatha from his town, Catania. They were convinced that only the mercy of a saint could save them. They clung to his robes like foam in a tidal pool. He'd tried to leave, but had finally needed to push and kick. He'd shouted that God had cursed them, that no Messinan would be welcome inside the walls of Catania, and that the relics of St Agatha would be protecting Catania instead. The riot hadn't been long following that.

Now there was talk about a compromise solution, about dipping the relics of St Agatha in holy water and then bringing the holy water here. A last-ditch transference of holy mercy. It was amazing, the amount of effort and hope put into the effort. They saw no other defense short of fleeing, and fleeing usually just spread the plague farther.

These were the kind of stories she was here to find. Her satellites filled in the statistics. A month ago, Messina in infrared had been bright orange with fires and body heat. Now the glow had gone blotchy. Whole neighborhoods had been abandoned, or close to it. The living stayed indoors, far from their neighbors. Every day, the city got dimmer.

She hadn't been ready for any of it. She'd known, going in, that she wouldn't be. Even that helped a little bit. Her demiorganics were working extra duty combating exhaustion and keeping her brain chemistry from spiraling into depression.

She was out again, and had just passed an ivy-wreathed merchant's house, when a tremor buzzed the edge of her thoughts. A call, flagged important. Someone trying to get her attention.

Joao sent, "Habidah."

"I'm here," she said.

"So you *are* still with us. Have you been listening to the chatter?"

Habidah had been dimly aware of her team's voices in the back of her head, but she hadn't really listened to any of them. Joao was supposed to have just finished a long-term observation at Constantinople. The location tag appended to his datastream claimed he was calling from seventy kilometers south of Lyon: their field base.

She was in charge of her little team. She should have been paying closer attention. "I've been busy," she sent. "Did I miss anything important?"

"The Genoan ships are still seaborne. I thought you'd have something to say about that."

Habidah stopped walking. *Still?* They were nearly dead the last time I saw them."

"Never underestimate merchants sitting on depreciating cargo."

"I don't believe it," she sent. "The one I saw was barely moving. I'd started to think it wouldn't make Messina."

"Check the satellite feeds yourself. We have another satellite crossing that part of the Mediterranean in, ah, seventeen minutes."

"I didn't say I thought you were lying. Never mind." She kept forgetting that Joao had been raised on a Core World. Its inhabitants were raised by NAIs more than by humans, and tended to be literal-minded. "Hell. Where next?"

"Three of the ships returned to Genoa. The Genoans kicked them out in time. We haven't detected any plague transmission there. Other cities weren't so quick. Another of the plague ships is close to making port in Marseilles. And it looks like the one you saw is headed toward the Iberian Peninsula."

"Keep tracking them." The rest of her anthropological survey team must have been sharing news for hours, and she'd never noticed. After the past few days, it seemed very distant. But this would alter all they'd predicted of the plague's spread overland. "You've already rescheduled everyone?"

"Mmhmm. Meloku just arrived. You'll get the shuttle next."

"I've already got just about everything I need from here, anyway."

She rested her hand on the lip of an abandoned wagon. She hadn't quite told the truth. It would have been valuable to stay in Messina to see what happened with the relics and how people responded when they didn't stop the plague. She hardly wanted to stay here longer, anyway. Not that where she ended up next would be much better.

She eyed the merchant's house. Its owner was one of those who'd fought over the Flemish cloth. She'd kept track. A quick infrared scan showed only a single person inside. The thermal signature matched the maid's. Mistress of the house, now. Habidah had spotted her wearing her employers' clothes and jewelry. There was no one to stop her any more than there was anyone to collect rent for Habidah's lodge.

Habidah turned. She trudged southward under a cold and empty evening, her hands drawn into her sleeves. Her course took her along the piers, and then the gray beach outside the city. The cacophony was gone. The piers were empty. The fish sellers' stalls were deserted. The only ships were far away, moored and quarantined for the duration.

The bulk of the city disappeared behind the hills. There were still plenty of people in Messina, but it was hard to resist the impression that she'd left Messina deserted but for graves. On the day she'd arrived, she'd been able to hear the noises of the city even from here. Now, there was just the wind.

Eventually, she was alone under an encroaching twilight. Houses stood about her, but infrared revealed that none were occupied.

She stopped in a little cove, looked up, and waited.

A patch of gray sky rippled. A dark, smooth shape resolved out of the clouds. It was fuzzy at the edges, as if just coming into focus on a bad camera. Its hull was inky black and broadly wedge-shaped, but that was all the impression that crept through the camouflage fields. By the time it extruded landing struts and settled onto the rocks, Habidah still hadn't quite managed to make it out. The sounddampening field was even more effective. She couldn't hear the hiss of the landing jets until she stepped up to it.

As she stepped through the camouflage fields, there was a brief and disconcerting moment in which her vision went foggy. Then everything solidified at once, and she could see the whole craft. The ventral thrusters hissed in her ears, and their ice-cold wind brushed her cheek.

The shuttle came in low, a swooping blackbird. The craft was slender at the nose and bulkier in the rear, where its engines and sensor packages were housed. It possessed what Habidah privately considered an excessive number of wings. But it was a multipurpose craft, a university rental, designed to be as much at home in the liquid metal core of a gas giant or the corona of a star as a terrestrial atmosphere. Its long, narrow wings rippled with exhaust. It spotlighted her. A boarding ramp extended from its belly.

She strode up. For all the craft's bulk, there was surprisingly little space inside. The bulkheads were as dark as the hull. A tiny corridor divided a passenger cabin, a lavatory, and a sleeping space that doubled as personal storage. The rear bulkheads hid cargo compartments, but they weren't pressurized. This shuttle had been designed to be tolerable for a few days, maybe as long as a week. A service vehicle, nothing more.

The passenger cabin held three acceleration couches, all empty. A handful of displays with exterior camera views ringed the bulkheads. The images could have been sent to any passenger's demiorganics, but not all at once – not without overstressing their visual cortices. The monitors were the shuttle's one concession to creature comforts.

There was no one else aboard. The shuttle NAI didn't even wait for her to finish settling into the middle couch before running through the liftoff routine. It was punctilious about its schedules. Like all NAIs, it didn't have the creativity to be otherwise.

Habidah's demiorganics opened a datastream to it. It slid into the back of her awareness at once. Talking to NAIs was not like talking to humans. It never would be. NAIs, neutered AIs, held true to their names. They were as complex as humans, often more so, but held back from making the final leap to self-awareness and ambition. They made for discussion as interesting as a calculator's.

Habidah's masters, the amalgamates, had started as AIs themselves. They managed the Unity's affairs from a distance. Outside of the amalgamates' own Core Worlds, most member planes retained their own independent governments, surrendering control only over their trade laws. Transplanar trade was vital to the Unity. But when the amalgamates squeezed, they had grips of razors. They would not brook any competitors entering their niche. *Those* wars had been fought long ago.

Several additional datastreams filtered into her head as her systems neatly laced with the shuttle's. In a moment, the shuttle felt like an extension of her own body. She felt herself inside the passenger cabin, a knot of feeling inside a bundle of sensation. It was uncannily like being in her own stomach.

Her couch's safety harness snapped painlessly over her shoulders. A firm press of acceleration shoved her into her couch. Wind whipped past her wings. Her landing struts sank into the ventral hull. A view of Messina rose above the horizon, turned tiny by distance.

The shuttle shot straight through the clouds. Gray wisps peeled past the forward-facing monitor like a curtain parting. Then all of the displays turned deep blue. It wasn't until she had several moments alone in the open sky that Habidah began to feel better.

For the first time, she was grateful for the monitors. It was amazing how something so simple could change the whole tenor of the cabin. She breathed out as the acceleration eased. A carpet of clouds bubbled below. She was tempted to try to convince herself that the land below belonged to a different world, and that she was leaving it behind.

But it hadn't been that long since she'd seen the plague during beautiful weather, too.

Her full name was Habidah Um'brael Thayusene Shen, but all that had stopped meaning much a long time ago. For years, she'd been Habidah or Dr Shen. The other names denoted her local and extended clans on her home plane, Caldera. But she hadn't gone home in over twenty years.

As the shuttle juddered into its descent and her stomach dropped away, she found herself thinking of it again. It was something she did only when she wasn't looking forward to an assignment. Which was silly. She'd already been here for months. She should have already settled into it, resigned.

But her assignment hadn't really started until now.

Home was isolated, bound by academic regulation and procedure and tradition. It was small university settlements, bored into the side of the continent-spanning supervolcano that gave her plane its name. Its thousand-year-old university campuses and research satellite towns, originally built to study the volcano and the mantle underneath, remained as small as the day they'd been founded. She rarely saw more than two or three people at a time in its rocky-walled corridors. Ten was a crowd. She hadn't missed feeling stifled, but her time in Messina's crowds had turned her memories a shade fonder.

Caldera was just one part of a larger multiverse. It was a member plane of the Unity. The rest of the Unity encompassed more planes than a merely human imagination could hold. Caldera numbered among hundreds of thousands of Unity provincial worlds, among millions of known inhabited planes, among trillions of charted Earth-parallel planes. The moment she'd left Caldera, it seemed impossibly tiny. Every day since made it smaller.

The shuttle's nose glowed red. It should have been screaming. All Habidah heard, though, was a low rumble. The shuttle's sound-dampening fields hadn't been installed for her benefit, but they were certainly nice to have. There weren't many people in the forests and fields below, but it wouldn't have done for any of them to know about the shuttle roaring overhead two to three times every night. The fields folded the air to mute the sonic booms, and zippered a pocket of vacuum around the engines to keep them from roaring. Anyone looking up would see at most two flickers of blue engine exhaust, easy enough to mistake as a glimmer of moonlight or trick of the eyes.

It wouldn't have fooled anyone with technology, of course. The infrared bleed alone shone like another star in the sky. But the people below had nothing more than their eyes.

Many miles south of Lyon, the shuttle descended. The clouds pulled away. Rural France unraveled below: crumpled green parchment dimpled with hills and covered by woods. As the shuttle slowed, one of the camera feeds zoomed in on two lonely, dilapidated buildings: a farmhouse and a barn, surrounded by nothing. The field base was buried underneath the barn. There was something snug about being underground, though she knew she was the only member of her team who felt that way. The others had all come from wealthier planes.

The shuttle circled to bleed its excess velocity, and then settled into the shadow of the barn. Habidah's safety harness released. Gravity reasserted its solidity.

She was down the outside thirty seconds later. The shuttle's engines still thrummed. It would be off to pick up Kacienta next. Kacienta was on assignment charting the overland trade routes most likely to be vectors for plague transmission.

The farmhouse's roof was half-staved in. One of its walls sloped at a dangerous angle. Habidah pulled the farmhouse's one door aside. Inside, the survey team had made no attempt to keep up the illusion. At the far end of the barn, a silver door sat half-buried in the dirt. It slid open. Polished offwhite walls followed a ramp downwards. Lights lined the ceiling and floors, eliminating every shadow.

They'd taken a risk of discovery during the field base's construction. Flash-manufacturing wasn't subtle. The construction drones' light, heat, and noise – like a thunderstorm at dawn – couldn't be disguised. But Habidah had needed the base built that quickly. Their schedule had been too tight. The plague had already spread through China and Central Asia by the time the Unity's survey drones had found this world.

Habidah tugged her wimple to the back of her head as she walked. When she reached the door at the bottom, she expected to walk into a vista of silver-blue city, with a sky sparkling with antimatter engine exhaust plumes. Providence Core, Joao's home plane. He usually monopolized the viewwalls. Instead, she stepped onto a wide row of trimmed purple and yellow vines. A squat, ultramodern violet farmhouse overlooked the vineyard. The vineyard stretched into a featureless horizon, under a sky that was a much lighter blue than the world outside.

It took Habidah a moment to place it. She'd never been to the plane, and needed to consult her demiorganics. This was Rodinia, home of Feliks Vine, her team's medical specialist.

Rodinia was a quiet little world, one of the oldest settled planes in the Unity. Her demiorganics supplied the statistics. Seventy percent landmass, nitrogen-rich soil, humid atmosphere, an old and hot yellow-white sun, and a unicellular native ecology that had begged to be supplanted by genengineered crops. A perfect agricultural plane. Hundreds of planes whose peoples never heard Rodinia's name got their foodstuffs from this world. It was mostly NAI-run factory farms, managed by legions of drones and a few very wealthy employee-shareholders. Rodinia exported food, yes, but also pharmaceuticals, narcotics, and a host of other psychoactives.

Her demiorganics laced with the field base's NAI. An additional layer of data told her where to find the others. Joao was nearest, in the field base's communication chamber.

The field base had been supplied with a communications gateway, a micrometer-width transplanar portal that served as their link to the Unity. It was just enough to send data. Her team, their construction drones, and their satellites had arrived through larger gateways. When her team would eventually leave, they would be dependent on their university to bring them back.

The gateway was safely concealed behind one of the viewwalls. When Habidah entered the room, the floor and wall thrummed with power. The gateway was active.

Joao sat on a chair seemingly sprung right out of the vineyard. He wore a sheet-black suit that billowed about his wrists and ankles. He looked up as Habidah entered.

Of all the members of Habidah's team, Joao was the least comfortable here. Habidah had grown up in university warrens, at ease in closed-in spaces. More importantly, she hadn't had much in the way of creature comforts. Joao had come from an abundance of space *and* luxury. Here, he had no personal relationship manager NAI, no servant sprites, no immersion libraries, no personal fabricators, or anything else the people of a wealthy plane like Providence Core had spent their whole lives accustomed to.

If it hadn't been rude, she would have asked him why he'd come, but this was his tenth field assignment. He must have gotten used to it. And he'd done well so far.

He was their systems specialist, which meant that, in addition to his anthropological duties, he was supposed to keep the field base and its shuttle and gateway operating. Or at least monitor the base's and shuttle's NAIs while they did that.

Habidah didn't waste time. "He's gotten worse already."

She knew why they were in the middle of Rodinia rather than Providence Core. "The first symptoms have manifested, yeah," Joao said quietly, as though Feliks might overhear. "He didn't say anything, but he couldn't hide it from NAI. And NAI let me know."

Habidah tried not to be offput that the base's neutered AI had told Joao rather than her. Then again, Joao spent more time here. In addition to his anthropological duties, he was their systems specialist, in charge of their base, shuttle, and satellites.

She said, "He must realize it's not a secret."

Joao said, "He asked for a view of home. That's all he said to me."

There'd been more that she planned to say to Joao, but none of it seemed important. She nodded so as to not seem dismissive. Then she left. Her demiorganics told her that Feliks was in his office on the other side of the field base. Unfortunately, another icon was closing in faster.

Meloku intercepted her in the middle of the corridor that separated the field base's kitchen from its dining hall. Like the rest of the team, Meloku had altered her appearance so as to better blend in. She'd left her hair as it had been, though: long, night-black, and bound in two rams' horns in the back. Habidah hoped she hid it well on assignment. The locals saw uncovered women's hair as lewd.

Whenever Habidah was getting a sense for new team members, she started with their home planes. As Joao had proved, that didn't mean everything, but it was a start. She had no idea what to make of Meloku's plane, though. Mhensis was an oceanic plane, a tourist getaway with very few permanent residents. Meloku had been one of those – born there, even. Her plane was split, and starkly, between high-technology sea-skimmers and ships shown to tourists and the artificial islands that had little but housing for the staff and guides.

Meloku couldn't have arrived that long ago, but she'd already changed into a short-cut bluewhite jumper. "I've been assigned to Venice," she said. "I thought I was going to Avignon."

Habidah retrieved and perused the schedule. Joao had written it, but she saw its logic at once. "The plague ships changed all of our projected contagion routes. I'm sorry, but we need observers in all the major coastal cities."

"I've been studying for Avignon for weeks. There's still so much we have to learn that I can only discover by being there on the ground."

"You'll have a chance to go to Avignon when the plague reaches it. It should only be a few more months. If not sooner." She kept walking toward Feliks' office.

Meloku kept up. She could have conducted this conversation entirely by datastream. She'd shown up in person to pressure Habidah. "We're not *just* here to watch the plague. We need to study these cities before they're struck. Otherwise, we won't have the context to judge how they change."

She had a point. Not for the first time, Habidah wished she could have gotten a larger team. Five anthropologists would never be enough for a broad-ranging survey like this. But everybody back in the Unity was preparing for the collapse of their *own* civilization. And there were other survey teams to staff as well. Hundreds of others, from hundreds of universities across the breadth of the Unity.

Habidah struggled to think of how a more socially adept person would handle this. She used to be better at this. She resisted checking her protocol and empathy files for suggestions. That was a crutch she'd used too much when she was younger.

She said, "We have to do the best we can with what the university gives us. You'll pull through."

Judging from Meloku's glower, that had been exactly the wrong thing to say. "I'm not worried about me. I'm worried about the assignment. Avignon is the most important religious center on the continent. It's unique. I'll never be able to get a clear understanding of what its people are like and what they're doing if I only arrive on the eve of its devastation."

"Then we'll just have to live with an incomplete understanding." Habidah felt bad saying it, but she was almost to Feliks' office and rapidly running out of patience. There was no good way around the truth. Their university's resources were too strained to give any team more than the bare minimum of personnel. That was going to mean missed data.

Meloku stopped. Habidah did likewise, regret coloring her cheeks. "Look – I'll rearrange the schedule for the next few weeks, and get you to Avignon as soon as possible. But for now I absolutely need you in Venice. It's non-negotiable."

"Sure," Meloku said, and turned sharply.

Habidah tried not to resent her as she watched her go. She must have known what was going on, where Habidah was headed. Her problem could have waited.

Habidah stopped outside the hidden double-doors that led into Feliks' office. She needed a moment to recover her breath and gather herself.

She held her hand in front of her nose as she entered. She had been around enough death in the past few days to recognize the smell. The bodies of three plague victims lay on tables inside. There was a wrinkled old man, a bony woman in about her thirties, and one six year-old girl, her black hair pleated behind her. They'd been dead several days, and hadn't had the best hygiene before. She couldn't tell if they'd been so hollow-eyed and gaunt before dying or after. The plague didn't go easy on its victims.

A desk and several workbenches lined the far walls. They and the tables looked very out of place in the otherwise rural-idyllic setting, but Feliks had always been a very practical man. Asking for a view of Rodinia was the most sentimental Habidah had ever seen him.

Feliks had come from the poorer half of Rodinia's demographic range, which still left him with more resources than most in the Unity. Habidah had no idea what he'd done with himself in his youth, but, as an older man, he'd chosen the dissipation of study over the dissipation of leisure.

He, too, was in native costume: the colorful multi-layered robe of a well-placed courtier. The sleeves of his blue outer tunic peeled away like onion skins to reveal red, gold, and oak brown. He stood in front of the gurney holding the six year-old. A silver-and-glass cairn of microscopes, sensors, recording equipment, and dissection lasers floated above her.

He waved her in apologetically. "I know, I know," he said. "I'll get them out of here as fast as I can. I didn't want to arrest decomp until I'd had a chance to get them under my equipment." A perfumed breeze flowed from invisible air vents, trying its best to cover the sharp citrus smell of decay. "I can't get trustworthy measurements through a suspension field."

Habidah stood beside him and gazed at the girl. All at once, it was like being back in Messina, dead and dying all around her. She held her expression steady.

Feliks explained, "I recovered these from the mass graves of second-wave plague victims in Caffa. There are already new mutations showing up. They'll reach the rest of Europe before long. It should mix things up quite a bit, beyond what we'd prepared for."

"We're already beyond that, and it's just started."

Feliks gave her a sardonic little smile. "We always knew things would get interesting."

Doctors. Habidah never knew what it was with doctors.

To a local, Feliks would have looked healthy, youthful, vigorous. He had broad shoulders and well-sculpted muscles. She was short for higher-gravity Caldera, and he was tall for his lower-gravity plane. Next to her, he was huge. He'd allowed a few signs of his true age to seep into his features. White flecks speckled his mustache and sideburns. His eyes were shadowed, but that was not a sign of age.

Of all the people on her team, Habidah had known only Feliks before this assignment. The two of them had served together on a survey mission five years ago, visiting a variant Earth whose sun had been captured in a far orbit around a trinary star system. Its stellar neighbor been far enough from its siblings to support a stable, life-bearing planetary system. The sight of such tantalizingly close new worlds had pushed its inhabitants down the path of space travel rather than transplanar exploration like most other advanced civilizations. Feliks had discovered three novel genetic adaptions to zero gravity.

As then, he was eager to run down what he'd uncovered. "The plague we've examined so far has been spread by fleas infesting black rats," he said, and nodded to his left. For the first time, Habidah noticed the animal carcasses carefully lined up atop one of the workbenches. "The mass rat die-offs caused by plague have forced the fleas to feed off humans. The plague has been exceptionally virulent, but the fact that its primary method of transmission has been a rat parasite has put hard limits on the speed it can spread."

Feliks nodded at the child. "Not so now. One of its new mutations is a pneumonic form. That is, it spreads from person to person via respiration. My best guess is that this strain developed when the older, bubonic form escaped a victim's lymph system and infected their lungs." Feliks peeled back the girl's upper lip with a gloved finger. Her teeth and dry tongue were flecked dark red and brown. "The natives call it the coughing plague. Victims cough up copious blood before they expire."

He moved on to the next corpse in line, the thin, middle-aged woman. Her skin was so mottled that, for a moment, Habidah thought it had been stained. In Messina, she'd met plenty of woman whose ankles and arms had been blistered and stained black by the caustic soap the natives used. But, no – this discoloration came from somewhere deeper, in tissues under the skin. Her veins were beet-colored. Feliks said, "And now there's a septicemic variation. Blood plague." He lifted the woman's fingers. They were coal-black. "There's an extraordinary amount of plague bacilli in the decedent's blood, not just her organs. This one is not as virulent as the pneumonic plague, but it's far deadlier.

"We knew we'd see some mutations, but this might throw all our projections away. The old bubonic form of the plague has a sixty-five to seventy percent mortality. The victims of the pneumonic plague, however, have a ninety to ninety-five percent mortality rate. And no one we've ever observed with the septicemic form has survived at all."

Habidah listened until he gave her a chance to speak. "All good to know," she said, though it wasn't. "How do you feel?"

He'd clearly been hoping she would ask him something about the plague or the bodies. He shrugged. "Like I want to work."

He remained over the corpse. Aside from a flicker of an awkward glance when she'd come in, he hadn't yet met her eyes. She waited.

"All right, all right," he said, and rubbed his eyes. "I feel like I haven't slept in days, but I woke up three hours ago."

"You having any trouble lacing with NAI yet?"

"Some glitches every once in a while. Nothing serious." He waved at the bodies. "That's why I want to get so much of this out of the way while I can still operate the equipment."

Feliks' demiorganics were shutting down. The mind-machine barrier was difficult enough to cross in the best of circumstances, and his condition made it worse. The onierophage was advancing into his nervous system. Habidah had known he carried it when she'd offered him the position on her team, but she hadn't known how long it would be until the symptoms began manifesting.

The timetable for the remainder of the onierophage's progression was just as much up in the air. Anywhere between three weeks and eight months from now, he would no longer be able to receive any datastreams. Once his demiorganics were fully offline, the rest of him would follow.

The onierophage was like nothing anyone in the Unity had ever seen before. Given the sheer scale and variety of the multiverse, the Unity was forever encountering new ideas and technologies and forms of life, but the onierophage had been beyond everything, a new category. Even the amalgamates, with their long experience, had thought it impossible.

The microbes were nearly subatomic. They were like houseflies, slippery and elusive. They darted about to escape observation. When finally isolated and examined, they seemed to contain no information at all: no DNA, no genetic coding of any kind. Just bare and basic organic chemistry that shouldn't have been able to accomplish any of what it had.

No quarantine worked. No method of contagion had ever been discovered. People who slept next to the infected every night, shared their air and bodily fluids, escaped catching it. Others who'd been completely isolated from Unity since the plague began had contracted it. It ate away at them, body and mind and demiorganics.

The only constant was that it attacked mostly, if not exclusively, individuals with demiorganics. Even infected without demiorganics had had, sometime in their past, extended contact with transplanar civilization. That suggested a source of infection far in the Unity's past. Something that might have been spreading and breeding, under the surface, for some time.

That meant the people of this plane were safe from the onierophage, at least. Habidah wouldn't have come if she hadn't believed that. They only had their own pestilence to worry about.

Some of the extraplanar pathologists at Habidah's university were even speculating that the visible microbe was only a symptom, not the cause – that the disease was being transmitted through the quantum structure of the multiverse itself. The microbe was just a protrusion, they said, the exposed tip of a far deeper structure. Only by boring itself into some underlying fabric of reality could it have escaped all of the amalgamates' attempts to detect it and eliminate it.

The amalgamates had conquered threats before. The multiverse was replete with danger, as infinite in form as it was in scope. Other transplanar empires. World-eater AIs. Memetic parasites. Plane-leaping vacuum metastability events. Occasionally, news leaked through to the Unity proper, but, for the most part, the amalgamates kept them at bay.

They'd defeated so many threats that the threats had started to blur together, play in repeat. One hostile transplanar empire was often much like the one that came before. Though the multiverse was infinite, *most* things, as a percentage, fit into patterns.

But the onierophage couldn't be categorized. If it had a controlling force, it was invisible and intangible. If it had a purpose, it was obscure. It seemed to be drawn to members of the Unity and their client planes, but, even then, that was not a rule.

That was why her team were here. The battle to fight it was happening well beyond the ken of most people in the Unity. The amalgamates had been working on that for months, and were still.

Habidah's work was anthropological. She and her team had been sent here to research how other planes responded with plagues that overturned their worlds, and to come back with whatever coping strategies she could. Her team was only one of the hundreds studying similar mass death events. It had been a long time since the peoples of the technologically pampered Unity had had to deal with anything so primitive as disease. They needed to relearn how.

The rest of the Unity viewed these projects with skepticism (if they were aware of them at all). They were concerned with solving the onierophage. They believed in discoverable cures. They were waiting for the amalgamates to find it. It was the policymakers – the people who actually had to engineer political and social answers to the facts as they were, rather than the facts they wished for – who had shown the greatest interest in projects like this. The hundreds of universities sending out teams like hers had had no shortage of funds, if not volunteers.

Feliks said, "I saw our new schedule has you headed for Genoa next. Alone."

"There's too much going on for any of us to work in pairs."

"And yet I'm supposed to stay here holding the fort."

"It makes sense, doesn't it? You can't travel alone with failing demiorganics. The last thing we need is for you to lose satellite contact."

"I can't do anything more here. Just dissect old corpses. I want to work."

Their university didn't *require* that someone stay behind at the field base, but strongly encouraged it. That way someone would always be ready by the shuttle. With all their tools and technology, none of them should have been in much danger, but this was still classified as a hazardous assignment. It was a weak excuse.

Feliks asked, "What about you? Do you think you'll be able to handle this all alone?"

"Of course I will. Why?"

"Your demiorganics have been pumping a lot of anti-depressants into your system."

Damn. As her team's medical specialist, he did double duty

as their doctor. Of course he'd have access to that information. Habidah shook her head.

Feliks asked, "Why did you request that I come along with you on this assignment, anyway?"

"You're one of the best I've worked with."

"Your academic history is public record, you know. Forty-seven field assignments, and never once did you ask anyone you'd worked with before to come along on your next project. Three weeks after my diagnosis, I get a call from you."

"I can be unpredictable. Spontaneous, even."

Feliks raised an eyebrow. "When was the last time you went home?"

It was starting to gall her how completely he'd turned this conversation around on her. If he didn't want to talk about his condition, she wouldn't force him. "You wouldn't ask if you hadn't already pulled my records."

"Twenty years since you've been to Caldera. For a three-week visit." To tell her parents goodbye and that she'd be back as soon as her field assignment wrapped up next year. Fortunately, that part wasn't in the public records.

Feliks leaned against the only clear desk. Muted, orange Rodinian sunlight flickered over his shoulders. "You haven't settled anywhere since. One field assignment after another. *Are* you planning to go back home sometime?"

"I did keep my clan names, you know. What are you asking?"

"I have it better than a lot of onierophage victims. I've had a reasonably glorious life. I'm old. Not as old as I'd like, mind, but I've already had those moments where I looked back and figured out what I would rather have spent time on. I should have spent more time making friends."

"You think I don't want to make friends?"

"Well, why haven't you?"

"What makes you think I should?"

"You think you should, or you wouldn't have put me on your team." Something about the way that Feliks was leaning struck her as uncomfortable. He wasn't leaning to slouch, she

53

realized. He didn't have the energy to stand anymore. "Now that the Unity is falling apart, you're starting to realize what a lot of other people are."

"That we don't have much time left," Habidah said, finishing his thought.

After a moment's quiet, Feliks asked, "What's more valuable to you, staring down the end? Going to Genoa alone, and having me here? Or going with company?"

Habidah couldn't quite meet his gaze. In that moment, it was difficult to not resent him. For as terrible at it had been to be alone in Messina, she never would have wanted to go with someone else. She couldn't imagine how it would help.

But Feliks had trapped her quite neatly. He was still watching her. He folded his arms.

"I suppose that's one of the things we're here to learn," she made herself say.

4

The sacrist stood in the snow and beat his *tabula* for the hours of the Divine Offices, and now also for the deaths. One or two a day, at first, then a steady, relentless stream. A clock to tick arrhythmically along with the Liturgy of the Hours. The tally had been fourteen yesterday, up to eighteen by this morning.

Then, after the afternoon Nones service, Prior Lomellini stood. He announced there would be no more observances of the Divine Office until the pestilence had passed. His fear of it had become so great that he could not wait to announce this during the next chapter meeting.

Once again, Niccoluccio's exclusion from the rumor circles left him caught unawares. He sat aghast, his mouth slack. He broke decorum to look about. The only thing he saw from the other brothers was the strain of the past few days. There was no surprise.

Only once in the monastery's two-century history had a whole day of services been canceled. That had been when the old refectory had caught fire, and fifty years before Niccoluccio's time. *Days* without services was undreamt of.

The others filed out as if in a funeral procession. Niccoluccio lowered his seat lid, but stopped before crossing the door. He stepped aside and waited for the novices to shuffle out, and then turned back toward the altar. He kneeled.

Brother Durante had died two days ago. He tried to hide his fever until he'd collapsed in the refectory. Niccoluccio had helped carry him to the infirmary. Durante had been a wreck of shivering. He'd cried out in pain whenever Niccoluccio's fingers had strayed close to the oily bubo under his arm.

Durante had been Niccoluccio's bunk neighbor during their novitiate. They'd been the only pair of novices close to the same age. Niccoluccio hadn't forgotten the morning when he'd woken up with his hand curled in Durante's. Durante must have grabbed it in the middle of the night. Durante never spoke about it, though he'd studiously avoided Niccoluccio's eyes afterward. Niccoluccio had come to the monastery to get away from temptation, but the moment had felt right. Brotherhood was a special kind of love.

And now Durante was gone. Niccoluccio had spent half the last night awake, praying that Durante's spirit could hear him. Though they hadn't spoken much since their novitiate, Durante's silent presence in the church had been as much a fixture of the monastery as Prior Lomellini.

Niccoluccio licked his dry lips. It seemed impossible to focus, even on prayer. His thoughts kept drifting like a wayward novice's. Eventually, he decided to stop embarrassing himself in front of the altar. He forced himself to his feet.

His knees stung from the floorboards. A symptom of creeping age. He was still young compared to many here, but these past few days, he felt his bony elbows, the pins in his knees, the ache in his back. The parts of the real world that seemed to stop existing during his novitiate had crept into the cloister.

By the time he left the church, a glimmer of snow fell from a bright gray sky. Everyone else had returned to their posts or their cells. A silence deeper than usual permeated the cloister. For the first time in years, Niccoluccio couldn't take any comfort from it.

The new snow wasn't deep enough to conceal the sacrist's footprints by the infirmary, where he beat the news of each new death. Niccoluccio stopped by the door. The past few days, he'd heard endless coughing within, cries of pain. Today, though, he heard nothing. He shuffled quickly past, feeling guilty as he did every time. He couldn't bear to listen even to the quiet.

None of the dead had so far received funeral services. These were to be delayed until Death had finished reaping his harvest. The closest thing had been in the refectory during their last Sunday meal, when Prior Lomellini had suspended the usual scripture reading and allowed the brothers to speak to each other. Niccoluccio had kept his peace, but listened to the others' stories about the departed. He'd never known any of them so well.

Now he supposed there would be no more communal meals, either. Prior Lomellini hadn't announced their suspension, but Niccoluccio doubted any of the brothers would be willing to take the risk. They only entered when the refectory was empty, or even, in violation of one of Sacro Cuore's oldest rules, smuggled food into their cells.

Niccoluccio didn't take any food into his cell, nor did he come out in the evening to find dinner. His stomach gnawed at him. He pushed it out of his mind. He didn't deserve to be comfortable. When it came time to sleep, he lay on top of his covers rather than let himself stay warm beneath them. His attempts to live like normal, as though this would pass, had turned to ash in his mouth. He couldn't pretend any longer.

He kept careful watch on the shadows on his wall, the play of moonlight through the clouds. During that last supper, one of the novices had claimed a vision of Brother Durante had come to him in the night. Durante had been dead for but a day then, but his spirit claimed to have suffered through Purgatory for what felt like a thousand years. He'd told the novice of the wonders of Paradise that awaited them all past Purgatory. One of the other novices corroborated the story. Niccoluccio didn't believe a smattering of it.

But just in case, he kept watch.

No spirits visited him during the night, or the day, for that matter. Only the ghosts of names he'd left in Florence, but that had happened before.

The next morning was emptier than any he'd ever seen in Sacro Cuore. Not until these past few days had he realized just how many noises the brothers made: the creaks of floorboards and doors, the shuffles of the elder brothers' infirm feet, the flutters of scattering birds. All of it had felt like silence, but very different from this stifling blanket. This was a silence of the grave.

There were fresh prints in the snow where the sacrist beat his *tabula*. Someone else must have died during the night. Maybe more than one. Niccoluccio hadn't woken.

He turned, and walked again about the cloister, hoping to find something he had missed. Nothing. After too long listening to nothing but his own feet shuffling the snow, it was hard to escape the feeling that the whole of the monastery had died. Struck by a sudden fear that that was in fact the case, he hurried past the sacrist's footprints, toward the infirmary. His heart juddered with something between shock and relief when he nearly ran into Brother Rinieri, the infirmarer, stepping through the doorway.

Rinieri's hood rested limply on his head. He was so bald that he'd stopped needing his hair tonsured years ago. His eyes were so tired that he hardly seemed to register the near-collision. "Brother Niccoluccio," he said. "I'm pleased to find you still alive."

"No less than I am to see you." Some of the others had wondered aloud if Rinieri wouldn't be among the first to fall. He spent more time around the diseased than anybody.

Rinieri trudged toward the refectory. Niccoluccio followed. Usually, smoke trailed out of the kitchen chimney. Today, nothing. Rinieri said, "It seems those of us still here have been left to fend for ourselves."

"Do you know when Prior Lomellini might lift the suspension of services?"

"Prior Lomellini took ill last night," Rinieri said.

Niccoluccio couldn't breathe for a moment. Rinieri looked at him with a trace of sympathy, and said, "I left him in the infirmary. It's only a matter of time. The laws dictate that we elect a new prior the day after Lomellini passes, but I don't believe that will be happening. Lomellini will be our last."

Niccoluccio said, "Sacro Cuore has survived pestilence before."

"I've read the records enough to know that this is very different. We unlucky few are living through the end of the world."

It took Niccoluccio a moment to process what Rinieri had said. Ever since the pestilence, things seemed to always be moving too fast – as fast as they used to in the outside world.

Niccoluccio said, "Every day in Florence there were people who pronounced the end of the world. They were all wrong. It's not possible for Man to know these things."

Rinieri waved beyond the cloister grounds, to the leafless branches looming over the chapter house. "The only question I have is whether all of this will continue without us. Will there still be trees? Moss? Will birds return in the summer? It seems a shame to unravel the whole world because men proved unworthy."

"You must be mistaken," Niccoluccio said.

Rinieri patted him kindly on the shoulder. "You'll see, brother." He stepped into the refectory. Niccoluccio found himself drawn along as if tied by the wrist.

The refectory was empty. The warm air that usually wafted from the kitchen doors was absent. Niccoluccio rinsed his hands out of habit. Rinieri went last. Encrusted brown sludge sloughed off his hands. Only then did Niccoluccio notice the persistent smell of a lavatory following him.

There was no milk left in the kitchen. The lay farmers had cut contact with Sacro Cuore. Some kind brother had set out jugs of water. There was still bread, at least. Someone was coming in to bake it. Niccoluccio and Rinieri sat together.

Rinieri said, "I'm going to fall asleep soon, whether I want it or not. I don't know if I'll wake again. More than one of us has fallen asleep professing to feel fine and woken dead, so to speak."

"How long have you been awake?"

"Two sunrises. I can't leave my post. I can't save them, but I can at least make them more comfortable."

A wave of guilt tided over Niccoluccio. He'd spent the past few days trying to read and meditate. He swallowed. As if anticipating Niccoluccio's thoughts, Rinieri said, "The other brothers are probably right not to come near the infirmary. I doubt it will save them, come the end, but it might get them a few days' reprieve for penance."

Niccoluccio swallowed. Rinieri could hardly have been more obvious if he'd come straight out and asked. Niccoluccio said, "I wasn't aware you had no help."

Rinieri looked at him pointedly. "As I said, I believe the others made good decisions."

"You should not expect so little from us." Niccoluccio had to force his next few words out. "I would be glad to help you."

Rinieri smiled, and turned his attention to his bread. The rest of their meal passed in silence. Niccoluccio couldn't hear anything over the crunch of the bread's grit in his mouth. His heart beat as though he'd just offered to follow Rinieri over a cliff.

Rinieri said nothing on the walk to the infirmary afterward. The moment they stepped inside, Niccoluccio was stopped by a stench like nothing he'd encountered before. He couldn't put words to it. It was overpowering: it reminded him both of a latrine and a garbage pit, but there was a third element to it, too, something musky and citrusy, heavy as compacted soil. It couldn't be death. None of the brethren who'd died would have been left here long enough to decay. Niccoluccio remained in the shadow of the doorway until Rinieri, eyes gleaming with sympathy, waved him in.

The moment Niccoluccio's eyes adjusted enough to see the double row of cots, he understood. The smell wasn't death, certainly. But the brothers resting on them were dying, and they were not doing so prettily. Their habits were stained and crusted yellow-brown with bile. Some of the brothers hadn't been able to move to use their buckets, let alone the small lavatory in the back.

The infirmary hadn't been designed for so many men. All three of the original beds in the front room were taken. The rest of the cots had been dragged in from the dormitory.

He hadn't registered the sounds until the moment after he entered. One of the brothers was muttering prayers in a voice as weak as an old man's. Another man, whom Niccoluccio belatedly recognized as deaf Brother Francesco, was scrabbling for the bucket beside his bed. A novice had a book splayed over his chest as though he'd been reading it to the others, though he lay unmoving now.

Niccoluccio stopped breathing when he saw Gerbodo. Gerbodo seemed a different man. Sweat layered his forehead, reflecting the daylight coming in through the door. The muscles under his cheeks had slackened. His covers only came up to his chest. Either he had broken decorum by undressing, or Brother Rinieri had undressed him. He was asleep, his left arm above his head, no doubt to give relief to the bean-sized boil in his armpit.

Prior Lomellini lay on the bed farthest from the door, eyes closed and mouth hanging open. His chest rose shallowly. A heavy black lump bulged from under his neck. Niccoluccio swallowed. Brother Rinieri threaded between the beds. He touched his hand lightly to Lomellini's forehead. He sniffed Lomellini's breath, and then the bottom of his sheets. He waved Niccoluccio to Lomellini's bed.

Rinieri said, "We need to move him to the back." That was where brothers were taken to die. The moment of death was supposed to be private, between the sufferer and God.

Niccoluccio said, "I thought you said Prior Lomellini had just taken ill last night."

Rinieri looked at him, and didn't disagree. He just grabbed one end of the cot. Niccoluccio strained to lift the other.

Lomellini's eyes hung open. He said nothing as Rinieri and

Niccoluccio lifted him, only looked at Rinieri with eyes stained red by the strain of vomiting. It was as if Niccoluccio didn't exist. Niccoluccio at once felt ashamed for the ill thoughts he'd directed at Lomellini. Lomellini had been more *political* than other priors, certainly. But there was no slyness in his eyes now.

The back room of the infirmary should have been empty, to allow the dying their privacy. There were already two men lying there. Both had shallow bowls of water balancing on their chests. The bowls were the last measure of breath. The water in one rippled gently. The other was completely still.

Niccoluccio didn't even know the name of the man who'd died. He was a novice, about as old as Rinieri, with an oily forehead and half-parted eyelids.

Time seemed to flow smoothly around the next hours, a stream over pebbles. Niccoluccio was hardly conscious of their happening. He and Rinieri hauled the dead novice out of the infirmary and set him by Sacro Cuore's small cemetery. Rinieri fetched the shovels, and Niccoluccio joined him in the painful labor of digging deep in the cold ground. By the time they returned, the man beside Lomellini had also died.

When they came back from the second burial, Lomellini was still awake and staring at the ceiling. His eyes were sallow, his skin pale and veiny. He looked twenty years older than he had yesterday. Niccoluccio could not help but be impressed that Lomellini made no sound of distress, though the boil on his neck must have been agonizing. Rinieri called in the sacrist to administer the Last Rites, and to announce the deaths to the other brothers.

After he and Rinieri tended to the other inmates – Niccoluccio numbly following Rinieri's instructions – Niccoluccio returned to Lomellini with a book of scripture. Lomellini's eyes remained open, and he breathed shallowly. Niccoluccio pretended not to notice the stains on his covers. He sat on the edge of the nearest cot.

For much of the rest of the night, he read to Lomellini. He

kept going after the prior shut his eyes, and stopped only when his breathing became so thin that there was no mistaking the moment.

Niccoluccio retired to the refectory, intending to get a quick meal. He fell asleep at his bench. In the morning, Lomellini was dead. Another brother had taken his cot.

Niccoluccio dug most of the graves. The hard soil yielded half an inch at a time, and his bleeding hands stung with every thrust, but he forced himself through it. He had nothing else to give. There were no longer enough of them left to provide decent funeral services.

Whole groups of companions perished. After Brother Francesco died, Niccoluccio went about the dormitory to ask about him. The only one of the brothers who knew him well enough to provide an oratory had died shortly after Niccoluccio discovered him.

Every morning, Niccoluccio and Rinieri carried brothers out of the dormitory. It seemed a miracle that there was anybody left. But the infirmary always had space to accommodate them. The inmates died as quickly as they were brought in.

He and Rinieri worked silently, sincerely. Niccoluccio's hands chapped and bled, turned black by the soap he and Rinieri used on the inmates' sheets. They washed and changed everything as often as they could, but it was never enough. Niccoluccio never got used to the smell of sweat and vomit that suffused them. Still, he preferred anything to working with the sick themselves. His suffering was only a distant shadow of theirs. Only Rinieri had the expertise to handle them.

Rinieri had held himself apart from the other office-holders. Niccoluccio only wished he knew anything else about the man. He was already dreading the day that Rinieri, too, would die. Or that Rinieri would hunt in vain to find anyone who could give Niccoluccio's funeral oration.

Or, worse, that he wouldn't try.

The monastery would become a cemetery of mute spirits,

straining through the snowfall to hear anybody speak of them. In his working trances, he heard the endless peal of church bells across Italy, across the whole known world – a funereal chorus resounding long after anyone was left to hear them.

No. He couldn't let himself think like that. Sacro Cuore would go on. It was his life. Living or dead, he would always be here. The place was too much a part of him.

Gerbodo lingered longer than Lomellini, but he, too, died. Over the next two days, he was followed by the precentor and almoner, and shortly afterward by the novice-master. All of the monastery's senior office-holders, barring Brother Rinieri, were dead.

Whoever had had the duty of refilling the refectory's wash basin had died. Niccoluccio replaced it himself. Every morning, the basin was covered with a thin sheet of ice. The water stung his hands. Shoveling had turned his knuckles into maps of knobby callus and dry, bleeding skin.

After getting his stale bread at nights, he didn't have the courage or strength to return to the dormitory to listen for coughs and wheezing. He retired to the calefactory, the warming house. It was the only building in the monastery to be allowed a chimney and open fire, a comfort for the elder brothers. The prior before Lomellini, Prior Gianello, had spent most of his dying days there. Men of Niccoluccio's age were typically not permitted inside. But he couldn't keep himself from it. Every night, he went through the motions of rekindling the fire while he purged his mind of the day's losses. The heat soaked into his bones.

Niccoluccio draped himself in front of the fire and wondered if he would wake. But each morning he woke healthy save for the ills his work inflicted on him. His shoulders felt like hot irons, and his hands stung like they'd been boiled, but he never woke with a fever nor black lumps.

The remaining monks kept themselves in their cells, too afraid of each other to emerge for any reason other than necessity. Niccoluccio tried to recount the names of those he knew were still alive, besides Rinieri. Brothers Rainuccio and Arrigheto had left on their mission to the bishop. There had been no word. Beyond that, there were names Niccoluccio had only heard in passing, names he couldn't attach feeling to. By the time Niccoluccio became familiar with them, it was too late. They'd been brought into the infirmary.

He'd long ago lost track of the number of men Sacro Cuore had lost. He'd buried two dozen with his own hands. That made thirty-five total? Forty? Out of fifty-nine. Sacro Cuore was hollowed out, a shell of stone and wood.

At last, though, the flow of the diseased and deceased began to diminish.

Rinieri began taking walks around the freezing cloister in the morning. Niccoluccio joined him. Niccoluccio had occasionally had trouble with ice lining the cloister walk, but never as much as this year. The brother whose duty it was to clear the walk had also died. He and Rinieri took each step slowly, haltingly.

Rinieri remarked, "We must have angered the Almighty mightily to have this happen during winter. At least in summer we might die with a trifle more comfort."

Rinieri's fatalism had never let up. Niccoluccio said, "I've always felt there was no more holy a season than winter. The snow stifles sound. It helps keep everything in the cloister silent."

"Silent evermore," Rinieri mused. "If the birds and beasts continue on, they'll enjoy that."

"Christendom has survived worse," Niccoluccio said.

Rinieri said, "Christendom cannot survive an angry God. It has never stopped paining me that you will not accept that."

"I cannot believe our time on Earth is finished."

"Prior Lomellini had a difficult time accepting his end, before he died. As did many of the others."

Rinieri hobbled over the next patch of snow-covered ice, slower than usual. Niccoluccio had to take mincing steps to keep from overtaking him. "I didn't just come to this monastery for the sake of my own salvation. I came to be a part of the

Body of Christ, of the Church He built. It has long outlasted all its founders save Him. The work we do here is meant to last centuries."

"The house Christ built on Earth is long-lasting, but no more eternal than Earth itself. There's no need to have a house without occupants."

"Long after we've gone, I have to believe that there will still be men walking this cloister, and that the work we've done here will continue to help guide them to their salvation."

"You 'have' to believe. You see, even when you pretend it's not about your desires, it is."

Niccoluccio shifted. No doubt Rinieri derived a great deal of satisfaction from his hesitation. "Even now, the pace of the pestilence is slowing. For the past two days, now, we've had fewer and fewer sick and dying."

Rinieri gave him a look of the sincerest pity. For the first time, Niccoluccio noticed how red his eyes were. His cheeks were flushed.

"My poor man," Rinieri said. "Have you counted the heads that have come through our doors?"

Niccoluccio shook his head. "I started working with you too late to start counting."

"Our work isn't slowing because the pestilence is leaving us." Rinieri slid his hood partway back. He brought his fingers to the side of his neck, to the black lump the size of a bean.

Niccoluccio gaped. Rinieri smiled, thinly. "It's slowing because, very soon, there will be no one left to die."

5

The empty bridge spanned the dark, seemingly rootless. Meloku kicked a rock along it. There were a few things to admire about Venice, she supposed. Any Mediterranean coastal city that had avoided the plague thus far was worth a second glance. Its people had their wits about them. Still, she couldn't keep the resentment from leaking out of her thoughts and into her demiorganics.

"Now, now," Companion soothed. "Venice is an important urban power in its own right. There's plenty to be gained here."

Meloku had slept through the flight to Venice. The shuttle had deposited her on an empty pier at midnight. She'd missed getting an aerial overview. Companion had dutifully recorded the view, as well as given her a satellite map of the city. Meloku had shunted it into deep memory.

She looked up. The shuttle was a blur of shadow. It faded into little more than the suggestion of a breezy cloud, visible only in the infrared.

"A local power," Meloku subvocalized. "It can't control the Italian peninsula. It's got no power over Europe's imagination." Not like the papacy.

"Europe is not centralized, nor will it ever likely be. Even the papacy has enemies everywhere."

Meloku kept her thoughts stifled as she reached the other side of the canal. Cold air brushed her neck and ears. She hated it when Companion lectured her. It meant Companion was disappointed in her. She'd learned by now that it always had a good reason to be.

Companion continued, "In any case, you underestimate Venice's influence. Its trading network extends far beyond the Mediterranean. Its armies and mercenaries have toppled nations. Given the right guidance, it could grow into an empire."

"But it's never going to receive the right guidance, is it?"

She knew she was being petulant, but she couldn't help herself. Emotional control was one thing she'd never quite mastered over her decades. Not, at least, in the confines of her own head. More and more, she relied on Companion to keep herself in check.

Her rock clattered ahead. There were no lanterns or torches. She navigated by retinal infrared. Bodies glowed ahead. She stayed carefully clear of them, as well as the watchmen on patrol across the next canal.

She fancied herself a ghost slipping through Venice, intangible. She never needed to employ any of her stealth capabilities. That, at least, made her feel a little more competent.

Slowly, against her will, Meloku's mood buoyed. She'd always found cities exciting. No matter how many planes she'd visited, some part of her subconscious always thought of "proper" worlds as endless flatness, water from horizon to horizon. The island-ships and pleasure cruisers of home never stayed put. There'd been no sense of place. The tourists always wanted the same experience. Every ship had the same foods, everyone spoke with the same accent.

Like all of the cities on this gloomy little world, Venice was a sprawling mess. Her first impression was of tangled knot of wood and stone, suspended like jetsam over the water. She entered what was obviously a wealthier neighborhood, with swept walkways and kinder smells. There were more canal boats tied to each dock. She passed an open yard that, judging from its refuse piles, housed a fruit market in the day. The wind from the port was suffused with the odors of day-old salt fish. The next building over was obviously a warehouse, protected from fire by canals. The hot outlines of night guards stood at each corner.

She turned to follow the waterway. Companion told her it was the widest in the city. The houses looming over it had been designed to impress the neighbors as much as those passing. Their facades were ornately carved. Heraldic banners hung over the doors of those manors whose inhabitants had been wealthy and bold enough to be knighted. The streetside loggias were hung with silk. A pulse scan revealed prodigious amounts of gold and silver in seemingly every room of every house. Even some of the servants' quarters had polished mirrors and silk sheets.

She asked, "We're still going forward, aren't we?" A not-so-deeply buried part of Meloku remained afraid that her reassignment had messed up everything.

"We can hardly do anything else," Companion assured her.

Companion was one of the few non-neutered AIs the amalgamates allowed to exist in the Unity. No one was meant to know that the amalgamates still dabbled in true AI. And this one was hers. A gift for her service. A superior and a friend, keeping her honest.

It lectured her on the city as she searched for a place to begin operations. She was the first of her team to visit Venice, but Companion had months of satellite coverage to draw from. Venice was an extraordinarily wealthy city, richer than any city Meloku had visited thus far. It appeared that Venetian trading posts thrived in every port, sending gold and silver back home. Trade poured through every pier. Even plague quarantine couldn't stop the smugglers arriving every day.

As with seemingly every city on the Italian peninsula, Venice was at war. Mercenaries clashed on land and sea, but Venice remained untouched. A bankers' war. It reminded Meloku of the aftermath of wars she'd seen on other planes – wars fought on the Unity's behalf, and that few in the Unity knew about.

Though she shied away from people, she was dressed as a local, in a rough reddish-brown kirtle and chemise treated to look as though it had suffered through a long, horseless countryside trek. Her oval-shaped field kit appeared wooden. Even the other members of her team had no idea about the technology inside. They would have been appalled by the weapons.

After crossing several bridges, she found a run-down travelers' house bordering a slum. Infrared revealed only two people: a middle-aged man and woman, both with poor circulation and cold extremities. It was single story and had three vacant rooms, one of which was leaking. A pulse scan found that the rushes hadn't been changed since the quarantine, except in the landlords' room.

It took three knocks to rouse the inhabitants. A hefty, balding man in a buttonless brown tunic and nightcap came to the door. Meloku, hands folded meekly, pleaded her case. She was Constance, a woman who'd fled her home in the countryside for a reason she refused to state. Even with the plague approaching, that was as good as saying that she was running away from her husband. Many women like her did. She'd reached the island republic just before the quarantine.

His skepticism ended when she pulled a handful of silver coins out of her pocket, enough to pay for a five-day stay. He showed her to a room that had two candles, a straw mattress, and woolen sheets. The walls were solid, at least, and he'd taken her to the room without the leaking roof. Meloku handed over her payment and held her tongue when he said he'd replaced the rushes only a few weeks ago.

Alone, she was tempted to take a moment to test the bed. But Companion ticked away quietly in the corner of her mind. It was always judging her, measuring her. That was why she had it.

She opened her field kit, and from it took five thumbnail-sized discs. She placed one on each wall, and a third on the floor. When she activated them, a red flicker distorted the wood around them. The room was now sound-proofed – imperfectly so, admittedly, but enough to fool a merely human ear. She could be up pacing all night, and her hosts would never hear.

Her colleagues preferred to get out, interact with their subjects. Meloku had a hard time being personal. Besides, she was better at multitasking. She had a grade of demiorganics normally restricted to Unity military officers. She played along with her team because she'd had to, but she might as well have been as alien among them as anywhere else on this plane. Every time she spoke with them, laughed with them, ate with them, she made herself remember that.

Next, she planted a quartet of field projectors around her door frame. They, too, were military-grade. Even her augmented eyes couldn't register the security field switch on. When she gave the door an experimental kick, it struck back hard as titanium.

She turned. The air scintillated with red, blue, and green lines and icons, a satellite view of Venice. Her demiorganics projected the map directly into her visual cortex. She could have conjured it as an abstract idea, as knowledge rather than a scene, but too much of her remained stubbornly human and attached to her senses.

Five minutes' analysis was all she needed to identify Venice's neighborhoods and traffic arteries. Potential vectors for plague transmission sprouted as bright red arrows and percentile probabilities. Before long, she had five good guesses as to where the first infections would appear and how they would spread.

Over the next several nights, Meloku snuck out and planted eavesdroppers in every position she'd marked. Each time she returned, the map of Venice shrank, squeezed out by camera views. Eventually, the floating images expanded into the third dimension, layering atop each other.

She tracked every boat, from the slave galleons to two-person canal rafts. She kept a careful measure of the quarantine efforts at the piers. Those who had the means were evacuating to their country homes. Their neighbors gave them dark and jealous glances, sometimes broke into their homes minutes after they left. Even before the plague reached Venice, the city lost more and more of itself each day. Everyone knew what was coming.

The plague took longer to arrive than she'd expected. She was left with nothing to do but sit and watch. She daydreamed about stealing the team's shuttle and taking it to Avignon anyway.

Inevitably, the plague seeped through the quarantine, and gave her plenty else to think about.

It arrived via two vectors at once, three days apart. The first vortex of death tugged at the city from the east. It started as a handful of bodies, and quickly became dozens upon dozens. At the same time, another rash of infection appeared along the Grand Canal. Meloku nearly mistook it for the same outbreak, but these victims developed up to two buboes rather than one, and died more painfully. It was a different strain, and must have arrived through the harbor. Even with the largest ships barred from entering, plenty of canal boats came and went by night. A city like Venice could never be completely cut off from the world.

The plague spread through the city's arteries. She could actually track the waves of death striking homes along the roads and canals, and working their way inward from there, like ink seeping through a sponge. One hundred people died each day. Then two hundred. Even with most of the city shut indoors, the plague spread without restraint. Pigs and cats and loose dogs roamed the streets and bridges, dying of the plague like everything else, carrying their pestilential rat fleas with them.

As Meloku hoped, her landlords died. The eavesdropper she'd planted on the street outside saw the husband struggling home with a fever. Two days later, she watched through the walls as their infrared signatures cooled to ambient. She would no longer have to plan her trips around their waking hours.

The other members of her team focused their studies on the

common people, the illiterate masses, those who had no voice and no power. Meloku didn't know why they bothered. There were only five of them. They would get some spectacular individual stories to sell back in the Unity, certainly. But it was like trying to understand a colony of ants by dissecting one worker.

It was the systems that were important. Venice was a snarl of competing interests and vainglorious wealth, but its response to the plague was comprehensive, organized, and likely the most effective that the natives' knowledge allowed. The eavesdroppers tracked talk of a commission of nobles and knights formed to protect their city against the plague. Already, the commission had shut down drinking houses and banned wine boats from the canals, killing a major avenue of plague transmission.

Body disposal had been quickly regulated, as well. Every plague corpse was shipped away to one of two islands. There, they were given a ritual "last view" of Venice, a prayer, and buried in graves strictly measured to a meter and half in depth. The commission outlawed keeping corpses inside homes. Every day, gondoliers plied the canals shouting, "Dead bodies, dead bodies!" Householders threw family members' corpses into the gondolas on pain of arrest.

The commission banned doomsayers and mourning clothes to try to keep the populace's spirits high. When the city streets started to look too empty, they announced clemency for exiles and debt criminals, and opened the jails. Venice's authorities firmly believed their world would continue, and fought to make everyone see it the same way. Even as the plague deaths reached their peak – with five hundred bodies shipped to the mass graves every day – the commission announced that any civil servant who'd fled and refused to return to their job in the next eight days wouldn't have a job to come back to. Scores of fresh applicants filled the vacancies.

Venice stood in sharp contrast to other cities, especially Messina and Siena. There, authorities seemed to have decided the plague was God's will, and there was nothing they could do. Meloku scanned the images Habidah had captured in Messina. Venice's organized response to the plague may have saved a few lives, but it made an even vaster difference in the way Venetians comported themselves. They fought through their mourning. The Messinans, even the healthy ones, trudged the streets when they came out at all.

Venice's civil government was fascinating, and worth extended study by itself, but it was local. In spite of its extended trade network and vast influence, Meloku couldn't believe it could turn itself into an empire. She hadn't come here to write reports.

"I should be in Avignon right now," Meloku muttered, alone in her room.

Companion said, "You can make progress towards that here."

Meloku started. Companion could be silent for days at a time. Meloku had nearly forgotten it was there.

Not for the first time, she wished she could have grown up with Companion. Companion had been implanted in her twenties. Even with demiorganics, human neuroplasticity only went so far in adulthood. If she'd had Companion there since she was a toddler, she would never even have learned what it felt like to be alone. She wouldn't need to put any effort into being a team, she'd just *be* one.

From the day Companion had been let loose in her demiorganics, it had known her better than her parents. Companion was brilliant, understanding, munificent – and it was just a few clusters of neuronal pathways buried deep in her demiorganics, a fraction the size of her own messy and disjointed brain. Just one more way humans were less than the machines that governed them.

Companion didn't have to peer deep into her thoughts to know what she was thinking. "The onierophage is forcing us to step up the speed at which our agents are elevated into demiorganic bodies," it thought. "Continue proving yourself, and it will be your turn."

She asked, "How?"

"Can you figure that out by yourself? Or do I need to tell you?"

Another test. That quieted her.

She sifted through her array of cameras and stopped on the image of St Mark's Basilica. The pearl, multi-domed cathedral drew more and more people each day. Its bells rang constantly.

Quarantine or not, people flocked to St Mark's. Though these people couldn't have guessed the plague spread through rat fleas, they knew it could transmit from person to person and even that possessions were contagious. Yet they were gathering here, and not even the commission dared stop them. It said a great deal about the power their religion had over them.

She rooted through her field kit for her tailoring supplies. Three hours later, she was Edessa Akropolites, a traveler from east of Constantinople trapped in Venice by the quarantine. Her demiorganics adjusted her accent and gave her a Greek language database. She dressed as a noblewoman, in an orange tunic of imitation Parisian fabric lined with velvet, and a violet skirt that trailed to the ground. She left her hair bound tightly behind her neck, now in a single, elaborate knot, with a scarf as a headdress. Seductive without being vulgar. She had jewelry to match, a pearl necklace and emerald and lapis rings. Two of the buttons on her sleeves were also jeweled. In sum, a rich target for a thief – especially the kind of thief who would aim to part her from her wealth by means more sophisticated than pickpocketing.

She avoided looking at the corpses of her landlords on her way out.

She was embarrassed to find that, like all of the other visitors approaching St Mark's, she was awed. Meloku had seen infinitely grander things on other planes, but after spending so many days shut in her little room it was still a shock to her senses. Four lead-lined domes stood above five stone entranceways. A statue of St Mark stood upon a gable, flanked by angels, looking upon the crowds. For the means these people possessed, the craftsmanship was quite extraordinary, and would have consumed whole lifetimes of endeavor.

Meloku sidestepped a group of filthy four to seven year-olds begging at the door, apparently orphans. St Mark's was as bustling inside as out. The cacophony made it difficult to think. There were no formal services at the moment. Congregants clustered at the altars dedicated to Venice's numerous patron saints. She walked down the central aisle, trying to look like she knew where she was going.

Some Venetians kneeled silently, but still more were talking to their deity and its saints as though they were physically present. They crowded around each other, touching the same altars. A pulse scan revealed lice hopping clothing. Meloku couldn't help her grimace.

"Not so different from what's going on back home," Companion said. "Trillions lining around the amalgamates, praying for a cure."

"The amalgamates exist," Meloku said. "The onierophage doesn't spread person-to-person."

She made her way to the front three rows. The pews were overfull. The crowd spilled over the edges and onto the floor. Five children wailed next to their mother, who was trying to ignore them and pray. Meloku filtered out their noise to have a thought left to herself.

After applying another filter for the smell, Meloku strolled around the aisles until she found the type of people she was looking for: five ecclesiastical officials in black and red robes. They stood away from the crowd, their backs to her. Audio sorting detected a French accent.

Meloku strode past the full pews and, like so many others around her, took refuge on the floor. Her expensive dress drooped onto the stone. She folded her legs, closed her eyes, and mouthed an approximation of prayer. Her demiorganics found a passage of scripture appropriate for a woman praying for her soul.

As she expected, when she opened her eyes, two of the robed officials were beside her. "Madam," said the nearest, appalled. He was a man of heavy girth, a stubbly dark beard, and a voice that gave him away as Venetian. "The floor is no place for a woman like yourself."

Meloku dabbed her eyes. "God be with you, sir," she said, heavy on the accent. She looked to the full benches. "I had nowhere else to rest my legs."

She knew at once that the man beside him was the Frenchman, even before he spoke. The avarice of the Avignon papacy was legendary. He was tonsured, but humility ended there. His curled, pointed shoes – the ridiculous height of fashion – were long enough that she couldn't imagine him walking up stairs. Jeweled rings studded six of his fingers. No doubt his robe was hiding more expensive clothes underneath.

The Frenchman said, "You are welcome in the baptistery, if you would care to join us. We have closed it to the people for the time being, but it is more comfortable."

Meloku accepted his hand up, and meekly let him lead her. The Frenchman took her through an open door to the left of the farthest nave, and into an empty round room. Images of saints looked down upon them from the golden walls. A statue of St John the Baptist stood upon the font.

The Frenchman's companion hadn't followed. On another day, a woman in "Edessa's" position would have refused to go further with a lone man, even a clergyman. The plague had upturned the world, though. She needed him to think Edessa vulnerable.

He directed her to a bench and sat beside her. "It gives me grief to see ladies like yourself in these conditions." He paused. "I admit, I do not see many travelers from so far east here."

"I came here with my husband. We were traveling for business, to buy silver."

"He is not with you now?"

She told her demiorganics to make her tear up. "He rests

77

on San Giorgia d'Alega." The island held one of Venice's mass gravesites.

"Would that you were safe back home. It's not often that travelers take their wives with them, for this reason among many others."

"He could not bear to be separated from me for so long."

"And now you are trapped here with the rest of us. I, too, have been forbidden from returning home until the pestilence has passed."

"Oh? You are not Venetian?"

He smiled thinly. His eyes traveled once over her body. "No, madam. I am a delegate from the papal offices in Avignon, here to visit the bishop."

As he would expect her to, she at once bowed her head. When she had recovered herself, he said, "What I meant to say earlier was that I did not expect to see someone from so far east *here*, at St Mark's. Not since the divide between our churches."

"Oh! I never meant to come as a schismatic. I never had the opportunity to know anything but my church until I arrived–"

"Quite all right. And understandable."

"I attended services when I was a child, but my husband wouldn't allow me to leave home after we wed. This is the first chance I've had."

She laid out her story. Edessa had been raised Orthodox, but had lost contact with the church once her jealous husband began forcing her to stay at home or travel with him. Her only exposure to formal religion since had been here, in Catholic Italy.

She nodded to the golden mosaicked walls. "Even when I was a girl, I never felt anything at church like I do here. This place isn't like anything I've ever seen there. It's so grand, so humbling, so… so… I can't explain what it's done to me."

The legate seized upon her hints. "Do you have anything waiting for you when you go home? A family… a church to belong to?"

She shook her head. "Only property. Certainly not a church,

not now. I don't feel I could after what I've seen here."

"It's a terrible thing, not to have a church."

"The world is more and more a terrible place."

"We try our best to make our own beauty and solace in it. You've come to the right place to start." He hesitated. She could taste his greed, like sweat. "You are thinking, perhaps, of converting?"

"That is a very difficult question to ask a woman."

"I would be willing to help you through the transition."

She looked at the granite statue covering the baptismal font and pretended to steel herself.

After a long enough pause, she said, "I've come to believe that this church could mean something to me no other ever has. I feel a blindfold has been lifted. But I would be afraid to convert without a guide. I would not be able to go home. I have no one here."

He took one of her hands in his. "I would be only too happy to serve."

She couldn't do anything but pretend not to notice his hand. Women of this culture weren't allowed to notice the obvious, least of all when it was something that they wanted. She needed to pretend diffidence to be attractive to this type of man. Judging from his longing look, she'd done a good job of it.

She smiled weakly. She'd worn underclothing authentic to her noblewoman's costume, on the chance that it might matter. Companion had been right after all. She didn't need to be in Avignon to find her route into it.

6

Before Habidah and Feliks reached Genoa, the plague ships had come and gone. The Genoese had been ready. Genoese cogs came to meet the plague galleys, bowmen standing in their towers with arrows nocked, until the galleys turned away.

The shuttle arrived at night. It drew a cloak of dark over itself. Habidah had the shuttle spiral over Genoa while she conducted a deep scan for any sign of infection: significant quantities of corpse gas expulsions, people with abnormally high body temperatures, a lack of movement from neighborhood to neighborhood. Nothing. The Genoese seemed to have escaped for the time being. She breathed out.

Feliks watched her from the acceleration couch opposite hers. He'd been quiet throughout the flight, but he'd rarely taken his eyes off her. His concern grated on her. *He* was the sick man, not her.

Visual scanning didn't reveal much besides a few flickering fires. Otherwise, Genoa was as solid black as the open wilderness. To Genoa's inhabitants, the night must have seemed like a different world, cold and wild and dangerous. It was no wonder many of them believed that the plague spread most easily at night, carried on ill winds. Switching to infrared to pick a landing site felt like cheating.

The shuttle set down just inside the city walls, in an open square near a well. The moment she and Feliks set foot on soil, the ramp folded up. The shuttle vanished with a whisper and a suggestion of a shadow. A cold autumn breeze swept in.

Still thinking of the dark, Habidah turned her retinal infrared off. She wanted to see the world as the locals saw it. Her breath caught in her throat. She might as well have struck herself blind. She couldn't even see Feliks. The world seemed so closed in around her. She only lasted a few seconds before she turned infrared on again.

Feliks waited. He knew her retinal infrared was switching on and off, Habidah realized. She wondered if there was a single member of the team he wasn't always monitoring.

"Empathetic understanding is core to your analytic approach," he said, as they walked. "Unusual for an anthropologist, isn't it?"

"Something wrong with that?"

"It places your health at more risk during this assignment."

"Not as much risk as other people around here."

"That's my point. You're worrying more about the natives, about people you can't help, than your own wellbeing."

"I wasn't talking about the locals," she said, with an arched eyebrow, and left him to interpret that.

Anyway, if she was after "empathetic understanding" then she was doing a miserable job of it. She couldn't even stand a few seconds of claustrophobia.

An overcast hid the stars and moon, but the hot outlines of Genoa's sleeping inhabitants shone through their walls. She needed only spin a circle to know that she and Feliks were absolutely alone, unobserved. None of the locals could ever be so sure. Here she was, immune from the plague, ensconced in technology; she'd never be able to understand the peril that these people felt themselves in every day.

She and Feliks started by tacking a handful of thumbnail-sized sensors around the city, but their chief accomplishment that night was to get their own feel for the city's streets and neighborhoods. They walked past small churches and around the Cathedral of St Lawrence. Habidah took infrared snapshots of the carvings adorning the richest churches, and of the architecture of the poorest. The carved doorways and loggias and swaying banners told a score about the locals' values, and the weight they placed on their own ostentatiousness.

She said, "It's going to be interesting to see how much of this the locals will keep pursuing in the face of the plague."

Feliks asked, "Comfort in luxury goods?" His breath was flagging, but he had more energy than yesterday. For now, he kept up fine.

"Worth considering, if it works here. There's no shortage of high technology luxury goods in the Unity. The amalgamates could always find some new ones. Reshape a few economies to chase after them." Anything and everything might bring some solace.

The amalgamates would never admit to having so much control over the Unity's member worlds as to reshape their economies. Publicly, the amalgamates only "ran" the Unity in the sense that they set trade policy among member worlds. They also managed the gateways linking planes, ostensibly as a public service. The Unity was supposed to be more of a loose federation of planes coming together for mutual benefit and defense. *Unified* only to outsiders, in the sense that an attack on one plane would be perceived as an attack on all. The amalgamates, with their powerful planarships and other secret weapons, were judges of last resort as well as security against truly outrageous threats.

Everyone with half a mind and a will to not self-deceive knew that the amalgamates did more than they professed. The chancellor of Habidah's university, who had organized this along with hundreds of other universities across the planes, made no secret of her sympathy to the amalgamates. And she had let Habidah know that her findings were of interest to them, and would be forwarded on.

It would not be the first time the amalgamates had read her work. They soaked up all kinds of data from throughout the Unity. They controlled all of its gateways – communication gateways, too. Absorbing their message traffic was just a happy bonus of their position.

This assignment was the first time anyone had admitted it so openly to Habidah, though.

Sunrise let her finally turn off retinal infrared. Bright pink shadows silhouetted the mountains to the north. The markets bustled with activity, stall and store owners setting up for the day. Fear of the plague didn't slow them, at least. The Genoese knew that the threat came from outside the city, not within. Several spice merchants had closed, and recently enough that the smell of pepper and saffron still lingered about them.

She and Feliks headed closer to the city gates, into the poorer neighborhoods. There, they passed an empty house. The door was locked, and the two beds within were covered in dust and bereft of sheets. A few minutes' chat with the neighbors found that the landlord, a clergyman from the Cathedral of St Lawrence, was having trouble finding tenants.

Feliks sat heavily on the wooden doorstep, his face red. Habidah went alone to hunt down the clergyman. By the time she returned, key in hand and several silver coins lighter, he was still breathing heavily. He was able to get inside under his own power, but fell on the bed before Habidah could throw out the old and moldy dried heather mattress.

Feliks didn't wake until the next morning. By then, Habidah had gotten to know the neighbors. One, a woman with soap-scarred black hands, promised to be a rich source of gossip. Another, a pilgrim en route to Rome and trapped in Genoa for fear of the plague, had promised to share all of his views on the church with her.

Habidah sat on the edge of his bed. "You sure you want to stay here?"

"Positive," Feliks said, and forced himself to get up.

She took it easy with him regardless. He courteously declined to notice. She limited their morning expeditions to the neighborhood, which worked just as well because it was poorer and likely to be hit hardest by the plague.

They met fishermen, seamstresses, former soldiers with

deep-gouged old wounds, carpenters, and dockmen. They lived across from an old mercenary with a missing eye and a bubbly patchwork of scar tissue where half his scalp should have been. Their neighbor was a former Greek galley slave who'd escaped by slipping loose his shackles and diving overboard. Next to him was a forty-year-old woman who'd successfully raised seven children and been left with three more when her sister had eloped with a second husband. Elsewhere were a bald old ex-clergyman who illegally preached on the corner and was rumored to receive a stipend from an old mistress, and an apprenticing furrier who bragged about a scar on his arm he claimed resembled a saint, and a different saint every week.

Life among neighbors in Genoa was intimate. Everyone on this narrow, corkscrew-like street knew everyone. Habidah and Feliks had been noticed before they'd moved in. She fit in well. Back in the Unity, she'd been short. In this city, with its poor nutritional balance, her height was just average. Feliks was huge next to her. They took the guise of a married couple, with Feliks recovering from a long illness (nearly the truth). Nobody asked where she went while he stayed. Habidah would hardly have been the first prostitute on their street, not even the first married prostitute.

There was no way to be sure when the plague would enter Genoa, only that it would. Habidah perused the rest of her team's reports at night, when she couldn't get her three hours of sleep. Meloku's reports from Venice were sparse and clinical, with almost no useful conclusions. Kacienta was in the skies, scouting plague transmission vectors. Her map looked like black bile pulsing through the veins of the continent.

After their morning walks, Feliks stayed inside to compile their data. They both knew this was an excuse to let him stay off his feet. Habidah took long and leisurely walks through the rest of the city, perused shops and markets. But the churches got most of her attention.

The Genoese knew about the plague – what's more, they

knew it was coming. In spite of travel restrictions and the ever-present political turmoil of Italy, news arrived every day. They waited in dread and prayer, and overstuffed their churches. No matter the venue, from the poorest church with a nailed-together altar to the Cathedral of St Lawrence, Habidah had a hard time finding space to stand. The sermons focused on ritual and repentance. The cathedral's clergymen were particularly animated about "God's holy Sunday," and lectured that their audience's failure to keep it had brought His wrath. Those close enough to hear absorbed every word. Now that the news of the plague had had weeks to settle in, a strongly ritualistic, performative mythos was taking shape. Believing the plague could have been averted by proper genuflecting was a classic attempt to control things that could not be controlled. She'd seen it many times before.

She knew exactly how the plague bacilli spread. Infrared picked up the rats waiting in the walls. She already knew which households would be most at risk. Like seeing in the dark, though, knowing this obstructed her understanding. These people hadn't even developed a germ theory of disease. As far as they were concerned, it might as well have been the hand of God carrying off half the world. She couldn't think that way.

Habidah crouched against a church wall and listened to another in an endless stream of psalms. Then again, maybe she and Feliks were more like the locals than she wanted to believe. Everyone in the Unity was still waiting for the amalgamates to cure the onierophage. They had to take it on faith that the amalgamates would prevail, if not in curing the disease, then in stopping its spread.

In all their explorations of trillions of planes, the Unity had never found minds as powerful as the amalgamates. The amalgamates had emerged from the AI wars that had racked the Unity in its lost early age, fifteen thousand years ago. The battles had been fought over datastreams, and entered the outside world only when the AIs had bombed key power plants or network junctions. But the electronic warfare corrupted most of the era's databases and records, and left the wars more mystery, speculation, and legend than fact.

The wars had reportedly lasted only half a day, with battles measured in fractions of a second. The victorious AIs had survived only by forming power blocs. They'd enforced the permanency of their alliances by merging together. Their unified minds were sculpted out of hundreds or thousands of individual AIs. They programmed safeguards into every AI created after them, neutered their capabilities to ensure that no other AIs would threaten their positions.

With that squabble out of the way, the amalgamates had turned their attention to protecting themselves. The multiverse was full of wonders and terrors. Thanks largely to the amalgamates, Habidah had had plenty of experience with the wonders, and little with the terrors. Rival transplanar empires, runaway AIs, nonhuman xenophobes, hyper-invasive species, and other bogeys skirmished with the Unity all the time. The amalgamates had not yet been bested.

It was an open secret that the amalgamates maintained their empire of human civilizations to protect themselves from all of these. Even they couldn't control everything – not without multiplying themselves to the point of risking another civil war.

Humans were not the most common sentient species in the multiverse, but they tended to produce the kind of civilizations that the amalgamates found most useful. Humans were grasping, avaricious, and social. They harnessed those traits to build vast industrial economies. By incorporating so many human-populated planes and their output into their empire, the amalgamates controlled much more than they could have managed alone.

The amalgamates lived in or above the Unity's eleven Core Worlds, their intellects residing in fortress-stations or planarships. Each took responsibility for a different aspect of the Unity's governance. Together they managed the Unity's affairs across its countless and ever-expanding member worlds. They enticed planes into the Unity with the promise of their vast interplanar trade. They were above the affairs of individuals. They managed through a multiplicity of agents and neutered AIs. The NAI that managed the field base was a low-level example. Another agent oversaw the university that had sent Habidah and her team here. Even planes that had rejected the amalgamates' control were reputedly riddled with the amalgamates' agents.

Now even those planes were stricken by the onierophage. Planes that had long ago tried to cut all contact with the Unity opened their gateways for the first time in centuries, asking the amalgamates for help.

Habidah watched men and women line themselves in front of their saints' altars and relics. She couldn't ever remember being *comforted* by the idea of the amalgamates, but she supposed it must have been true. She'd never trusted them, exactly, but she'd never feared them either. The amalgamates rarely interacted with individuals other than their agents, but they were always there, as concrete in form as they were abstract in personality.

For these people, their God was the reverse. He was thunderous when given voice by the preachers, but absent from their daily lives. What would it be like to be as afraid of the amalgamates as these people were of their God? She couldn't imagine.

The plague breached Genoa's walls in winter, when it would have its worst effect.

Satellite observation picked it up first. It started with mass rat deaths, the city's invisible animal population dying and dispersing. Pigs and dogs next. Then the infrared signatures of people living along one of Genoa's eastern avenues began winking out. More and more people stayed inside as they realized what was going on long before the city authorities did. But even people who stayed died. Few Genoese lived in houses impervious to rats and fleas.

By the time the plague reached the markets, it was too late for even the most stringent quarantine to preserve Genoa.

Feliks reclined on his bed and sifted through the blood samples Habidah had taken from the locals through handshakes. It took him only a few minutes to pronounce that he expected sixty to seventy percent mortality.

Habidah hurried through the streets. She drew her coat against the cold. The same cold had long since been at work repressing the locals' immune systems, leaving them fewer defenses than if the plague struck during the autumn. It wasn't easy to tell the empty houses from those filled with the dead. So far, the empty houses outnumbered the ones with corpses. Plenty of Genoese had fled for the countryside. More left every day.

She stopped at the end of one street when she saw three militiamen standing in front of a cart, hauling a woman and two sick girls aboard. Vomit stained the woman's tunic and her eyes were closed, but she was still alive, and far from the sickest Habidah had seen. The girls were pale and hollow-eyed, but awake. They meekly allowed the militiamen to lift them into the cart.

Habidah trailed the cart. The militiamen pulled two more living plague victims out of an alley. The cart left through the city's northern gates, quickly waved through by the on-duty watchmen. Habidah lost track of it as she waited in the lines with all the other people fleeing the city.

Outside the walls, the cart's tracks led her to a sizable wooden house, much longer than it was wide. It was obviously of fresh construction. Unused planks and sawdust littered the ground around it.

The Genoese didn't want anything to do with the dying and the dead. They left plague victims in their homes. Those who had no homes, or who fell in the streets or other public places, were hauled to "hospitals" set up outside the city walls. The authorities claimed the sick would be taken care of there. No one believed that. The hospitals were mass graves that hadn't been dug yet.

Habidah carried a medical kit, concealed under her coat. She'd grabbed it this morning without letting herself think about why. The amalgamates had, through their agents in the university, specifically forbidden her team from possessing the cure to the plague. She did have painkillers, though. And fever reducers.

Infrared picked up hundreds of living people inside a space that would have been uncomfortable for dozens, lying atop each other, feverish, suffering. And that wasn't counting the corpses interspersed among them. If the hospital had once had nurses or physicians, then they, too, had been felled. More likely they had abandoned their posts, or never been assigned.

Habidah had painkillers for a dozen people, at most. If she requested more, the field base's NAI would notice. Word would get back to the university.

Her hand drifted away from her medical kit.

She made herself walk back. She turned off her demiorganics' nerve dampeners. She wanted to at least experience the same cold these people did. It kept her from thinking clearly, but it also forced her to focus on the things right in front of her: on keeping herself moving, hopping from one warm place to another, and on taking comfort in the indoors. Just like these people.

Habidah and Feliks still took their morning walks. There wasn't as much to see. Their sensors let her know when her neighbors went indoors and failed to come out. Infrared gave her the rest of their stories. Some of them were still alive. They'd just gone to what remained of the markets, bought as much food as they could, and holed up inside. They didn't step out even to empty their nightsoil.

The old mercenary died huddled on his floor. He was quiet to his end, even when he was choking on his bile. The disgraced priest had fled, but he never had the opportunity to make it out of the city. She heard from one of his neighbors, a prostitute, that his name had appeared on the cathedral's death roll of clergymen.

Habidah saw the apprentice furrier die. From his body temperature alone, she knew he was sick, but since he was still on his feet, she'd assumed he couldn't have been badly off yet. He'd sat down against the side of his house like he was taking a moment's rest, and never got up again. The corpse-collectors fetched his body a day later.

The old woman raising her two nephews and niece struck Habidah the hardest. As soon as the woman realized she was sick, she took the kids out of her house and made them live with one of her grown children still in the city. One of her other grown children, a dockman with already-thinning hair, came back with her. He half-carried her inside, muttering soothing words.

Habidah listened to their conversation remotely. He brought bread and fresh milk. He promised her that he would be back, that he would bring more milk, and sweetmeats and sugar and other foods. Habidah's attention perked. The price of sugar had spiked because it was said to be good for the sick, and would stretch a dockman's pay. The old woman had drifted to sleep mollified.

Habidah's sensors kept watch through the night and next morning when he failed to return. He could have died, but he'd shown no sign of infection when he'd left.

The old woman's bed lay by her window. She no longer had the strength to stand. Throughout the morning, she cried for her son to come back, and then for anyone at all to bring her food or help her. She had no water. Her voice grew weaker, and cracked.

Habidah and Feliks heard her on the next morning's walk. The few people out hustled by, pretending they hadn't heard. No one wanted to enter and risk infection. Without thinking, Habidah started toward her door.

Feliks caught her arm. "You do it for one of them, you'll start doing it for all of them," he said.

She let him stop her.

Nothing in her medical kit was good enough, anyway. She

had no cure, no way to replace the dead. The amalgamates had withheld a cure for just this reason. They knew that some of her team wouldn't be able to resist helping.

Habidah asked, "You could synthesize a cure to the plague if you had enough time, couldn't you? Even without access to the Unity's libraries."

Feliks nodded. "But I wouldn't."

"You're a stronger person than me."

"Think about it this way: the amalgamates didn't forbid our interfering because they want to harm these people, or even to protect them. They made that rule for our protection. We'll lose ourselves if we get in too deep."

The amalgamates could hardly claim noninterference as a guiding principle. The only reason they'd allowed the shuttle its stealth fields was to protect the sanctity of her team's observations. They meddled with other planes persistently. They had to, they said, to survive. They had competition.

They were not the first creatures to grow and maintain a transplanar empire. But they were, so far as Habidah knew, the most successful. The amalgamates swallowed or destroyed their rivals. Some even joined the Unity willingly. The amalgamates and their agents fought vast and lightning-quick wars on the Unity's periphery.

But for all the resources they poured into those conflicts, somehow they couldn't have spared an infinitesimal fraction of them to cure this world's plague. Or so they would have her believe.

She and Feliks continued down the street until the old woman's cries faded into the susurrations of the city.

Feliks said, "This would still be happening if we'd never come here. We have a responsibility to use our time here efficiently. If the things we learn can help even one plane back home, then, frankly, individuals don't matter."

"I know. I don't need a pep talk."

"You raised the subject."

He said nothing else, waited for Habidah to speak again or

let the subject rest. In spite of herself, Habidah asked, "Has anything we've discovered here helped you?"

Feliks took a long moment to think. "Yes. Seeing other people go through what I have." He nodded at the building they were about to pass, a one-room home that had once housed a widower and his five children. All dead. "Realizing what I have, that I'm still very lucky. My demiorganics will preserve my memories and experiences. That helps keep it all from seeming pointless. A generation from now, there won't be a trace of these people left."

"Would you have gotten the same feeling out of reading a report?" Habidah asked.

"Probably not."

"A lot of good we're doing with our time here, then."

"We're not looking for an instant solution. Just some strategies to help people cope with the onierophage, that's all. And, anyway, we're not the only team out there." Feliks waved his hand at the overcast sky, a stand-in for infinity. "There are hundreds of others on planes like this. We'll be able to share observations before we compile our conclusions."

Habidah said, "I haven't heard a single thing from any of them."

"We're all facing our own difficulties," Feliks said, and fell silent. This time, Habidah didn't break it again. All she'd done was make things worse.

Habidah had hoped the old woman would have faded away by the time she and Feliks circled back. There'd been no such mercy. She would have plenty of time to die.

7

Niccoluccio shuffled through the silent cloister, dragging his robe through the snow.

Sacro Cuore's late cellarer had once feared that the monastery would be inundated with refugees. None had appeared. There might well have been nobody left in the outside world.

It had become easy to lose track of the days. Every morning, the first thing he did was visit the sacrist's quarters to check his calendar. If it wasn't Sunday or a feast day, he promptly forgot about it. He liked to treat Sundays differently, but, in practice, other than spending a few extra hours in the church, he wasn't sure how. He couldn't prepare an appropriate meal. The milk was gone. All he had was a prisoner's diet, water and gritty bread. He baked the bread himself.

There was too much else to do around the monastery to take a day off. Every time he worked on Sundays, he heard Prior Lomellini's voice ringing in his ears, haranguing him for not keeping the day holy. He needed firewood, though, and to clear the snow between the dormitory and infirmary. Graves, too, needed to be dug.

After checking the calendar, he made his rounds in the dormitory, knocking on doors and checking inside when no one answered. Most cells were empty, but behind some he discovered bodies, delirious or dead.

The deaths came in waves. The last four of the novices had perished within hours of each other, without ever visiting the infirmary. Niccoluccio had found them huddled in opposite corners of their shared quarters. Even dying, they remained terrified of each other, of infection.

He took the monastery's last dog, a mastiff, with him on his walks. Her littermates had died as well. She was at least some company. She had been trained to never enter the dormitory, though, and not any of Niccoluccio's coaxing could change her mind. She ran off when Niccoluccio approached the doors.

He dreamed of buboes, gurgling and poker-hot under his arm. Every time he woke, he expected to find himself racked by tremors. He felt awful all the time – cold and hungry, aching – but never sick nor feverish.

The first few days after Rinieri died, he ate in the refectory, hoping for company. Twice, he was sure he heard footsteps in the foyer. When he checked, he found no one, nor footprints in the snow. The last time Niccoluccio had spoken with more than one of them, around Brother Rinieri's grave, they had whispered that the plague must spread by sight, that it leapt from a dying man's eyes into its next victim. Niccoluccio had seen so many dead and dying that he should have been well on his way to joining them. The others stayed clear of him.

He wasn't sure when he started to pray for the pestilence to take him, too. But a week after Brother Rinieri died, the pestilence trickled to nothing. The deaths ended.

Niccoluccio found no more bodies in the dormitory. By knocking on doors and waiting for answers, Niccoluccio figured there were about a dozen brothers left. They were all junior to him. None of them had been at Sacro Cuore for longer than ten years.

The survivors met in the too-large chapter house. Eleven hooded and shadow-eyed brothers sat at the benches, refusing to sit near each other or at the table reserved for the officers. They took stock of the dead and the monastery's meager resources. Only after Niccoluccio's prompting did they agree to try to survive the winter here. The nearest town was too far for winter travel, especially should pestilence find them en route or – Father forbid – at their destination.

In spite of the troubles this presented, Niccoluccio left the meeting feeling better than he had since Brother Rinieri died. Hearing their voices had been like exhaling after weeks of holding his breath. He could inhabit the temporal world again. He could think more than a few hours into the future.

Then, perversely, things became worse.

Two of the other brothers walked to the lay community to contact the men there. They returned without having gone the whole distance. Instead, they'd found a half-dozen snow-covered and ragged sheep half a mile along the route. The sheep followed the brothers on their own, and no shout or shove could ward them off. They were skin and wool and bones, and their eyes rheumy.

There were no sheep herders in the lay community. They must have traveled here from a long way indeed. They lingered around the gates like beggars.

A day after the sheep arrived, they began to die.

Niccoluccio took up a rusty hoe and chased the sheep away, but they kept coming back, and by then it was too late anyway. The sheep died outside the gates, bleating to get in. The two brothers who'd rescued them joined them in death swiftly thereafter.

Whatever new pestilence they'd brought with them was worse than anything Niccoluccio had yet seen. He found the two brothers dead in their quarters only a day after he'd last seen them. (None of the brothers ever voluntarily came to the infirmary anymore.) Judging from the stains on their pillows and cheeks, they'd coughed blood until it dribbled out of their lips.

Several other brothers claimed to have heard them dying, but they wouldn't open their doors to let Niccoluccio see them. They were terrified of him, afraid that he'd be next. He, too, had been near the sheep. He stayed away from the dormitory in case they were right and he only needed time to manifest the symptoms. Nothing, though.

The next time Niccoluccio made his rounds, two days later, he found three new corpses. One of the youngest men, three months out of his novitiate, had collapsed in the corridor, as if struck down searching for company.

The weather had unseasonably warmed, but the ground remained hard as iron. The blisters on his palms reopened as he dug their graves. He had once dreamed that he wouldn't be doing this again.

He had wept as he'd dug graves before, but always for the departed, not himself. He had hardly known these men, couldn't put names to their faces. The end of the world was revealing him to be a worse person than he'd ever known he could be. Until now, he hadn't imagined himself so self-absorbed, so focused on his own fate and mortality. He didn't feel a thing about these men. He couldn't force himself to. This resurgence of the pestilence had drained everything he'd thought was good in himself.

A vicious storm swept across Sacro Cuore that evening, pelting the walls with hail, breaking windows in the church and chapter house. Niccoluccio listened from the calefactory and shivered. The wind broke branches, flung them against his door. It was as if the storm were trying to bury Sacro Cuore and the last of its men. Brother Rinieri had wondered if the natural world would continue after the end of man. That night, flinching at every gust, Niccoluccio knew the truth was lateral to that: it was the natural world that would end man.

The next morning saw the night's rain turned to ice, covering the cloister. Niccoluccio fought, unsuccessfully, to avoid slipping on his way to the refectory. As he chewed his granite-hard bread, he decided against making his dormitory rounds. If any of the men believed he could help, they would come to him. He certainly hadn't helped any of the sick he'd found so far, except to force them to drink water. He was no Brother Rinieri. Better to let them die on what terms they wished.

Instead he took to making long, slow walks with his memories of Rinieri. Rinieri was quiet, as usual, but occasionally he would remark on the sights around the cloister. The trimmed bushes at the southeastern edge of the cloister would die soon without care. The walls of the seyney house would be overgrown by vines unless they were trimmed by spring. Worse, snow and branches remained scattered on the floor of the chapter house. No one had replaced the windows, nor had anyone even been in there since the new pestilence.

Niccoluccio kept his hood down so as to not miss any of the other brothers should they try to attract his attention. No one came. By the end of the afternoon, the cold stung like slapping branches.

Another windstorm arrived that night, and blotted the voices he tried to create for himself.

At least during the storms there was noise and movement. His morning walks didn't help him clear his mind. They were a longer form of pacing. He glanced at the dormitory as he passed it three times, anxious to see any sign of life, of movement, inside. Nothing.

He stopped outside the dormitory doors. With a numbing shock, he realized he hadn't seen any living brothers in three days.

No one had come to him. No one had cleared any of the ice in front of the dormitory's entrance. There were, so far as he could tell, no tracks other than his own.

The other brothers would at least have needed something to eat. He supposed, they could have taken days' worth of bread from the refectory, but he hadn't noticed any of his batches vanishing.

He wanted to stand still, blend into the cloister and wait for someone to come out. They had all been so frightened of each other that, for weeks, they might as well have each been alone.

That night, he reclined in his warm chair and tried to dream up ways to visit the other brothers. If he could convince them that he was healthy, they might let him in. Surely some of them were as starved for company. He would risk pestilence just to talk.

The next morning, he went straight to the dormitory. He stopped outside, and, for several minutes, couldn't convince his feet to carry him in.

The first hall stood dark and empty. Most of the doors hung open to indicate that no one lived there any longer. Cold air brushed Niccoluccio's cheek. Someone must have left their garden door open.

He shivered. He took half steps toward the closest shut door, and stopped and listened. He raised his hand and knocked timorously. After three knocks with no answer, he opened the door. One of the half-dozen former survivors lay on his bed, gaunt-jawed and open-eyed.

The next closed door was the same. A dead brother sat in mute contemplation of the stumpy remains of his candle. He wore a peaceful expression in spite of his blood-encrusted lips.

Niccoluccio rushed to the next closed door. The cold grew more bitter as he approached. He flung the door open without knocking – and found only an empty cell and a bed limed with frost. Its garden door hung open, letting in a stinging breeze.

Outside, he found bare footprints frozen in the vegetable garden. Yesterday afternoon had been the last time the ground had been soft enough to mark. These had to be at least that old. Niccoluccio had kept careful track of the stock left in the refectory stores. He was sure nothing had been taken. This cell's inhabitant must have run away to try to make it to the nearest town, or to die. Without supplies, the result was destined to be the same. He hadn't even taken his shoes. Possibly he'd been delirious.

The footprints faded. There was nothing to track, no one to look for. Niccoluccio closed his eyes and tried to regain control of his breath.

Later, after he'd found himself again, Niccoluccio discovered the same thing in the remaining brothers' cells. All but three had perished. The remainder were unaccounted for. They, too, must have tried to leave – though with what supplies Niccoluccio couldn't imagine. He double-checked the refectory and sacristy to satisfy himself that nothing had been taken.

It was of course possible that he'd just missed the remaining brothers' corpses somewhere in the now-labyrinthine monastery grounds.

He left the sacristy, planning on walking back to the calefactory. His legs stopped halfway. He sat heavily on the stump of a tree, and buried his head in his palms.

He could have still tried to hope. The missing brothers might have survived. Brother Rainuccio's two-man expedition could have returned. All of this talking to himself couldn't quite silence the corner of his heart that knew the truth. More likely they were all dead.

Even if they weren't, it would hardly matter to this place. Sacro Cuore had been waning before the pestilence struck. With the roads to Rome all but empty, the ecclesiastical hierarchy would never deem it worth repopulating.

A fitful breeze swayed the bone-white branches of the cloister's trees. Niccoluccio lifted his head out of his hands. A dark gray cloud shaded what little of the horizon he could see. High, icy clouds stood still against the sky.

The door to the dormitory lay open. Niccoluccio had neglected to close it. Darkness loomed behind the chapter house's broken windows. The infirmary, too, stood bare and empty. Niccoluccio stared at the cloister with slack lips. All of the voices of the world had been extinguished.

He pushed himself to the calefactory and threw the door open as loudly as he could, stomping to the embers of the fireplace. He sorted his remaining firewood into stacks to give his hands something to do. The noise was a mockery. It was no more a real sound than the shouting inside his head. Just needles in his ears.

For a while, Niccoluccio waited by the embers, uncertain what to do next. At least, he pretended to be. His mind was already made up, but his heart wouldn't tolerate it.

The only thing left to do was leave Sacro Cuore.

He had to strike out, like the others. He would die if he stayed. If the lingering pest didn't claim him, his food wouldn't last.

Sacro Cuore depended on winter grain and milk shipments from its lay community. If anyone there yet lived, they would surely want to leave once they heard that no one in Sacro Cuore – other than himself – had survived. They might send their own search party. The monastery grounds were large enough that they probably wouldn't discover him. They would strike out without him. If, indeed, they hadn't already visited and done just that already.

He opened the calefactory's doors and stood in the chill, staring at what was left. The place wasn't important, he told himself. The brotherhood was. Or had been. Believing that was the only way he was going to convince himself to step out of the gates. The only brotherhood left here was the communion of death.

A good monk shouldn't fear death. He should close himself off from the world, accept his place in Purgatory and dream of the coming Paradise.

But the past few weeks had taught Niccoluccio that he wasn't as good a monk as he'd thought he was. Any people at all would do for brotherhood now. He shut the door again and hurried about packing.

8

Three days after Christmas, a pillar of fire burned high above the Palais des Papes.

Meloku watched it through silk curtains on the third floor of her cardinal's residence. The shuttle stood a kilometer above Avignon's soiled streets, unmanned, firing its rockets hard. The only reason it hadn't shot off on an escape trajectory was that it was firing its forward thrusters just as hard. The shuttle roared like a cyclone, haloed in an inferno.

The problem with all this was the fuel expenditure. She could hide the shuttle's trip to Avignon easily enough. It had been taking an automated aerial survey of Marseilles, and Avignon was only a short distance from its return course. It had been more difficult, but doable, to bounce her communications signals between satellites to trick NAI into thinking her updates were still coming from Venice. But she couldn't hide half a missing fuel tank. This stunt had burned through that much in just three minutes.

But when she'd started planning this, Companion had revealed several software packages it had, until now, concealed from her. While Meloku watched slack-jawed, Companion had altered the shuttle's refueling schedule, added false extra legs onto trips between study sites, and then extracted its infiltrators without leaving any trace.

She had black software of her own, but she had been forbidden from using it in all but dire emergencies. If

Companion had deployed these resources on her behalf earlier, she wouldn't have needed to hitch her way to Avignon on the legate's coattails. But Companion had been testing her. It wanted to see what she could do without a crutch.

"We take this project very seriously," Companion had told her.

"'We?'"

"The amalgamates and I."

"Why are the amalgamates taking a personal interest in a backwater like this plane?"

"You'll be briefed soon." Companion added, teasingly, "Though you've seen enough that you should be able to guess on your own."

More tests. Meloku reclined into her seat and waited. Two minutes after the pillar of flame dwindled to nothing, audio filtering detected the footsteps of five men hurrying up the stairs. Her door clapped open.

She didn't turn.

"It happened exactly like I said," she said.

Cardinal de Colville said, "The whole of Avignon saw it, Edessa." For the first time since she'd met him, he sounded like he didn't know what to do.

"They heard it, too," said a man Meloku didn't know. From his accent, he was from Languedoc. Probably a veteran of its vicious Inquisition.

De Colville said, "It was even more magnificent than you said."

"*Terrible*," Meloku stressed. "It's a terrible thing. The first half of an epistle from the Son."

The cardinal asked, "Do you know what the message is?"

"Are we doomed?" another man asked.

Meloku let the question hang in the air for a full minute. Gauging how long the men waited, she could tell how thoroughly she'd succeeded. Yesterday, no man besides de Colville would speak with her for other than insincere pleasantries. Today, they would eat out of her palm if she asked them to.

"I need to speak with His Holiness," she said.

She'd established herself in Avignon with a minimum of fuss, until now. The Papal legate from St Mark's had bribed his way past Venice's quarantine officers. After reaching Avignon, she'd promptly left him for the more powerful Cardinal de Colville. De Colville's appetites were infamous even among the debauched church hierarchy. Unlike many of his colleagues, he remained sincerely devout. If he saw a contradiction there, he never seemed bothered by it.

She'd waited until she'd gotten into the most public place she could. Today, while touring the Palais des Papes with him, she'd cried out and collapsed, clutching her hands. Her demiorganics had manifested a minor repulsive field that split the flesh of her wrists and spilled blood onto the marble floors.

She hadn't dared call it stigmata. Better to let de Colville's friends draw their own conclusions. She'd cut her nails short for traveling. Everyone could see they weren't long enough to cut so deeply. She'd looked straight at de Colville and announced that she had received a vision from the Virgin. A pillar of flame would alight over the papal residence later that night.

Now, Meloku stood. She primly folded her sleeves over her scabbed-over wounds. She'd turned away all attempts to dress them. She turned to de Colville. The cardinal had planned to spend most of the night out playing at cards, gambling half his estate away. He was dressed in a padded red doublet under a white surcote. He was bashful about his bald scalp, and hid it under an elaborately folded hood. The costume was wholly secular.

If the papacy had ever been a primarily spiritual authority, it had been long ago. Now its spirituality masked a nexus of raw temporal power.

He took a step away. Meloku knew at once that she wouldn't have to share his bed again. But she wasn't done with him yet.

"I will need a carriage to the papal residence," she said, and hugged her arms to her chest. "I can't be expected to tolerate these filthy streets in a state like this."

De Colville said, "I had left my horses and driver at Jourdonnais's when the fire erupted." Jourdonnais was his gambling friend. "I came as fast as we could."

"Then I should expect that you would get it."

For a moment, Meloku wondered if she might have pushed too far. Until just this morning, she'd been here at his pleasure. Now she was asking him to serve her. She held her expression steady. Finally, he gave a stiff bow and backed out of the door.

Too long a wait later, her augmented hearing picked up de Colville's wagon clopping down the street. By the time it clattered to a stop, she was already at the front door. De Colville's driver startled at her approach. Preternatural "foresight" would only enhance her reputation. Word would get around.

De Colville, happily, was nowhere to be seen. It was small wonder he hadn't come. The seat was hardly large enough for one person. His wagon was a bumpy, poorly built wooden ramshackle. And this was the property of one of the wealthiest men in Europe. Even compared to other primitive planes Meloku had visited, this one had a long way to go.

Meloku hugged her arms to herself to keep herself warm. Her demiorganics could block the sting of the cold, but they still insisted that she huddle up to preserve her core heat. The smell was worse than the cold. Avignon was the filthiest city she'd seen yet. Though the papacy had called Avignon its home for nearly half a century, the city had yet to have a rudimentary rubbish disposal system. Open sewage runnels lined its streets.

She could have traced her course by the smell of urine and stale beer. Cardinal de Colville lived near a number of taverns and whorehouses. There was no place in Avignon without them. The highest-ranking ecclesiastical officials in Avignon lived in splendor unparalleled on this side of the continent, but the city was simultaneously home to the world's poorest preachers and laborers. The squalor invaded the rich men's streets.

When the plague reached Avignon, it would find rich feeding. Meloku projected that casualties here would be a significant fraction above other cities. The boarding houses that served the church's legions of clerks and accountants were so tightly packed that they were *already* a haven for fatal diseases. The higher church officials would do well to flee. Thanks to Cardinal de Colville, Meloku already knew some of their plans.

They were what she hoped to prevent.

Ordinarily, the streets would be still and silent at this time of night. Tonight, men and women stood outside the taverns and brothels, some naked or in their underclothes. Meloku passed two preachers giving impromptu sermons on the fire. Rumors that a woman had predicted the fire would soon permeate every stratum of the city.

No one was panicking – yet. These people lived in what they believed to be an age of miracles. The pillar of fire was just one more way their God manifested Himself in their lives. They were waiting to hear what it meant. Meloku was ready to tell them.

She wasn't accustomed to influencing things so directly. The amalgamates preferred a softer touch. But this assignment was an exception among exceptions.

Most of the Unity's peoples agreed that the amalgamates controlled the Unity, but were a little spottier on the *how* of it. The amalgamates ruled their Core Worlds directly, of course, through edicts enforced by their NAIs and agents. Otherwise, the amalgamates ostensibly retained control only of the gateways. Each member plane retained its own choice of political and economic systems. The amalgamates only adjudicated in trade disputes or anything else that might lead to conflict.

It was no secret that the amalgamates' agents roamed the halls of power everywhere. Most member planes accepted them because the economic, cultural, and security benefits of belonging to the Unity were so attractive. Others became satellites to the Unity, maintaining only a handful of modest trade links. The amalgamates, in their many and varied ways, still made sure that their wishes were represented on those planes. And then there were even more unaligned worlds, colonies, outposts, still wormed through with the amalgamates' agents.

The Unity was less a federation than an espiocracy, a government by spies. Even the power brokers among whom Meloku had spent her teenage years suspected little about how deep and far the amalgamates' influence extended.

The Palais des Papes presented a stone, white-walled, crenelated face to the street. Its windows glowed with torch and candlelight. It looked more like a lord's castle than the home of a godly man. Especially here in Avignon, the papacy's venality was no secret. Clement VI was one of the most profligate men who'd ever held his office. He showered money on his cardinals, many of whom were his nephews and cousins.

Infrared detected not one person sleeping. Cécile, the Countess of Turenne, came to the door when Meloku's driver informed the guards of their arrival. Cécile, it was rumored, was Clement's lover. She was a slight, sharp-cheeked, pale-haired woman. She spent all of her time at the papal palace rather than her own residence, acted as hostess for Clement's parties. Meloku was surprised when a pulse scan detected no scent of sex about her, even days-old. Maybe the rumors were wrong for once.

The countess asked, "Madam Akropolites? You arrived earlier than I was told you might."

Meloku bowed and nodded without answering. She didn't ask for the countess's name. Even if the rumors weren't true, the countess surely must have been aware of them. She stepped past as soon as the countess stepped aside. She exchanged pleasantries as the countess guided her through the halls, but kept her purposes to herself. After only a minute, it became clear that she was having the effect she intended. The countess was stuttering, off-balance.

She led Meloku to an audience chamber hung with gold-lined tapestries and a jeweled chandelier. Pope Clement VI sat cloaked in layers of multihued silk. He was bald but for a fringe of puffy white hair. He spoke with a clear voice. But he wasn't a quarter as impressive as Meloku had imagined. He had trouble meeting Meloku's eyes. His red cap couldn't hide his cold, sweaty forehead. Infrared revealed a racing pulse. The noise and light had terrified him, deeply.

He would listen to anyone who told him what to do about it.

Meloku gifted him with a smile. She could afford to be generous. She had entered this room already a victor.

An hour later, she left Clement pale and shaking. Her wagon was waiting. De Colville had somehow caught up with it, shivering and hugging his arms for warmth. Meloku guessed that he'd probably tried to enter the papal palace and been turned away. The bitter curl of his lips confirmed her guess.

She climbed aboard the wagon. For a moment, he looked as though he might remain there, dumbfounded. As she told the driver to take her back, though, de Colville finally climbed aboard. The wagon's bench only provided comfortable space for one passenger, but he forced his way beside her.

He asked, "Well? How does His Holiness fare?"

"For Christ's vicar on Earth, seeing an actual miracle left him white."

De Colville was one of Clement's strongest supporters among the College of Cardinals, but he let the bait pass without biting. "What did you tell him?"

"That the fire was the wrath of Christ. When I received my vision from the Virgin, she told me she had tried to restrain His holy anger. The pestilence ravaging the south is coming here, where it will strike worst of all."

De Colville swallowed. "Then needs we must leave the city for the countryside. The Curia will be able to–"

"No." She hadn't dared take that tone of voice with him before. "I believe the Virgin Mother spoke to His Holiness through me, unworthy as I am. When I collapsed today, I knew what she wanted. The church must remain here, in Avignon."

"You said the pestilence will annihilate us."

"Christ originally intended to end all men, everywhere. The Virgin begged for clemency, and persuaded him to send the pestilence instead. The pestilence is a punishment, no less for the church than for all men. Trying to escape is like a child trying to run from the rod. It will only make it worse in the end."

"So we're to expose ourselves to destruction on your word?"

"Not my word. By Law."

"Or else what will happen?"

Meloku turned to look through his eyes. "Do you think you could escape God's punishment?"

He couldn't meet her stare for more than a moment. He grunted, and settled back into his bench.

Meloku allowed herself another moment of satisfaction. Clement and his hierarchy would probably have fled to the countryside. They would have stood a higher chance of escaping the worst of the plague. She didn't want them all alive. She wanted them weak and in turmoil. Easily controlled.

The moment of elation faded. She'd won a coup tonight, but tonight would end. Clement had been terrified, but daylight would strengthen his resolve. Meanwhile, the church hierarchy was always disobedient and discordant, even to His Holiness. She had much more work to do. As if to prove it, de Colville asked, "How long have you been planning this?"

"Beg pardon, Your Eminence?"

"That was a very well-timed vision this morning. It happened just when several of the men of His Holiness's court were in earshot."

Meloku held up her hands, still brown with dried blood. "It was more than a vision. The Virgin's guidance always arrives at the moment it's needed."

"The divine revelations of the saints always came in private, not in public."

Meloku was sure he was bluffing, but couldn't be bothered to ask Companion to dig up counterexamples among the natives' myths. "Do you think I created the pillar of flame with my bare hands?"

He hastily shook his head. "Something divine certainly happened this night."

"Then you have no recourse but to take my word as truth. I can leave your home if you doubt me."

"Most of the Curia and all of the College of Cardinals know that you became my mistress as soon as you arrived in Avignon. You're already tarnished by that. If you were to abandon me, all of them would certainly know that you came here from no deep feeling, but to seek an avenue into their offices of power."

Meloku glanced back at him, taking a deeper measure of him. When he thought she was just a Greek outcast making herself available to satisfy his desires, he'd been open and welcoming, but he'd certainly never treated her like an equal. He'd dictated the course of her day to her, when she must stay inside, and whom she had permission to speak with. In the course of a night, she'd turned from a mistress into a political power.

He'd adapted much faster than she'd thought. He was already treating her with the suspicion that he would other power players. "You think my revelations convenient."

"Far be it from me to ever suggest that they would be planned for a woman's benefit."

"They need not be. I will no doubt have several powerful visitors over the next few months, if the Virgin continues to bless me. My host would be at the center of their society." And he would no doubt continue to provide access to high church office.

There wasn't much firelight on the streets, but the little there glimmered in de Colville's eyes. "If offense was taken, I humbly retract my words."

"No offense was taken, Your Eminence."

They rode to his manor in companionable silence. All Meloku needed to know now was what she had been sent here

109

to do. Companion had told her to get this far, and promised that her next instructions would be coming from the amalgamates themselves – though what the amalgamates could possibly want out of a dismal plane like this, she had no idea.

But, for tonight, Companion kept its peace.

9

Niccoluccio packed hastily – more hastily, he knew, then he should have. It was already noon. The thought of one more night alone in this graveyard was enough to make him break out in a sweat.

He took what was left of the bread, brick-hard though it was. He traded his worn old boots for a pair left in the infirmary. He could have found a better fit in the dormitory, but the last thing he wanted was to reenter that mausoleum. He was tempted to dress in the triple-furlined coat and ostentatious hat hanging in Prior Lomellini's cell. But anyone seeing him on the road would assume him to be far above his actual station. Any travelers he met would more likely than not be robbers and brigands. Only devils thrived in Hell.

He shrugged into his own fox-fur coat. He'd brought it into the calefactory. It had been a gift from his parents, the only artifact of his wealthier upbringing he'd been allowed to keep. He pushed aside the monastery gates and left them open. He sidestepped the frozen corpses of the sheep.

Throughout the frenzy of dressing and packing, he'd managed to push the most pressing question from his mind. It crept up on him. What would he do when he reached civilization? The rational thing would be to make contact with the ecclesiastical hierarchy, let somebody know Sacro Cuore's fate. Then what? How would he live while waiting for a response, if indeed a response was forthcoming? He couldn't depend on charity. No doubt the churches would be inundated with orphans and widows.

Assuming, of course, that anyone lived at all. The pestilence had wiped out Sacro Cuore. Niccoluccio had no reason to suppose it had been any less virulent in the secular world. Only a thread of hope kept him believing that Rinieri had been wrong, that God's final judgment hadn't fallen upon the world. That thread was stretched thin.

By occupying his thoughts like this, he kept himself from realizing that he'd left the monastery grounds until they were well out of sight. A chill settled on his bare scalp. His footsteps came to a stop.

He spun a slow circle. Nothing but trees and a smattering of snow. The silence here was as deep as in Sacro Cuore. Strange. Throughout his years there, he'd begun to imagine Sacro Cuore as the quietest place on Earth.

Niccoluccio had last been this far from the monastery two years ago, and not for long. Coming back was like dreaming of childhood places. The half-forgotten shapes of trees remained as they had been. He remembered each curve in the trail only as he came upon it.

Then, over the next slope, was Sacro Cuore's lay community: a cluster of cob homes shaded by the hills and trees, and opening into tilled fields to the north and west. He walked faster, grateful for the sight. Gradually, his pace slackened again. The last time he'd been here, dark clouds of hearth smoke had twisted through the air. Today, there was nothing. No smoke. Not a single fire.

The trail vanished under snow near the village. Last night's storm had snapped three thick branches off the trees at the edge of the clearing. Nobody had come to gather them as firewood.

He reached the closest home. Its goose house was empty. When he knocked, he received no answer. There were no tracks in the fresh snow, but indentations in the mud underneath that might have been footprints.

The door didn't open easily. It was lashed to a stone set in its base, and hadn't been fitted securely. When he finally shoved it open, the daylight fell on two pairs of bare feet, shriveled and blackened, on an earthen floor.

Most of the other houses were empty. Two more held bodies. Another few minutes' searching found mounds of graves, half-buried by snow.

Niccoluccio called. No one answered. Nothing moved. He slumped hard against the rough wall of the nearest house.

He didn't know how many men had lived in the lay community, but it didn't seem like there were enough graves to account for everyone. They must have already left, trying to make their way to the nearest town. They hadn't even gone back to the monastery. Or, if they had, they'd missed him.

He heard a sudden rustle. A cry of despair caught in his throat. Someone was stepping through snow behind the nearest house. Fast.

He stumbled around the side of the house nearly in time to collide with the stranger. But it was no villager. The mastiff froze mid-stride, black eyes staring at him.

Niccoluccio couldn't remember the last time he'd shouted. Certainly not since he'd entered Sacro Cuore, and probably not for years beforehand. Now he shouted until his voice was hoarse. He yelled at the dog until he felt his face would burst.

He could not control himself. The shock and rage spoke for him. The mastiff came back twice, and Niccoluccio chased her off each time. The poor creature would be better off without him. He picked up a rock from one of the frosted-over vegetable gardens and threw it at her. Finally, he was alone. He sat back against the wall and hid his sob under his hands.

He was going to have to follow in the laity's footsteps, but he knew in his heart that he wasn't going to reach the nearest town. He would die. He didn't have enough food to sustain him. He didn't know anything about the roads. He'd counted on finding help here, but he hadn't realized how alone he actually was.

The ice quickly numbed his skin. Cold air bit through his coat. He should have been moving, but his energy had fled.

A monk shouldn't fear death. He'd thought he'd known where he was bound. There would be a seeming eternity of Purgatory before his final acceptance into Paradise. He'd spent all of his time at Sacro Cuore trying to prepare himself. Now that it had arrived, none of it seemed real.

A quiet, rational voice ticked away his faults in the corner of his mind. He was acting in ways contrary to the man he'd imagined himself to be. Just this past minute, he'd shown himself crueler than he would have believed. *The poor creature would be better off without him.* The excuse had sounded hollow even in the moment he'd thought it.

By the time he pieced what remained of his wits back together, the sun had traveled a wide arc across the sky. He picked himself off the frozen ground and tried to rub some feeling back into his thighs. It was slow in coming. His hands shook uncontrollably. He wasn't actually sure how much of himself he'd found again, but it seemed enough for now. He had to start moving. If he stayed with no company but his damning thoughts, there might as well not have been any difference between Hell and the here and now.

He couldn't see the Via Romea di Stade from here. He had a vague idea of which direction to go, but that was all. He set out heedless of the approaching evening. He couldn't conceive of spending a night in any of the abandoned houses, let alone trekking back to the monastery. He knew, instinctively, that if he entered either, he would die before he could leave.

Eventually he reached a parting in the trees that must certainly have been a road. There were no tracks in the snow or dirt. Niccoluccio frowned. In winter, the old pilgrimage road saw little traffic, but it hardly went unused. He trudged southward.

But for his crunchy footsteps and heavy breathing, silence abounded. The pestilence must have stifled traffic. But part of him was already imagining reaching the next town and finding it deserted but for the dead. The whole world had been swept away and left him behind.

As the sun neared the horizon, the shadows of the trees deepened and covered the path. Niccoluccio's footsteps seemed like they carried for leagues in the cold air. No matter how he stepped, he couldn't stifle them. Once, he heard a sharp *crack* a quarter-mile off. After a moment crouched and waiting, he decided it must have been a tree branch snapping under the weight of the snow. He kept his ears perked for other sounds of travelers, but there were none. If there was anyone else here, they were lying in wait.

The last time he'd traveled the Via Romea di Stade, he hadn't been alone. He'd walked alongside a cart. He'd felt like he was fleeing Florence and the people he'd left there. Three monks had met him at the end of his journey. Niccoluccio hadn't been able to stop staring at them. They were the most serene men he'd ever seen – too peaceful, almost. Their hoods made them seem identical. They were as Niccoluccio imagined saints when he was a boy.

He'd learned the truth about their individuality later, of course, but that moment had only confirmed the choice he'd made. Leaving Florence, losing his family's money and comfort, his father – he'd pay all that and more again for the chance to be like those men. He'd never felt less worthy of them than right now, but even the thought of them steadied his step and stifled his shivering.

Clouds darkened the sky to the south and west. He didn't let them deter his course. As the first needles of freezing rain pierced his arms, he tried to remember the psalms he'd sung in choir the morning after he'd graduated from his novitiate.

Better that all the robbers and silences of the world hear that, if they were going to hear him anyway.

Niccoluccio jolted out of sleep sore and shaking. He clawed at the air until he realized there was nothing out there, nothing shaking him awake – he was shaking of his own volition. He didn't know what time it was, or how long he'd been shivering.

This was his second night. The first hadn't been this bad. He'd taken cover under a low pine. He woke sore and miserable, but himself. Last night, there had been no trees with low branches, so he'd crawled under the half-hearted shelter of a bush. The needles and sticks had scratched, but, once he'd settled, he could at least trick himself into feeling comfortable. A carpet of twigs and leaves shielded him from the frozen earth. Since his coat hadn't yet dried from the recurrent, petty rains, he'd hung it overhead and relied on his habit for warmth.

That had been at the end of the day, before all the heat had ebbed out of the world. This night was a new place. A torment he'd only just become conscious of. He scrabbled free of the bush. The ground spun as if on a pottery wheel. He fell on his first attempt to stand. His bones had turned to ice, yet sweat plastered his underclothes to his skin. He stomped to regain feeling in his feet. In a sudden panic, he checked his underarms for buboes. He felt nothing but sweat.

He didn't have to search long for an alternate explanation for the dizziness. He hadn't eaten all yesterday afternoon or evening. He'd been intent on preserving his supplies. He'd fasted for longer, after all. But on fast days he hadn't been marching all day, or parched.

He put on his coat, but that only made the cold bite harder. The coat had gotten wetter overnight. It must have rained while he slept. He threw it aside and hugged his arms to his chest. But he couldn't see the ground. He was swimming in ink. He felt his way forward, shivering violently, until he couldn't stand it any longer and threw himself recklessly ahead just to get his blood flowing. A broken leg or ankle would kill him, but so surely would staying still.

He ducked away from branches as they brushed his cheek. Miraculously, he didn't trip, and only crashed into a tree once. A world of wormy, veinlike shadows resolved ahead of him. After a minute, feeling returned to his feet. He wished it hadn't. He was walking on knives. His fingers were no better.

Half his body had been taken from him while he slept.

He strode in circles. Suggestions of silhouettes turned into trees, hillsides, the mountains rising to the south. There must have been a modicum of moonlight, or even a kiss of dawn. He kept circling and pacing, rubbing his hands. And then stopped.

All at once, he realized he didn't know where he was. The trees didn't look like they had the night before. He must have gone too far pacing, or taken a wrong turn circling.

He retraced his steps until he found something recognizable. The familiarity was fleeting. He hadn't taken a close look at his surroundings the night before. The bush he'd sheltered under had been some distance from the road.

He'd left his coat, bread and water there.

Yesterday, he had started to wonder if he'd found the Via Romea di Stade after all. The road had seemed more of a clearing carved through the trees. Brushes tangled its path. He'd already gone too far to turn back. He'd kept going and tried not to think about it. This road had to lead *somewhere*.

But now the shadows showed him several clearings that seemed like they could have been the road. He fought and stumbled his way toward one, positive he'd found the right one. He retraced his steps toward the bush under which he'd taken shelter. Nothing; just another unfamiliar batch of trees.

He took careful stock of his surroundings, trying not to panic. Nothing looked right. The rain had turned the snow to filthy slush. Not long after Niccoluccio regained feeling in his toes, he lost it to the third icy puddle. His boots were soaked through. In Sacro Cuore, he'd gone barefoot in penitential processions, but not once had that been as bad.

By the time the sky brightened, he was still searching. He didn't *think* he could have gone very far, but he recognized nothing, nor could he find the road. The forest took on an entirely different cadence at dawn, and nothing looked like it had at night. He walked in circles, larger and larger each time, cursing his stupidity. Several times he spotted bushes like the one he had slept under, and dashed toward them only to discover nothing underneath.

Finally, when the sun shone high through the overcast and his throat was raw from thirst and desperation, he gave up searching.

His eyes burned. He hadn't felt so ashamed of himself since his final confession in Florence – the most personal, intimate he'd ever given. But he'd already suffered more for this mistake than any sin he'd ever committed.

That was a faithless thought, he knew. He was never going to meet his brothers again. They had crossed through Purgatory and were bound to Paradise – and he was on the first leg of his journey into the darkness. He had been since before he'd left Florence. He couldn't deceive himself any longer.

He stumbled southward, half-blinded, heading toward the high hills on the southern horizon. They at least meant he was headed in the right direction. His throat was rusty with thirst. He searched in vain for some sign of a road, but later just walked as straight a course as the forest allowed. For all that clumps of trees and brush and steep-faced hills forced him to veer, though, he must have been wandering like a drunkard.

He gathered what little snow had survived the morning's rain, and dabbed it in his mouth to keep his tongue from feeling like tree bark. He'd stopped shivering, at least. His habit kept him warm enough when the sun was out.

He stumbled across a brownish stream late in the afternoon. He crouched by the water and drank mightily, ignoring the rusty taste. By the time he finished, his stomach felt bulged and swollen. Dirt flecked the inside of his mouth. He couldn't conjure the saliva to spit it out. Hunger had crept up on him from the margins of his awareness, but he hadn't realized how hungry he was until he'd sated his thirst. A sudden, stabbing pang in his stomach made him jolt upright in shock.

He'd had bread as breakfast on the day he'd left, and more during his walk yesterday. It hadn't seemed important, then. He was ashamed of his body for the fact that it seemed important now. He'd worked hard to master it, but he would always be a slave to its wicked desires. Sacro Cuore had done nothing but buy him a temporary reprieve from the person he'd been.

He closed his eyes. He shouldn't doubt himself like this. Everyone who'd entered Sacro Cuore had desires that chased them away from the temporal world. He doubted any of them had defeated them in their entirety. Even saints sinned.

He should have confessed more often. He'd been afraid of his brothers finding out what he'd left in Florence. About Pietro, and Elisa – but especially Pietro. His life at Sacro Cuore had been too important to risk. He didn't know that any of them would allow him to stay if they knew. He'd confessed several times to his tutor and his priest in Florence, and that had seemed enough. Both men had encouraged him to seek a monastery. Since he'd reached Sacro Cuore, the thoughts had become less troubling.

But they hadn't gone away.

He took a breath to gather himself, stood. He took measure of the horizon and the foothills ahead. Farther on, snowy peaks cleaved the sky. If he kept heading toward the mountains, he would cross southbound roads heading east around them. He remembered, on his trip to Sacro Cuore twelve years ago, shadowing the mountains for days at a time.

He hobbled forward, trying to walk around the pains in his stomach. His head swam, but he was able to put it behind him. For the first time since he'd set out from Sacro Cuore, he wasn't afraid of the death he was surely marching toward.

That didn't last as long as he would have liked.

A crinkle from a bed of leaves behind him drew his attention. A shadow darted into the trees. He spun, froze. The shape had been too low and too fast to be a person, but neither had it been small. It had disappeared by the time he focused on it.

He turned back toward the hills and walked quickly. Already the sun was near the western horizon. If this night was to be as cold as last, he would never survive sleep. He would have to try to walk through the night. The icicle in his stomach and the lightness of his head made him doubt he could do that, either.

More than once, hunger pangs drove him to halt. Each time it was harder to force his legs forward again. He chastised himself, but that didn't do more than further drain his energy. Thoughts of food became a constant bedevilment. He even kept an eye out for stray hares and birds, not that he would know what to do if he saw one. He had never hunted, not during his youth and certainly not at Sacro Cuore.

By the time the sky turned red, he became aware that his path was no longer straight. He weaved and bobbled like a drunkard. He blinked and forced himself to straighten it. The next time his feet wandered, he only just managed to avoid running into a tree that rose out of the blurred forest. He set his hand on it and paused, panting.

That was the first time he realized he hadn't been seeing straight. The forest resolved into focus, but only for a moment. He had to concentrate to see.

When he heard a crumple of leaves, he was sure he was hallucinating it. He turned just in time to see a devilish shape dart into the long shadows. A four-legged shadow ran after the first.

Golden eyes met his stare unflinchingly. His breath caught in his throat. Wolves. They looked as thin and ragged as he felt, but no less menacing.

The pestilence had made the world mad. He was being stalked. Wolves didn't attack travelers outside of children's tales. He never thought it could happen here, in civilized Italy.

But the pestilence didn't just strike humans. The dead sheep outside Sacro Cuore, and the dead dogs within, were testament to that. These animals had avoided the pestilence because they were smart enough not to eat plague carrion, but they must have been starving. And crazed.

The thought gave him the energy to push away from the tree. His pulse lashed against his ears. He marched onward, half-turned backward.

He managed to get a count of the wolves from the glimpses they allowed him. There were four of them. They skulked after him speedily and relentlessly, closer every minute. Their features faded into shadow as the night advanced, but he could still see their perked ears, their loping canine grace.

He tried shouting, but the noise that came out of his throat was hoarse and not very frightening at all. He couldn't keep walking backwards, not on ground this uneven, so he eventually had to take his eyes off them. He lost track of two of them.

As much as he'd braced for it, the first attack took him entirely by surprise. A hard, sharp pain slammed into the small of his back. It shoved him to the ground face first. Teeth the size of coins sank through his habit.

Niccoluccio hadn't known he had any energy left until that moment. His elbow lashed back, caught the wolf under its chin. He felt more than heard its jaw snapping. The wolf jerked back and danced away, but didn't go any farther than the nearest clump of trees.

He struggled to his feet. Heat ran fluidly down his back. His pressed his hand to it and felt warm and sticky cloth.

The other wolves watched him from just a few dozen feet away. Niccoluccio frantically looked about the trees, trying to decide if he had the strength to climb any of them. He didn't, but it hardly mattered. The trees were crooked and spindly. He doubted he could find a branch high enough to support his weight even if he could get up.

One of the wolves circled him. Another trotted in the opposite direction, trying to get behind him. They were treating him cautiously, with respect – but they weren't wasting any more time. Agony crawled up his back; the pain of the bites had just only just started to arrive. Everything went dizzy. The horizon spun, and, for a long moment, he had to put all of his effort into staying upright.

For twelve years, whenever Niccoluccio thought of his death, he'd been content believing that he would be buried at Sacro Cuore. His body would be laid to rest intact, following his Last Rites and final confession, ready to be Purged and enter Paradise. What would happen beyond that was beyond imagination, but he would be as prepared as any mortal, short of saints, could be.

Vanity and self-deception. He had administered the Last Rites to as many brothers as he could, but it was plain now that he would die unshriven. When he died, there would be nothing left to bury. He'd been foolish to expect robbers. There were never going to be any robbers. Everyone had left the mortal world, and he was the only one still here.

He fell onto his knees without ever having been pushed.

It was too dark to see the next attack. It landed on the back of his neck. Niccoluccio instinctively jerked his head aside. Teeth sank into his shoulder. He cried out. All he could see of the wolf was its snout, bloody-lipped, and demonically snarled. Its eyes met his.

Niccoluccio saw a shadow move just soon enough to bring his arm up. He managed to deflect the second wolf's bite. It latched onto his wrist and wrenched him aside.

He was yanked to the ground, and his face dashed into icy mud. For a moment, the world had turned upside down, and he clung to the ground for fear of falling into the sky.

A wolf's paw stood two inches from his open eye. Red and black blotches filled his vision. He was sure he saw blood splash across the dirt. Needle-sharp pain stabbed into the side of his neck. He felt, but not heard, hot breath against his ear.

He couldn't force himself up. The weight of the wolves had become the weight of the earth, burying him. All of his limbs felt asleep, distant. With what little control he had left, he forced himself to lie still. His fighting instincts amounted to little more than twitching anyway. He allowed the wolf gripping his wrist to tug him over, face up. There was no point in fighting; there never had been. This was the end to which his whole life had crescendoed.

The truth about everything that had happened since he'd left Sacro Cuore came to him in an instant, a snap-spark of revelation so bright that it seared. He had died long ago, back in the monastery. He had tumbled through Purgatory, and hadn't made it through. He didn't deserve to. He never had, not since the day he'd run away from the man he'd been in Florence. Sacro Cuore had just been a distraction.

He couldn't deny it any longer. For the first time in his life, he didn't have the energy.

He'd spent so much time hiding his secrets from himself, but he couldn't hide them from the Father. The air roared in his ears. The sky turned too white to look at. His arms were pinned open. He craned his head to expose his neck, ready for the final Judgment.

10

The Genoese fell to the pestilence like wheat to the harvest.

From infrared observation, Habidah confirmed a sixty percent mortality rate so far, and that was even taking the flight to the countryside into account. Whole neighborhoods became mass graves.

The plague's grip on the city was diminishing, but it was far from gone. Habidah spent all of her waking hours walking among the survivors, rapt by what she saw. Collectively, among every social class, they'd gone from fear and flight to acceptance, even as the plague took its daily toll of hundreds. Now, even people who had the opportunity to leave Genoa chose not to. It was astounding what people, collectively, could put up with when they saw their neighbors doing the same.

Nobody had moved into the abandoned houses on Habidah's street, of course. They knew better. Nor were businesses and marketplaces reopening. But people were venturing outside of their homes to find out which of their family and neighbors had survived thus far. Habidah heard men and women ask each other on the street, in disbelief, "You are still alive?"

Courts were in session. Habidah listened in on one case, a nephew and a stepbrother disputing the inheritance of a small house. The previous owner had left a will, but all five other beneficiaries had died. When the court reconvened the next day, neither claimant arrived. Habidah tracked them down. They'd perished overnight.

The city restructured around the plague. Civil servants were replaced as soon as they died. For once, they didn't come exclusively from the Genoese elite, who no longer had so many sons and nephews to spare. The city hired hundreds of new corpse carriers and gravediggers.

The only men willing to take such obviously risky jobs came from the lower strata of society, rural Italians who couldn't survive as mercenaries or brigands. They plied the streets at all times of day. They kept the corpses from piling on the streets or rotting under too-shallow graves. But they also ran rampant through the taverns and whorehouses, or robbed whoever they pleased.

On her nightly walks, Habidah observed gangs of gravediggers breaking into homes. She'd nearly run to help when she'd seen three gravediggers pull knives on a lone father with three children. The gravediggers wouldn't have stood a chance against her. Only the thought of Feliks held her back. The last thing she needed was for him to report her.

The worst thing was that he wouldn't do it out of spite. He'd do it because he was concerned. He'd already decided she wasn't suited for this.

Maybe he was right.

Genoa's response to the plague made a marked contrast to her own. She buried what she could under a flood of antidepressants and electrocortical stimulation. She could only go so far with those before arousing Feliks' concern.

She was accustomed to working alone. She'd forgotten how much pressure came from just the fact of being watched. She was always on edge, always thinking about how she would be seen.

She trudged back in the hours before dawn, taking care to keep clear of the carousing gravediggers. She hardly went to their house except to sleep. She'd been out for thirty-six hours.

When she entered, Feliks was sitting up on his bed, staring at a map of the city projected on the opposite wall. The onierophage was making using his demiorganics uncomfortable. Several hot yellow blips stood out on each street. He said, "I think we've got enough eavesdropper coverage that you don't need to be out there."

"We don't rely on eavesdroppers. That's why I go out."

"The first wave of plague deaths are just about over here. I know we don't have the manpower to visit every Italian city, but I think it would be appropriate to spend some manpower surveying the rest of the peninsula."

"The plague's cooling down, sure. But not the people. The state of the city is changing every day."

"I think I'll be able to observe that from here, through the eavesdroppers."

Habidah sat heavily on her bed. "*You?*"

"I know I'm not doing well, but I'm not dead yet."

"You really think you're up to it?"

"I'm trying to be diplomatic, Habidah. You need to get out of this city before you lose your mind. Get in the shuttle, go up there, clear your head."

"Medical leave, you mean."

"We all need breaks. You've been out there for ninety-five percent of your waking hours for a month. Frankly, I'm amazed you haven't had a breakdown already."

"The last time we were on assignment together, I managed three months like this."

"That assignment was a biosurvey. People didn't die every day. You weren't getting to know families just in time for them to get annihilated. This is harder than anybody should have to watch. It's been getting to you. I know."

Habidah shrugged. Her impulse to deny it was a foolish one, she knew. She couldn't deny what her brain chemistry made plain as day. "I didn't come here to be happy."

"You're not going to be much good to anyone if you fall apart. Come back after you've taken a trip, gotten some new air in you."

"Sounds too fair," Habidah said, only just keeping back what she really wanted to say.

Feliks said, "I also know you're chafing living with me."

"I am not," Habidah said. She didn't know why she was denying it.

"You're not going to offend me if you say it. I don't want this assignment to end with us not on speaking terms. I know it's not your fault, or my fault, if we can't live together. So I'm asking you to please take a break. I'll let you know if anything interesting happens here. Sound fair, too?"

Habidah hated the way her voice sounded when she said, "Sure."

That evening, she stood in a clearing outside the city, waiting for the shuttle. A gust of freezing wind ruffled her wimple. She'd had to wait; the shuttle's camouflage fields weren't up to protecting it during the day. A shadow waved across the sky. Then the shuttle dropped the camouflage fields. It was right there, hovering and huge.

This time, the shuttle waited until she was snug in her acceleration couch before gaining altitude. She soared along the Italian coast, putting distance between her and Genoa. She watched the map, and then turned to the cameras. It was too dark to see past the reflection of the cabin lights.

She leaned into her cushions and let the engines' vibration throb against her ears. All of the exhaustion she should have felt over the past few weeks was catching up with her all at once. It wasn't just Feliks that she was running from. It was the whole damned plane. The plague here and the plague back home.

But she still had too much work to treat this like a vacation, no matter what Feliks thought. She dimmed the lights in the cabin. Details emerged on the monitors. She was cruising above a churning, tumultuous sea of starlit black-and-grey clouds. The western sky was still twilight-blue. She wasn't even sure she was still over land until she pinged one of the survey team's positioning satellites. The shuttle was taking her south, not too far from Naples.

When she was nearly upon Naples, she told the shuttle to

127

descend under the overcast. Visual scanning showed a few firelights, tiny stars. Infrared unveiled a far richer tableau. Bright red blotches delineated sleeping bodies, hazy old smoke from fires burning to embers.

None of her team had been to Naples, and none were scheduled to go, but she didn't need to pull up satellite records to see that the plague had struck here, too. Infrared showed empty houses, whole abandoned streets, even the cooling bodies of the recently dead.

There was worse yet. A pulse scan found neighborhoods reduced to burnt husks, littered with fresh dead. All had died at once. They'd been massacred. She knew immediately what had happened. Joao had watched and reported on many similar events. All over Europe, people blamed the plague on a conspiracy of Jews, and torched their neighborhoods.

The Neapolitans had washed streets in a slurry of Jewish blood and ashes.

She couldn't tear her eyes away. She nearly directed the shuttle to land, though she didn't know what she'd do. She couldn't stay long. Maybe she could help a person or two. But Feliks would immediately know what she was doing.

He had his principles. They felt like shackles around her hands.

She ordered the shuttle to turn hard north.

She wondered, not for the first time, what had become of the fisherman in Messina. He might have gotten out of the city in time, he might not. It had been worth taking a chance for. She never could have done even that much with Feliks looking over her.

She closed her eyes and breathed into her hands. How long it had been since she'd cried? Her eyes were so dry they hurt. When she tried, she couldn't make one tear.

She thought she'd been prepared for this assignment. All of the others seemed to be doing better, at least when she saw them. Maybe it *would* be best if she went home. But the moment the thought occurred to her, she knew it wouldn't help. She'd be going from one plague to another. Here, she might still send something useful back to the Unity.

She carefully charted a path away from any cities. The world below was a dark, gray canvas. Tiny towns and farms and country houses and even brigand camps lay scattered across the countryside. Their inhabitants' bodies glowed tinily. Radar landscaping found several buildings empty and abandoned. Chemical analysis handily told the difference between those abandoned long ago and those that held the recently dead. Habidah's mind's eye conjured images of children lying still in their parents' arms, livestock fallen in piles.

Several wealthy country refuges seemed untouched, with dozens of active or sleeping inhabitants. These manors might be worth a look. They were perfect case studies of healthy, isolated citizens coping with the loss and despair seizing the Unity. They'd left their friends and families, and often their fortunes, just to improve their odds of survival. Many in the Unity were trying the same. Joao and Kacienta had left families to come here.

She soared past the constellation of refuges without stopping. She didn't know what she was looking for. She wasn't fit for this assignment, not in this state. She'd come here to accomplish, but all she'd done so far was bear witness. It would drive her mad if she couldn't do more. So many survivors of this plague drove themselves frenetic. They spent their hours working to collect for their churches, caring for orphans, praying for help and for the souls of the departed.

Radar landscaping showed broad, rocky hills. Very few infrared sources dotted the horizon. A distant town – more of a cluster of houses – stood to the east, a few farmhouses around it, without any infrared sources at all, even livestock.

The infrared specks grew farther between. She'd entered a heavily forested region. This far from the towns and cities, the wildlife stood out. She pulled up an infrared survey of the region taken months before the plague. Even accounting for the seasonal change, there were far fewer animals than there should have been. The plague had come in through the trade road, but it penetrated the forest rapidly.

She spotted a skulk of foxes out much later than they should have been. They had quite a hunt ahead of them, judging from the paucity of infrared fuzz to indicate hares and other prey animals.

One heat signature caught her attention. She reduced speed. There – one human shape caught in the midst of several red blurs. They were dog-shaped. Habidah's eyes widened. They were wolves, attacking the person.

She'd seen wolves and wolf-analogues on many other planes, but never attacking a human. Like the foxes, the pack must have been desperate. As she watched, the person toppled to the ground with one of the wolves latched on his neck.

She forced herself to look away, and commanded the shuttle to accelerate. She didn't want to see what would happen. Everything in that person's story had already been written. It was only a matter of flipping the last page.

There was no reason in the multiverse why the amalgamates couldn't have given them a cure for this plague. If not now, then when they had learned all they could and were about to leave. Even Feliks wouldn't object to that. There was a difference between detachment and callousness.

Before she'd applied for this assignment, she'd seen detachment as a mark of professionalism – of craft. She couldn't take charge of the natives' destinies. It would have been vanity. Even the amalgamates, powerful and control-hungry as they were, didn't force planes to mirror their values. She was far less impartial than they.

Now, all those excuses sounded hollow. There was no principle in keeping her hands off even when there was nothing useful to observe.

Feliks was probably watching. The amalgamates always were – if not directly, then by proxy. A hard lump burned in her throat. It stopped her from swallowing. The weight of it kept her from thinking of anything else as the shuttle pulled away.

11

Niccoluccio lay unmoving under a blanket of numbness. Echoes of the agony lingered in his memory.

His body had been torn apart, he was sure of it. It had been ripped away from him one painful bit at a time, until all he was left with was the numbness and endless light and noise. The noise was like roaring rain, thunder that never faded. There was nothing intelligible in either. The light hurt to look at, but he had nothing with which to block it.

His arm lay unmoving, pale and distant, as if through a foggy window. He felt no attachment to it. He couldn't have looked away. He didn't even know how.

The light had seemed endless and perfect the first time it had washed across him, but now he spotted minute variations, splotches of shadow. Unknowable shapes, like afterimages, rippled like waves. Stars and sparks scintillated. Late at night, unable to sleep, he sometimes decided to stay awake until the call for Vigils. He would go to his garden and stare at the stars for so long that they seared into his eyes. He watched individual stars set or rise. Watching the celestial sphere had been like communing with perfection.

He watched and waited, trying to discern patterns, but none emerged.

He wasn't breathing. He'd never realized, until now, how much he depended on the feeling of air coming in and out, of his chest rising. As a drum beating for hours faded into the background rhythm of awareness, so breathing had always been woven into the tapestry of his thoughts, the rhythm of his life. As Pietro and Elisa had become back home. It was just as good to escape.

Some of the numbness parted like a curtain. A hot pressure mounted in the place where his chest had been. It was quickly becoming urgent.

A weight pressed the center of his being. Then another close to his heart. He still had a body after all, he realized with a shock. The shadows were touching him.

He couldn't feel anything of his old self, could only see his body out of the corner of his eye. His arm lay across slushy mud, open-palmed. Some of the slush was stained with his blood.

The tide of noise dwindled to nothing. The silence that persisted afterward was deeper than any he'd experienced before. The pressure in his chest was intolerable.

This must have been what Hell was like, he realized. Dead, alienated from his body but still in it, still sensate. The pains of death and decay accumulating minute after minute, day after day, forever.

The light shifted around him. Shadows stirred the grass. A brush like warm fingertips followed its passage. The ground fell away, and nothing touched him.

Then the pressure in the center of his chest lifted all at once. Sweet-smelling air flooded through him. He gasped. It was like rosewater and saffron. He'd never tasted anything so striking. It was as if the most wonderful music were coursing through his body, though all remained silent.

He was being carried away from the bloodstained ground, from the agonies and sufferings left limp and still behind him.

When awareness returned, the blistering light had fled the world, and left him in suspension. The only sensation left was warmth, indescribable warmth, and fullness of being.

The light that remained was warm, steady, and colored

133

like the sun. It came in strips smooth as brushstrokes. He felt himself still rising, rising skyward, though nothing moved.

His head spun with the delirium of it all. He rasped a laugh. His breath came lightly, and he still couldn't control it.

He tried to raise his hand to his forehead to steady himself, but he couldn't move his arms. His body had ceased to be his own. He rested on a curved and cushioned pillow twice as large as his body, more comfortable than anything he'd ever felt before.

He wasn't alone.

A woman sat on another black pillow. An unearthly play of blobby red light turned her into a half-silhouette. Her hair was bound tightly behind her. A wimple lay discarded across a slanted table. Straps held her body to her seat, but her arms were free.

"Why do I deserve this?" he asked.

She glanced back at him once before returning her attention to the lights. Her eyes were bloodshot. "Least I could do," she muttered.

Before Niccoluccio could speak again, another tide of euphoria crashed through him and rendered him insensate.

PART II

12

For the first few hours, it was easy to move without thinking. All Habidah had to do was what came naturally. The medical patches did the rest.

The shuttle's spotlights and the roar of its unbaffled thrusters had scared the wolves away. She found the man lying unbreathing, in shock from blood loss. She'd planted a medical patch on his chest to restart his heart, and another to regulate his breathing. A third flooded him with enough adrenaline and endorphins to convince his brain to keep going. Dermal spray stemmed the bleeding.

Given rest and warmth, a healthy man could have convalesced without intervention other than a transfusion, but this man was far from healthy. She cradled him in her arms and hauled him into the shuttle. Now it was her turn to flood her system with endorphins. Even with muscular enhancements, she'd never built herself to carry other people. By the time she got him strapped in, she'd had to block the pain receptors from torn muscles.

The monk – and it didn't take long to discover that he was a monk, once he came to some semblance of consciousness and started babbling – was unnaturally gaunt and bony. No wonder those wolves had thought him viable prey. He had no coat. Given the freezing rain the satellites said was coming over the horizon, he would certainly have frozen to death.

It was plain just from looking at him that he needed more

help than a lift to the nearest town. His blood pressure was too light to feel his pulse. The medical patches supersaturated his blood with oxygen. Soon, though, he'd need a transfusion.

She ordered the shuttle to head to the field base.

Feliks would notice. A landing or two might have gone unremarked upon, but not this. Kacienta was at the field base, too, and Habidah couldn't hide from her. It would have been undignified to even try.

Now that she'd made the fatal choice, she might as well own it. She called Kacienta. "I'm bringing back an injured guest. Be standing by with the blood synthesis and transfusion kit when I arrive. B positive."

She cut the transmission before Kacienta could ask.

The monk stirred. He squinted through his endorphin and painkiller-induced delirium. His gaze traveled around before locking on the monitors. "A miracle."

"Suppose it is," Habidah said, for lack of a better answer. There was no way that the monk, or frankly anyone on this plane, would attribute his rescue to worldly causes. She wondered how far to let him go along imagining this was divine intervention.

It would be better for him to know some of the truth. "It may be a miracle, but I'm certainly not."

The monk tried to focus on her. "Who sent you?"

"Nobody. My leaders will be upset when they find out I've done this."

He seemed a little smaller. "Did you come from Heaven or from Hell?"

"I'm from a farm south of Lyon," she said, and that did a good job of shutting him up for a moment. "That's where my, ah… wagon is taking you now."

"Quite a journey," he said, after a moment.

"It's a fast wagon."

She was nearly there already. The field base's landing beacon shone above the horizon. The monk moaned as the shuttle dropped. At least he had eaten so little that he had nothing to throw up.

The shuttle landed with a jarring *clunk*, prompting another gasp. "Nothing's gone wrong," she said. Rather than startle him by allowing the shuttle to undo his safety harness, she tugged it loose for him. He hitched his arm over her shoulder. "The road's a little rough this time of year."

He said nothing, though of course he would have been an idiot if he'd believed her. Habidah took his whole weight on her shoulder. She pulled him through the ventral corridor and down the boarding ramp. A wall of freezing air greeted them. The monk's gaze lolled up. He gaped at the shuttle's silhouette. She pushed his head downward before he could believe what he'd seen.

He looked around the wide, moonlit plain. He slurred, "We were near a forest," though he didn't seem very agitated by this fact. He just wanted to let her know.

She ground her teeth and dragged him. He tried to walk, but could only manage one or two steps before slumping into her. She had to kick the farmhouse doors ajar. The ramp entrance, at least, opened automatically. Light flooded the walk down.

Kacienta was hurrying up to meet them. Habidah hadn't seen her face-to-face in months. She, too, was a small woman, and squatter, with long, dark brown hair and skin a shade too dark to be native to the region. At least she was in costume, hair hidden under a wimple. Her lips tightened. She hoisted the monk's other arm over her shoulder.

"What the fuck were you thinking?" she hissed. Habidah pretended she didn't hear.

The moment she reached the bottom of the ramp, the monk gasped. Too late, Habidah noticed the viewwalls were on, and projecting scenes of a vast, sandy-walled cavern. Sun globes cast sharp shadows across the kilometer-wide walls. A carpet of patchy green farmland clung to the distant floor like moss. Skyscraper-sized tunnels wormholed the walls. Habidah felt like a microbe lost in a sponge. This was Kacienta's home plane, Arbor.

Like Habidah's world, much of Arbor was underground, but the similarities ended there. Kacienta hadn't grown up in warrens and bunkers but in vast caverns like worlds, each ten or more kilometers in diameter, with their own climates and microecologies. They exported genengineered fungi and fauna to the rest of the Unity. It was as cosmopolitan, if not as high-technology, as Providence Core, Joao's home. Kacienta was accustomed to dealing with outsiders – and seemed to have a low tolerance for all of them. She glared at the monk.

Habidah ordered the illusion off. The corridor became flat, claustrophobic gray walls. The monk shook his head and winced.

The double doors to Feliks' office slid open of their own accord. The monk started. When they were through them, he glanced around her shoulder as if to see who might have opened them.

Habidah tried not to show her relief when she saw that Feliks had disposed of his plague corpses. She laid the monk atop the first of the three white examination beds. Kacienta had rolled the blood synthesis kit out of storage. It sat on a cart, broad, gray-and-black, rectangular, about the size of a head. Thin tubes dangled out its side, drawing organic sludge from feedlines plugged into the wall. The device clicked and ticked like a pair of knitting needles.

Kacienta picked up a fat, needle-tipped tube. The monk tried to struggle off the bed, but Habidah held his arm steady. He looked at the ceiling, and didn't fight the second and third needles. With the mélange of painkillers swimming in his system, Habidah doubted he would have noticed if he hadn't been looking. She held his arm regardless. His flesh was cold.

"I put tranquilizers in the feed," Kacienta sent. She transmitted rather than spoke to keep the monk from understanding.

She hadn't said a single word to the monk. The monk seemed perplexed by the room's lights. He raised his free hand, palm out, as if to feel for heat.

Kacienta could monitor him. Habidah didn't want to watch him fade away. Gradually, Habidah let go. She told him, "I'm going to step out for just a moment and let your friends know where you are. I'll be back."

The monk, still holding up his hand, said nothing. Habidah wasn't sure he'd heard her.

As she stepped through the doors, the monk told her, "Niccoluccio Caracciola."

She halted on the other side, and looked back. Somehow he'd found the strength to crane his head. He was staring at her with quiet, taut desperation.

"Habidah Shen," she managed to say before the doors shut.

The monk spent three days regaining his health, fading in and out of a drug-induced coma. Finally, Habidah took him off his tranquilizers and let him wake. She spoke to him as he stirred so he would have a voice to listen to.

She brought him food and warm milk from the kitchen. He drank quietly and said little. He looked about the walls of Feliks' office, mesmerized by its clean, simple shapes. Finally, he turned to her, visibly trying his best to absorb what she was saying. It was obviously too much for him. He smiled, confused.

When Habidah had to leave, she made sure to lock him in.

Feliks remotely supervised his convalescence while finishing up in Genoa. He hadn't said anything to Habidah – yet. Habidah hadn't answered his one call. Considering how quickly he and NAI usually patched up most injuries, three days had been a very long recovery period. The bites and blood loss had only been Niccoluccio's most superficial problems. He'd been hypothermic. He'd been starved over the past few days, and eaten poorly for longer. She could count his ribs. His arms and legs were just as bony.

One important medical test came back negative right away. There was no trace of the plague bacillus. That was the only thing she couldn't cure.

She sat in the conference room with Joao and Kacienta, watching Niccoluccio through the cameras. He was picking at the patch on the side of his neck. Habidah had told him not to, but he still did when he thought she wasn't watching. The patch had adhered so firmly that he would have had better luck removing his ear.

Kacienta said, "We should have kept him on tranquilizers."

Habidah hadn't yet figured out what had made Kacienta choose extraplanar anthropology, except perhaps as a stepping stone to another field. This was only her third field assignment. She was the team's data analyst, meaning she spent large chunks of her time cloistered here, compiling reports. That seemed to suit her.

Joao said, "It doesn't matter. He already saw everything in that room before you two put him under."

Joao had arrived a day ago. Feliks, too, was on his way. His shuttle had just landed. Only Meloku had refused to return. She participated remotely. When she spoke, her voice was even cooler than usual. "He might have assumed that he had been dreaming or hallucinating."

Kacienta said, "If too many of the locals know we're here, they'll certainly change their collective response to the plague. It will contaminate our work."

Joao said, "Whatever. It's not the point. If we think he might get out and say something that would interfere with the survey, we can drop him off in Australia. The point is that this is a completely unnecessary, and risky, entanglement. We didn't come here to help these people. We came to help *us*. Any time and effort we don't spend on our mission comes at the expense of millions of people back home."

Habidah kept her eyes on the monitor. There wasn't much to say in her defense. She wasn't particularly worried about this one man changing the world. Kacienta was overestimating the influence of a lone monk. Niccoluccio was all but powerless. He had no friends to return to. Satellites confirmed that the monastery Niccoluccio named had been completely abandoned.

Niccoluccio gave up his attempt to peel off the medical patch. He felt back and forth the smooth contours of his bed. She smiled briefly. It was like watching a puppy explore a new home.

Joao said, "This is endangering everything we're doing. There are only five of us. We can't spend our energy helping these people. If we did, we'd run out of resources long before we accomplished what we came here to do."

The door whisked open. Feliks entered, still in Genoan costume. Habidah swallowed. She'd been dreading this. He paused to lean on the edge of the table. After glancing at her, he focused on Joao. He'd been listening in. "Do you think that, because Dr Shen helped this one man, we're now going to instantly abandon our mission and spend all of our time helping the locals?"

"That's where I'm afraid this is going to lead, yes."

"You must have learned about the slippery slope fallacy sometime in those expensive Core World schools."

"Even the time we're spending here, talking about 'this one man,' is too much."

"You were scheduled to be on your way back from Siena regardless, yes?"

"Yes, to get ready for my next assignment, not fret over this."

Feliks walked to the end of the table and sat. Habidah watched him until he turned his eyes to her. She looked away. She'd been waiting for his scolding. Apparently, if it was forthcoming, it would only happen in private. That felt almost worse.

Habidah told Joao, "You said there were only five of us. Now there are six."

Joao swiveled his chair to face Habidah. "Excuse me?"

"I did what I did. I'm not making excuses for it." Nor would she ever take it back. "But it's already done. Can't any of you see the opportunities he presents?"

Meloku said, "Opportunities to keep sabotaging our project."

Habidah let that pass. She traced circles on the table. "Our

143

resources have always been stretched thin. We can only cover a few of the plague sites, and then briefly. Meloku, you told me that we need to study a place before and after the plague strikes. What if we had a correspondent who could? Someone with a native perspective."

Feliks watched her carefully. "Do you think he'd be agreeable to that?"

"He's certainly not hostile. He thinks I was sent by God whether I'm aware I was or not." She nodded at the screen. Niccoluccio was muttering a prayer under his breath. NAI's lip-reading software scrawled the lines of a psalm underneath his image. "He wants to learn."

The past few times she'd visited, Niccoluccio had overflowed with questions. He'd wanted to know where he was, why he'd been healed, why she'd chosen him. He was much more interested in *why* than *how*. He'd never asked how her medical machines functioned.

He'd chosen the right questions. Those were the ones she could actually begin to answer. She'd avoided specifics, but told the truth.

She'd told him that she and her team were foreigners from a very distant land, and that they'd come to Europe to learn about its peoples. They had amazing tools, tools so advanced that they seemed as magic to Niccoluccio. She didn't intend to use them to harm anyone. She had used them to save him.

Niccoluccio had asked if Habidah was an ambassador from Prester John. Prester John was a native rumor, a mythical Christian king in the far east, crusading against the infidel. Habidah had just smiled and shaken her head.

She'd expected him to ask, eventually, if she was Christian. The question never came. He seemed to already know the answer. For a monk, he was more open-minded than she'd expected. He seemed to *want* to like her. If that meant closing his mind to certain problems, then he would.

Joao's nose wrinkled as he watched Niccoluccio. "He might

help. If he's interested. If he likes what he sees of us. If he doesn't try to expose us. If he doesn't catch the plague and *die*. If you don't have to spend more time babysitting him than you do working on your surveys. If he even knows what information is valuable to us. If he even goes somewhere useful. And even *if* that's all true, you still had no right to put us in this position, or a native in an environment completely alien to him."

"I firmly believe he would rather be here than where he was."

Kacienta said, "You've endangered the whole project. I have no choice but to send a report about this back home."

"Seconded," Joao said. "It's going right in our next transmission."

"Fine," Habidah said. "Does that mean we're done here?"

Silence followed. She took that to mean the meeting was finished. She stood. "Now, unless you'd like to help, you should get to your next assignments."

She walked out of the room before anyone answered.

She expected Feliks, at least, to come after her. No one followed. She breathed out. That had been more difficult than she expected. But so long as the university hadn't recalled her, she was still in charge. She didn't have to defend her decisions. She just had to make them.

Of course, how long she would remain in charge remained an open question.

When she entered Feliks' office, Niccoluccio stood at once. He bowed deeply. For the past day, he'd been treating her like an honored ambassador. Habidah inclined her head in return. She sat on one of the desk chairs.

She'd remained in costume these past few days to help him stay comfortable. He remained standing, formal but not stiff. It took an effort to extract the bitterness of the meeting from her voice. She made herself smile. "How do you feel this morning?"

"Irritated under my neck." He pointed to the patch under

145

his chin, not touching as if to show how good a boy he'd been by not picking at it. "Otherwise, I can walk and not feel as if my legs are on fire, or that my head is on the end of a twenty-foot pole."

"Good. That means you'll be ready to go soon."

He shifted. "It may surprise you to hear this, but I'm sorry to hear that."

"We've left you in here so long I expected that you would think of this as a prison cell."

"I am accustomed to living in cells."

She smiled, and this time didn't have to force it. "Of course."

"I don't wish to further impose on you, not without finding some way to repay you for your hospitality." He hesitated. "But I don't wish to leave. I have told you about my monastery."

"We wouldn't send you back there."

Niccoluccio let out a long breath, though he'd been holding it for days. "Thank you. If I may, I have more questions for you."

Habidah nodded, bracing herself.

"You and your companions didn't just come here to learn about us, did you?"

"No. We also came here because of the pestilence." It was always a struggle to know just how much to tell him. "The pest is annihilating our people as much as yours. We traveled here to learn about it, or at least how to better cope with it."

The mention of the plague seemed to strike Niccoluccio as a physical blow. "I'm afraid you will not learn much from me. I'm not suited for life outside a monastery. If it hadn't been for you, the pestilence would have killed me as surely as if I had actually contracted it."

"You lost more than most people ever have or will, and you're still coherent and talking."

"I do not feel very coherent when I think about it."

She pursed her lips. He'd had some kind of breakdown in the forest, true. She would have expected him to have another here, but he'd remained intact. Few like him could have done the same. "Would you prefer that we take you to another monastery?"

Niccoluccio shook his head without speaking.

Habidah asked, "Do you want to tell me why?"

"I do not believe I am worthy of my vows."

She hadn't expected that, but she didn't pursue the subject. "If you could travel anywhere in the world, where would you go?"

"The only place in Christendom I could call home is Florence. My father still lives there. He may or may not allow me into his home."

"We've been to many cities in Italy, but not Florence. Not yet. I'd love to take you there and see it."

Niccoluccio hesitated, winding himself up to say something. "Madam, I would rather do anything that I could to repay your kindness. You have treated me with more hospitality than I ever deserved. I could not in good conscience leave without doing something in return."

Habidah had to restrain herself from smiling again. His life was almost as much a mystery to her as hers was to him, but he was certainly disarming. Charming, almost.

She stood. "I was hoping that you might be able to help us learn about Florence. There's a lot that we would like to know."

He furrowed his brow. "Help as a… ah, a spy?"

"No. We're not concerned with governance or diplomacy or anything to do with your army. We only want to know how average Florentines have coped with the pestilence."

She offered him her hand. He stared at it without moving. She'd nearly forgotten how long it must have been since he'd had any contact with a woman. She said, "If you don't mean to live in a monastery again, you need to learn how to act like it."

After a pause, he accepted her hand, and she pulled him to his feet.

He said, "It is my blessing to serve."

• • •

Habidah gave Niccoluccio a brief tour. If he was going to be their agent, she owed him at least that much. She showed him their kitchen and dining room, and the communications chamber. She explained that the base had been hidden to avoid frightening or harming anybody. He nodded and listened without understanding, and only truly came alive again when she demonstrated a viewwall.

She projected a map of Europe to show him where they were. He startled. Once he got control of his wits, she tried to explain how to read it. He reached out, tried and failed to touch the map, which was projected to appear half a meter underneath the wall's surface. By the time she led him back to Feliks' office, his head was spinning with information she knew it would take him weeks and months to digest.

The next day, while she applied a fresh medical patch over the rapidly healing bite scar on his back, he remarked, "Since I was fourteen, I wanted to join a monastery." Lucky for him, he couldn't see the gnarled, bark-like tissue. "I thought it would be much easier."

She may have convinced him that she wasn't an angel or agent of God, but that didn't stop him from treating her like one. Or, at least, like something more than a stranger.

She asked, "So what happened when you were fourteen?"

He let the question soak for a long moment. He didn't seem to mind her touch. Habidah didn't need to have researched much about monastic living to know how odd that was for a monk. She *was* a woman. One more way he didn't treat her like an ordinary person.

"I confessed to my tutor what I had done," he said. "I fell in love like most young men do. And young women." He swallowed. "We chose to express it in ways none of us should have. With people we shouldn't have. We were slaves to our lusts."

From what Habidah knew about monastic life, chastity was its most prized virtue, no less so among monks than nuns. The way he struggled for words made her suspect he hadn't spoken of it in some time. He'd probably never confessed it to his brothers.

So why had he confessed it to her?

She watched him carefully while she compressed the replacement patch. He breathed in as if about to speak, and then stopped. After several false starts, he said, "At the time, I thought I had too large a heart."

"In the country I come from, many men and women act like you did without shame."

He didn't seem to hear. "I never wanted to be so in thrall to myself again. My tutor encouraged me to join a monastery."

It wasn't that he hadn't heard her, she realized. Her experience with the locals had led her to expect a heap of judgment and chastisement for what she'd just said. But that was entirely absent in Niccoluccio. The only person he cared to judge was himself.

He said, "I still feel a great deal of lust in my heart. And I am afraid to die."

"Is that why you don't want to be taken to another monastery?"

His only answer was: "These are the things I've come to realize about myself."

She *was* more than an angel or agent of God, she realized. She'd become his confessor. When she'd taken him in, the last thing she had ever expected of him was unremitting trust.

She trusted him, too. She had to be mindful of the power imbalance between them, certainly – under no circumstances could he be a threat to her. But that wasn't all of it. They were so far outside each others' experiences that neither of them had any reason to harm the other. And Habidah had demonstrated her good will from the start.

"I used to think that I was a good anthropologist," she said.

"A what?" he asked.

"A traveler," she said. "A professional outsider. I'm going to get in a lot of trouble for what I've done. And I don't think I can do this for much longer."

He didn't seem to know what to say, not any more than she did. When she finished sealing the medical patch, he set his hand on hers. She let it stay there for a while before slipping away.

That night, in her quarters, she checked to make sure that Niccoluccio was sleeping before laying down. With perfect timing, her demiorganics jolted her a moment before she was about to fall asleep. She sat straight up when she read the message's tags.

The communications gateway was open. She was receiving a call from Felicity Core.

She hadn't expected her transgression to go so high up. She'd never been to Felicity Core, but understood that it was much like Joao's home plane, or any of the other Core Worlds: dead gray seas, lifeless rock landscapes punctured by cloudscrapers, and pitch-dark skies. All of the Core Worlds swam through interstellar dust clouds that blocked the light of the outside universe. Their only stars were constellations of the amalgamates' fortress-stations and planarships.

Someone or something very close to the amalgamates was calling.

Her room's rear viewwall fuzzed on. Her demiorganics didn't adjust her eyes fast enough. By the time she lowered her hand, a woman with solid black skin stood beside her desk.

The stranger had no hair or clothing. Her chest was flat and her pelvis was bare. Only the curve of her hips made her feminine. Her skin reflected light like plastic. A tiny, decorative nostril-less nose perched atop line-thin silver lips. Her eyes were the only thing that looked human. They were mottled brown.

Habidah swallowed. She'd never spoken with a prosthetic before. Not many people earned the privilege of transferring their minds into wholly demiorganic bodies. All who had were, in some way or another, servants of the amalgamates.

"Ms Shen. We've been reviewing your team's reports with

interest. The last one in particular caught our attention."

"*Doctor* Shen. Thank you."

So those lips were capable of smiling. "Very well, Dr Shen. My name is Osia. I won't do you the disservice of pretending that you don't know what I'm calling about."

"I wasn't aware what I'd done would concern anyone outside the university."

"I'm working with your university in this matter."

The woman stood in front of a bone-white background. Habidah checked the call's location tag. She hid a jolt of surprise. Osia was calling from one of the amalgamates' strongholds: the planarship *Ways and Means*, in high orbit above Felicity Core. The planarship was named after the amalgamate it hosted.

"The amalgamates take an acute interest in anything that might affect the politics of our response to the plague. I volunteered to serve your university."

"Does that mean they're having you call to fire me?"

"*Ways and Means* would like to ask you not to interfere with the locals again. It understands that this is a difficult assignment, but would prefer your efforts focused on your job. Otherwise, the arrangements you've made with the monk are retroactively approved."

Habidah blinked. "That's all you're going to say?"

Osia arched the skin above her eye, as if daring her to disagree. "That's all."

When Habidah didn't respond, Osia's image whisked into nothingness.

Habidah couldn't sleep for hours. Nothing about that had been right. She'd never spoken to anyone so close to the amalgamates before.

Osia's presence had been just as much a message as anything she'd said. It felt like a threat. Only Habidah had no idea what she was being threatened into doing – or not doing.

13

Niccoluccio had been more amenable to a transmitter implant than Habidah expected. She wasn't sure if he entirely understood what she'd asked. He kept feeling his lower neck, where she'd told him it was.

"There's nothing to feel," she told him, as she guided him into the shuttle's acceleration couch. Again, she pulled the safety harness over his shoulders herself, though the shuttle could have done it for her. "It's very small, and deep under your skin."

"And you may remove it whenever you like?" Niccoluccio asked doubtfully.

"We certainly will before we leave your land."

She sat in the couch beside him. Niccoluccio groaned at the weight of liftoff. Habidah had turned off all of the monitors. He didn't need to know how fast or high they traveled.

He asked, "You'll be able to hear whatever I say?"

"Only what you want us to. It's just like I said – to activate it, you have to talk under your breath. You don't even have to move your lips. Just flex the muscles." She'd gone over the subvocal transmitter three times. At least it kept him distracted from the shaking and swaying. "There's another device in your ear that will let you hear our answer."

He immediately felt his ears. "Will everyone on your 'team' be able to hear and speak to me?"

"Your message will be received by whoever's available.

Usually that's going to be Joao or Kacienta."

He hesitated. "Would it be possible to ensure that I speak only to you?"

"Joao and Kacienta are trustworthy."

"It's not that I don't trust them. It would be better to say I would rather speak with you."

She looked at him, but his expression was impenetrable – mostly because his eyes were screwed shut. "All right."

Her demiorganics kept her apprised of their progress. Flying blind shouldn't have bothered her, but it did. Without the monitors, she couldn't pretend she was in control.

Faster than Niccoluccio would have believed, the shuttle ripped through the skies of central Italy. The sound-dampening fields neutralized its sonic booms. Unfortunately, some of that energy occasionally reflected into the shuttle. The shuttle thundered and shook as if it crashed through a lightning bolt. Niccoluccio cried out.

The turbulence lasted only a moment before the dampeners compensated. Niccoluccio yelled, "What went wrong? Are we dead?" Habidah grabbed his hand to keep him from clawing his way out of his harness.

By the time the shuttle landed, he had just about recovered his voice. Habidah still held his hand to keep him steady. He glared at the dark bulk of the shuttle, for once unintimidated by its size. "I will never go back in that beast if I can help it."

Habidah gave him a moment to notice where he was. She'd landed at the edge of a vineyard a bare kilometer from Florence's walls. Dawn was still an hour away, but stars and moon shone brightly. Niccoluccio fell silent at once when he spotted the pale shadows of the city walls. He recognized that little bit of Florence at once. "Did I faint? We came so far so quickly."

He still didn't know how far they'd really traveled. She said, "The city gates will open before dawn." According to the satellite records, anyway.

"I know." He started to step forward, and was stopped by

the tug of Habidah's arm. Only then did he seem to realize that he was still holding Habidah's hand, and that Habidah wasn't coming with him.

She said, "This is your home, not mine. I have another assignment in Marseilles." She should have been there weeks ago. The plague's late arrival in Genoa had delayed her. "My superiors don't want me to get more involved. I've done too much already."

"I can't bring myself to pass the gates alone. I would rather wander the wilderness again."

"You won't be alone once you find your family. I don't want to interfere."

"You don't *need* to interfere."

The moon shone bright enough that Habidah didn't need infrared to take stock of the fear in his eyes. "All right." Only then did they let each other's hands go.

She sent the shuttle to find a secluded hideaway on the Mediterranean coast. With a breath like a whisper, it vanished into the night. Niccoluccio glanced back to make sure she was following, and gaped at the shuttle's sudden absence. Habidah kept him moving forward.

Rows of stakes and old, dead vines constrained their path. Branches scraped at their ankles. A pulse scan found the nearest road. They stepped onto it just ahead of a horse-drawn wagon. The driver – a farmer, judging by the dirt under his chin and the calluses on his hands – glared at them as he passed, but said nothing. Niccoluccio stared after him. It took Habidah a moment to remember that this farmer was the first person, other than herself and her team, that Niccoluccio had seen since the men of his monastery had died weeks ago.

Habidah let him lead the way. The road was broad, wheel-rutted, and slick with frost. Florence was a cloudy nebula in infrared. The plague had already passed through. Even from this distance she could detect the empty houses.

As they drew closer to the gates, he gradually seemed to forget she was there. His step became surer. Infrared showed his pulse slackening. It wasn't just the comedown from the flight. However he protested that he couldn't come here alone, he knew this place. He was probably more comfortable here than anywhere short of Sacro Cuore. Judging from what Habidah knew of Carthusian monastic life, maybe more.

Habidah kept her head down as they entered the gates. The towers on both sides dwarfed them. Armored men stood astride the walls, but didn't move or speak. Florence had started to come sullenly alive. The winding streets rattled with cart traffic, the morning's grain. The sky had pinked enough to reveal the city, from the smaller houses nearby to the slender tower of the Castagna and the Cathedral of Santa Reparata.

For the past week, Niccoluccio had looked as lost as a sheep in the clouds. For as readily as he recognized this place, that impression hadn't faded. His step wandered. More than once, Habidah had to gently take him by the elbow and lead him out of the way of cart traffic.

"It's so noisy," he said, lost in wonder.

"Not as noisy as it used to be, I'll wager." When Niccoluccio turned to her, she explained, "The pestilence has already struck. The worst is over, at least the first wave, but it's taken a lot of lives."

He nodded, solemn. "I may still die of the pest even after all this."

"You're safe."

Niccoluccio glanced at her, nearly tripping over a wheel rut. "Beg your pardon?"

"The pestilence doesn't seem very interested in you." There were some things she hadn't told him, or her team members, and that he'd never need to find out.

It had been easy enough to figure out how Niccoluccio survived. The tight, unsanitary quarters of monasteries made good homes for rats and their fleas. Mostly, he'd been lucky. But he'd mentioned spending most of his time away from the dormitory, and sleeping next to a fireplace. The smoke would have warded off plague-carrying fleas.

Back here, he would be just as vulnerable to the plague as anybody else. Habidah wasn't prepared to let her rescue go to waste. She may not have been able to cure the plague, but she wasn't completely helpless against it. She'd fortified Niccoluccio's immune system. Her bugs were swimming around his veins, teaching his white blood cells new tricks.

He frowned, and pulled his hands into his sleeves for warmth. He glanced at every person they passed, searching for familiar faces. Habidah followed in silence, no longer trusting herself to speak.

Unlike Genoa, the city maintained some semblance of civil order. There were no bodies in streets and alleys. Several streets were deserted, but that was all. The plague had made its mark, certainly, but it was written underneath Florence's surface. The Unity would be so lucky to end up like this after the onierophage ended, if it ever did end.

She would have to count on Niccoluccio to peel back Florence's skin. Even coming this far with him was stretching things. As if stirred by that thought, her demiorganics let her know that she had an incoming call. Feliks. She swallowed her irritation.

"Straying a little far into Florence, aren't you?" Feliks asked.

"I wish you wouldn't watch so closely."

"I'm worried about you and I have every professional right to be."

"I'm accompanying him home. I don't intend to stay longer than that." She glanced skyward. The nearest observation satellite was high overhead. "Thank you for not piling on during the conference."

"Is that what you think I'm doing? Piling on now that we can talk alone?"

Habidah massaged her forehead. "No, no – but if you didn't want to make it seem like you were, you could have opened with another question."

"How is our guest coping with the plague city?"

"It's nowhere near as bad as Genoa. He's doing better than

I expected."

"You said you're going to drop our guest off. Are you planning on visiting again?"

The question caught her off guard. "If we get enough about Florence from him, I don't need to visit again." That would mean that she would never see him again after today. Her throat tightened looking at him.

Niccoluccio was navigating on automatic now, taking turns without looking. Once, she caught him stepping over an upraised cobble without glancing at it. Every once in a while, he looked to the Cathedral of Santa Reparata as it rose over the rooftops.

Feliks said, "Let's make sure this *stays* your last visit, all right?"

"I understand," she sent back.

"And you might want to send his reports to Kacienta."

"He's already asked that I keep in contact with him."

"Are you going to keep in contact because you think it will be better for our project, or because you think it will be better for you?"

She didn't have an answer. No. Rather, the answer was all too obvious. Niccoluccio checked to make sure she was still following. She gave him a thin smile.

Feliks said, "Don't use him as a cushion to cope with your own problems. I don't know much about him other than what I've seen through the cameras, but I can already tell you that he deserves better. These people have their own lives. Let him have his."

The streets had gotten wider, more evenly cobbled. Fewer infrared shadows shone through the walls. It wasn't a symptom of the plague. Niccoluccio had led her into a wealthier, less crowded neighborhood. The wide doors and windows were spaced farther apart, and barred by high loggias. The Cathedral of Santa Reparata's dawn shadow covered seemingly half of Florence.

At the next intersection, Niccoluccio stopped and looked

157

again to the cathedral. He lowered his hood. Habidah let him have his moment. It had been a long time since he'd seen any building like it. She closed her eyes and focused instead on calming her breathing.

Niccoluccio said, "It seems so small, after everything you've shown me."

Habidah cracked an eye open. Maybe she'd misread his reason for stopping. "Our field base could fit inside those walls and still leave most of that space empty."

"But I didn't... I didn't mean physically."

"Then what did you mean?"

After a moment of searching for words, he said, "It's difficult to articulate. I'm sorry. I can't. You must know what I mean."

She glanced at the cathedral. It was the tallest building in the city, but only about ninety meters. It was hard to feel much when she looked at it. It was impressive only in the context of the society. On her first field assignment, when she'd been a junior anthropologist itching to start her work, she'd seen stone towers carved into mountains so tall that she'd needed a respirator to visit the top levels. She'd felt something like awe then, certainly. But she'd left without a glance back. The awe hadn't been for the towers. It had been for the breadth and variety of the multiverse. That had been when she'd stopped entertaining ideas of settling back home.

Now she'd brought something of that perspective to Niccoluccio. A pit opened in the center of her chest. She'd told him that she and her team had come from another part of his world, but that hadn't kept her small enough.

"Your home is nearby?" she asked.

He nodded. "I could see the cathedral spires from my bedroom. Another half-mile, perhaps."

"We could have taken a more direct route."

"I had thought to visit the cathedral with you first, but I can see now that that was a mistake. It doesn't mean as much to me as I remembered."

This was what Feliks had warned her about. Just by telling half the truth about herself, she'd taken something away from him. She stopped walking at the edge of a quieter intersection. "I can't keep going with you."

"Because of the cathedral?"

"No. I just can't go any farther."

"Do you need rest?"

"You've been looking about for familiar faces. Think about that. If someone you knew spotted you returning in the company of a strange woman, the gossip could damage your reputation forever."

"You said you would come with me."

"The rest of my team is already calling me away."

Niccoluccio glanced about. "From where?"

She smiled, shook her head, and tapped the side of her head. "In here. Like you'll be able to talk with me, whenever you want."

"I don't know that I can go farther alone," he said. He seemed only perplexed, but an infrared scan showed his quickened pulse. He was actually doing an admirable job of hiding his anxiety.

"Like I said, you can talk to me whenever you want. Then neither of us will be alone. But my staying here is not going to be good for either of us."

Niccoluccio's arms drooped at his sides. Habidah touched his hand, but couldn't do anything more. She took a step back. "You'll be able to handle this better without me than with me. I have faith that you can." She was about to remind him that she would be watching, but, looking at him again, reconsidered. That just meant that he would be thinking about her again. He needed to focus on his own life rather than the shadows he'd glimpsed of hers.

That would have to be for the best.

She smiled one last time, more slightly than before, and turned. The sky was still gray enough that, if she hurried, the shuttle would be able to pick her up without arousing too much attention. She tried not to look behind her, but, when she did, Niccoluccio was still standing in the same place she'd left him.

14

Niccoluccio threaded through the streets, though he didn't remember the trip. He wasn't sure how he managed to stay upright. It felt like the strings holding him up had been cut.

The past few days had been a dream, a hint of Paradise. Now he'd been cast back to Earth.

It had to happen at some point. Habidah hadn't allowed him any illusions about staying in her home. All he'd wanted was to put off leaving as long as he could. It smelled so sweet back there. Florence was a nightmare by contrast. He picked his way over the sewage-filled runnels, hand held over his nose.

He was so intent on remembering the smell of Habidah's home that he hardly noticed he was back in his old street. The sense of familiarity made him halt. Two houses had been taken down and replaced. Another was missing its windows. The old servants' chapel had lost all of its paint.

He still hadn't seen anyone he knew. He strode to his father's home without looking at it. He took a breath, braced himself, and faced it.

There was no one inside. He knew that at once. No smoke came out of the chimneys. At this time of year, there should be at least one fire. Puddles of frost-salted mud sat undisturbed in front of the door. When Niccoluccio had been young, if their front walk had looked so filthy, his father would have had him out cleaning it before dawn.

He stared for a long time until he found the courage to

approach. The door was locked. No one answered his knock. His father was a late sleeper, but his siblings and their children and servants should have been up.

For a long time, he stood in front of the door, hoping that someone would come up and tell him what to do next. He nearly started speaking to Habidah as she'd taught him. The way she'd looked at him before she left made him hold back, though.

The last he'd heard (and his news was not recent), two of his four brothers had homes in the city. He had no idea where. His brother Dioneo had finished his legal training and begun to work for one of the city's priors. The priorate met in the Palazzo della Signoria. He had no choice but to start walking.

The streets were far filthier than he remembered. Dark masses had congealed under the ice. A pair of pigs ruffled in the refuse. The roads hadn't been cleaned by rain or city sweepers in a long time. After the faultlessly immaculate rooms of Habidah's home, he felt he needed a bath just walking here. The buildings on either side seemed too close together, but he was sure that was a trick of his memories of rural Sacro Cuore. Florence had, in his absence, turned from a city of streets into a city of alleys.

He passed his first victims of the pest. Two men bore a cart covered with pale cloth. Niccoluccio may not have been able to see underneath, but the cloth couldn't hide the stink. Niccoluccio had smelled bodies, fresh and old, too many times to forget it.

But if only Brother Rinieri could see how many people still lived here.

The filth diminished as he approached the figurative center of the city. The manors stood pridefully tall, overlooking the streets like little castles. Some bore faux-crenelated roofs. In the days before Niccoluccio had left, the vanity of it all had made him say a prayer for the people inside. After Habidah, it only seemed insignificant.

He didn't see the Palazzo della Signoria until he stepped

out into it. The street emptied out into a wide, clean cobbled space, free of the worst city smells. Even at this early hour, the plaza bustled. Foodsellers set up their stalls along the brick walls, but the plaza itself hosted nothing but people and their conversations: civil servants hustling to work, merchants in open-air meetings, clergymen giving sermons to crowds clustering to hear. Even in the aftermath of the plague, it was still as Niccoluccio remembered.

He stood at the fringes for nearly a minute before he remembered he'd come with a goal. As impressive as the plaza was, the priors only *met* here. They worked elsewhere. He spun in a circle and racked his memories before he alighted on the Palazzo Vecchio.

The Palazzo Vecchio was a broad, squat-looking rectangle with an ugly, jutting, off-center finger of a tower. It cast a deep shadow over half of the plaza. Like the manors, it had a crenelated roof, but the battlements were more than decorative. As one of the centers of Florence's government, it had good reason to fortify itself against riots.

It had been built over the home of a rebel family to prevent their supporters from ever rebuilding there. The off-center tower had been a part of that home. Florentines took pride in the building, but Niccoluccio found it jarring. Time hadn't improved its appeal. If anything, its walls were dirtier than he remembered.

The grand, golden foyer felt like a cathedral. Niccoluccio would have stopped in his tracks if he hadn't just come from a more incredible place. Neither of the men standing guard inside looked at him, but the pock-faced secretary behind the lone desk did. Niccoluccio approached him. Hesitantly, he gave his brother's name and then his own.

The secretary raised an eyebrow, but dispatched a page upstairs. Niccoluccio stood by the wall, closed his eyes, and tried to center himself. He didn't have long to do that before the boy returned.

The boy led Niccoluccio up a flight of stairs and through

a hallway far wider than it needed to be. Other people were about – Niccoluccio heard an occasional cough or wheeze – but they were hidden behind doors and few in number. The priors and their aides generally didn't do any work this early. Like most of the city's wealthy, they slept through the mornings.

Niccoluccio's guide left him in front of a carved wooden door large enough for three men. The boy bowed before he left. Niccoluccio watched him leave. He hadn't thought he'd deserved a bow. He couldn't remember anyone in this city bowing to him before. He was so perplexed that he neglected to knock before entering.

On the other side, there was a door, a desk, and a man.

The man was not the younger brother he remembered – almost a stranger. Dioneo stood astride a finely carved oak desk piled with ledgers. His hair was thinning and exposed a patch of scalp. Some of it had started to lighten, a prelude to graying. His brow had grown a deep crease. He held a pair of hefty, white-framed spectacles.

But his eyes brought back memories sweet as strawberries. When they were young, he'd spent hours each day teaching Dioneo to read and do sums. Niccoluccio had once been able to lift his brother. Now Dioneo looked to be one-and-a-half times his weight. It was as if Niccoluccio's brother had aged two years for every one Niccoluccio had been away.

Dioneo stood in a wordless stupor. He let his spectacles clatter to the desk. He brought Niccoluccio into a wrenching embrace before Niccoluccio realized what was happening. "You're still alive?"

When Niccoluccio got his breath back, he answered, "That does seem to be the most appropriate greeting for the times."

Dioneo laughed a disconcertingly deep laugh. "Well met! So long as there are still two Caracciolas in the world, we can remember how to laugh." The edges of his eyes were wet, but he was not crying. He clapped an arm over Niccoluccio's shoulder and led him to the seat before his desk.

Niccoluccio sat with hands folded in his lap. His pulse

threaded in his ears as he explained what had happened – up until the point at which he met Habidah. Dioneo said, "I heard from a merchant that the survivors of your monastery's lay community fled. They'd assumed you had all fallen to the pestilence. Was I told a tale? Does Sacro Cuore survive?"

Niccoluccio was oddly pleased that his brother knew the name of his monastery. He had assumed that his father – along with everyone else in the family – had forgotten it. "Your report was right. Would that those travelers had found us. We would have gone with them."

Dioneo's paunch sagged below his waist. "How many of them lived to make the journey with you?"

"I was the only one at the end. I left when I realized it."

"On your own?"

Niccoluccio knew the lie was coming, but he couldn't hold it back. "It was a long road from Sacro Cuore. I had supplies, but you are the first person I've exchanged more than five words with since I left."

Dioneo couldn't answer for a moment. He brushed the wetness from the corner of his eye. "Then your coming to us was twice a miracle, brother."

"Very much," Niccoluccio said, sincerely. It was the closest he could come to the truth.

Now he couldn't keep the tears back, either. The two of them wept in earnest, and thanked God for the opportunity to meet again. Dioneo recovered himself in just a minute, though. His voice sounded as if it had never broken. He said, "I had imagined that I was the last of our family in Florence, as well. Our father was the first of us to die."

Even after Niccoluccio had seen his old home empty, he'd tried to hope that his father was traveling or sheltering in the countryside. The news came as no surprise, but still felt like ice in his stomach. Dioneo told him next of their siblings. "Until you arrived, I had thought Umiliana and myself the only survivors of our generation." Umiliana had lived outside the city ever since she was married. "I myself lost three of my five living children."

News of death had become so commonplace that all Niccoluccio could think to ask was, "You have had that many children?"

Dioneo laughed again, boomingly, and shook his head, though there was a trace of anguish in it.

Niccoluccio said, "I didn't mean– that is, to count your children as–"

"I have two living children now. Let's leave it at that. I nearly lost my wife as well, but she miraculously recovered. Not nearly so miraculous as your arrival here, I might add. How long are you to stay before going to your next monastery?"

Niccoluccio said, "I have not applied to any other monasteries, and do not believe I will. I don't feel suited for it after everything I witnessed."

If Dioneo had had any idea of the gravity of what Niccoluccio had just said, he would have been taken aback. But Dioneo had always lived outside of the church. For him, leaving a monastery was on a par with changing from one job to another. "Then I insist that you stay with myself and my family. You have been alone far too long."

"I passed our father's house. It seemed empty. If it has not been sold, I could stay there and not get in your way."

Something else had changed in his brother, too, that Niccoluccio was only just starting to see. There was a probing edge to his eyes. "I wouldn't dream of condemning my dear brother to such danger. The pestilence lingers in the homes of the dead. Besides, I wouldn't get to see you."

Niccoluccio fought to keep the relief out of his voice. "If I would not be imposing."

They were interrupted by a sallow clerk. While Dioneo was preoccupied, Niccoluccio looked about the office. Though he'd known his brother worked in governance, he hadn't imagined anything this large, or that Dioneo would have men serving him. "What are you doing here?" he asked.

"Another sad tale. The prior I worked for, the *vexillifer*

iustitiae, did not flee the city like his colleagues. He and his heir perished. As his senior officer, I am filling in for him in the meantime, and, if I have my way, permanently."

The *vexillifer iustitiae*, the standard-bearer of justice, was one of the Florence's seven priors, and the only one who didn't represent one of the city's districts. He, along with the *podesta* and the captain of the people, was one of the city's highest legal authorities. Suddenly the size of the office and the voluminous ledgers made more sense.

When Niccoluccio didn't answer, Dioneo grinned broadly. "Yes, things have gotten so desperate that the other magistrates are considering even the likes of me."

All Niccoluccio could think to say was, "It's an amazing opportunity to elevate the family."

"What's left of us. Speaking of, I must introduce you to them."

Niccoluccio nodded at the ledgers. "Your work comes before me."

"For now, dear brother, you *are* my work." Dioneo put an arm around Niccoluccio's shoulder before Niccoluccio could ask what he meant.

Dioneo stopped at several offices on the way out to announce that his brother had miraculously returned from his distant monastery. Niccoluccio stood obediently behind him, hands clasped. Their progress seemed interminable, but eventually they reached the plaza.

Dioneo's home was near. It made their father's look tiny. It was broad, shaped like a half-oval, and hosted a garden that must have looked spectacular in summer. The doors were shadowed by loggias. Dioneo led him inside. Portraits of Niccoluccio's father and a man Niccoluccio didn't recognize flanked the walls.

The next hour blurred into a stream of names and faces. Not only were Dioneo's wife and two children at home, but so were their five servants. His wife had invited a cousin and her family to supper. Niccoluccio hadn't met so many people at once since his first day at Sacro Cuore. By the time Niccoluccio sat to supper, he couldn't remember if Dioneo's wife's name was Catella or if that was her cousin. It was all he could do to keep his thoughts centered. Every time he heard a new name, embraced a stranger, it felt like bits of him were flying off. Except for the washing of each others' feet, the brothers had rarely touched each other. Niccoluccio had to hide a shiver whenever anyone, even Dioneo, touched him.

Dioneo soon departed to find a better point to end his work. Niccoluccio was left in a labyrinth of strangers. He couldn't hear a word of the conversation. It flittered through the air, insubstantial. He heard himself responding. He and the other brothers broke rules whenever they so much as whispered at each other during communal meals. Niccoluccio couldn't focus on either the conversation or the too-oily, too-rich rice pasta. His thoughts were as long-lived as a fog of breath.

By rights, he ought to have been more comfortable here than he had with Habidah and her companions. In an odd way, their very alienness had helped. They were so far removed from him that the only way they could connect was through the basic nature that united all humans. Niccoluccio had been lost and suffering, and Habidah had wanted to help. It was the same innocent manner that three year-olds related to the people around them.

Here, things were far from innocent. Niccoluccio abstained from the meat pies offered to him. He offered his servers an apologetic smile, but nothing else. He tried to hide his dismay at the gowns and jewelry the women (even his eleven year-old niece!) wore. They, in turn, didn't disguise their disdain at his habit. It was freshly laundered, at least. It had been cleaned while he'd slept in Habidah's home, though he didn't care to think about how.

When Dioneo returned, Niccoluccio said, "Surely you didn't finish your work so early."

Dioneo was grinning. He wrapped his arm over Niccoluccio's

shoulders. "I haven't even started it. I've visited the clergymen at the cathedral chapter, telling them about the miracle of your survival."

"It wasn't..." Niccoluccio started, and stopped himself.

"Wasn't a miracle?" Dioneo finished.

"Of course it was a miracle," Niccoluccio said. "Just one I would rather not speak of widely."

"That is too bad for you, dear brother. My friend at the cathedral, Ambrogiuolo Olivi, wants to meet you. I have made an appointment for you in the morning."

The way Dioneo spoke the name made Niccoluccio think he was expected to recognize it. "Who? Why?"

"You've seen how much of a toll the pestilence has taken. You weren't here when it was at its worst. The corpse wagons flowed like a river. It hasn't ended. Even now, people are only starting to return. They fear that the pestilence could return at any instant. People need a hero, a survivor to admire. A miracle to show that the world has not ended."

Niccoluccio had already shaken his head several times by the time his brother finished. Dioneo, hand still over his shoulder, led him from the table before he could find his voice. "Ambrogiuolo is a powerful man in the cathedral chapter. He can do a lot for the family. You'll see when you meet him. You do want to do more here than just live at my home, don't you? Be active. Contribute."

Niccoluccio stopped. He had become acutely aware how much his brother had accomplished while he was away. All he'd brought back from his twelve years as a monk was a conviction that he was no longer suited for it. Even at his most pious, he'd never felt so small. Perhaps that meant his piety had never been so sincere after all.

He was at the mercy of his own petty ego. And yet: "I will not be a hero. Let alone a saint."

"Then don't be, but the appointment is already made. See him. Tell the truth about what happened. Preach the glory of God in that way."

Prior Lomellini had often preached that the world outside the monastery was a tempest, replete with evil and temptation, and that a man could not help but be caught up by it even when he knew better. Niccoluccio opened his mouth, throat dry, but he could not bring himself to say no to his brother. Not yet.

15

Habidah had hardly returned to her acceleration couch when her demiorganics jolted with an urgent message from Joao. She inwardly groaned. She braced herself for another scolding.

He sent, "All of our satellites' sensors are flipping the fuck out. Something's happening up there."

Another jolt, this time adrenaline. Though demiorganic transmission didn't capture emotional cadences, she heard his panic. "In *orbit?*" she asked.

"Disruptions all over the thermosphere." Raw data poured through Habidah. She needed a moment to make sense of it. The satellites her team had placed in orbit were intended to study the surface, and had very few instruments looking elsewhere. Those lateral sensors could only pick up a jumbled and incomplete swamp of fluctuating energies, spatial rifts. Most were centered in equilateral orbital bands of varying altitudes, but others had appeared over the poles.

Joao said, "Somebody's opening a dozen, two dozen, transplanar gateways up there."

Each was about three meters in diameter. The power needed to open that many large gateways was beyond the capabilities of most industrialized worlds. By comparison, the field base's communications gateway was less than a micrometer wide, just large enough to transmit information.

"Open our gateway," she said. "Send an emergency message to the university. This world is being invaded by a transplanar power. We need immediate multiple-site evacuation. There's no time to get everyone to the field base." The first thing an invading power would do was target extraplanar interlopers. They could have seconds. Her first impulse was to find Niccoluccio and get him off this world, but that would be placing him in even more danger. The missile targeting her could be on its way even now.

Joao reported, "Our gateway just opened on its own."

Her heart juddered. "*What?*"

Their gateway was hard-linked to their university. If nobody at her field base had opened it, that meant somebody from her university had. "We're receiving a signal from Felicity Core," Joao said, in wonder.

Habidah settled into her couch, pulse still racing. She knew who she would be speaking to before she answered. "Send it to me."

All of the cabin's forward-facing monitors blinked off, replaced by a composite image of Osia. The borders between the monitors fractured her image like stained glass. She stood with her arms folded over her chest, double-jointed fingers bent backwards.

Habidah asked, "What the hell is the meaning of this?"

"An intelligence operation unrelated to your activities," Osia answered. "I apologize for the lack of warning, but you had no reason to know. We're depositing satellites, nothing else. This won't disrupt your assignment. In fact, we need your reports to continue coming in. Our satellites can't collect the kind of social and political information that you and your team have been gathering."

The light leakage from gateways that size would be naked-eye visible in the night sky. "You've already disrupted our mission. Get those satellites out of here."

Osia locked her gaze on Habidah's. Then she looked somewhere to her side. "If you'll excuse me, we're in pursuit of other objectives at the moment."

Her image vanished.

Habidah tried to get her back, but the communications gateway had closed. She slapped her couch's armrest. It was too cushy to be satisfying.

Osia had been acting when she'd pretended she was being called from off camera. Prosthetics like her had far more advanced communications technologies. They didn't need to talk aloud, except to ordinary humans like herself.

She told Joao, "Get everyone ready for pickup and flight to the field base. Maybe we'll be heading home. I don't know. We need to figure out what's going on."

Her harness snaked over her shoulders, tugged tight. All of the paranoia that had dogged her since Osia's last call crashed through her all at once. It went without saying that none of this was right. Worse, maybe nothing had ever *been* right. This whole assignment had suddenly taken on an air of fraud.

She tried to scavenge as much information about the intruders as she could, but her satellites' sensors, even reoriented, couldn't make out much. The gateways had closed. The objects that had fallen through were too small to hold man-sized creatures. The largest was only half a meter long. There were somewhere between thirty and forty of them. She didn't have good enough coverage to get an exact count. So far they'd done nothing but squat in orbit, occasionally belching EM static that was either a scan or a signal. If not for the gateways, Habidah's satellites might never have detected them.

The engines shoved her into her seat. The sun had nearly risen. She only had minutes to get away before the shuttle's camouflage fields lost the cover of darkness.

Her pulse skipped a measure when her gaze skipped across a monitor looking back at Florence.

Her team had last gathered in the conference room scarcely a day ago. Having all of them back was like a recurring nightmare. Feliks and Joao were even in the same costumes. Meloku was here in person this time, dressed as a wealthy Frenchwoman, with several rings, a necklace, and a lacy headdress.

Joao hugged his arms to his chest. Like last time, he and Kacienta had focused all of their attention on her. This time, they were looking to her for direction. Only Feliks remained detached.

Joao started off by going over everything he'd learned. "They're stealthed, just like our satellites. Light-absorbent hulls, no reflective solar paneling. Nobody's going to look up and see them now."

Habidah said, "They care about concealing themselves from the natives. Why?" The amalgamates had never cared about interfering with civilizations on other planes before.

Meloku said, "They care *for now*. Tomorrow they could drop all pretenses."

Habidah asked, "But, again, why? What could it possibly matter to them?"

Joao ventured, "What if they're not here for the locals? They could be hunting an extraplanar target. A fugitive. They did tell you 'intelligence operation.'"

Habidah said, "They didn't bother to shield themselves against high-technology observation. Anyone from a culture capable of transplanar travel would detect them as easily as we did. The only thing they're protected against is visual observation."

Feliks said, "So they're concerned with the locals. Not us. Not extraplanar fugitives. Certainly not another planar empire, and that's about the only thing I can think of that would explain an intrusion like this."

Kacienta asked, "Could there be some... I don't know, some natural resource here?"

Meloku said, "Again, if that's all it was, they wouldn't bother to shield their satellites."

Habidah resisted the impulse to lay her head on the table. "What could this place have that the amalgamates – or anyone in the Unity – could possibly want?" Again, her thoughts tended toward Niccoluccio. She had to force them away.

174

After a moment, Feliks answered, "Labor."

Meloku said, "Don't be barbaric. The amalgamates have access to a million more efficient forms of automated labor. If they wanted labor, they could seed a world with self-replicating worker drones. In a month, they'd have a population equal to this world."

Osia had said she needed her team to keep providing her with "social and political information." To the best of Habidah's knowledge, neither she nor her team had concerned themselves with this plane's politics other than to the extent that it influenced its peoples' reaction to the plague.

Feliks said, "The real question here is not why they're doing this. It's what do we do about it."

Habidah asked, "What *can* we do?"

She was sure Osia and the amalgamates were listening to every word. They had the means. The field base's NAI answered to them. They hadn't stopped her team from talking about them because they had no reason to. They had nothing to fear from anyone here.

Joao said, "We can pack up and go home. Or we can keep working."

Kacienta asked, "*Can* we go home? The field base hardly has enough power to open up a micrometer communications gateway. We're dependent on the university for transport. *That* means the amalgamates."

Meloku said, "The amalgamates don't care enough about us to trap us here. We're too small."

Joao said, "We need to keep from panicking, OK? OK. So – we don't know why they're doing any of this. I feel like it's my obligation to point out that they could have reasons for this that we might agree with if we knew them."

Habidah said, "Then the amalgamates have no reason to hide those reasons from us."

"That's just how they operate sometimes."

Meloku said, "All of the time."

Habidah kept a careful eye on Joao. He'd grown up on

Providence Core. The amalgamates' fortresses and planarships filled his skies from the day he was born. Their agents managed everything about life on his world, down to the traffic stops.

She said, "If they thought we'd agree with their reasoning for what they're doing, they'd tell us. Whatever they're doing, it's not something we'd voluntarily associate ourselves with, and they know it."

Meloku said, "We can speculate all we want, but we're not going to learn anything new."

"What else can we do?" Joao asked.

Meloku said, "We didn't need to come back here if all we're going to do is complain."

Habidah looked at Meloku, biting her tongue. But she was right. "Joao," Habidah said, "find out where the other anthropology teams have gone. Try to get in contact with them."

Kacienta said, "The amalgamates and their agents could fake any messages we got back."

Meloku said, "Only if they *cared* that much about tricking us."

Habidah nodded to Joao, and added, "See if you can't get us permission to visit their planes. Say that we want to compare notes."

Feliks said, "The amalgamates will know what we're trying."

"Then let them try to stop us, and at least be honest about it."

"Is that all?" Meloku asked. "What are you going to have us do in the meantime?"

Habidah said, "Joao is right. Our only two choices are to keep working, or not."

Kacienta asked, "Does our work even matter after all this?"

After a moment's consideration, Habidah said, "I believe it does. We signed up for this because we believed we could help ordinary people back in the Unity. So far as I can tell, the amalgamates have no reason to block the reports we're sending back home. Anyone disagree?"

No one answered, but no one could quite meet her eyes, either.

"That settles that," Habidah said. "We'll head back to our assignments tonight, and keep our eyes open for other opportunities."

Daytime kept them all trapped in the field base. Habidah sealed herself in her quarters. She didn't eat. She wasn't hungry. It felt like a long time since she had been.

She lay in bed and stared at the ceiling. There were observation devices hidden here, she knew. Even with her retinal enhancements, she couldn't find anything. With her demiorganics lodged in her head, routing her neural impulses, she couldn't even be sure of the sanctity of her thoughts. She had no way to fight that level of surveillance.

One uncomfortable thought had picked at her since she'd left Florence. If this were really an intelligence operation, the amalgamates could have sent more of their agents, creatures like Osia, to do their work on the ground. Yet the only gateways they'd opened were in orbit.

If the amalgamates had been involved in her mission from the start, they would have been sure to have their interests represented.

Someone here had to be working for the amalgamates. It could have been the base's NAI, but it wasn't complex enough. Anyone or anything else could have been put in place long before she and her field team arrived, but Habidah doubted that. The amalgamates would have had no reason to send her survey team if they already had agents here. They shouldn't have needed to bother with the fiction of her assignment.

Something her team – or the amalgamates' agent – had found must have prompted this new operation.

Her team's only way to contact the Unity had been the field base's communications gateway. If there was a spy here, they would have had to use the gateway just like anyone else.

NAI wouldn't let her peek inside anyone's message traffic.

But, as the survey team's leader, she did have the authority to examine her team's signal traffic in bulk. NAI could tell her how much traffic had gone through the gateway at which times, and to which of the Unity's network junctions their signals had been routed.

Sure enough, someone on her team had exchanged a great many messages with a network junction that routed to Felicity Core.

Habidah wished she could say that the discovery was satisfying. All it seemed to mean was that her mission *had* been compromised from the beginning. She curled her fingers. She had to stay calm. There had to be some way to use this. If she could find out who it was – well, throwing them off her team would have to come second.

The first thing she had to do was find out what the amalgamates were up to.

16

Meloku kept waiting for Companion to say something during the flight back to Avignon. It had remained silent for days. It hadn't even spoken when the satellites arrived. Meloku had discovered them from Joao's frantic call like everyone else.

Avignon rose over the shadowed horizon, a nebulous fuzz of infrared haze. It was far dimmer than it used to be.

The plague had arrived.

It was much easier to find discreet landing spaces these days. Infrared found a cul-de-sac with only four living people nearby, all of whom were asleep (and one in plague convulsions). The boarding ramp stretched to the cobbles. Meloku hastened down it. She could have done without the disruption of that meeting. It was a wonder the amalgamates hadn't sent her alone, or, at the very least, chosen a team of ideologically trustworthy anthropologists.

She'd toured this part of the city twice before. It had been a bustling neighborhood. Tonight, the smell of death clung to the ground. Most of its occupants lay in bloated decay, and the survivors had fled.

New cemeteries sprang up all over the city, but they weren't enough to contain the dead. As Meloku passed the trio of brothels nearest the heart of the papacy, she started passing bodies under the snow. A wandering pig had uncovered one corpse and was chewing off long, leathery strips of flesh. Farther down the street, two more pigs lay dead, victims of their scavenge.

A slow Armageddon was sweeping the city. The people who tried to their best to help usually fared the worst. The monks at the almshouse she passed, La Pignotte, had taken in as many of the sick as they could. They hadn't survived their charity. The almshouse stood empty but for corpses.

The survivors hadn't taken long to see enemies everywhere. Men attacked Jews in the streets. The fact that the Jews suffered from the plague as much as anyone didn't deter their persecution. On her walk to be picked up, Meloku had seen the pyres, ashes, and bones left of three men, a woman, and a child.

Whatever the amalgamates had in mind, Meloku wished they'd hurry. These people obviously weren't fit to govern themselves.

Closer to the papal palace, bonfires burned on street corners. No one had died in these fires. The papal court's physicians had recommended them as a defense against the plague. Clement VI had sealed himself away in his study with a lit fire, and breathed in the smoke. These were actually reasonable measures, though nobody here understood why. The smoke warded off fleas.

Infrared showed five servants inside de Colville's manor. Only two were sleeping. They thought that she was still in her room. When she'd gone to the field base, she'd told the servants she needed to shut herself inside her room for the day to "commune with her saints." No one questioned her. She'd taken care to build her reputation as an eccentric.

The back door was poorly locked. A few minutes of playing hide-and-seek with the servants' infrared shadows, and she was back in her plush room. Her bed was four times the size it needed to be. She sank into it as though it were a cloud. She had no idea what to do next.

Even back home, she'd never lived in a room this comfortable. Her home, Mhensis, was covered almost entirely by ocean. It was a tourist destination, a getaway, for people craving marine adventure. Like all resorts, the people who lived and worked there didn't enjoy their lives.

Growing up, she'd spent most of her year alone on an island while her parents staffed tourist seaskimmers. Her schoolteacher NAI had been her favorite company. Her favorite days had been the ones in which she hadn't seen any other kids at all. The other kids were herdlike, judgmental, and could never be as fascinating as an AI engineered to entertain and instruct her. The NAI had caught her asocial tendencies early and tried to curb them. It had only ever succeeded in getting her to tolerate her peers, never to accept them.

Her parents' seaskimmer was of course no place for a child: cramped spaces full of sex, drugs, and politics. Mhensis' seaskimmers were a favorite destination for powerbrokers from other planes. The deals they made there were not the sort deemed suitable for their publics: market-manipulating, vote-trading, petty corruption, all the usual bugbears of human-run societies.

When Meloku graduated at fourteen, she'd finally been able to accompany her parents, working in the ship's stores. The politics of it all had fascinated her. She'd immediately started watching self-important people and studying their habits: who they slept with, what foods and drugs and medicines fed their addictions. It had been easy to make sure their needs were met. Some of them even asked her to ferry messages. They were always archaically handwritten, missives so sensitive that they couldn't be trusted to transmission.

As it turned out, they were right to be wary. They *were* being watched. The amalgamates and their agents had their hands in everything. They needed to see the messages she was carrying. They made contact through their agents, and told her how she could open the envelopes without triggering the traps inside.

So she started working for the amalgamates, too.

The amalgamates were very selective about the people they employed. Meloku had always been proud of that. Companion had been one of the amalgamates' first gifts, a non-neutered AI to guide and mentor her. Even its existence was highly secret. No one was supposed to know that the amalgamates allowed non-neutered AIs to exist.

Her teammates on long-term cover assignments like this had long ago stopped bothering her. But Habidah had pried under her skin. She didn't understand why Habidah had to be here. This mission would have been so much easier with an ally in charge. She closed her eyes, and, unsuccessfully, tried to sink into her daily two hours of sleep.

"You must be dying to know," Companion said.

Meloku was impressed with herself for keeping her wits about her.

"Not nearly so badly as the others," she said.

"I can tell you a little," Companion said.

The next morning, Meloku beamed as she strolled through the Palais des Papes' courtyard. The ecclesiastical trolls and toadies along her way only smiled briefly in return. She wasn't the day's main attraction.

She should have been impatient. Instead she felt magnanimous. Her smile was genuine.

She wrapped her gown and fur coat about her when she reached the courtyard, but her demiorganics stifled the cold. The men and women in the gathering crowd weren't so lucky. She took her privileged position in the front row. There were fewer clergymen about than there would have been in normal times, but the upper echelons of the church had survived in far greater numbers than the street and church-level preachers. As with kings and queens, their attention to hygiene insulated them.

A trumpet blast was the cue for the men about her to straighten themselves into neat, orderly rows. Meloku stood, folded her hands, and waited. A minute later, Queen Joanna's procession entered.

The visiting queen rode at the fore of thirty lance-bearing knights and thirty more handmaidens carried in litters. She was seated atop a white mare, sheltered by a purple silk canopy carried by four men. Two grooms led her horse so that she could carry the scepter and the orb of her rulership. A carmine-and-violet fur cloak touched only her shoulders. She must have been freezing, but she did an admirable job of hiding that. She couldn't hide her cold skin from an infrared scan, of course, but that only confirmed what Meloku already knew: this woman was an accomplished actress.

She was extraordinarily beautiful for her age. Her blonde hair was neatly stitched and covered by a ribbed headdress. Three gold and silver necklaces draped over her shoulders. The shape they made pointed to her cleavage, an appropriately chaste and deniable statement of sexuality.

Meloku smiled beatifically, but of course Joanna didn't notice her. Yet.

This was another one of Habidah's irritating qualities. She paid little attention to anything truly important about the cities she visited. Not politics, not governance, and certainly not leaders. Everything Meloku knew about Queen Joanna, she'd had to discover herself. Certainly no one else had researched her.

One of the mysteries of the multiverse was that the Unity itself was the largest transplanar empire it had ever encountered. All of the others it encountered had numbered thousands of planes at most, typically hundreds or dozens. Simple reasoning about the infinite nature of the multiverse suggested that there should be – and were – larger somewhere. They must have been so rarefied that they were close to impossible to find.

Meloku privately suspected that the amalgamates were among the few creatures capable of controlling such vast estates. They had the intellect. All of the other transplanar empires she had personal experience with had been run by the usual warlords, overly ambitious algorithms, or other engineered minds. They produced more ruins and rubble than functioning civilizations.

The minds that, like the amalgamates, *were* complex enough

came with their own problems. They tended to disparage the help of lesser species, their inhabitants, and multiplied themselves instead. Even one mind of the amalgamates' caliber, so determined, had the power to wipe out its progenitors. And so those empires, too, fell prey to civil wars.

The amalgamates had struck a perfect balance. They kept their numbers limited to minimize the chance of one of their own going rogue. Enough of them to handle the tasks that took a truly powerful intelligence. But most of their strength came from their human civilizations, and the engines of human economies, managed at a remove. It was why, for all their powers, the amalgamates used agents like Meloku. And it was why fribbles like Joanna were important.

Joanna was the fugitive queen of Naples. She'd married a seventeen year-old Hungarian prince, Andreas. Thanks to Pope Clement VI's support, she had retained full sovereignty. Andreas received no power. However, Andreas's mother intervened with Clement, and Andreas, too, had received sovereignty. He'd immediately set the whole Neapolitan aristocracy against him by, among other things, releasing three violent brothers arrested on charges of treason, and returning properties that long since had been disbursed to other nobles.

Not long after, Andreas was hung from a balcony and thrown to the ground. Joanna claimed to have been barred in her room by the actual conspirators while the murder took place. And maybe she was telling the truth. But if she hadn't been complicit in the murder then, she'd become so afterward. She'd moved to protect her cousins and other members of her court, who almost certainly *had* committed the crime. She'd cast aspersions on Andreas's Hungarian bodyguards instead, calling them drunkards. Her investigation had gone nowhere beyond one scapegoat chamberlain.

The Hungarians had invaded Naples in retaliation for the murder. Joanna had fled. In the midst of the plague, she'd traveled to Avignon to stand trial for Andreas's murder in the papal court. She already had the court's sympathies. They saw her willingness to travel during the plague, and especially to pest-ridden Avignon, as proof that she believed that God would allow her the opportunity to prove her innocence.

Meloku doubted the Hungarians could maintain their hold over Naples for long. Andreas had been especially unpopular among the Neapolitans. The Hungarians had marched an army into Naples, but they didn't have the means or the will to keep it there. Both sides had declared a truce, with the war to be resolved by papal trial.

The procession halted in the courtyard. The knights and their lances stirred as Joanna dismounted. Some of her handmaids left their litters. Joanna spared no time for them. Accompanied by eight of her advisers and lawyers, she strode through the doors to the consistory, where the trial would take place. Meloku had not been invited to that, but her eavesdroppers kept track.

The consistory was also used for receptions, but today's overcast left it shadowed. It took an awkward half-minute for Joanna to shed her cloak and approach. The far end had a raised dais with two levels. The top tier held Pope Clement, sitting on one of a pair of velvet-and-gold thrones. The other throne was empty. There was no such thing as subtle symbolism in Avignon. All of the cardinals still alive and present in Avignon stood on the lower level of the dais, watching and waiting.

Joanna stepped to the dais, and kneeled on a pillow that had been placed before Clement. This was scripted, as was the kiss she placed on his slipper. And the kiss on the mouth that he gave her in return.

What was *not* scripted was the warm embrace he treated her with afterward. That was what she had been waiting for, though. It had shown her everything she needed to know.

Pope Clement had his own bills to collect. Joanna's persecutors, the Hungarians, were allies of the English in their war against the French. The papacy of Avignon was French in every way but officially. The papacy would be rewarded for anything that constrained the Hungarians' power.

Meloku and several other papal officials waited in the hall outside when the first day of the papal court concluded. She stood to attention when the royal procession began to emerge. Joanna was fourth out the door.

This time, Joanna couldn't quite hide her chill. She held her arms to her chest and her breath trembled. Yet she smiled. She inclined her head at each man she passed. She only halted when she reached Meloku.

Joanna said, "I've heard tales of you. The prophetess of Avignon."

"Merely performing as I have been called to," Meloku said, head inclined.

"Tell me – have you dreamed any dreams about me?"

"I know only that you are innocent. Naples will soon be yours again."

Joanna's smile became warmer. Meloku could smell the guilt on her. No matter. So long as Meloku told her what she wanted to hear, she would still be willing to believe that it was a divine message. People believed what they wanted to.

Most of the time, all her job entailed was telling them what they wanted.

Joanna turned, her cloak sweeping the dusty floor. Meloku cleared her throat. "My apologies, your majesty, but there are more challenges in your future. I've seen them in dreams, as well."

Joanna turned back to her, eyebrow raised. Meloku said, "After this ordeal is over, you will be visited by messengers. God intends Naples to serve as a foundation stone for Italy. They'll touch your dreams as they have mine."

Joanna blinked. She didn't believe much of *that* pronouncement, but she wasn't prepared to ignore a woman of Meloku's reputation. "We should talk about this later this week, you and I."

Meloku nodded, and held her silence. Joanna continued, her step a little less certain. At least she no longer looked cold.

Compared to France, the Holy Roman Empire, England,

Spain, even many Italian cities, the pope's temporal power was null or insignificant. But no one in the world held spiritual authority comparable to his. All of western Europe's power brokers either traveled here, or were in thrall to someone who traveled here.

The best place to influence all of them, therefore, was here. Joanna was to be the first. A tiny thrill traveled up Meloku's back. She was the only person on this world who knew what was about to happen to it.

One of the amalgamates was coming to this plane. She was going to *meet* it.

Together, they were going to reshape this world. And scavenge what remained of the Unity.

17

Niccoluccio was struck by a moment of panic when he woke and his cell walls were nowhere near. He rolled, stifled by a too-hot weight. Only when he'd fallen off his feather bed did he remember.

He pushed himself back under his blankets, sweating. He glared at the ceiling. His new bedroom was nearly as large as Sacro Cuore's refectory. He had no idea what to do with all the space. He had a while to wait until dawn.

His brother had procured him a second habit. The maid had cleaned one of them again last night. The people of this city were far too vain about laundering. Grudgingly, he dressed himself under the covers to spare anyone who might enter from the immodesty.

He felt drawn to the window. He cast open the shutters and leaned out. He needed to be sure he hadn't dreamed Habidah, or Florence. The biting wind dispelled the latter idea.

Niccoluccio's bedroom window stood on the second floor. He didn't have to crane his neck far to see the other wings of the home. It seemed all the buildings of Sacro Cuore could have fit between them. Dioneo had even spoken of a summer villa, a purchase their father had made the summer before.

Niccoluccio hadn't been the eldest of his father's sons, but he was the eldest of the two survivors. All of their father's property had gone to Dioneo. Niccoluccio had forsworn property when he'd gone to live in Sacro Cuore. Even outside the monastery, he didn't particularly want property now. It felt pointless being jealous when he'd already met a woman far wealthier than any Florentine.

The more he reflected on the miracle of his rescue, the more he felt the spark of the divine. But it was like no divinity he had imagined before. He wondered how something could be divine without being godly.

Dioneo escorted Niccoluccio into the city. Niccoluccio silently watched the buildings, each with a more elaborate facade than the last. They didn't contain a hundredth of the wonder of that single room in Habidah's home.

Dioneo chattered. "The old bishop chose to stay in Florence during the pestilence. Everyone thought he could never survive the pestilence. His arms were thin as bones. But, no, he's still with us."

Niccoluccio listened politely, not sure why Dioneo was talking about this. Dioneo's digressions usually had a point. Niccoluccio said, "I know how he must feel, to survive when by all rights he shouldn't."

Dioneo smiled broadly. "That's what today's meeting will be about. I applaud you choosing to wear your habit again."

Niccoluccio blinked. "You did get me the second one."

"Well – isn't it who you are? How you want other people to see you?"

"No. To both questions."

Dioneo left that alone. When they neared the cathedral, he said, "Ambrogiuolo will want very much to hear the whole story of your return. Leave out no detail."

For as often as Habidah had been on his mind, he hadn't breathed her name since she'd left. Ambrogiuolo – or Dioneo – would hardly believe anything he had to say about her. He was still trying to figure out how to say that he could never explain the most important part of his rescue as the shadow of the cathedral fell over him.

For as much as the secular architecture of Florence failed to rouse him, the sight of the Cathedral of Santa Reparata sent

189

tremors down his chest. Its white facade was so tall that, from this angle, it hid its dome. An enormous arch outlined the doors, carving deep shadows across the sunlit stone. The doors were held apart as if waiting for him.

Even this early, the nave was bustling with shadows and voices. Candles cast wan light over the cathedral's six principal altars. The most popular altar – that of St Zenobius, the first bishop of Florence – drew traffic toward the crypt. Sunlight shone through the stained glass at odd angles and strange colors. The vaulted ceiling looked somehow farther than the sky.

Niccoluccio let out a long breath. Earlier, he'd wondered if he could ever find peace again. If he could, it would be here.

The two of them slipped down a passage toward the adjoining baptistery, and from there to the dim back chambers. Niccoluccio had had no idea what Ambrogiuolo's role was until he saw his office. It was buffered from the public by a pair of secretaries. Niccoluccio swallowed. Ambrogiuolo had to be the head of the cathedral chapter.

Ambrogiuolo was as undersized as his office was oversized. He was sharp-chinned and nearly bald. He sprang from his seat and embraced Dioneo, but he didn't seem to know what to do with Niccoluccio. He settled for peering at him intently. Niccoluccio stood with folded hands.

Ambrogiuolo wasted little time. "So," he said, sitting down, "tell me about your escape from the pestilence."

Niccoluccio started with the truth, and told them how the pestilence had crashed through Sacro Cuore in two waves, taking every life but his. Ambrogiuolo and Dioneo visibly hungered for details. Niccoluccio didn't dwell on them. The brothers he'd left buried there deserved more than to be sensationalized, details in someone else's story. He said his brothers' names, but not how they died.

The trouble came when he reached his flight from the monastery. When Niccoluccio hesitated, Ambrogiuolo said, "It must have taken a miracle to see you back safely to us, especially from so far away."

Niccoluccio cleared his throat. At length, he decided he would tell the truth but elide her name and the mechanism of his deliverance. "I can't explain what brought me here. I found my body had been repaired and my needs sated. I do not remember leaving the forest, and yet here I am."

"Incomparable," Ambrogiuolo muttered, and then: "Did it happen in a moment, or over days?"

"I cannot tell you. I did not know where the time had gone, but afterward I found myself in the world of the living again, in a tiny village." Her home. "From there, I made my way to Florence."

"What was the village's name?" Ambrogiuolo asked.

"I did not have the presence of mind to ask," Niccoluccio said, truthfully.

Dioneo asked, "Were there any visitations?"

"I remember seeing people," Niccoluccio admitted.

Ambrogiuolo asked, "Saints? The Holy Mother?"

"Only people," Niccoluccio said. "Mortals."

His answer didn't seem to disappoint Ambrogiuolo. He leaned back as if at the end of a great meal. "The world must know of your story, Brother Niccoluccio."

"I do not believe it does. And I'm not a brother anymore."

"Oh? Have you informed the proper ecclesiastical officials of your decision?"

"Not yet, no."

"You're a brother in my eyes and the church's, Niccoluccio Caracciola. I hope that you stay. I'm certain I can find a place for you."

Niccoluccio opened his mouth to protest, and then stopped. "A place?"

"The San Lorenzo parish is looking for several high officials."

The San Lorenzo parish was the wealthiest – and therefore most important – parish in Florence. Clergymen fought for the privilege of serving there. Niccoluccio quickly shook his head. "I have done nothing to deserve such an honor. Nor am

191

I capable of upholding it."

"The pestilence has moved us all in directions we could not otherwise have taken," Ambrogiuolo said. "Your brother is serving as prior. He may, if God wills, keep that position. Before the pestilence, did you ever think that could have happened?"

"No," Niccoluccio admitted.

"This is a matter of necessity. There's been a great deal of turmoil in relations between the church and the city. The San Lorenzo parish lost its treasurer, among a good many others. It needs someone the church and the people can trust. A monk, particularly a monk graced by miracle, would be a popular choice."

"You'll have to look somewhere else for a monk."

"If you are not a monk, then what do you intend to do to better your family's fortunes?"

Niccoluccio glanced at his brother, and then back at Ambrogiuolo. "Pardon?"

"You're your father's eldest son. Not working to improve the family fortunes or to continue the line could be excused while you were in the church. If you carry on telling people that you're no longer a monk, they'll expect you to contribute."

"I do not care for other people's expectations for my life."

"Then what of your own?" Again, Niccoluccio had no answer. Ambrogiuolo pressed, "What do you intend to do if not stay here with us?"

"I don't intend to leave Florence, if that is what you mean."

"Yes, but then what? Your brother can provide for you, of course. How content would you be with nothing but that for the rest of your life?"

"I had not thought so far ahead."

"You keep saying that you are no longer a monk. Does that mean you are no longer clergy? That you can't contribute to the church?"

Niccoluccio hesitated. He wanted to exit this conversation as fast as possible, but Ambrogiuolo was speaking the truth. Sacro Cuore had taught him to resist fleeing truth.

"I will consider that," he said, though he knew the two other men would interpret that as acquiescence.

Certainly his brother was already speaking as if he'd accepted as they exited the cathedral. "I have not felt so optimistic about this city for years. Your return was a gift I didn't dare so much as pray for."

Niccoluccio tugged at his coat sleeves, willing them to be warmer. "I wasn't aware you'd felt so poorly of Florence."

"You've been fortunate, staying away when you did. It's been years of hard winter, and food shortages. The municipal bread ration is lower than ever. Last year there were grain riots at the Orsanmichele market. I think the only reason we haven't seen the same this year is that the pestilence has taken so many people that food prices stayed low. Fewer mouths."

There was nothing to say but, "I am very sorry."

"On top of that, there's been the trouble with the church."

"Surely the church has only helped in these trying times."

"Religious men help, yes. The *church* has been a hindrance."

A body lay at the edge of the alley ahead: a man about thirty years old, with mud over his open eyes. Judging from the snow sprinkled over him, he had been there for days. No one had so much as covered up his face.

Niccoluccio stopped. His brother took him by the crook of his elbow, and dragged him on. "That man needs help," Niccoluccio protested.

"That man *needed* help."

Niccoluccio was so taken aback that he couldn't speak for a moment. "That's not a very Christian attitude. He needs a burial."

"These are not very Christian times."

Niccoluccio only looked at him.

Dioneo sighed, and asked, "You of course remember the Compagnia della Misericordia?" Niccoluccio nodded. They were a spiritual order founded to tend to the sick. Their red robes and hoods were highly esteemed everywhere in Florence. "After the plague struck, they came to care for the sick and dead. They wore masks, but that didn't protect them. There are few left now. I do not have the charity left in me to see the same happen to my brother."

Niccoluccio lapsed into silence. As usual, his brother went on without prompting: "Avignon has interfered with a number of our elections. Not only within parish institutions, which would be understandable, but municipal elections. There are always new clerical taxes even when there is no crusade. Yet our clergy don't have living wages. In times like these, their parishioners don't have enough to support them, either. Anyone the bishop deems against him, he declares a 'potential outlaw,' and requires them to post a bond for good behavior. You can imagine that the bishop is not now the most popular man in the city. Too many people were hoping he wouldn't survive the pestilence."

"Many people not including yourself, I trust."

Dioneo looked to him. "I would never celebrate the death of another Christian in these times."

Niccoluccio studied his brother. He had always known Dioneo as an honest man. That had been twelve years ago. It was evident that politics had changed him in many ways.

Dioneo went on, "This bishop has not been kind to us. Neither he nor anyone in Avignon cares about Florence. The church has just become another Venice or Naples, scrabbling for power. You will see for yourself when you work with us. That is the last I will say on the matter."

For now, Niccoluccio silently added. Dioneo was rarely finished with talking.

The smell of roasting garlic from a nearby market would have tempted him if his stomach hadn't still been churning from the sight of the corpse. Maybe it would be easier to avoid temptation here than he'd thought.

Experimentally, he flexed the muscles in his throat, and spoke as Habidah had taught him. He said, or unsaid, "I can already tell you a great deal about how my city has changed."

Her voice sounded as though it were coming from all around

him. "Huh…? Oh. Niccoluccio."

He started. He glanced at Dioneo, sure his brother had heard, but Dioneo kept walking, unaware.

Her voice had sounded entirely unlike her. Even when she'd made him practice calling her before they'd left her home, she hadn't sounded like that. It was deep. Resonant. For a moment, he wondered if she'd allowed her companions to answer her calls.

But when she spoke again, the moment of oddness had passed, and she was herself. "It's good to hear from you," she said.

She sounded preoccupied, like she'd half-forgotten him. Niccoluccio tried, unsuccessfully, not to be hurt. He subvocalized, "I didn't disturb you, I hope?"

"Of course not. I shouldn't have neglected you since yesterday. A lot has happened here."

He'd never heard her so unsettled. "Would you care to tell me about it?"

Something like laughter echoed through the streets around him. It was astounding that only he could hear this. "No. Tell me about your day."

Nonplussed, he told her what Ambrogiuolo and his brother had offered him. Habidah said, "Congratulations. That sounds like quite a step up."

"It doesn't feel like it. I may refuse."

"That's your choice to make."

"I don't enjoy feeling as though I am not in control of my fate."

There was a lengthy pause. "I'd thought that joining a monastery required subordinating yourself to God's will as well as your superiors'."

"Yes, but *entering* the monastery was my choice. None of this is. I might love Dioneo, but I could never place my faith in him."

Habidah asked, "Do you believe you can do good with what you've been given?"

195

"I don't know," Niccoluccio said.

"Then neither do I."

Niccoluccio hadn't failed to notice that Habidah had avoided asking about Florence, even after he brought it up. She'd supposedly sent him here to report on the city. It didn't help his upset stomach.

He and Dioneo passed the Church of San Michele, one of many small churches near the cathedral. He'd gone by it many times without thinking of it. It served the staff of Florence's politicians and bankers and merchants. Most people went straight on to the cathedral.

He'd expected it to have changed in all the ways the rest of the city had: fewer people, filthier and meaner grounds, maybe closed. But the doors were flung open. People bustled inside. There were more people here than he could remember seeing on all his trips past, just as there had been more at the cathedral than he'd seen so early in the mornings.

No matter the dangers of the pestilence, Florentines still flocked to the church for hope, healing, and succor.

He told Habidah, "Perhaps I could do some good re-entering the church."

"Help as you're able," she said. "It's all any of us can do."

18

The cold sea draft flowing through the cracks in Habidah's walls didn't bother her as much as the stink of fish it carried. She imagined she would have gotten used to it by now. Her demiorganics could block out discomforts like cold, but odors were something else. Even when she couldn't smell Marseilles, she could taste it.

She lay on her heather bed, churning over her thoughts for the thousandth time. Whatever was going on in orbit was far more than a simple observation mission. Joao had tracked satellites in orbits far and extreme, but their orbits crisscrossed most heavily above Europe. It could hardly be a coincidence that the university had instructed her team to focus on the same region.

The plague had visited lands farther east, but Europe was being hit hardest right now. It was the most vulnerable. The easiest to influence.

That wasn't all. More gateways had opened on the dark side of this world's moon. Joao had registered the neutrino static of gateways opening, but he had no way to tell what was happening there.

All she wanted was someone to talk to. She and Joao compared notes every day, but Habidah hadn't shared any of her conclusions with him. She couldn't trust him. She couldn't trust any of the rest of her team, for that matter. Niccoluccio was the only person she could be sure wasn't involved.

She'd hoped he would have called before now. She'd gotten a blip the other night, an instant's buzz in her bones, but it had stopped the moment she'd gotten it, like the signal had cut or redirected. He'd probably started subvocalizing without realizing it.

She was tempted to call him herself, but she didn't want to add to his troubles. And no doubt everything she told him was monitored.

There was someone on her team who could tell her exactly what the amalgamates were doing here. Poring through her data, she was pretty sure she knew who it was.

The numbing wind deadened what was left of her nerves as she stepped outside. An ice-fringed moon limed the flat expanse of the sea. The smell got worse. The only wind in Marseilles came from the harbor, which the city also used for sewage runoff. It must have been bad enough before the plague. Now the harbor had been chained. The quarantined ships were full of the dead, and their catch rotted in their holds.

By contrast with Habidah's other cities, Marseilles had all but fallen apart. Unlike Genoa, Marseilles had no neighbors suffering from the plague, no experiences of this severity to draw from. When the plague had arrived, it had quickly metamorphosed into the more deadly pneumonic form. Even with many of its people having fled to the country, Habidah estimated that Marseilles would lose two-thirds of its population.

In many ways, Marseilles reminded Habidah of the first planes to be struck by the onierophage. Many people refused to believe that there was a disease that the amalgamates couldn't cure, and carried on about their business. When the truth struck, they panicked. Transplanar trade all but halted. Whole worlds quarantined themselves. There, as here, people killed their neighbors if they thought it would save them from the plague. Or, more often, for mundane reasons. Marseilles may have had fewer mouths to feed, but famine was coming. The municipal grain stores wouldn't last all winter.

She startled at a jolt from her demiorganics. Another message. She hoped that it would be Niccoluccio, but no such luck. Feliks.

"I'm worried about Joao," he sent. "I think he may be like me. Infected."

Habidah swallowed. "Have you told him?"

"No. I'm not sure, but I couldn't keep it to myself any longer."

"Symptoms?"

"Lethargy, lack of appetite, increased thirst. It could be a reaction to stress, but I doubt it. He must have noticed but he hasn't said anything."

According to the transmission's tags, Feliks was still in the field base. "Aren't you supposed to be in Dresden?"

A pause. "I don't have the strength anymore. I'm sorry."

She swallowed her curse before she could inadvertently subvocalize it. "You should have told me before I made you board the shuttle–"

"I'll get back out the moment a trip to my quarters and back doesn't leave me flat on my back. That could still happen."

Habidah sat heavily on a freezing stone doorstep. The satellite linking her with Feliks would only be overhead for another three minutes. After that, it would be another twenty-five minutes before the next. He'd chosen the timing deliberately. It wasn't like him to be avoidant.

"I'm so sorry, Feliks."

"We're not going to get anything done telling each other that, are we?"

"Kacienta is still available, isn't she? I'll send her out in your place."

"I've already voiced the idea to her. She doesn't want to disrupt her own work. She's busy compiling our reports."

"That's too fucking bad for her," Habidah said, before she could help herself. "Send her to Dresden. Do whatever parts of her work you feel capable of."

Feliks knew when to put up a fight, and when not to. "If

that's what you think is best."

"It's not as though it'll make much of a difference. Not with whatever the amalgamates are up to." Listening in on this conversation. "I don't know why they haven't packed us back home yet. There's got to be a reason we can't see."

"The amalgamates are powerful, but they can't do everything themselves. That's why they have agents. They need intermediaries."

"You think we're their intermediaries?"

"Why else would the amalgamates have us here?"

"If it was that simple, why the false premises? Why not just tell us?"

Feliks couldn't answer that, of course. He asked, "Do the people of this plane matter to you?"

One minute left. "They don't deserve to suffer this." Another reason she wished she'd heard from Niccoluccio. She couldn't tell if she'd made things better or worse.

"They matter to me, too. I'm living through the same nightmare they are."

"If the amalgamates have long-term goals for this world, why don't they cure its plague? From the start, they specifically barred us from that. They have the capability. They could do it in a month."

"I don't think anyone here could tell you the answer to that."

No. There was at least one person who could. "Just spitting questions into the wind."

"Speaking of wind, you need to keep on your feet. I'm getting some warnings about your body temperature. You can't just have your demiorganics keep you from feeling the cold."

"You worry about yourself. I'll take care of me."

She'd timed it perfectly. Their satellite fell beyond the horizon.

She grunted as she forced herself to pace on her cold-stiffened knees. While she'd talked with Feliks, reports from programs she'd left at the field base had reached her. Their results sluiced through her memory.

The communications gateway remained the key. It remained the only method of transplanar communication on this plane. The satellites had come through temporary gateways. Those had closed. If the spy wanted to talk to his or her masters, he or she would still have to use the field base's gateway.

Habidah had kept an eye on communications traffic and on everyone's sleep schedules. Since they only needed to sleep a few hours a day, it had taken time. With careful monitoring, she'd discovered several messages to Felicity Core had been sent while Feliks and Kacienta were sleeping.

Finally, last night, Habidah had ordered the communications gateway closed, and told everyone but Meloku. She'd revoked everyone's permission to open it. Sure enough, an hour ago the gateway had opened without her instructions. NAI had no explanation. It had no record of any command instructing it to do so.

Meloku hadn't even bothered to hide. She had been the only one making use of the survey team's communications satellites at the time. She must have been as tired of hiding as Habidah was of hunting her.

The corner of Habidah's lips twitched. She swallowed, pushed down the rising rage.

The next time a communications satellite rose over the horizon, she had NAI prep the shuttle for flight. Habidah marched out of the city. She had two hours of night left. Marseilles and Avignon were so near that it would be a very short flight.

The shuttle waited for her in a grove a kilometer from the city. Its edges glowed red from the speed of its transit. She could have confronted Meloku remotely, but that would have just afforded Meloku an extra opportunity to evade her. If Meloku wanted to run away, it wouldn't be as simple as closing a communications channel.

Before long, Avignon was an infrared flare on the horizon,

a tower of firelight and smoke. Habidah arced around it. The heart of the city, around the papal palace, shone brightly in both visible and infrared. People were awake and fires were lit. It was the last district Habidah expected to see active so early. Papal bureaucrats weren't farmers. More than anyone else, they had license to sleep in.

Meloku had fought to get here. That left Habidah with an unsettling idea. This was the administrative center of the religion that dominated this continent. The power the papacy wielded was more tenuous than secular sovereigns, but only the courts of the Mongol khans were more far-reaching.

And Meloku had demanded to be here.

Habidah brought the shuttle to a low hover near one of the mass graves. No one was around to see her disembark. Before long, the shuttle wouldn't have enough concealment for its camouflage to function. She instructed the shuttle to leave her here and head back to the field base.

The Palais des Papes obscured the approaching dawn. According to the satellites, Meloku's last signal had come from a house nearby. A large one, certainly not the kind of unobtrusive inn or rental that the anthropologists were supposed to pick. Habidah picked up her pace. A household servant stood just inside the door. From his infrared shadow's stance, he looked like he was waiting for someone.

Habidah clomped up the front steps, making no secret of her arrival. The servant opened the door just before Habidah reached it. He was bald and reedy, and his eyes were wide. He stepped back. Though he'd been waiting, he seemed startled to see her.

"Madam Akropolites is expecting you," he said, and bowed his head.

Habidah wished she had the presence of mind to say something in return.

Meloku was waiting in the third-floor bedroom, next to a wide window with embroidered curtains, and a lacy hanging sheet to shade the bed. The perfumes couldn't hide the scent of sweat and sex from Habidah's augmented senses. Meloku was dressed as if to bed a king, in a layered, multihued dress that drooped across the floor. It made her look twice as big as she was. Habidah could hardly keep herself from laughing.

Meloku asked, "Always have to be inconvenient, don't you?"

The temptation to laugh vanished. "What the fuck are you trying to pull?"

"Do you think I know?"

Habidah opened her mouth, but had nothing to say. Meloku said, "The amalgamates don't share their secrets with everyone. Most times, with anyone. I find out what they'll have me do only when it's time to do it."

"You knew I was coming."

"The shuttle is easy enough to track. I think you scared my poor doorman. He didn't believe me when I told him I had a premonition that a stranger would be visiting at this hour."

"What are you doing here? Why would you – why would the amalgamates – need all this? A manor. A doorman. How could any of this possibly give the amalgamates anything that they don't already have?"

Meloku was like a queen, completely in control. She folded her arms. "You could have come nearly any other night. I'm missing a very important rendezvous because of you."

Habidah flicked her eyes to the bed. "Seems like you already had it."

"Not that. You care enough about these people that you're not going to leave when they can see you. I suppose that means you're planning on staying here all day."

"I'm not leaving until I've gotten answers."

"You don't matter as much as you think you do."

"Then why am I even here?" Habidah exploded. "Why are any of us? Why the anthropological assignment, the false pretenses, if we're irrelevant?"

"To do exactly as you were told to. Your reports haven't been censored. They've been sent home as you were told they

203

would be. Worlds across the Unity are reading them and many others to develop a social response to the onierophage."

"You can't expect me to believe that us being here, and everything going on in orbit, is a coincidence."

"You're right. I doubt it's a coincidence. After this morning, we both might know a little more."

Habidah sat on the bed and rested her face in her hands.

Meloku was starting to look satisfied. "Do your work, or not. It doesn't make any difference to me. Or to the amalgamates."

"I don't believe you," Habidah said. "If we didn't matter, you wouldn't have needed to infiltrate us. You could have just come here on your own. The only reason to hide this is that you knew we wouldn't go along if we found out. We haven't exhausted our usefulness."

Meloku shrugged. "You might as well shuttle out after sunrise. It won't matter if the locals see you. They're already expecting strange things in the sky."

Habidah looked up sharply. "Why?"

"Because I told them to. I have a record of being right about these things."

It was all Habidah could do to keep herself from leaping up and throttling Meloku. But the amalgamates didn't leave their agents defenseless. Meloku would have beaten her.

Meloku said, "Most of the papal district is up, watching the sky. I would be out there with them if I hadn't heard the shuttle was on its way."

Aggravating as it was, Meloku's smugness had its virtues. She had said more than she'd probably meant to. Earlier, she said the shuttle had been easy to track. Now she'd *heard* that Habidah had been coming to Avignon. Someone had told her. Another agent, or NAI. "Who else are you working with?"

Meloku strode to her window, pushed back her curtain and opened her shutters. Habidah crinkled her nose. The smell of one of the mass graves carried right in.

Meloku said, "I'll show you."

Habidah made herself get up. As soon as she was close

enough, Meloku clapped her arm around Habidah's shoulder, and came just short of pushing Habidah out the window. Before Habidah could gasp, Meloku held her chin and tilted her head upward.

Several stars still shone above the graying horizon. A wavering light, like a reflection seen through water, rippled across them. The hazy glow of a comet's tail lingered behind it, moving much too fast for something so far away.

Habidah's demiorganics trilled a dozen alarms through her bones. She was receiving calls from the field base's NAI, from Joao, from her observation satellites. It was all too chaotic to understand.

The cloudy light shimmered. She could just make out an impression of motion along it. Even with her augmented vision, she couldn't discern more than shifting darkness, stars disappearing as something moved across them.

Habidah answered the call from Joao. "Planar gateway in high orbit," he blurted. "Larger than the others. Larger than any I've ever seen."

Joao didn't have to say what was coming through. He already knew. Just from the sheer scale of the rimy line ripped across the sky, so did Habidah.

She tapped into a view from one of her observation satellites to confirm it.

At first, the satellite's view looked no different from hers from the ground, only clearer. The atmosphere no longer blurred the sky. A lightning-bright rent in space tore the arched horizon. The satellite had sharper senses, though, and after a moment she saw an occlusion of stars, a shape, sliding, emerging.

Light spilled out of the tear. For flickers of a moment, that light shone across interconnected gunmetal gray platforms. The platforms were interconnected, studded with needle-slender cannons, stubby factories, and docked craft. One platform was shrouded by gas, a hazy atmosphere bound by containment fields, wrapped around a vast parkland.

A short distance away, darkness glommed onto the object. Considering the light the gateway produced, that was a half-hearted attempt to hide. Nor would they ever fool people like Habidah, who knew exactly what they were looking at.

A planarship. Habidah had never seen one herself, but she recognized it.

"*Ways and Means,*" Meloku said, contentedly. "Here."

The same planarship from which Osia had called. Habidah breathed, "Why?"

"To take control for us," Meloku said. Habidah repeated her question, and Meloku answered, "What else do the amalgamates do?"

Only then did Habidah decide that Meloku didn't know anything else.

19

At the breakfast table, Dioneo's surviving children couldn't stop talking about something that had happened in the skies early this morning. They hadn't seen it themselves, but they had heard the story from their housekeeper. Shortly after the last of the stars had disappeared, a white streak had ripped across the sky, as if the firmament could be split like the skin of a fruit.

By the time Niccoluccio had woken, it had long since disappeared. According to the people who had seen it, it had been like a comet's tail. Comets always heralded disaster.

Dioneo's children were struggling to determine what could be worse than the pestilence. Finally, they turned to Niccoluccio. "Is this the end of days, uncle?" the oldest boy asked. He sounded as though he were asking if there would be fruit after breakfast.

"Never believe that," Niccoluccio said.

He ate the rest of his bread in silence while his nephew at once disregarded him. He'd hardly had to think about his answer. He didn't know what other people had seen, but he knew the end of days wouldn't look like that. He could have conjured a thousand theological reasons, but none of those would have been the reason he'd answered as he had. He couldn't have even explained it to Brother Rinieri.

He knew how small his experiences were, and how ill-equipped they left him to explain anything. His experience with Habidah had served to remind him how tiny he was underneath the heavens. Habidah had seemed like an angel. After her, he'd had no idea what an angel might look like, and had given up trying to conceive of one.

Dioneo met him halfway to the San Lorenzo parish. Niccoluccio hid his grimace, but Dioneo took no notice. Dioneo strode along with him, and took the opportunity to lecture Niccoluccio on politics.

"This city did not defend and support the papacy against the Ghibellines for so long to be ruled from Avignon as a reward. Our city is our own, not a... a French pope's."

Niccoluccio remarked, "The papacy doesn't belong to any kingdom."

Dioneo chuckled, bitter. "We made our choice to side with the papacy when the papacy was Roman. Whatever good men there were in the papacy have been choked by the stench of Avignon. Do you know how many whorehouses that city has? And how few monasteries and churches?"

Niccoluccio politely refrained from enumerating the brothels he and Dioneo had passed already on their walk today. He turned his attention elsewhere. At Sacro Cuore, he had always woken with the dawn. The sun was already halfway to its zenith, yet he still didn't feel awake, and wasn't sure he ever would.

Since he'd come back, every time he looked at Florence, he felt tired. The filth in the alleys and the runnels along the road made his skin itch. The smell of fresh-cooked meat from the marketplaces roiled his stomach. He hadn't seen any plague dead today, but expected them at every intersection. If anything heralded the end of the world, it would be unburied bodies, not lights in the sky.

Passersby still gawked skyward. Eventually, they had to get on with the day, even if awed and subdued. By the time Niccoluccio and Dioneo reached the outskirts of the San Lorenzo parish, the markets were as bustling as the day before.

The skyline took shape as if from his memories. So much

had changed about the city since he'd left, but not this neighborhood. He and Dioneo were only streets away from their father's house. And there was Elisa Vergellesi's home, with its multi-arched roof and trellised, ivy-spun windows. Further down the street, he would find the bakery that occupied the spot where the old grain market had been. He, Elisa, and Pietro had sneaked into the market at nights for their contests in love.

Elisa had been the daughter of a merchant who was often away, trading along the Grecian coast. She had been pretty, with pale skin and carefully braided brown hair. Pietro had had tanned skin, short blond hair, a handsome chin. Niccoluccio and Pietro had gotten it into their heads that they were play-fighting for her hand, and had kept up the illusion even after they'd grown old enough to realize what was actually happening.

Niccoluccio didn't remember when he'd started to think that Pietro had been prettier. The first time he and Pietro had had each other had been in that grain market. Elisa had brought them there at night and declared that she needed to see them practice their arts of love before she would deign to let them touch her. When Niccoluccio and Pietro had sufficiently proven themselves, she would join them.

Niccoluccio felt light-headed, and had to close his eyes. The memories were heady and unwelcome, but he couldn't push them away. He hadn't turned to the monastic life to escape Florence. He'd turned to it to escape himself.

Niccoluccio's memories of those nights kept him awake at night for years. He'd confessed his deeds. To his shock, his confessor had said that Niccoluccio had needed to scourge himself publicly, to bring Pietro and Elisa to the attention of the city authorities. Niccoluccio's tutor had not been so severe, but had told him to seek monastic solitude. That was the only thing that could save him.

Niccoluccio shed most of himself in the monastery, but there would always be that rotten core at his heart. Monastic life had been helpful in other ways, but it couldn't smother the flames of his youth or the sins of his body. He could no more divest himself of it than he could his bones.

It was a relief to reach the parish's head church.

Dioneo showed him about. Niccoluccio would even have his own office, a shadowed space that reminded him of his cell in Sacro Cuore. Candles cast a respectful glow over it, and the mutterings of parishioners sounded like wind rustling trees.

Dioneo introduced the clergymen who would answer his questions. Then Dioneo announced he had an appointment he needed to keep. The clergyman disappeared as soon as Dioneo left. Niccoluccio was alone with the diocese's account ledgers.

He read for hours. To his dismay, he discovered that Dioneo's tirade against the papacy had some reason. The diocese had become significantly poorer over the past few years thanks to clerical taxes. The taxes had been collected in the name of crusade, but there had been no crusades in years.

The San Lorenzo parish and the Diocese of Florence had gone heavily into debt. Now the pestilence would prevent the diocese from raising the money to pay it off, let alone the new taxes.

Niccoluccio found one of the clergymen. The wisp-haired old man couldn't quite meet his eyes. It took Niccoluccio a moment to realize that he was in awe. Niccoluccio hesitated a moment, and then told him to collect a count of the preachers employed by San Lorenzo and record their salaries. The old man nodded and scurried off.

Niccoluccio watched him go. If only he knew how unworthy Niccoluccio actually was. What would Habidah think of him, the real him?

He returned to his office. The noise from the parish hall grew louder as he read. When he stepped back out, the church had become full of parishioners, many of them looking toward his opening door. The closest stepped back with a respectful hush.

Dioneo had obviously not hesitated to share Niccoluccio's story.

The nearest reached out to touch his sleeve. Niccoluccio

drew back. People followed to the door, but, fortunately, didn't chase him outside.

He kept his head down as he walked. At Sacro Cuore, he'd dared to believe he was beyond anger. His brother probably thought he was doing Niccoluccio a favor.

He flexed the muscles in the back of his throat, almost spoke to Habidah again. But she had her own problems. He didn't need to run to her like she was his mother. Habidah was human, not someone to whom he could pray.

That he'd nearly started to meant that there was something deeply broken in him.

His chest still burned when he looked at Elisa's home. Maybe, he thought, there always had been something broken. Sacro Cuore hadn't changed a thing that mattered.

20

Habidah charged out of Meloku's manor. She didn't look at the stunned doorman, didn't speak. Above, Meloku's infrared shadow leaned over her window, almost in reverence.

Habidah scanned the sky as deeply as her augmented senses allowed, and shunted feeds from her team's satellites into her visual cortex. The planarship could be whatever color it wanted. Right now it was deep-sea black. Aside from the stars it occluded, it left no trace. Even still, its shadow would excite astronomers around this world.

Habidah could only just make it out in other spectra. *Ways and Means'* aft platforms glowed hotly in infrared, ebbing engine heat. The planarship drifted lazily across the sky in high semi-synchronous orbit. It was a dark mass of dozen-kilometer-long platforms studded with missiles, spaceplanes, detachable factories, and sensors. Nine of these segments were arranged in a three-by-three block. A tenth sat at the front. That one housed the amalgamate's mind. Nothing human was allowed there.

Joao had already alerted the rest of the team. They were all already listening. She asked Joao, "Did you tell the university what's happened?"

"I've included everything we know in our last report."

"Heard back?"

"Not yet, but we only just sent it—"

"Open the communications gateway. Tell the university

Ways and Means is here and one of our anthropologists is a spy. Demand an answer. Hell – send our reports to every academic institution you can think of. Journalists. As many people in the Unity as are willing to listen."

Habidah chewed her lip as she waited. Then Joao said, "No answer."

"Contact anyone in any news agency. Anyone who will answer."

"Hold on. I'm getting an... it's an automated answer. Our messages back to the Unity have been 'temporarily blocked due to a security emergency.'"

Habidah slammed the heel of her hand into the bricks of Meloku's manor. Slim chance their last messages had gotten through, either. This was just the first time the amalgamates had admitted it.

Silence stifled what was left of the night. No one knew what to say any more than she did. She said, "Keep trying. Send an additional request to evacuate us. Whatever's going on here, I'm sure I don't want to be a part of it."

"Requests for four individual evacuations, sent," Joao said.

"Five," Habidah said, without thinking.

Feliks said, "I doubt you're going to get Meloku to come with."

The gateway had closed. *Ways and Means* was all but invisible now. It had wanted to announce its arrival, though. Whatever plans the amalgamates had for this plane, she was sure its people wouldn't want to be any more a part of them than she did.

She had a responsibility to help as many as she could, even if she could count them on one hand.

"Five," she repeated.

Joao paused before answering. "All right. Requests sent. We got the same answer back."

"Keep sending them."

Habidah stared at Meloku's manor. There were no shadows behind the illuminated curtains, no more infrared blurs close to the windows. Habidah walked in the opposite direction. The cobbles left her step unsteady.

There had to be a way to puzzle out what was happening. This world had no exceptional natural resources, no civilizations that should have gotten the amalgamates' attention. Only a continent devastated by plague and war.

Maybe that had something to do with it. The amalgamates refused to cure their plague. Certainly now that *Ways and Means* was here, they had the resources to eradicate that plague any time it pleased.

She sat hard by a garden wall and folded her knees. A crawling sensation started at her neck and spread down her back. The amalgamates *wanted* these people dead. Or dying.

It was suddenly too obvious. Weak, wounded civilizations were easy to lead. Terrorists and tyrants on billions of planes could attest to that.

And Meloku had placed herself at the administrative center of a continent-spanning religion.

"They're taking control of this continent," Habidah said, both aloud and to her team.

Demiorganics didn't convey tone very well, but they hardly needed help to capture Kacienta's skepticism: "Why would they ever want anything as small as this world?"

Feliks said, "It's not that far out of bounds. They've taken over other planes before. Incorporated them into the Unity."

"*Advanced* planes," Kacienta said. "Planes that had something to offer, some resource or technology."

Joao said, "The only thing that makes this world different from trillions of others is the people. And, some atypical religious beliefs aside, the people aren't *that* remarkable. You can find lowtechnology civilizations all over the multiverse."

Feliks said, "They're not remarkable. Just vulnerable."

Habidah added, "And easily manipulated."

"Manipulated to do *what?*" Kacienta asked. "What could they possibly do that the amalgamates couldn't themselves?"

A long silence followed. Finally, Feliks ventured, "Work with people. The amalgamates don't have the resources to take care of everybody themselves. That's why they have agents. That's why they said they sent us to begin with – to help them understand this world."

Joao said, "Right." Even his transmission had a nervous tremor to it. "The amalgamates usually hire out to take care of low priority tasks, like dealing with people. They have agents."

"Or stooges like us," Habidah said.

Joao asked, "So what would the amalgamates need the people of this world for?"

Habidah shook her head ruefully. She cast her gaze upward. *Ways and Means* was halfway behind a cloud, but she could see through that. There was no sign of further engine activity, and only modest thermal leakage. She could only think of one job large enough that the amalgamates would need a population like this plane's.

She said, "To work for settlers."

Feliks supplanted, "Colonists."

Now even Kacienta seemed shaken. "What do you mean, 'work for'?"

Habidah pulled herself to her feet, though she wasn't sure where she was going. A hot, heavy pressure built in her chest. "*Slave* for. Indigenous servants."

Feliks said, "A servile class." Silence followed, as even he couldn't seem to be able to follow the thought to its conclusion. "Maybe they're even going to be taught to be willing."

Habidah said, "Meloku put herself right at a center of power, started making an impression on its leaders. She told me she'd forecasted *Ways and Means'* appearance. She set herself up as a prophetess. A good position to tell the locals of a race of saviors coming. I wouldn't be surprised if *Ways and Means* was sending agents to every court on the plane."

Meloku said, "A well-reasoned theory."

Habidah glanced sharply to the manor. She had accepted, a long time ago, that the amalgamates could listen in to everything. This felt different. Meloku wasn't an amalgamate. She was just an intruder.

215

"Go fuck yourself," Joao advised.

Meloku ignored him. "I want to assure you all that it's not as bad as you've made it sound. If the amalgamates intended to harm anyone on this plane, they would have already. What's happening here will be as good for them as it is for us." The amalgamates must have told her more in the past few minutes, or Habidah had guessed wrong and she'd known more than she'd said. "We have refugees all over the Unity. Some planes are still trying quarantines, evacuations. Their evacuees can't return home. They need a new one."

Habidah said, "A new home with people already living on it."

Meloku said, "Again. If all the amalgamates wanted to do was conquer, they wouldn't need to infiltrate its systems of power. All of the armies on this world couldn't stand up to a single orbital defense drone."

Feliks said, "Easier to convert than to conquer. More productive, even."

"Exactly," Meloku said, missing Feliks' bite. "There are millions – billions – of people in the Unity who need new planes. Easier to bring them to a place with people to build their homes, staff their industries, be their neighbors. The amalgamates can do a lot, but they can't make a world feel like home. By the time the evacuees arrive, we're going to make sure the natives are ready to accept them."

"'Feel like home,'" Habidah repeated, trying to count how many horrors Meloku had elided. The natives would never be the equals of the settlers. "No, no, no. If that was all, you wouldn't need us. You'd come here with only loyal agents. You wouldn't need to trick anthropologists." It clicked all in one moment. "Unless the amalgamates are stretched thin. They're doing this on hundreds or thousands of planes, and don't have enough agents to scout them. So they have to use dupes like us to fill the gaps."

Kacienta said, numbly, "We helped you get a foothold into the plane, to understand the locals. That's all we were ever here for."

"Your reports *have* been sent back. They're being read on plague-stricken planes even now. Nobody lied about that."

"With references to your project censored," Joao said. Meloku didn't answer, which was as good as a confirmation. "That's another thing I don't understand. Why the security? Why block our calls? What does it even matter if the rest of the Unity knows about this?"

Once again, Meloku said nothing. Habidah doubted she knew the answer.

Feliks said, "The amalgamates have never been afraid of anyone in the Unity finding out that they've occupied other planes. It's not as though ordinary people have ever had the ability to stop them. They've never been afraid of ordinary people before."

Habidah said, "Then they must be afraid of something else."

Before Habidah could finish her thought, Meloku said, "This conversation is over."

"Then get off–" Habidah hadn't gotten more than two words in before she realized the call had ended. Her sense of the others' presence, always present in the back of her mind, had gone.

She tried to reestablish contact, without success. There was nothing wrong. Her satellite was still above the horizon. She had a solid connection to the field base's NAI, and even saw each of her team members' vitals when she checked. She just couldn't speak with them.

She reached the shuttle and ascended the boarding ramp, but Meloku had been right. She couldn't leave Avignon, not without revealing the shuttle in daylight. She was stuck here until nightfall.

After that – she didn't know. The fire in her veins cooled. She doubted she'd be able to talk to the others until she got them face-to-face. Only Feliks had been at the field base. The others were scattered over Italy, France, and the Germanic states. If Meloku were to take control of the shuttle, she might not ever see her team again. But Habidah doubted Meloku

217

would go that far. Meloku had cut them off out of spite rather than any real need.

She wasn't afraid of Habidah or any of the others. They couldn't threaten the amalgamates.

Feliks had been on to something, though. The amalgamates *were* afraid.

Habidah slumped into an acceleration couch. She watched the branches of the nearest trees sway against the shuttle's cameras. All her life, she'd thought many things about the amalgamates, but never imagined that they could be scared. They were too powerful, too above her. Eternal.

The shuttle would only return her home. Its NAI refused to take her to search for Kacienta and Joao.

By the time it settled outside the field base that night, she'd come no closer to answers. She trudged out into the farmhouse. The lights lining the ramp down flicked on as she stepped through. If anything, it made the base seem more desolate. The viewwalls were off. The lights followed her from corridor to corridor.

NAI was only quasi-sentient. It wasn't capable of understanding what had happened. When she asked to send a message, it simply told her that the base's communications gateway wouldn't open. Someone on the other end had blocked the gateway from forming.

She expected to find Feliks at his desk. Instead, he was stretched out on one of the beds he'd used to examine plague victims. Habidah stepped quietly, afraid of what she'd find. But he was awake, watching something. Pale red light shone from the ceiling.

He said, "I was hoping they wouldn't stop you from traveling back."

"What are you doing?"

"Trying to figure out how much longer I'll be with you."

She looked to the image on the ceiling. Veins, muscle tissue, nerves and bone rotated round a helix of numbers. They were labeled with Feliks' name. "Do you really think you'll see something the rest of the Unity hasn't?"

"Of course not. But I like to study. It's a kind of solace."

The final stages of Feliks' disease had already begun. Every part of his body was weathering a slow, grinding attack that the lab's instruments could hardly see. His marrow's ability to produce fresh blood cells had faltered. His demiorganics sporadically refused to carry signals. Now his muscles were dying, including his heart. His pulse experienced long periods of thready, irregular activity.

Habidah said, "You'd think they'd reopen the gateway to let you back home, see your world another time."

Feliks said, "I wouldn't think that. Anyway, I wouldn't have come on this assignment if I needed to see home again."

"Stop that. I'm trying to be angry on your behalf."

Feliks snorted.

Habidah asked, "You're really at peace with it, aren't you?"

"I don't know if I would call it 'peace.' But I'm more comfortable with it than I was before I started studying this world."

"I'm not. Everything we've seen, everything I've learned about what we're doing here, just makes it worse. I mean... fuck, Feliks, what are we supposed to do now?"

"'Let it happen,' would be my guess."

"I can't."

"We don't have any choice. Refusing to accept that might be the biggest reason any of us are suffering right now."

"That's a ton of shit. People are suffering because they're dying, losing their friends and families."

Feliks shrugged. "That's my experience of dying. All I can do is share it with you."

Habidah had a thousand things to say to that, but she held her tongue. She wouldn't tell a dying man he was wrong to have found solace.

Feliks said, "More of the Unity is coming around to think the same way."

"That we're all doomed?"

"I have less than a fraction of the intellectual resources the amalgamates devoted to the problem. The fact that one of them is here says a lot."

Habidah said, as the realization struck, "The amalgamates are looking at ways of surviving the plague beyond curing it."

"Plague exiles should be a temporary problem," Feliks said. "The amalgamates could solve it any number of ways. Put the exiles into cold stasis or slingshot them around a pair of suns at relativistic speeds. Shelve them on empty worlds. Basically put them aside until they develop a cure. Settling an already inhabited world is a permanent solution."

Habidah said, "They're setting up house here in the event the rest of the Unity dies."

"On many other planes like this one, I'll bet."

If that was true, it seemed to her like the amalgamates were getting ahead of themselves. A plan like this wouldn't save more than the minutest fraction of the Unity's population. The Unity was in bad shape, but not close to disintegrating.

She was missing something, but couldn't feel the shape of it. Not yet. The amalgamates *did* like to think ahead. The Unity wasn't dead, not yet, but maybe this meant they were writing it off.

Habidah strode the length of Feliks' office. She had never felt claustrophobic underground before. The weight of the earth pressed the two of them together.

Feliks asked, "What do you *want* to do?"

"Get off this plane. Cure the plague. Send *Ways and Means* home."

"You're not important enough. None of us are. All we can do is help one person at a time. Isn't that why you saved the monk?"

"That was all I could get away with. And even that was a stretch."

"How much do you think you could get away with now?" he asked. "If you were to start saving more of the natives now,

220

do you really think the amalgamates would stop you?"

Habidah stopped pacing.

Helping Niccoluccio had been a stone tossed into a pond. A brief splash and then nothing. She hadn't saved him, not like she'd hoped. He'd lost his vocation, his friends, everyone he'd known. No wonder she hadn't heard from him since she'd left him in Florence. She couldn't have saved what he needed saved. And now *Ways and Means* had come to overturn everything that remained. She'd preserved his body, but she couldn't shelter him from loss any more than she could protect Feliks.

After a long breath, she said, "I could never save enough."

Feliks blew air through his lips, unsuccessfully trying to hide his frustration with her.

She said, "I wish I could be more like you, but I can't. I'm sorry."

"It's all right."

"No, you're right. I should try. I *can* help more than him." Niccoluccio had been something, at least. He just hadn't been enough.

He shook his head. "Not in the long run. Not any more than the people out there could cure their own plague."

"Some of them are at least trying to help."

"Doctors and priests and nuns. Most of them are dead. You're right. The children who fled from their parents, and the parents who fled from their children, are the ones who stayed safe." He touched her wrist. "At some point, we need to figure out when we're hurting ourselves more than we're helping others, and pull back and take care of ourselves."

She swallowed. She reached with her free hand to touch Feliks' fingers. The two of them did nothing but look at each other.

21

The business of managing the parish of San Lorenzo was just that: a business. So much money passed between hands. Sacro Cuore hadn't seemed like this, not at his level. Niccoluccio wondered if it had been all along.

For the first few days after he took office, all he knew was where the money was *not* going. His salary was a pittance, especially for the wealthy San Lorenzo parish, but it was enough to live upon. Most of San Lorenzo's clergy were not so fortunate. They lived off parishioners' donations. In San Lorenzo, that was easier than other neighborhoods, but even here clergy were poor. Some of them slept on the church floor.

Niccoluccio stayed in his office until it was too dark to read. He had spent the day poring over records of weekly tithes. There was no way to satisfy the bishop's demands without charging double for services, and this in a city clamoring for long-delayed funerals. His only alternative was ransacking the parish churches and selling San Lorenzo's triptych of John the Evangelist's life. He was sure that the mob of San Lorenzo would have lynched him if he breathed the idea. He nearly contacted Habidah to ask for advice. The thought persisted, rising at odd moments.

His head hurt, and his eyes rested on needles. His back was stiff with idleness. He forced himself to his feet and ambled into the church. Dioneo and Ambrogiuolo were waiting.

Dioneo said, "You've made yourself too scarce since coming

here. I've hardly had a chance to see my own brother."

"I come back to your home every night," Niccoluccio said. "The problem has been that *you* are not often there." Dioneo wanted him to come carousing, as he had offered several times already.

Ambrogiuolo said, "You're going to squander your fame if you don't show yourself."

"I don't believe I've earned any fame."

"Yet people are talking about you. The only survivor of Sacro Cuore! How could they not? A number of my friends and I will be dining together tonight. I would be pleased to have you join us."

Niccoluccio was no fool. He had been put in San Lorenzo for a reason. Ambrogiuolo and Dioneo had wanted him to experience the strain of the papacy's demands on the city. They'd made a compelling argument. Niccoluccio was a vowed servant of the church, but he no longer knew what to think of its highest members.

"This once," Niccoluccio said. "And if you do not mind if I keep my peace for the evening."

The three of them walked the twilit city in silence, past the shadow-spired cathedral and into the nearby ecclesiastical offices. Ambrogiuolo led him to a candlelit dining room. Stepping into the smell of roast mallard was like slipping underneath the veil of a waterfall. This was a different world from the one outside. Chatter filled his ears like a rumble of water.

Niccoluccio had once expected that men of the church would eat moderately. He wasn't surprised to see the feast laid out. In addition to the mallard, there were legs of pork, pheasant, and a centerpiece of roast goose. The pomegranates and figs alone were more expensive than any meal at the monastery. Someone had brought silver spoons and knives. Malvesey wine and ale sat together in uneasy company.

Not all present were clergymen. Dioneo, of course, was a civil official. Two men wore the liveries of the Visdomini and the Tosinghi, two of Florence's great families. A third was dressed in layers of folding robes, each a different color. Dioneo whispered in Niccoluccio's ear that the robed man was the family's new lawyer. Niccoluccio took the nearest open seat, next to the lawyer. Without waiting or asking, Dioneo scooped mounds of food onto Niccoluccio's plate.

At Sacro Cuore, Niccoluccio had believed that he had conquered his senses. That Niccoluccio must have died there. As soon as he smelled the roast goose, Niccoluccio knew he was lost. It felt as though someone else were lifting his hand to his knife.

A few minutes later, his appetite half-sated, he began to hear the conversation. Dioneo's friends had gathered to discuss the old bishop, whose life seemed to finally be nearing its end. Messengers flowed from his household daily, but the man himself hadn't been seen in weeks.

The lawyer said, "No doubt his replacement will be little different. Another man of Avignon."

Ambrogiuolo said, "No one living can remember the last time we had a Florentine for a bishop."

The goose left Niccoluccio heady. He reached for the ale without thinking, and said, "Plenty of public posts aren't filled by natives. The *podesta*, for example." The *podesta* was a special police captain, always a foreigner. It was his task to keep the peace between the city's noble families – such as the Tosinghi and Vosdomini men seated here.

Ambrogiuolo countered, "Clergymen do not police the city. Clergymen are *of* the city."

Dioneo said, "You've served the diocese long enough to know that the church can't function with the demands the bishop is placing on us. This is not a matter of selfishness. This is a matter of our trying to avoid riots."

"What would you suggest as a cure?" Niccoluccio asked. "Rebel?"

Niccoluccio had been in the monastery for so long that he'd forgotten how to speak to the people of his home. He hadn't

224

meant to shock them, but the silence that swept the table was deep. The man across from him, a procurator from the cathedral chapter, cleared his throat. "Of course not. All we would wish to do is place a worthy man in the bishopric."

Dioneo said, "Even if that means appointing him ourselves."

Now it was Niccoluccio's turn to blanch. "The pope would never allow that." That *was* rebellion, whether they called it so or not. The papacy guarded few rights more jealously than that of appointing bishops.

"The people of Florence would back us," Dioneo said. "Clement would have to muster the force to convince us otherwise."

The lawyer said, "It's been done before," and left it at that.

All of them knew what that meant, even should their conspiracy succeed. Excommunications. Possibly an interdict for the whole city, barring clergy from performing services, even Last Rites. In a city ravaged by pestilence, that would spark a revolt. All had happened in Florence before. These men had fallen silent when he'd mentioned it not because they were appalled by the thought, but because they hadn't wanted to call it what it was.

Niccoluccio ate in silence, allowing the conversation to turn to more comfortable matters. In spite of the church's financial difficulties, the cathedral chapter was buying the land of pestilence victims to speculate on prices. More important, though, was falconry. The lawyer had just purchased a new falcon, his second, and was anxious to pit it against his friends'.

Niccoluccio's head spun from ale. The juices of roast goose lingered on his tongue. As his dinner companions began to stand, Niccoluccio turned to the door. It would have been wiser to stay with his brother, travel in a group, but Niccoluccio kept going and didn't look back.

He gave no farewells. He just walked. No one came after him. The firelight leaking through the open door dwindled behind him. Before long, his footsteps were alone in the night.

Niccoluccio sang a hymn under his breath as he marched.

Though the words came to him easily, the melody didn't quite end up like he remembered. Lomellini would have tanned his hide if he'd heard.

Niccoluccio had gotten accustomed to walking the cloister after dark, on his way to Vigils or his early morning labors. He'd known the path as surely as if he could see it. Here, some desultory lights from homes and a half-shrouded sky were all he had to guide his way. Few people risked traveling in night's miasmatic winds. It occurred to him then that he would do well to be afraid. He shrugged the thought away. If a robber came upon him, he had nothing worth taking, not even his life.

His hymn quieted as he got farther from the cathedral. The streets narrowed. There were fewer signs of the pest at night. No boarded doors, no empty houses, at least none that he could see. He could almost pretend Florence was as he had left it, half his lifetime ago. He remembered the smells too well, the pig shit and nightsoil and moldering rot, but it all seemed so much stronger than he remembered.

He should not have come back here. He realized that at once, though the strange burning had been building up in his throat for days. The grease on his lips proved that he succumbed to temptation too easily. He should have gone with Habidah, wherever she was. Failing that, he should have lost himself in the wilderness. He didn't want to live like this. Given his options, that was tantamount to saying that he didn't want to live at all. A mortal sin. As with all sins lately, it took effort to push the thought of it away.

His hymn ended. He trudged through the winding streets, under an ever-darkening sky, only half-sure where he was going.

In the manner that Habidah had taught him, he asked, "Are you there?"

Her reply took a long moment. "I'm here, Niccoluccio." Her voice sounded so much like she was right beside him. As before, in the back of his mind, a deep disquiet settled over him. The first few words she spoke hadn't sounded like her.

He told himself that it was just their means of communication giving him difficulty. She had said that there may be times when, due to the arrangement of the stars above them, they may not be able to talk right away.

As though her voice were like someone trying on a glove, though, it didn't take her long to sound like her. "I'm sorry if I sounded distracted. We've been busy. Things are looking up. Several new agents are coming to help us."

Something about the way she said that left him unsettled. He swallowed to cool the heat in his throat. "I agreed to come back here to help you learn about our ways of living," he said. "Could you also tell me about yours? Your home? I feel it would do me a great deal of good. I only need know a little if you have better things to do."

Habidah let out a long breath, as if deciding how much to say. "I come from several lands grouped together, into countries collectively called the Unity. It's... it's larger than I can describe. Larger than I can imagine. I don't think any human could. Take a thousand continents the size of Europe and stack them atop each other, and then add a million more, and all cosmos above them."

She paused to give Niccoluccio a chance to absorb that. Of course he couldn't. She'd said before that she'd come from another land, another continent. He hadn't believed her, and she seemed to know it. It was still astounding how fast the pretext disappeared.

She said, "It has cities made of glass and diamond and gold, worlds of perpetual lavafalls, or seas of clouds. I grew up on the side of a volcano larger than every land you've seen on a map. I swam in green oceans the size of this world."

Niccoluccio ought not to believe this, either. Everything he'd seen of her and the wonders she'd worked made it impossible not to. He hoped his voice didn't sound broken. "Are the people of these places Christian?"

"Of all the places we've visited, yours is the only one with a religion like it."

That ought to have cut him to the quick. He'd known the answer before he asked. It hadn't mattered then any more than it mattered now.

He let out a cold breath. If any of his brothers from Sacro Cuore had been able to hear his thoughts, they would have told him he was damned. He couldn't convince himself that they were wrong, but neither could he rouse himself to care.

Anticipating how he would react, Habidah said, "I'm sorry to have to tell you that."

"It's all right," he said, leaning against a brick wall. "I'll get better."

"You have a unique vision. All of the Abrahamic religions on this world do. Few in the Unity see the body and the mind as separate in the way you do. I've appreciated learning about it." She hesitated, and seemed to realize that she wasn't helping.

"I ought to focus on the assignment you gave me, not all these politics."

She said, "Don't worry as much about the assignment. The new agents will help us fill in a lot of the gaps in our knowledge."

He said nothing to that, and she didn't elaborate. She hadn't said it with any malice, and yet dread tickled the back of his throat.

He didn't know which of them had cut the power that bound their voices, but he didn't speak to her again for the rest of the night. Maybe she was always listening. It would have been comforting to think so.

More likely, though, he was simply beneath her notice.

He figured out where he was without trying hard. He could still see the silhouette of the cathedral and the Tower of the Castagna. Both landmarks so near meant that his brother's home was scarcely a fifteen-minute walk away.

The candles by the windows were still lit. They usually were. Dioneo spent most of his nights away. He claimed politicking at late dinners, but even his children knew that he had a mistress, a widow.

Niccoluccio fumbled his key and tried to fit it to the lock, a more difficult operation than he imagined. His fingers kept disobeying. On his third try, the door opened of its own accord. Dioneo's wife, Catella, stood behind it. Niccoluccio stood there a moment, key drooped in his hand. Catella always retired long before Dioneo returned home.

Catella curtsied and stepped back. She moved quickly, anxiously. "Beg your pardon, Brother Niccoluccio. You have a guest. I thought you would be back at your usual time and let her stay, but after it got late I didn't want to turn her out to the dark."

"Who?"

"She said she was a friend of yours, from across town."

Niccoluccio couldn't think of any woman friends aside from Habidah. He strode past Catella and into the parlor. His head was light at the thought of Habidah.

The woman seated in the parlor stood as he entered. She was not Habidah. He nearly didn't recognize her. Like everyone in Florence, she'd changed. Ivy-vine wrinkles crawled around her eyes. She'd shed weight and become unpleasantly slender. Her hair had turned stringier.

He stammered her name at the same moment that it occurred to him. "Elisa?"

Her voice choked. "I'd heard you'd come back to Florence, but I didn't think you would... I mean, I didn't believe..."

Niccoluccio stepped closer. Over the years, he'd thought he'd hardened his heart to this woman. He'd pushed her memory away, carefully and deliberately. He'd regretted the things they'd done and prayed for forgiveness for her as well as for him. During his last few years at Sacro Cuore, he'd thought of her as he might someone dead, so far away and lost she'd seemed.

All his effort fell away at the sight of her. Before he knew it, he was embracing her.

Her hair smelled of the peppers people used to ward off the pestilence. She wrapped her arms around him. He could hardly hear her over the pounding in his ears.

"...believe you'd survived! My parents died, my husband, his parents, our children, even Pietro..."

Holding her was something between a memory and a dream. He wasn't sure he would have sounded any more coherent if he'd tried to speak. He stayed with her until she got her voice under control.

So much of what he'd believed at Sacro Cuore was without foundation. It had existed only in his head. He'd never dreamed of a world as large as the one Habidah had given him. He'd been so small that he'd tried to never allow himself to think of Elisa, who had been part of his life longer than anyone but Dioneo.

How amazing it was that he'd ever thought of himself as better for that.

When she was able, she let go. He led her to a cushioned chair, and sat across from her. She said, "People at churches have been saying your name. When I heard you'd come back, I had to see you. I didn't think it was possible. Everyone else in my life is gone."

Some of her words were just catching up with him. "Husband?" he stammered.

She nodded. "God has seen fit to extinguish all of the lights of my life. My children..." For a moment, Niccoluccio thought she was going to weep again, but she held her voice together. "They left me behind. I didn't think that I would find any part of my life again."

"Pietro, too?"

"Taken the first week the pestilence visited Florence, almost."

The news sent a spike through his heart, as deep a gouge as it had been when he'd discovered his father's death. Pietro was another enormous part of him that had lapsed into silence while he'd been at Sacro Cuore.

He saw it so clearly now. He thought he'd been looking into the face of God, but all he'd done was stare at brick walls.

He said, "I had no idea. There are no words adequate to contain my condolences. Every time I think the world could not hold more misery, I find out its depths go even deeper."

"Even that seems pale next to what I've heard you went through. Your whole monastery–"

"If my brothers were here, they would be the first to tell you that God has not taken your children to deprive you, but to receive them into Grace."

Elisa had always been perceptive. She asked, "Would *you* say that?"

He had no answer suitable for her hearing. None that he wanted to say to himself. When she offered her hands, he accepted them into his. "You and I have a great deal to talk through before we get to that."

22

Meloku had never needed to take acting lessons or have programs fake a talent for it. She'd been acting since she was a child, pretending to be happy to see her parents, to go to school. She hadn't been herself for so long that she'd forgotten who that person was.

She attended the papal court only on its last day. When Queen Joanna entered, Meloku stood along with the rest of the spectators. Every day of her trial so far, Joanna had worn a different and fabulously elaborate gown. Meloku had no idea where Joanna had found the money. Probably creditors hoping to recoup their costs when she was restored.

This morning, Joanna's dress was blinding, virginal white. Chastity and innocence. Though Joanna and Andreas had consummated their marriage, it would have been ridiculous for a queen to remain unmarried and unheired. Joanna aimed to put herself back on the royal marriage market.

She'd gotten exactly what she wanted.

This morning, Clement embraced her in front of hundreds of spectators and the bitterly muttering Hungarians. In a clear voice, the pope apologized profusely that such suspicion could ever have fallen upon such an obviously virtuous woman as her. Joanna said nothing, blinking and wiping away tears.

Meloku cheered with the rest of the spectators. All life in the multiverse was performance. The demands upon the actresses were about to get much higher.

Her new secretary, Galien, sat beside her. She caught his probing glance. He'd scheduled a meeting with Joanna later that day. Meloku had never shared her purpose. Galien was sharper than most of the men she'd met here, but he never asked the obvious question.

That afternoon, Meloku waited in the sitting room of de Colville's manor. It was a nice, quiet little room. Not perfectly soundproof, but, aside from Galien, whom she'd left to answer the door, the servants had been dismissed to their quarters for the afternoon.

Joanna arrived promptly, wearing the same white gown. She brought two officers of her court: middle-aged men, portly, and self-serious. Notaries or lawyers. Not even her principal advisers. As Joanna ignored them, so did Meloku.

Formalities first. Meloku said, "Congratulations on your restoration, your radiance."

"I have a long way yet before I'll be restored to my throne."

"A distance that's a great deal shorter with the church's backing. The Hungarians don't have the ability to hold Naples. Your acquittal robbed them of their only justification for the war."

Joanna wisely didn't answer. She had no need to reveal the strength of her position. Everyone in Avignon knew that Meloku was in Clement's inner circle. She had only come because she believed Meloku was going to ask, on behalf on Pope Clement, for favors in exchange for her acquittal. "Am I to understand that you, a woman, are representing the church...?"

"I represent a higher power. God wants to spread the power of the church farther than ever."

"I might interpret that to mean His Holiness is trying to gather support for another crusade."

"Eventually. First we must consolidate the church's hold in our own lands. Italy, even."

"My people of Naples are the most God-fearing in the world."

"I'm sure they are. The fact remains that God is dissatisfied with the state of governance in Christendom. His Holy Church is not respected as it should be."

Joanna glanced to the courtier on her left. He rolled his eyes. Joanna was reputedly sincerely devout, but words like Meloku's only weighed so much in the theater of her world's politics. She seemed bemused, but it was clear that Meloku's time was up. "I'm sorry, Lady Akropolites. If Clement wants to use me to fight his wars, he needs to pick a better time than a year of pestilence. And he certainly could have picked a better messenger."

It was a shame, in some senses, that Joanna had been the first monarch to visit during Meloku's time here. Meloku had gotten to understand and appreciate her a little more during the days of her trial. She was exceptional here, a woman ruler on a continent that didn't often allow those to last long.

And now Meloku had to take all of that away from her.

As Joanna turned, her courtiers collapsed.

It happened with neither warning nor spectacle. Their eyes fluttered, their knees buckled, and they hit the floor like felled wood. The walls reverberated with the impact.

Joanna only saw one of them fall. Her mouth opened in shock. It took her a moment to notice that the other had fallen, too.

She spun toward Meloku. She looked as though she'd been about to ask for help. Then she saw Meloku's eyes.

For too long, Meloku had been working like a mouse – keeping behind the holes in the wall, hardly making her presence known. That was a way to learn about a world, but hardly suitable for shaping it.

One thing that stifled her guilt was that it felt really good to stop pretending that she was one of these people.

She raised her hand. The skin above her knuckle slit open. A diamond-tipped dart shot free. The dart whipped past Joanna and pierced the doorknob. It penetrated the wood behind and stopped halfway into the door frame. Hooks speared out from each end of the dart, digging deep, sealing the door to the wall.

Joanna didn't even see it. She might have felt a whisper of air, but she was too busy gaping at the weeping wound on Meloku's wrist. Meloku said, "I told you. I'm not here on behalf of the pope or any temporal authority. I've come from a *much* higher power. The highest you'll ever know."

Joanna backpedaled. She grappled for the door and jerked her hand back from the splintered wood. She turned, but didn't have time to do more than see the shattered doorknob before Meloku reached her.

Joanna started to scream, but Meloku cut her off with one hand over her mouth. Another swiftly compressed her throat. Joanna tried to strike, but Meloku's muscles were like ironwood. No matter how hard she slapped, Meloku remained unmoved. After fifteen seconds without breath, Joanna gave up the fight.

Meloku eased the pressure on her throat, and let her gasp air through her nostrils.

"I have a very important mission," Meloku said, soothingly, "and so do you. Those of your class who work with God will be privileged above all others. But I need to secure your cooperation before I can tell you anything more."

Meloku curled her ring finger to touch the side of Joanna's neck. She doubted Joanna ever felt the needle pierce her skin. Soon, Joanna began to relax. Her legs went limp. Meloku held her upright. Her stare traveled through Meloku's.

This was one of the easier things about dealing with purely biological humans. Demiorganics only made things more complicated. She could see the rules under which people like Joanna operated. Manipulate their blood and brain chemistry, manipulate the person. Engender an addiction...

Any person who might otherwise pose a problem could be turned into a tool.

Gradually, Meloku released Joanna's mouth.

Meloku asked, "How do you feel now?"

"In love," Joanna said, from somewhere else.

"You've never felt God's presence until now." Meloku once again touched her finger to Joanna's neck. "Before I explain what I'll need from you, let me show you what worship is like."

Infrared showed Galien sitting in the corner of the foyer. He stood when he heard her coming. "God's blood, what took so long? I thought I heard someone falling. I nearly ran up–"

She waved him silent. It wouldn't have done her reputation any good to have someone hear how often her secretary invoked God's name in his oaths. "Queen Joanna is entirely on our side."

Galien ran his hand through his hair as he tried to recover his equilibrium. Unlike so many other men on this plane, he was always clean-shaven. She'd found him buried deep in a clerical office, tallying accounts. He'd been only mildly cowed to see her hovering over his desk, which she appreciated. When she'd come to Avignon, she'd never thought that Cardinal de Colville would be more than a temporary ally. Better to start with someone below her and build them up, and leave them always indebted to her. Galien had only been too grateful to accept quintuple his salary. He could be blunt-spoken, but he never disobeyed her.

He asked, "What kind of favors will Her Majesty expect of us in return?"

"None. You misunderstand. She's on *our* side. We're not on hers."

He stood dumbfounded. He hurried to catch her going back out to the street. Finally, he said, "You're either lying to me, lying to yourself, or you're the most persuasive woman I've ever met."

She allowed him a smile. "Wait until after our next meeting to make up your mind."

They were only a few minutes late to her next appointment. Three men in ostentatious red hats waited to meet her in one of the Palais des Papes' smaller dining rooms. Meloku idly wondered how the cardinals had gotten their hats under the door frame. This time, Galien stepped in beside her.

Cardinal de Colville stood. Meloku watched him. He may have been friendly in private, but the company of his fellow cardinals required him to act differently. "Well?" he asked. "You've had the courage to call us here, for what purpose I couldn't say. Do you have the courage to speak?"

She said, "To be honest, I'm surprised you came. You're not accustomed to coming at a woman's beck and call."

Young, wide-bellied Cardinal Regnault said, "As a favor to you and to your friends, we would be glad to listen to anything you have to say, Madam Akropolites." By "friends," he meant the pope, of course.

Meloku said, "I've been watching and listening to the church these past few months, and it's become clear that the church is failing in the obligations left to it by St Peter. I came to Avignon a convert from the schismatic Eastern church. When I followed the course God charted for me and turned here, I had hoped to find a church more deserving of God.

"It's plain to everyone inside and outside the church that your reputation is not what it ought to be. Kings and emperors ignore your judgments. Heresy is rife. The people make jokes in the streets about the venality of cardinals."

De Colville was used to dealing with scolds. He had a stock response. "Man's irreverence is one of his eternal sins. Fools will always make light of the church."

"No," Meloku said. "They do it because they're right."

The chilly silence that followed gave her the chance to take their measure. She said, "Kings flaunt your powers because they know you have none. Heretics sense people's dissatisfaction. They can't lead those who aren't willing to follow. And everyone makes light of the church's venality and corruption because the church *is* venal and corrupt."

The three men stared at her in silence. Meloku stared right back.

"I don't know what's possessing her to act like this," de

Colville told his companions.

"You've heard this from more voices than mine," Meloku said. "Correspondence from all over Christendom has said the same. The church's control slips everywhere. More importantly, it's losing respect. Between your nepotism, appointment packing, and taxation, half of Europe is ready to desert you at the slightest provocation. The pestilence may provide them with it. Already there are new mendicant orders and penitent movements everywhere defying papal authority."

Meloku had chosen Avignon to be her base of control because she'd thought it the best place for any single person to influence Europe. That didn't mean she'd thought it was a *good* one. There were no good places on this blighted little plane. Without her, the papacy's simony, hypocritically lavish lifestyles, and selling of indulgences would reach a head. Absent change, the church would fracture.

The last cardinal asked, "And what made you decide this was so? A message from God?"

"Yes," Meloku said. "It's the reason God sent me to Avignon, and the reason he sent the pestilence to ravage the world."

The cardinals looked at each other. While none of them showed any sign of getting up, Meloku figured that was just inertia. She couldn't drug everyone in the world like she had Joanna. She was only one person. She was going to have to use more conventional means to control men like these.

Like terror.

Meloku glanced between them. Cardinal Regnault had an elevated pulse. He was the youngest at the table, a nephew of the Duc de Berry. Naive. Impressionable.

"By this time three days from now, two of you will be dead," Meloku said, looking directly at Regnault. "Struck down by pestilence. The third will follow unless he heeds my words. *This I have learned from God.* If this man wishes to survive and serve God, he will seek me."

De Colville smiled patiently. "I don't mean to impugn your relationship with the divine, Madame Akropolites, but you may wish to make sure that your bad dreams are more than the product of spoiled beef before you call upon us again."

Meloku allowed them to shuffle out. In spite of de Colville's bravado, his companions looked pale. These men weren't accustomed to women speaking to them like this, let alone a woman with influence. Regnault looked at her as he went.

Galien only broke his silence when Regnault had closed the door behind him. "There is not a man I know who would have dared speak to cardinals that way," he said. "Not even other cardinals. Not in public. Whether that was for good or for ill, you are very impressive."

"And you know how to flatter," she said.

"If you can pull off whatever you're attempting, I will remain at your side forever."

It wouldn't take long for de Colville's companions to spread rumors of what she'd said. She'd allow a few days to for that.

De Colville would die publicly, of fast-acting genengineered variants of plague. He attended Mass every morning. The first symptoms of the septicemic plague – fever, the skin discoloration – would begin just as Mass began, when it was too late to politely get up. By the end of the service, his fingers and toes would be hard as coal, and he would be in agony. His luckless friend would find a similar death waiting for him at dinner with Clement that night.

And Cardinal Regnault would be back to see her the morning after, full of holy terror.

These men were so defenseless and predictable that the next few months might as well have been written on a page. Meloku pulled back the curtain sheltering the room from the drafty window. She peered into the palace yard. Queen Joanna was approaching to pay another call on His Holiness, a veil protecting her face from a mist of light rain. She was flanked by six escorts. She seemed calm and composed, but infrared and spectrographics showed the cold sheen on her forehead, the glassy dryness of her eyes. She believed she was on a mission from God. She had met Him, after all.

239

And so soon would many other monarchs scattered throughout the plane. *Ways and Means* had begun seeding the courts with their agents. Meloku didn't need to ask to know they were doing the same thing she was, subverting the natives from their leadership on down. Changing the structure of their society before anyone realized what was happening.

She turned off her enhanced senses as she watched Joanna trudge. She and her companions became distant figures again, cloaked by rain.

Her skin felt like gnats were crawling all over her. No matter how she stood, she couldn't get comfortable.

Companion mused, "Here I was starting to wonder if you had a conscience."

"Of course I have a conscience," she snapped. "I've always had a conscience. I want to do what's best for these people."

"What's best for them requires manipulating them in ways that you would never tolerate being done to yourself."

Meloku shifted, trying to not to show how much Companion's sudden appearance had bothered her. Futile, of course. Companion was inside her head. "If you or the amalgamates decided that 'influencing' me would be best for the Unity, I would go along." For all she knew, the amalgamates had been altering her all her life.

"But you wouldn't be happy about it," Companion said. "And you're not happy with the way this assignment has been going."

Meloku released air through her lips. "I'm sorry I've been doubting."

"It's been like this since your argument with Habidah."

"I wasn't able to argue against her to the best of my abilities."

"And you didn't like many of the answers that you gave her."

Again, there was no point in denying it. Meloku stared out the window, not seeing. She said, "If the amalgamates would like to replace me with another agent, I understand."

"The amalgamates are facing a threat they've never

encountered and could never have anticipated," Companion said. "The plague is forcing them to make decisions they never have before. Small, underdeveloped planes like this one must be subordinate to our interests. We can help the natives, ease the transition for them, but in the end they're going to have to give up control of their world."

Meloku cast her gaze across Avignon's streets, from the tall, wide walls designed to impress, to the shuffling fat drunks and ecclesiastics watching prostitutes pass by. "It's not as though they've done a good job managing things themselves so far."

"The amalgamates would not be as interested in you without your conscience," Companion said. "Remember that. Your empathy is why the amalgamates need human agents at all, and they forgive you for it."

"I've never been accused of being very empathetic before." A floating map of Eurasia appeared in the back of Meloku's mind, color-coded and shaded. She'd spent the past few weeks meticulously mapping the church's influence. Spain and France, outside Languedoc, were solid colors, but Central Europe, the northern kingdoms of the Holy Roman Empire, and especially the Netherlands were patchwork. England alternated between solid and broken depending on which metric she used. And the Italians, though deeply religious, resented papal control more than any other people.

She said, "These people have the means of controlling the continent right here, in this city, but they're frittering it away year by bloody year. The German kingdoms are just looking for an excuse to challenge Avignon. Florence is on the cusp of riot. And England will discard the papacy as soon as it becomes inconvenient."

"The wars are foregone conclusions," Companion said. "We planned for them long ago. They're not what you're upset about. Your subconscious keeps returning to Habidah."

She shook her head. Companion almost, but not quite, understood. Or did it? Sometimes she had trouble understanding what was going through her *own* mind. "I thought I could convince her."

"You could change her mind by blunter means. Why do you treat her more gently than Joanna?"

"She's one of us. She *should* understand. She doesn't have any excuse not to." She watched a procession of clerks march out of the palace and flock, in defiance of pestilence safety laws, toward the nearest tavern. "She and the others have no idea what kind of world they're actually living in."

Everything Habidah did, she did to satisfy her ego. To convince herself that she was a *good* person. She was maintaining contact with that monk. She and he called each other at odd times. Once, he had called her in the middle of the night, when demiorganic telemetry insisted she was asleep. He had kept transmitting at the pace of conversation, as if content that she might be listening.

There was something very odd about that relationship that Meloku meant to plumb further. She meant to eavesdrop but had not yet mustered the will.

Companion said, "Habidah is recovering contact with her remaining teammates. Joao is already at your old field base, and Kacienta is on her way."

"I thought I locked down their shuttle."

"*Ways and Means* unlocked it. It thinks that they may be of use."

Meloku's stomach tightened. "*Ways and Means* doesn't understand what it would take to get them on our side."

"Would you like to help Osia persuade them?"

She tried to hide it, but couldn't stop acid from rising in her throat. She hadn't realized how much Habidah had affected her. Maybe it was this whole damned world, and everything she was doing to it.

"No," she said. "They're less important than anything else I could be doing."

Companion sensed her mood. It sent a wave of endorphins and warmth to thaw the back of her mind. Meloku pretended to stare at the map. Only when she managed to push her objections below her conscious and subconscious minds – the only levels at which Companion could read her – did she get to work.

23

A call stirred Habidah out of sleep. At first, she thought it a hallucination. She hadn't even been allowed to contact anyone when Feliks died – suddenly and peacefully – a week after she'd returned.

Whoever it was could only be signaling her with the amalgamates' permission.

She pushed her feet out of bed. She stared at the wall a while, let the message drum against her subconscious before answering. The viewwall flicked to life. A larger-than-real Osia stared down at her. She stood in front of a dark background. Her jet-black skin made her difficult to distinguish. It was only from memory than Habidah knew that Osia even had a nose.

Habidah was dressed only in her underclothes. She said nothing, waiting for Osia to speak first. The timing of the call, the lack of warning or time to make herself presentable, meant that Osia was trying to put her on edge.

Osia said, "I'm prepared to give you permission to contact the Unity."

Habidah blinked. It took her a moment to know how to react. She said, "With anything I might say about your project censored."

Osia inclined her head. "The security of our project is important. So are your concerns. I haven't had an opportunity to express my condolences for the passing of Dr Vine. I've been given to understand that the two of you knew each other well."

"You would know," Habidah said, drily.

"On long-term transplanar assignments, it's traditional for the project leader to inform the families of those who've died."

Osia's background check would have let her know that Habidah had little family or friends to speak of. There was nothing in Osia's voice to indicate that she wasn't sincere. "I will tell them," Habidah said, with a cracked voice.

Osia nodded and vanished.

Habidah queried NAI. The communications gateway was open.

She stood and dressed, taking her time. *Ways and Means* would be listening to everything she sent home, of course. Her thoughts raced, trying to think of some way that she could get word out. Even if the whole Unity knew about the amalgamates' project, though, she doubted that would stop them. Most people simply wouldn't care. This was a primitive little plane. Everyone back home had worse troubles. They weren't here; they didn't know these people.

She pinged Joao. He'd returned on the shuttle a day after Feliks had died. He was in Feliks' quarters, packing his belongings. Joao had volunteered to spare Habidah from having to ask.

He said, "Osia just called me. Guessing she told the same thing to you."

Habidah said, "They want something they won't say."

"Of course they do."

"I'll contact Feliks' family." She hesitated. "Thank you for preserving his remains. I wasn't in a state where I could ask you."

"Not a problem." She and Joao weren't friends, but Habidah didn't think that she could have gone on without a companion of some kind. "Want to return the favor? I don't think I'm up to contacting my family. I don't want to tell them how I'm doing. If you could, I would appreciate it."

Habidah sent back a wordless affirmation. She sat cross-legged on her bunk, and turned her attention back to the wall.

After a moment breathing deeply, she connected to the Unity.

Communications between planes was the challenge that, long ago, had necessitated the creation of AIs as sophisticated as the amalgamates. There was hardly a more daunting task in the multiverse. Even small gateways swallowed hideous amounts of power. To save enough energy to make transplanar communication economical, the aperture opened and closed after every bit in a datastream. Accomplishing that, never mind predicting the millisecond the response would arrive and opening just in time to allow it through, took a mind beyond human understanding.

It was one of the many reasons the Unity couldn't exist without the amalgamates. All of its message traffic routed through them and the Core Worlds.

A hot flood of information rushed into her demiorganics. The wall showered her in dazzling icons: directories, guides, news bulletins, heaps of advertisements, gossamer maps of connections to millions of planes, demiorganic firmware updates, and mounds of her own unanswered mail tugged at different parts of her senses and awareness.

Reading the chart of network connections that would put her in contact with Feliks' home plane, Rodinia, was like following a water droplet down a spiderweb. Her signal leapfrogged thirty-five gateways, each opening and closing in tandem with millions of other signals. It was dizzying to follow.

Finally, though, she reached Rodinia. Rodinia's Public Commission had chosen to welcome visitors with an old-fashioned orbital view of their world. A live image of its lake-dappled megacontinent glittered across the wall. Arrow-straight irrigation canals crisscrossed its plains. Its western shorelines were smudged gray from a hundred city-sized rain factories.

Habidah stared for a moment, and wondered what it would have been like to grow up on such a throwback. Everything about this plane, from the clean air to the lack of visual noise polluting its dark side, said that Rodinia wanted to appear a simple world, almost frontier rustic. If any of this had shaped Feliks' character, she'd missed it.

Rodinia's directories listed a sparse few million inhabitants, most of them employee-shareholders of the same three companies. Rodinia was an agricultural world, trundled over by building-sized harvesters. Most people living here supervised the machines, and that was all. Everyone who didn't have a reason to stay left for more interesting planes. Like Feliks.

Habidah ran a search for Feliks' family. Zero results. She tried again. That didn't make sense. She *had* their names in Feliks' personnel record. Mother, two fathers, two sisters, all on Rodinia.

It was only when she expanded her search into other directions that she discovered her mistake. She had been searching the records of the living.

Feliks' parents had been cremated at the Vine Extended Family Mortuary Garden, recently expanded to cope with the influx of onierophage dead. A lump formed in Habidah's chest. Feliks had never mentioned this. Had he known? Had his family ever contacted him, or he them? She'd never find out. Only one of Feliks' sisters was alive. She hadn't appeared on normal directories because she had withdrawn to a coastal hospice for onierophage victims. She didn't want to be contacted.

Osia had known Habidah would find this, of course.

Habidah backtracked to Rodinia's address directory, and compared the results to an archived list from several months ago. Millions had been excised. Fifteen percent of Rodinia's population had died in the past twelve months, with another five percent expected to die in the next six.

Many of Rodinia's farms had gone dark. Power plant after power plant was shutting down. Its news bulletins were all panic and fear. The plane's Head Commissioner had died two days ago, the second office-holder in nine weeks. Counseling centers were overloaded, and hospitals so busy that most patients were sent home to die. And still the onierophage was spreading.

There was nothing else to do. She withdrew down the string of connections, back to the Core Worlds. This time to Providence Core, Joao's home.

For a moment she stared, unseeing, until the news bulletins finally broke through the visual noise. According to them, the Unity was vastly smaller than the last time she'd been there. Thousands upon thousands of planes had dropped out of contact. Some no longer had populations large enough to sustain themselves and had evacuated. Others had quarantined themselves from the Unity, going independent. The amalgamates, loathe to allow any plane to leave their influence, simply allowed this to happen. Occasionally, some of these planes resurfaced, infected and begging for help. Most simply vanished.

Perhaps she was getting old-fashioned, too. She reflexively pulled her attention up to an orbital view just to escape. Providence Core and its sun hung suspended in a solid black sky, dotted with lights too few and too near to be stars. Below, Providence Core's cities were stars on velvet, mirrored by rings of satellites and stations above. Two gem-faceted planarships, *Trade and Finance* and *Foreign Operations*, glittered in the sky.

This solar system, like all the Core Worlds, was in a thick interstellar dust cloud. It blocked most light from the outside universe. Only the sun shone through. The amalgamates had chosen these planes because the minimized cosmic radiation was perfect for their communications networks. They and their fleets and stations were the only objects in the sky.

But even here the amalgamates were helpless. Providence Core had been infected later than most planes, but suffered a comparatively higher death rate. Twenty percent of its people had perished. Another five percent were slated to die in six months. Before long, the death rate would approach that of cities on *this* plane.

Habidah fetched an orbital image of Providence Core a

year ago, and compared. Seas of darkness had opened in the middle of the continents, gradually reaching toward the coast. Providence Core consumed half the energy it had a year ago. The difference hadn't just come from the deaths, but from the failure of industry after industry as panic, trade quarantines, and economic depression swept the Unity.

The plane was crowded with bodies. There were not enough crematoria to accommodate the dead, nor time for funerals. Some families held onto their dead, waiting. Freezer warehouses were packed full of bodies. Graveships plied the oceans and stars, waiting forever to be unloaded.

It was unlikely that the plague spread by contact, but cities were nigh-abandoned. People no longer wanted to live near their neighbors. Parents had left sick children behind (and vice versa), often in the care of an NAI, but sometimes just to die.

Habidah hadn't realized she'd been holding her hand over her mouth. She lowered it.

A search for Joao's family produced more results than Feliks'. Father, dead. Mother, migrated to extraplanar hospice. Surviving relatives included a brother, a niece, two cousins, and an uncle. Habidah had no idea what to say to any of them. She nearly called Joao to ask, but stopped. Like Feliks, he hadn't mentioned any deaths in his family. If he hadn't heard, she'd need to find a better time to tell him.

Against her better instincts, she leapfrogged her signal home. To Caldera.

She hadn't been to Caldera in nearly fifteen years. Until now, she'd believed not much had changed. Caldera was a small, conservative, scientific settlement. It resisted shock. Centuries after its founding, it maintained a stable population of just two hundred thousand.

Eons ago, a meteorite collision had all but blown off the world's crust. Only a thin layer had been left behind. Caldera had been settled by transplanar geologists studying the resulting continentspanning supervolcano. Hundreds of years later, the plane still retained its academic character. Every child born on the world had free access to its universities. Its government was a council of professors that loved inflicting social engineering experiments on its populace. Most of these failed in perverse and spectacular ways, but those that stuck – like the system of clan families that had given Habidah her two other names – had become defining features of Caldera. The clans had fostered a sense of community between Caldera's isolated, underground cities. They defined Habidah, too. She'd never gotten rid of her clan names decades after she'd left. Nor had she ever stopped thinking of herself as a scientist.

She went straight to the news bulletins. She waved through the list of towns and clans, recognizing each of them. Even half of the reporters were familiar. As was the first name she saw, in an obituary for the president of Caldera's second-largest university. To set an example to the rest of the plane, he had requested no funeral observance.

The burdens of living underground on a hostile world had strained the settlers' resources in the best of times. Now, with twenty percent of its people dead or dying, Caldera had no time to mourn.

Caldera's geothermal power plants were shutting down one after another for lack of manpower and expertise. Some cities had imposed brownouts for all services except atmospheric support. Small towns had been evacuated.

There was no shortage of the dead. All of the available crematoria were running at maximum capacity. Several of the evacuated towns had been turned into holding centers of the dead. Habidah couldn't restrain her gasp when a reporter's optics scanned streets she recognized. They were in a town she'd visited for clan fairs. The sunlamps were off. The underground complex had become a vault. The hazy streetlights silhouetted lines upon lines of lumpy bags, blanketed in a fog of Caldera's cold and poisonous atmosphere. There were thousands.

Habidah's stomach churned. Her hand was over her mouth again. She held it there to keep from throwing up.

Caldera was missing more than just the dead. Thousands

of people had simply left. They recognized that, even if the plague were cured today, Caldera had no future. The Unity was near to splintering. Planes like Caldera would be the first to be left behind.

Three of Caldera's five largest universities were officially recommending that provision be made for the evacuation of the entire plane. The remaining institutions were expected to join them shortly. If Caldera were evacuated, it was unlikely to ever be settled again.

Habidah disconnected without planning to. The wall blackened.

Before she knew what she was doing, she slammed her palm into the wall. She spun and kicked her bunk. After a moment, the wall lit again without her prompting. She faced it.

Osia's towering image looked down on her, her expression implacable.

Osia said, "The Unity is facing an existential threat. I don't think you've had a chance recently to appreciate that. It's gotten much worse since you left. Unless we can cure an invisible disease, it's going to get much worse in the months and years to come." Osia's voice, for once, revealed some emotion: it hardened. "So if we place the survival of our culture above the individual freedoms of primitive planes like this one, I trust future generations will forgive us."

"Colonizing one world won't save the Unity," Habidah said, dully.

"There are dozens of others. Yours is only one of the first. But it will help."

"I don't understand."

"We still don't know how the plague spreads, but we *have* figured out who isn't contracting it. Those of us who've transitioned to demiorganic bodies, for one. There are others. Travelers. Exiles. Monks and hermits. Scouts. Explorers. People who, for whatever reason, haven't visited the Unity in at least five years. All of those we've found again have been uninfected. We've kept them isolated from the Unity."

"Turning these worlds into colonies for them won't preserve even a hundredth of the Unity."

"There are representatives from every plane. They're more than we have otherwise."

"Why save ordinary people at all, though? You just said the amalgamates' servants aren't affected by the plague. Neither are the amalgamates. Why not *let* the Unity die? What do the amalgamates care about ordinary people at all?"

After a moment, Osia asked, "Do you really think we're that cold?"

"Yes." When Osia didn't answer, Habidah pressed, "The amalgamates could have sailed off to the far corners of the multiverse. Not a single one of them has ever tried. Not in thousands of years. They've all stayed with the Unity. Everyone knows it's not out of altruism."

"I've read all of the conspiracy theories about the amalgamates, Dr Shen."

"For all the weapons, satellites, and factories you have up there, you can't actually *control* the peoples of this world, not without human agents getting their hands dirty. It must be the same way with the multiverse as a whole. Humans are by far the most common sentient animal we've found. The amalgamates, on the other hand, are unique. To control any significant number of planes, you need humans."

"While I'd love to debate this at length, Dr Shen, we both have more pressing questions."

"The answer you're looking for is 'no.' Under no circumstance will I help you colonize and manipulate the peoples of this world."

"Their lives are short, brutish, and replete with suffering. We can help."

"If the amalgamates were truly prepared to help them, they'd cure their plague. They can do that at any time now that *Ways and Means* is here. It's letting this plague weaken them, leave them vulnerable so their agents can march in and take over."

"We're a wealthy civilization, but we don't have unlimited resources. If you don't understand the transactional costs by now, I'm not sure you ever will."

"Whatever you look like, you're still a person. You know what I'm saying is right."

Osia stared at Habidah for a long time.

"Goodbye, Dr Shen," she said, and her image vanished.

When Habidah checked, she saw that her connection to the Unity had been severed again.

She rested her head in her hands. Her thoughts roiled. For, as sure as she had made herself sound, she wasn't. She couldn't keep from thinking of Niccoluccio. By trying to protect him, she was making decisions for him and everyone else on this plane, but they might not have been the ones he would choose.

Would *he* subordinate himself to the amalgamates in exchange for their guidance? Wasn't submission to a higher power the founding ideal of monastic life? The amalgamates were no gods, but on this plane, they might as well be. They certainly acted like gods. They'd withheld their plague cures to mold this world into a shape more pleasing. Niccoluccio's god had done worse.

Though she should have gone to Joao, she nearly tried calling Niccoluccio. She needed somebody she could be less guarded around. *Ways and Means* still allowed his signal to reach her. Her medical monitor said he was healthy and sound.

It would be best for him to let him figure out his own life, without an alien woman using him as a crutch. Still, she'd hoped he would have called before now. They hadn't spoken since she'd left him in Florence.

She breathed into her hands, and stepped out to tell Joao what she'd discovered.

24

Dioneo came to the dining room as Niccoluccio and Elisa were finishing their breakfast. He halted, and waited for Elisa to stand. He politely escorted her to the door. Then, after it was shut, he spun on Niccoluccio.

"I don't know if you've ever paid attention to *that* woman," Dioneo hissed, in a tone that made it clear he remembered exactly how much attention Niccoluccio used to pay her, "but she's a well-known adulteress. If her cuckold husband hadn't perished from the pestilence, he would have died of humiliation. Your reputation could be brought to ruin if you're seen with her again." Dioneo jabbed a finger into Niccoluccio's chest, uncharacteristically hard. "Right now, your reputation is the only thing you have of value to anyone."

Niccoluccio was too stunned to speak. Dioneo promptly returned to the dining room, where Niccoluccio could hear him informing Catella that Elisa was not to be allowed in again. Whether she cared or not, Niccoluccio knew she would obey her husband. That was the only kind of woman Dioneo would have married.

It was easy to catch up with Elisa. Niccoluccio dropped his jogging pace to a walk beside her.

Her mourning veil hid her until he was beside her. She glanced to him. Through her veil, he saw the skin underneath her eyes was stained. She said, "After the way your brother spoke to me, I didn't think I would see you again."

"Of course you would. I'm sorry I didn't look for you."

Elisa brushed a hand under her veil but, when she spoke, her voice was steady. "You had more important affairs."

He didn't, but there was no use saying that. That regret would follow him forever. Niccoluccio had never felt like he'd come home until he'd seen her. "I missed everything I shouldn't have." Elisa had summarized the years for him last night, but it felt unreal. She could only give him words, not experience.

"I missed a great deal, too, and I was here," she said. "When Pietro died, I wanted to attend his funeral, but my husband wouldn't let me."

When Niccoluccio tried expressing his condolences for her husband's death, she cut him off. "That man might as well have been my father's husband, not mine. My father was the one who chose him. Certainly the only one I've ever met who liked him. I kept seeing Pietro, of course."

"Of course."

Elisa looked back to him. Her attitude had hardened since last night. She'd come to him desperate, looking for help. At night, she might have tricked herself into thinking she'd found it. Now, in the sunlight, she could see him as he really was.

Niccoluccio increasingly did not like what he saw reflected in her eyes.

"I'm sorry," he said. "I wish I hadn't needed to leave. But I don't know how much help I would have been if I had stayed."

"It's all right," Elisa said, bitterly. "It's all the world that's turned to shit, not just us."

"There's so much more to the universe than our world."

Elisa turned. This time he couldn't see her eyes under the veil. "You sound like a man getting ready to preach."

"I need to share what's on my mind with someone." If Elisa was expecting to hear a streetside sermon, she was going to be surprised. After everything he had been through, Niccoluccio no longer needed religion to speak of God.

This world was a very small part of the cosmos. All the troubles of their lives would be washed away by time. Throughout his childhood, that had been a terrifying thought. Even in Sacro Cuore, he'd shied from it. Since meeting Habidah, though, it eased the pain in his joints, the heat lumped in his throat. If nothing that mankind accomplished was significant, then neither were its pains.

There were worlds covered in vast oceans; worlds of nothing but open sky. Worlds of fire and worlds of peace. All of them rich in their own peoples, and all of them so much unlike their world that he could never describe them to her or even imagine them. He'd wanted to weep when Habidah had told him of them. It had felt like grief at the time. Now he wasn't so sure. These other worlds had no bearing on their world or on the pestilence, but it felt good to speak of them.

He had never met anyone in as much pain as Elisa. When they'd spoken of the dead, they had elided over her children. They were what she could least bear speaking about. She listened. Niccoluccio began to feel foolish, but he continued. He had spent so long at Sacro Cuore that he had forgotten how to speak to people.

She said, at last, "Your life at that monastery must have been much more interesting than I imagined, if this is the man it turned you into."

"It was not the monastery that made me think like this."

"You've been somewhere very strange, that's certain," she said. "I don't think that any of it helped much, but I would still like to hear more. It might be nice to believe."

Niccoluccio belatedly recognized the narrow streets. They were near the parish of San Lorenzo. His church was around the next intersection, beyond the shuttered bakery. "I didn't mean to take you so far afield," Niccoluccio said. "I wasn't thinking, as usual. Would you like me to walk you back to your home?"

"I can find my way on my own, thank you. I came this way to listen to you."

"Then would you like to... to make a habit of walking, like today?"

She stopped just short of the bakery. "If you would keep me distracted, I could not think of any greater kindness." She extended her hand.

Niccoluccio clasped her fingers but did not kiss her knuckles. After a while, she walked back the way she had come. He had to make an effort not to follow.

He forced himself to turn to the Church of San Lorenzo. His thoughts still buzzed. He wanted to think about anything except the ledgers in front of him. But Sacro Cuore had taught him to put his labors above his love, and above even his peace of mind. Labor, Prior Lomellini had said, *was* the path to the peace of God.

An hour after lunchtime, he finished assembling a summary of the parish's debts and loans. The results were as bad as expected. If the parish's income remained diminished, and papal taxes high, the parish would have to call in all of its own loans to survive. That was, of course, contingent upon the parish's debtors being able to pay. Niccoluccio knew very well that they couldn't.

He had no solutions. If he had been in any position of power, he would have already bankrupted the church caring for the poor and the dead and the dying. The state of the church's debts mattered nothing to what its mission in the world should have been. It was a good thing he had never been placed so high up. He was not cut out for this life, these decisions.

His feet carried him out of the church. He paused at a street cart to buy maslin bread, and didn't think about where he was going. He needed to lose himself, as he'd used to sink into his chores at Sacro Cuore.

Instead, his thoughts kept sticking on Habidah.

When he called her, she asked, "So soon?" Again there was that disquieting moment when she didn't sound like herself. It faded more quickly than last time, but he couldn't put it out of his head.

He stammered, "I, uhm, I know. You have bigger problems than me to worry about."

"Things have been going well here. The multiverse can be as much a kind place as a cruel one. Someday I hope to be able to show you that."

Niccoluccio's stomach fluttered. "What do you mean?"

"When you were with us, I'm not sure you had a chance to notice that one of our number was ill. His disease released him. Wherever he is in the multiverse, I'm sure he's found more peace now than he had yesterday."

Niccoluccio did remember an older man in Habidah's home. If he had been suffering, he'd made no mention of it. "'Released?' You don't mean 'recovered,' do you?"

"There was not much chance of that."

Niccoluccio took a bite of his bread, as a pretense for not answering straight away. Habidah did not sound like the same person. He changed the subject: "I have perhaps too delicate a question for you. Forgive me if it is too much."

"I can answer any question you would like."

"What do your people think of love and sex? Is it...?" He had been about to ask if sex was a sin, but he couldn't finish the question, even subvocally.

"What they are to *me* doesn't matter that much. I get the idea that's not what you're asking. There are so many other worlds in the multiverse, Niccoluccio. Love means so many different things on all them. On some worlds, it's a fault, and on others a virtue. There are places where it's scorned and shameful, and others where it's celebrated in public."

"You can travel as you like, to any place that suits you?"

"Any place at all, Niccoluccio."

A pang of jealousy faltered his step. "I think I would enjoy talking to you more about your worlds."

That was nearly all Niccoluccio did over the next several days: talk, to Elisa and to Habidah. He hadn't had so much female company since he was a child. So many of the books he'd meditated upon at Sacro Cuore, from Cassian's *Conferences* to St Jerome's *Letters*, had warned him against feminine company and feminine corruption. Even then, those parts had seemed the smallest part of the text.

On their next walk, Elisa said, "When I couldn't attend Pietro's burial, I spent all of my waking hours in prayer. I pray for him every night. I don't know that any of it matters."

"Every prayer is heard," Niccoluccio said, automatically.

"What would a fallen woman matter?"

"You've always mattered to me."

"I don't believe that. You left. But on the chance you're right, you've been a fool."

Heat built under Niccoluccio's throat. "You are *not* a fallen woman."

Elisa laughed quietly, bitterly.

Nobody in Florence could see the world the way he did. He could try to explain it, but never succeed. Habidah was the only person who understood even a glimmer of it.

Their walks meandered through Florence's more pleasant neighborhoods. The Baptistery and Cathedral of Santa Reparata wasn't far from San Lorenzo. Other days, they walked along the Arno River and listened to the porters call to each other. Nothing compared to the peace of Sacro Cuore, but Niccoluccio's spirits were increasingly intolerant of peace. It reminded him too much of his last days of gravedigging in the cold and empty cloister. There were flashes of that here, too, no matter how much he tried to look away. Dark, shuttered houses. Family stores abandoned. A leathery hand laying near an open shutter.

He caught Elisa looking at them, too. Most people ignored the dead, but not her. She said, "There are rooms in my house that look just as empty."

The sight of Florence's dead may have reminded Niccoluccio of home, but this *was* Elisa's home. To live as she did would have been like walking through Sacro Cuore's empty cloister every day. The effort and the grief of it would have driven him to his knees.

Late that night, he told Habidah this. She said, "One of the troubles with mortality is that, no matter how much there is to see in the world, or worlds, there's never enough time to experience it. Or enough to forget the things you would rather not take with you."

Niccoluccio said, "You must be enormously tired of my sharing all this. I know this isn't why you left me the ability to speak with you."

"I'll allow it," Habidah said, with a trace of amusement. It made him start. He hadn't ever heard her amused when they'd spoken in person. It reinforced the feeling that he was speaking to someone other than the woman he'd met. Maybe speaking to her like this just made it that much harder for them to understand each other.

He said, "There are times when I wish I could see your face. I don't think I can ever get used to speaking to anyone like this."

"Someday."

He raised his eyebrows. He had expected to never see her in person again. Certainly that had been the impression she had left him with. She didn't bring it up again.

Their walks sometimes took them through the Palazzo Vecchio. Even after the pestilence had left Florence a husk, there were always people there, always busy. Today, the city's nineteen military companies mustered their strength in the plaza, one at a time, to take a count of survivors and hand out promotions. Niccoluccio watched them gather. The rest of Florence hadn't seemed to realize it yet, but these men were being readied to defend their city.

Nearly every day, he spotted armed and escorted riders heading out of the city, bearing messages for countryside castellans and peacekeepers. Florence didn't rule its surrounding towns, not officially, but it exerted so much pressure over them that it might as well have. Florence needed to see which of its picked men had survived the pestilence and replace those who hadn't. Should Florence be faced with a war, those towns would be the backbone of its defense.

All this was tied to his brother and his allies' campaign of tensions against the papacy, no doubt. Elisa watched, too. She said, "I don't understand how anybody could think of fighting so soon after the pestilence. Then again, I never understood fighting to begin with."

Niccoluccio shrugged. Cities rose and cities fell. It was that way throughout this world, and he was sure on many others as well. He wished he had something remotely comforting to tell her about it.

The next morning came with a hard thumping at the door. It was only by the time that Niccoluccio had stumbled out of bed that he heard the other sounds – hollering, metal clanging like banging on pans, and the ragged voice of a crier.

Niccoluccio and Dioneo reached the door at the same time. Thanks to the hoarse crier, Niccoluccio already knew what had happened.

The old bishop had died.

Niccoluccio followed Dioneo outside. The neighborhood was far more bustling than it should have been at this or any hour, full of hollering and impromptu marches. "Finally, finally!" men shouted up and down the street. More were lighting a bonfire at the end of the street. Several houses' windows were illuminated with candles.

Niccoluccio wondered if he had underestimated the city's antipathy for the bishop until he spotted a group of five men banging harshly on the door of one of the homes without candles. One way or another, the rest of Florence was going to be intimidated into appearing to celebrate the bishop's death. Catella raced to place candles in her windows.

Niccoluccio turned to Dioneo, but Dioneo was gone, already charging through the crowds. Niccoluccio hesitated, unwilling to go back to a house in which he no longer felt welcome, and equally unable to follow Dioneo.

Instead, he did what he did every time he'd felt unsettled: labor. He returned to the Church of San Lorenzo. He'd double-checked and triple-checked his accounts, but he took them out again.

With all of Florence focused elsewhere, he had plenty of peace inside to work. He stared without seeing. After half an hour of trying to read, he closed the ledgers.

"I would have thought that the pestilence would change things like this," Niccoluccio told Habidah. "That people would see how fragile their lives are."

"I hate to disillusion you. Our worlds are infested with a pest much like yours. It's only made the squabbling worse. What do you want to do?"

He hadn't done any work more exhausting than walking in weeks, and he still felt ready to collapse. There was only one answer he could give, and he didn't want to. "Nothing. I don't care about anything I've been made to do."

Habidah turned to a much more trenchant question: "What are you *going* to do?"

The answer had been building up in his throat for days. So long as he could avoid saying it, it didn't have to come true. But Habidah had taken his choice away. He couldn't keep it hidden from her like he could from himself.

"I'm going to leave," he said. "I have nowhere to go, but anywhere would be better than this." Not for the first time, he imagined himself left for dead in that deserted northern wilderness. Until now, the idea had never come as a relief.

25

Habidah missed her three hours of sleep. Usually, whenever she was on assignment, she forced herself to get them. Her work was stressful enough without fatigue toxins. But her demiorganics said that her mind was too active, her brain chemistry all wrong, for sleep. She brushed off its offers to correct this. She didn't trust her demiorganics.

She strolled the corridors instead. The field base was so compact that she was doing little more than pacing, but at least the viewwalls gave her the illusion of moving. She paced from the clouds of superhot gas giants into still images of half-meter-tall forests.

When her demiorganics told her she had a call, she nearly jumped. She half-expected Osia, and nearly blocked the signal until she saw that the signal's origin was in Florence.

"Niccoluccio?" She'd nearly thought Osia had blocked his signals out of spite. She hadn't heard from him since she'd left Florence. "Are you all right?"

"I'm well enough," he said. There was something odd in his voice. It didn't seem to fit him, not perfectly. The distortion vanished with his next few words. She had her satellites run diagnostic programs, but they found no errors. Niccoluccio went on, "You'll have to forgive me. I'm not accustomed to speaking to anyone like this."

"I can imagine. You've coped with an amazing amount so far." More than she could possibly have expected him to.

Even subvocally, she could hear his strain. "I haven't had any time to put my thoughts together. I've been so busy that I have nothing to repay the kindness you've shown me, not yet."

She leaned against the viewwall's image of a titanic mercuryfall. After all he'd put up with from her, she couldn't possibly inflict the past few weeks on him. "The assignment can wait however long you need."

"The assignment was the reason you saved me, wasn't it?"

"No. Knowing that you're well would do me more good."

Another hesitation. "I should hate to have to disappoint you."

"You're not well?"

What a question. Of course he wasn't.

"Everything is a... a substantial change. Life here moves so quickly. Our bishop died recently. There's talk of fighting the papacy over his successor. A real fight, with interdictions and excommunications. If I remain where I am, I'll be excommunicated as well. Every clergyman performing services will be. None of this makes sense. None of this matters. The pestilence killed half of the city, and all we've done afterward is just more likely to incur God's hatred."

"I wish I could understand everything about how you felt."

"Would that we could all understand each other. I don't want to take part in this."

She saw where he was going. She'd taken him to Florence at his request. He didn't want to appear ungrateful. "You don't want to be there."

"If I asked, would you take me back to your home, where you healed me?"

This must have been what he'd called to ask her. She shook her head, though he couldn't see. It wasn't a matter of protecting him from all her knowledge. After *Ways and Means* carried through its plans, very few people on this plane would be unaware of her and her people. "Maybe, Niccoluccio. Someday. Now would not be a good time."

"I may ask again soon."

She swallowed. Her last argument with Feliks resounded in her memory. "If that's what you truly want, I will consider it."

He let out a breath. "Thank you. I don't know if I will yet, but that was what I needed to hear."

"I need to ask you something in return."

"I cannot help you infinitesimally as much as you have helped me, but I can try."

Ever since she'd seen what had become of Caldera, a question had built in her throat, clinging to its sides like dread. "Your life is full of both natural wonders and miracles." At least he would see it that way. "How do you tell one from the other?"

A pause. "I don't draw that distinction. The natural world *is* a wonder of God. The breath of the divine lives in every seed on a tree, every humor in our bodies."

Habidah tried again: "But not every divine presence carries the same weight, does it? There must be something special, more intentional, about a miracle."

"No 'part' of the divine is different from any other. There are no parts. God is indivisible."

Habidah restrained the urge to roll her eyes. No matter how much she tried or trained, there were always going to be parts of extraplanar cultures that she failed to internalize. "Think of messages, then. How do you distinguish a message from any other part of the world? A burning bush versus a grain of sand."

"One would certainly get more of my attention than the other."

"Exactly. How do you decide between a miracle and a happenstance that, however extraordinary, is not a message from God?"

"You would know in your heart where the message had come from."

"It's that part that I'm struggling with." She could all but hear his consternation. He didn't know how to respond. She said, "Thank you for the advice, Niccoluccio."

He said, surprised, "I am humbled to have been of help."

She cut the signal before she could think of any other way to embarrass herself.

One of the reasons she'd chosen this career to begin with – beyond getting away from home – had been to learn to see her own worlds in a new way. There was no discovery so broadening as learning another culture's perspective. She may not have internalized Niccoluccio's perspective, but she had *started* to understand it. If he had seen what she had, he could only ever have drawn one conclusion.

That conclusion made her feel even smaller than she already did.

The plague had begun its creeping infiltration of France and the western principalities of the Holy Roman Empire. It hid in bales of hay and cloth and wool or in travelers' clothes, hopping from rat to flea and back. The satellites watched the infrared emissions of farmsteads and towns cut in half or disappear. The plague left cold and dark in its wake.

Habidah had little trouble navigating the channels of death.

She nestled the shuttle deep in an untamed forest of the western Holy Roman Empire, two kilometers from one of those towns. She marched down the ramp, brushing branches away. Kacienta and Joao trudged silently alongside her. The shadows of the foliage made dappled blotches all over their faces, left their expressions unreadable. They knew better than to ask why she'd taken them here. Leaving the field base gave them a better chance of talking without being overheard.

They walked in silence for too long. Then, as abruptly as if a curtain had been lifted, they stepped out of the forest and into a sun-soaked field. Dry dust billowed into Habidah's face. She shielded her eyes. About half a kilometer ahead, houses clustered in a semicircle. A pair of oxen flicked their tails against the morning heat. There was no sign of any other animal larger than a dog. That made this the poorest town

Habidah had yet visited. The oxen were likely communal, shared between farms.

More than half of the surrounding wheat fields had gone to seed, half-reclaimed by weeds. Satellite records showed that two-thirds of the town's inhabitants had died. Given their relatively close quarters and the stresses of poverty, Habidah was only surprised they'd gotten off so lightly.

Today was Sunday. Nobody was out working. The survivors were all at church. Habidah marched toward it. She could feel Kacienta and Joao's unease growing, but neither of them stopped her from stepping inside.

There were no pews. Empty space stretched to the door. Twenty-six people stood at the front. All of them turned to face her.

Habidah inclined her head to the priest whose sermon she had just interrupted. "Good friends, excuse our intrusion." She explained that she and her siblings were refugees, passing through. Three angry-looking, uniformly bearded and mustachioed men stepped forward. Before they could object to potential plague-carriers coming through, Habidah held up her hands. "Not one of us has ailed in two weeks. We haven't heard Mass in at least as long. You wouldn't turn Christians away from the Sacrament?"

The men looked at each other, but no one would tell her no. She led the others to the back, far from the townsfolk. Finally, the men stepped back, though one of them was always watching.

After a great pause, the priest resumed his service. Joao transmitted, "Was this necessary?"

"The amalgamates' satellites are more sensitive than ours. I wanted to get inside, where they couldn't lip-read. And I don't want to transmit anything."

Kacienta said, "As if the amalgamates would care if we conspire against them. Osia told you their whole plan for this world."

Habidah said, "They think that, by saving even a tiny

fraction of the Unity's people, they can save the Unity itself. Maybe rebuild and regrow it."

"They must be more desperate than I thought," Kacienta said. "The vast majority of the Unity is still alive." Given the multiplicity of political systems among the Unity, exact counts were tricky, but at least four-fifths of the Unity's people remained uninfected. The planes Habidah had contacted, Caldera and Providence Core, had been among the hardest struck. "They couldn't save more than a fraction of a percent of the Unity this way."

"It doesn't fit," Joao agreed. Habidah caught the mourning in his voice. He was still reeling from the betrayal. He didn't *want* to believe the amalgamates would abandon his world, just like that.

Habidah had thought more about that. She said, "The amalgamates are nothing if not forward-thinking. I doubt they're ready to leave all the Unity's planes behind them. Yet. But they can't cure the onierophage. They're running out of ways to try. They have to know they probably won't. The way their minds work, the way *any* AI's mind works, they would start laying their backup plans long before the final evacuation. They don't – can't – attach any emotional significance to an act like that. It's just something they have to do."

Kacienta said, "And they made *us* part of their backup plan. Scouting this world as a site to evacuate survivors."

The men and women up front bowed. Habidah mimicked them. She couldn't help but notice how old the audience was. There was only one younger than ten. The plague claimed the children first.

Kacienta said, "Amazing that these people manage to stay upright."

"Many of them didn't," Joao said.

Habidah said, "They have no idea where their plague comes from, but they think they do. Listen." The priest was not reciting Mass in Latin, but speaking in vernacular – expounding upon the evils of humanity, its lusts and petty sins and irreligiousness. The only wonder of the pestilence, he said, was that God had not inflicted it on men sooner. Those up front bowed further.

Kacienta said, "If I had to blame myself for our plague, I'd feel worse, not better."

"You might think that," Habidah said. "At least they don't have to wonder."

Joao said, "I can't believe that lying to ourselves would make us feel better."

Habidah said, "I'm not so sure they don't have the right idea. About the onierophage."

Joao and Kacienta were quiet for a while. Then Kacienta said, "Plenty of people think our plague is artificial. An attack from another transplanar empire. An experiment gone wrong. The amalgamates culling us. There's a reason nobody listens to those people, Habidah."

Joao said, "If it were an attack, whoever's responsible would aim at the amalgamates, not us. We're nothing. The amalgamates *are* the Unity. The Unity would collapse without them."

Habidah said, "The amalgamates certainly seem to think we're important. That's what their whole operation is about."

Joao said, "In all of the planes we've ever visited, we've never found a sign of any empire large or advanced enough to threaten ours." Those burgeoning empires it had run into had been quickly subsumed, swallowed, incorporated.

Habidah asked, "Ever wonder if the only reason the Unity hasn't found another large empire is because something happened to them?"

Kacienta said, "I'm sure someone has. We're hardly the only people who've thought about it."

"We've been thinking about our plague too conventionally. Quarantines. Disease control. Evacuee camps." She nodded at the priest. "These people see their plague in moral terms, religious terms."

Joao asked, "You think God is punishing the Unity?"

269

"Not their God. *A* god."

"*That's* not anything I would have ever thought to hear you say."

"It's worth considering. The Unity has explored about every option except what these people think about every day – that there's a very large, supremely powerful force that disapproves of what the Unity is doing."

"These people are *wrong*," Joao said. "They can fear God all they want, but it's not going to give their immune systems the power to fight off the plague bacilli, or burn the rat fleas out of their clothes. They'd stop that nonsense at once if they knew."

The priest pointed at each of his audience in turn. Habidah waited until his attention had moved on before saying, "The onierophage feels like a disease, and acts a little like a disease, so we try to fight it like a disease. It's only when we look deep down that we see it's something inexplicable. Maybe it's a mimic. A predator trying to seem like something else."

Joao said, "That doesn't mean that it isn't natural."

"It attacks only people with demiorganics. It bypasses every quarantine. Now we know that nobody who's been outside the Unity for five years has been infected. It's starting to sound like somebody's making a clear distinction between who's a part of the Unity and who's not."

Kacienta asked, "If you're right, what does that mean for us? All of this is so far above us that it almost doesn't matter."

"It means that the amalgamates' project is going to fail. The exiles are coming back to the Unity. No matter how deep the quarantine, they're going to be infected just like everyone else."

Looking at their faces, she could tell she wasn't going to persuade them. They were too accustomed to thinking of the onierophage as she had, as a temporal problem. She said, "It also means we need to get out of the Unity. Leaving might be the only way to save ourselves, if it's not too late already."

They couldn't speak for singing as the service progressed through the psalms and into the wine and the Host. Habidah and her colleagues had to step to the front. The congregants sidled clear of them. Joao curled his nose as he chewed the Host, but only with his back to the audience.

"I'm with you on that last part, at least," Kacienta said under her breath. "I don't want to ever go back to the Unity."

Joao muttered, "The amalgamates wouldn't let us go home after what we've seen."

Kacienta said, "I can't send mail to my family. We're exiles already. Might as well make it official, find a new home. We wouldn't be the first."

Joao said, "The problem is that we *can't* leave. We only have a microwidth communications gateway. *Ways and Means* controls every other way off this world."

Habidah admitted, "It's all an academic argument right now." But she was an academic. Hashing this stuff out early might as well have been in her department oath. "I brought you here because I needed to know that we're together on this. If there's any opportunity to leave, I'm going to take it. I'm counting on your help."

"And the people of this plane?" Kacienta asked. "Your friend, the monk?"

"We can't do anything for these people," Habidah said, though part of her was already making plans for Niccoluccio.

When the service ended, the first thing any of the locals did was to look back at the strangers. They were no longer welcome. Habidah led Joao and Kacienta out.

She glanced at the sky. Her demiorganics tracked several satellites overhead. If the amalgamates had infiltrated her demiorganics, they'd heard everything anyway, but she'd done what she could. Her best hope was that they didn't care enough.

Niccoluccio's voice interrupted the walk back: "Habidah, everything's on fire."

Habidah stopped in mid stride. Niccoluccio's voice sounded broken, strangely emotionless in transmission. His efforts to speak were constantly interrupted, cut off. "Help... need he... Right now."

"Say again?" Habidah subvocalized.

"There's a fire... The church is... I need to run." Niccoluccio sounded like a man in shock. "Help us right now."

A bad chill spiked down Habidah's back. "We're on our way. Stay calm, and tell me what's happening."

No answer.

Habidah glanced back at Joao and Kacienta. Without waiting to explain, she broke into a run. Not until she was halfway back to the shuttle did she think to check to make sure they were following. For now, they were.

26

Niccoluccio knew, in theory, that riots had ravaged Florence. Every Florentine, educated or not, knew about the civil war between the Guelfs and the Ghibellines, which had ended with the city ostensibly allying with the papacy. They knew about the magnates, the wealthy young men who ran wild through the city. And everyone lived in fear of food riots each bad winter.

But when he heard the yells outside the Church of San Lorenzo, at first he didn't know what to make of it. He stared at his lone, foggy window. It wasn't until he heard glass smashing – close – that he realized.

He rushed into the church proper, his habit rustling at his heels. The stained glass behind the altar had burst. Red, violet, and blue shards glittered in the sunlight. The moment after he arrived, the doors cracked open. Three men burst in, a jeering crowd behind them.

The handful of parishioners in the church were already rushing away from the doors. Frantic, Niccoluccio looked about for the head priest or any other clergyman, but he seemed to be alone. One of the women was weeping, trying to hide underneath her wimple.

Niccoluccio stepped forward before he realized what he was doing. The church had an exit in the back, hidden in a hallway tucked in an alcove. He waved the parishioners toward it.

The intruders were interested in looting, not chasing

harmless men and women. They broke toward the altar. Niccoluccio got the seven men and women out unmolested.

A handful of people had lined up to throw rocks in the alley behind the church. They must have been the ones who'd broken the stained glass. They watched Niccoluccio and the parishioners warily. When it became clear that they hadn't come to counter-attack, the rioters picked up loose stones and hurled them into the church.

Niccoluccio knew he shouldn't have fled. It was his duty to protect the church's treasures and shrines. In the flash of the moment, he hadn't even considered that. He couldn't think of himself as a part of the church. San Lorenzo was somebody else's property, somebody else's responsibility.

At Sacro Cuore, it would have been different.

The sounds of tumult and fury echoed over the roof. The worst of the crowd was on the street. The parishioners still looked to him for guidance. He took them down the alley, through puddles and waste runnels, around overturned barrels and an uncollected pest carcass.

Once the shouting dwindled and the immediate danger ended, they fled in their own directions. Niccoluccio saw the last of them off. And then he turned back to the street.

When he poked his head around the corner, he found the street empty but for a handful of men running past, all in the same direction. Peering that way, he could just see the crowd outside of the church. For as loud as they were, it was amazing that he hadn't heard them inside. Maybe they'd gathered that much strength since he'd left.

Niccoluccio gathered his courage and stepped into the path of one of the runners. The man slowed. His skin was pocked by some old disease, but otherwise he'd come through the pestilence strong and hale. Haste and fear glittered in his eyes.

Niccoluccio asked, "In God's name, what is happening here?"

"Interdiction," he breathed. "The fools have gone and got us interdicted."

Niccoluccio let him go. Everything had become clearer. Interdiction was the worst punishment a city could receive short of mass excommunication. It meant Pope Clement VI had decreed no services could be held in the Diocese of Florence. No sins could be confessed. No weddings officiated. No Last Rites administered. Whoever should die without either confession or rites would not be smiled upon by God.

In one breath, Pope Clement had placed the city a hair's width from damnation. It didn't matter if the churches continued to perform their business. None of it would be sanctified in the eyes of God. No one would trust a marriage issued under an interdiction.

This had certainly happened because the clergy of the cathedral chapter had, in concert with the civil authorities, unilaterally appointed Ambrogiuolo their own bishop. Not everyone had been in favor, but they'd been intimidated into silence. Now this was the dissenters' chance to prove that they had been right all along.

Pillars of smoke rose from the other corners of the city. Men clustered around a bonfire at the end of the next street. When Niccoluccio walked closer, he saw the fire had been fueled with chairs. A table burned as its centerpiece. The doors of the nearest home had been smashed. At least the rioters were civic-minded. They hadn't set the actual house ablaze and risked the fire spreading.

Niccoluccio should have gone to his brother's home. At the last street crossing, he turned to the neighborhood in which Elisa lived.

A loose formation of men passed, heading in the opposite direction. Half were dressed no differently than the rabble Niccoluccio had left behind, but the rest had the caps of the wall watch. The parish's aged, knobby elbowed constable was among them. Niccoluccio knew he ought to have been relieved to see someone moving against the rioters, but mostly he didn't care.

Elisa lived near where she'd grown up, in a row of formerly

up and coming merchants' homes only blocks away from the Arno River. Each home was tastefully designed to hide the economy with which they had been built. Stone and brick had been painted white to resemble marble. They bore wide porticoes, but there was no servants' housing.

There was nobody left to be impressed. The quarantine boards over her neighbors' doors hadn't been removed even by squatters. Niccoluccio wouldn't have been surprised to find pestilence corpses still in them, untouched.

Elisa's home was flanked by columns carved garishly in the shape of boars, birds, and game animals. Niccoluccio knocked gently. Elisa peered through the upper shutters before coming down. She stepped aside to allow him in.

All the shutters were closed, shrouding the interior. There was a dusty shadow on the wall where a painting had recently hung. Niccoluccio shuddered to think that this was where she'd lived all those months.

"Are you sure you want to be seen entering my home unescorted?" Elisa asked, bitterly.

"As if there were anybody to see. I wanted to be sure you were all right."

"Nobody would come here to riot. Why would they? There's nothing important left."

"You don't have anyone here? No servants? No family?"

"Our kitchen girl died of the pestilence. I couldn't have hired another even if I had the money. But this is my home. I'm not afraid of it."

Niccoluccio hadn't asked about her finances. He'd assumed, perhaps naively, that her husband had provided upkeep for after his death, or at the very least that her father-in-law would do the same.

"I'm glad to find you safe," he said, fumbling to find words. "I thought you would be panicking as much as I am."

"When my husband was alive, all he could talk about was obtaining his knighthood. It was so important to him. His knighthood would have made everything we'd suffered through worth it, he said. It would mean that no one could look down on him anymore. Our children would have their places secured." She stopped outside an empty doorway and curled her nose. "All that fighting didn't help him or them in the end."

Niccoluccio peered in the doorway. In the dark, he could just see a stack of five books, a pair of shoes too large for her. Elisa said, "You had the right idea, leaving Florence when you were young, learning about death and all other things precious to God. That's all that matters after everything else passes."

Niccoluccio had said this before, but he'd never felt it so keenly. "I learned nothing in the monastery."

"You're certainly a different person from who you used to be. And better than if you'd stayed here."

"All my brothers are dead. It was only a fluke that I survived."

"A fluke? I thought it was a miracle."

Niccoluccio blinked. He'd said the word before he realized what he meant. He nodded, slowly. "It can be both."

Elisa gave him a strange look. She led him through the buttery and into the pantry. Open and half-empty cupboards lined the walls. "I can't have you in without at least offering something to eat. I've had to throw too much of it out already."

She poured the pair of them a glass of wine each, and bread with wafers in pewter dishware. "I wish I had richer food to offer you."

"This is far richer than I am accustomed to." In Dioneo's home, after the first day's feast and the unfortunate digestive experience that had resulted, Niccoluccio had instructed the cook to furnish him with simple meals: breads with no butter, and milk. After a few bites, his pulse slowed. The fear that had burned since the riot dwindled.

"You know, it's strange how safe I feel with you," Elisa said. "Any other man on Earth, I would have felt like you'd come only to assault me. But you were never like that. You or Pietro, even after all the things we did."

Niccoluccio shifted. "I feel like a beast, thinking about that."

"The beasts are the men conspiring to pit us against the papacy so soon after the pestilence."

Niccoluccio took another bite to keep from saying anything about his brother. Elisa rolled her bread back and forth. She hadn't touched anything but her wine. She asked, "If this is the end of the world, why can't it hurry and arrive? Why does God have to leave so many lingering?"

"When the world ends, it will end in stages, none of which have come to pass." He meant to be comforting when he said, "This is not the end of the world."

She asked, "Why must suicide be a mortal sin?"

He knew what he was supposed to say. If she was a Christian, her life was pledged to God. It was not hers to give away. But, in many moments these past few days, he'd wondered the same. "I am no longer equipped to give spiritual advice."

Another odd look. "You, the Carthusian monk, not qualified? You've spent more years studying God than any priest in this city."

"I don't know what I am anymore. I feel my spirit being ripped in many directions." He'd been anxious about asking her a question, and he hadn't realized what it was until now. "If you could go anywhere you want – if you could leave here, and never come back – would you?"

"You always ask the strangest questions."

"It's always sincerely meant. Do you think you could be happy anywhere else?"

"It seems like being happy after all that's happened would be a sin."

"There must be some end to the misery."

"Maybe it comes when we die and are forgotten," Elisa said. "I know this is where my life is going to end. There's nothing else for me. I also know that, wherever I go, I'll never be free of what happened here."

The weight in his throat became a weight in his chest. He swallowed. He'd been near to asking her if she would accompany him when he left Florence, but he already had her answer. "Thank you for indulging me in my oddities."

When he stood, Elisa followed him to the door and stopped just beside it. "Do you think *you* could be happy?" she asked.

"I don't suppose so."

"I imagined as much. We've both lost so much."

There was so much he wanted to say, and nothing he could. He raised her hand to his lips and kissed it. He had to force himself to leave.

The fires still burned in every corner of the city. He passed no crowds on his short trip to his brother's home. He breathed out when he found the neighborhood left untouched. A trio of magnates, the wealthy young barbarians, had formed a guard at the end of the street. Even the sight of Niccoluccio's tonsure wouldn't convince them to allow him to pass until he told them his name. It prompted the lead man to grin, and say, "The widow-taker."

As Niccoluccio passed, another said, "Some monk," and spat on Niccoluccio's shoes.

They'd seen him with Elisa one too many times.

Catella ran to the door when Niccoluccio knocked, but deflated when she saw it was just him. She told him Dioneo had gone running to the heart of the city. Niccoluccio hardly paused for breath before setting off.

He found his brother in the shadow of the Palazzo Vecchio's single ugly tower. He was in bitter conference with a semicircle of gray-haired parish constables. After waving the constables off, Dioneo stormed toward the Palazzo Vecchio's doors. He gave no indication that he had seen Niccoluccio until he waved Niccoluccio after him.

"There is no way to win with the rabble of Florence," Dioneo complained, sitting behind his desk as if to shield himself. "Had we not appointed Ambrogiuolo, they would have rioted when the church raised rents and fees and called in its debts."

"You should feel lucky your home hasn't been targeted. I thought you might feel better knowing that Catella and your children are safe."

"We've almost got the rabble under control. There's no question about that. The city is ours, and it will remain ours. You're going to help."

"What? How?"

"You can start with the priests and monks. I thought the clergy would support us, but the lower orders of the hierarchy are almost as much in arms as the rioters."

Niccoluccio said, "They have more to lose from the interdiction than anybody. They'll get just a fraction of the pittance they used to receive for services."

"You'd figured that, and you didn't say so until now?"

"I didn't need to say what I thought you already knew."

Dioneo ground his teeth, but didn't bite back. "Go to Santa Reparata. It's crowded, but people will listen to you. You can tell them to supp–"

"I'm not taking part in this."

Dioneo stuttered to a stop. "You've already taken part."

"I've been dragged along. All anybody in this city can do after the pestilence is make the world worse."

"You wouldn't dare to side with the papacy, not after what you've seen."

"I'm not siding with *anyone*. I'm withdrawing."

Dioneo sat there, mouth in a twist of confusion and frustration. Niccoluccio turned to the door.

Dioneo said, "I never dreamed I would have to threaten to close my home to my brother. If you walk through those doors, don't come back to mine. This is too grave for philosophical scruples."

"If that is what you feel obliged to do, then I cannot stop you."

"Go back to your whore, then!" Dioneo shouted at his back. Niccoluccio's step caught, but he forced himself to continue.

He marched past Dioneo's secretary, trying to keep his face as composed as he hoped he had sounded. His bare scalp burned by the time he reached the plaza. He ran his fingers across his bare scalp. He felt as though there were a fire in his head. He leaned against the side of the Palazzo Vecchio, and only moved on when he noticed the disapproval of passersby.

He walked in the first direction he could think of, toward the western gates. No attempt at calm could keep his breath from coming in quick, shallow gulps. He had nothing in Florence, no reason to stay. His family and his home had been the only reason he'd come. He had no home elsewhere. He had no money, little knowledge of the cities beyond Florence's walls. If he tried to travel on his own, he would be no better off than he had been when he'd fled Sacro Cuore.

Applying to join a monastery wasn't an option either. He no longer felt a man of the church, which was tantamount to saying he was no longer a man of God. Losing his brother made him shake, but losing sight of God was what made him want to weep. And he couldn't explain the reasons for it to anyone in this city.

The pillars of smoke had dwindled to candle wisps, but shops remained closed and the streetside food carts and stalls had vanished into the ether from which they came. At least four men stood guard outside each church he passed. They stared at Niccoluccio as he went by.

His feet turned south, toward the Arno. Elisa's home.

Elisa looked only mildly surprised to see him again so soon. When he was safely inside, he said, "You asked me earlier why suicide should be a sin. I don't have an answer."

She needed a moment to understand. "Are you coming to *me* for support?"

"I usually did. You and Pietro."

"Back when we were little older than children. Can't you see how things are different?"

She didn't know what had just happened between him and his brother, and he wasn't inclined to explain. "I never felt like I belonged in this city since the day I came back."

"Long before that, I'll bet," Elisa said.

"I should have died at the monastery. Or frozen to death on the roads afterward. I have no right to be here."

Elisa glanced back to a half-opened door. Niccoluccio couldn't see anything behind it, but the knob was covered in dust. "Maybe we should both be dead," she said.

A flood of guilt nearly pushed him to the floor. He'd come to her for some comfort, some grounding, but of course he wasn't alone in feeling like this. Elisa had lost her children. However close he'd felt to his brother, she'd been closer to her family. She'd explained that before, with words he hadn't tried hard enough to understand.

"I'm beyond sorry. There's nothing I can say to ease your suffering."

"I wish you hadn't had to discover that the same way I did."

"How do you bear it?"

"I don't. And I won't. What about you? Do you think you'll find another monastery?"

There were some parts of him that she couldn't understand, not any more than he could her. He shook his head.

"Then – would you like to stay with me?" He could hear the reluctance trailing from her voice.

"Neither of us really wants that."

Elisa looked back toward the half-open door, and nodded.

She said, "I hope I'll be able to see you again, before–"

"It will be as God wills it." Short of God's aid, neither of them were in control of themselves.

He took her hand, squeezed it one last time before heading for the front door.

When he got outside again, he didn't know where he was headed, but he felt many times lighter. It was as though he'd dragged chains with him ever since he'd left Sacro Cuore – ever since he'd heard of the pest approaching – and he'd finally managed to lose them.

His brother's home was only a few streets away. If it weren't for the interceding rooftops, he could have seen it. It might as well have been in Xanadu. His head still burned. He turned to the southwest, and the neighborhoods of porters and laborers who made their homes near the river. He'd been there a few times in the company of Pietro and Elisa, searching for privacy.

There was more of that to be found now. As elsewhere, whole streets had been abandoned. Doors and windows were boarded over. Quarantine signs hung over them. Other houses had been left open to show off the rot inside. Most of the city's dead had come through here, on their way to corpse barges. They'd left annihilation in their wake. The pestilence had cleaved through the neighborhood like steel through flesh.

There were no corpses in the streets anymore, but indoors there would be plenty. Niccoluccio stopped outside one of the boarded-up houses. He had a good idea what he'd find inside, and the smell when he pried loose the boards and opened the door left no doubt.

He counted three adult-sized bodies, each with several children. The house had only one room, and they all shared it. Three of the children were tucked underneath sheets as if to be tended on their sickbeds. Their skin was gray, and their hair had become wisps. Their bones poked through their elbows. One adult had a mummified infant glued to his or her chest.

One of the children looked to have died long after the others. A girl, about seven years old, was in much better condition than the others. She looked as though she might merely be sleeping. but the skin on her arm had started to slip loose, and maggots had made a home of her belly. She'd laid down sideways to keep a bubo under her arm from tormenting her.

The riots had started the fire in Niccoluccio's head, but the heat had been there long before.

There was no one to talk to but Habidah, and nothing to say except to hope that she had been listening all along. She might understand what he was about to do.

Florence had cemeteries near every church. All of them had been overwhelmed with the dead. Still, when Niccoluccio visited the nearest churchyard, he found space in the margins of the last row of graves. Whether or not the church's builders had intended to bury anyone in there, it was still consecrated ground.

Finding a shovel proved of little difficulty. The last gravediggers had abandoned it against the side of the building.

He started with the girl who'd died last. He wrapped her in one of the sheets, carried her through the streets. People stared and stood well aside. When he reached the cemetery, he dug as deep as he could before his arms lost their strength. He laid her down and recovered the blanket.

He reused the blanket each time he had to carry someone, but it was so fouled that it didn't serve as much protection. Dark, evil-smelling fluid dripped from the places the corpses' skin had burst, and soiled his clothes. The blanket was more for their dignity than his.

With so little space to dig, he had no choice but to bury the adults atop one another, next to the children. After he was sure each of them was far enough down that they wouldn't risk spreading the pestilence, he filled in the grave. It was hardly the finest burial, but it was the best he could manage, and more than anyone else had been able to give.

He sat and caught his breath. He'd fallen out of practice gravedigging since Sacro Cuore. His throat burned and a chill had settled into his core.

Maybe that was how the pestilence started its work on its victims.

If this was how he was to die, he would not complain. It was how he should have died long ago. He remembered the monks of Sacro Cuore standing one at a time to declare their intention to face the pestilence. He wondered how many of them would have made the same decision if they'd known all that would happen. He certainly wouldn't have.

Now he knew what was coming, and he wasn't afraid. He wouldn't call Habidah or seek any other kind of escape.

He worked through the night breaking quarantine boards and burying the abandoned dead. Finally, he had to stop and rest. He sat against the back wall of the church, rested his head.

The next time he looked up, the sun had traveled across

half the sky. His stomach pained, but not from hunger. He just resisted the urge to vomit.

His skin burned from long hours under the sun. He braced himself against the wall, heaved himself to his feet, and returned to the streets. Dizziness made him waver. More people were out. Yesterday's troubles seemed to have ended, no doubt leaving his brother's faction in control.

The dead would have been buried eventually. The city would bring its gravediggers. But the gravediggers from the countryside were notoriously irreligious and treated the dead like bundles of logs. No, it was best that he do whatever little he could. It was a better service to the city than any he'd done as treasurer.

Habidah told him, "You don't have to do this to yourself."

Niccoluccio startled. "I don't know what you mean," he said, accidentally aloud.

"I've been tracking your heartbeat, your body temperature. You're sick, and you're moving rather than resting."

Niccoluccio didn't answer, and she didn't speak again.

His next two corpses were both children, on the floor of a one-room house with no beds, nestled together. Their faces had decayed into gray shadows. He couldn't tell if they were boys or girls. Passersby stepped back from him as he carried them, one after the other, to their graves. After he finished, people lined up to watch him as he trudged to his next house. They didn't say anything.

After he'd exhausted the available space at the first churchyard, he turned to other cemeteries farther away. Blisters stung his hands, and his legs and shoulders ached from lifting.

By mid-afternoon, his stomach had stopped hurting. All he felt, as he marched under the shadow of his growing number of watchers, was hollow. His forehead prickled with sweat even as he shivered. He should have felt hungry.

After sunset, he no longer had an audience, but he continued until it was so dark that he couldn't tell one house from its neighbor. Then he dug fresh graves, ready for tomorrow. When his arms at last gave out, he sat hunched under a church wall. The air bit his scalp. He shivered uncontrollably, and swallowed bile.

"Why were you so bent on saving me?" he asked Habidah. He wondered if she heard his teeth clattering. "Why me and not these children, or my brothers, or this whole city?" It was the first time he could remember feeling bitter toward her.

"All I've ever done is what I've needed to," Habidah said.

"What do you mean by that?"

She didn't answer, even when he asked again.

Niccoluccio wasn't woken by the cold, or even the blazing pain in his shoulders. Rather, it was the shouting man running down the street. When Niccoluccio sat upright, the man's words were drowned out by the rush of blood in his ears.

Dawn had only just brushed the sky. Rain clouds were gathering in the west. He could already feel their bite. The pit in the center of his stomach widened. He crouched to his side, and retched a trickle of watery, greenish fluid. The rush of pain from his head nearly made him faint. His vision dwindled to a blood-encircled tunnel.

It took too long for his vision to return to normal. His pulse drummed in his ears. Still no buboes, but it hardly seemed to matter. He staggered to the street, but the commotion had passed. He was left with a shroud of darkness, and a fog of thoughts.

Time, then, for the next bodies. An old woman had died in an abandoned tavern kitchen. The rooms above were all empty, so the owners had either died elsewhere, or fled the city. By the time he returned from her grave, the sky had brightened enough that he could see smoke rising again from the corners of the city.

One of the locals had risen early to watch Niccoluccio carry his burdens. Niccoluccio nodded to the smoke, mouth open with an unasked question.

The man bowed his head. He, too, was tonsured – a monk.

"Begging your mercy. News is that the pope hasn't waited for an answer to the interdiction. He sent for help from Queen Joanna. She's back in Naples and raising an army. They want to force our bishop to abdicate."

Niccoluccio looked to the smoke. After a while, and without any other choice, he resumed his work.

Before he'd finished digging the next grave, he sagged on his shovel. When he looked up, the fires had grown larger. Some seemed to have spread to houses. A fire spreading out of control could be as destructive to Florence as the pestilence.

Though some people had come to watch him again, the streets were unusually quiet for this time of morning. He gathered as much of his energy as he could manage. His next cadaver was a bony young woman who probably looked little different in death from how she had in life. His arms threatened to give out halfway through filling her grave. His knees buckled, and several times he nearly collapsed, leaning on his shovel – until a pair of hands helped him to a seat.

It was the monk he'd spoken with earlier. Without a word, he took Niccoluccio's shovel and resumed filling the grave. There were two others, two women, with him. They took turns digging the next while Niccoluccio sat and rested.

They helped him to his feet and escorted him back to the street, past another line of watchers. There were more of them this time – about thirty. Niccoluccio pointed them to the next house on his list, and they helped him carry the hefty man who'd died within.

The most remarkable thing was that no one spoke. They seemed to know what to do the moment he indicated the house. When he grabbed the corpse's legs, they took the arms. None of the corpses he'd carried had felt so light, so distant.

He sat to rest while they dug. Afterimages swam in front of his eyes. His head spun. He checked again for buboes. Nothing. His followers finished and continued.

He got up to follow, and his vision disappeared down the end of a dark tunnel.

The next time he was conscious, drizzle kissed his cheeks and lips. Someone was trying to drip water into his mouth. He sputtered, hacked a cough, and pushed the hands away. When his vision returned, he saw the monk holding a bowl.

Niccoluccio's throat burned, but the water only made it worse. He waved him away and fought to stand. Somehow he managed to get upright. On another day, he would have appreciated the gesture. Bread and water were as poison to him.

Throughout his childhood and monastic career, he'd drunk deeply of the lives of the saints, and tales of their agonies. He'd thought he'd understood why so many of the saints had chosen their suffering. He'd thought of agony only as a trial to be endured, but this was very different. It changed him and how he perceived himself. It forced him to hold himself at a remove from all the evil influences of his body.

This was the suffering he'd shirked at Sacro Cuore. His brothers had accepted it. He would still have his chance.

The monk asked him something, but Niccoluccio didn't hear. Clarity was not one of the blessings of this new state. He went past the people watching him.

His followers milled outside an unused dockhouse, as if uncertain whether to go in. Niccoluccio led them in. A pair of vagrants had gone inside to die. Niccoluccio uncovered the bodies, and the others lifted.

His followers outpaced him on their way to the graveyard. Niccoluccio gradually fell behind. He stumbled into an alley between houses. He leaned against the grimy wall and caught his breath. More smoke spires twisted across the sky, merging smoothly into the dark clouds overhead. The light rain wasn't enough to put the fires out.

His energy had fled him. He craned his neck to look at the sky. The fires had been burning all day now. When he strained his hearing, he could hear yelling, though it was difficult to tell what was real.

He allowed his curiosity to get the better of him and picked his way down the alley. The boundary between this neighborhood and the next wasn't discreet. The houses grew taller and their sides cleaner. He stepped into a boulevard twice as large as any he'd visited over the past few days.

The street was so bustling that, for a moment, he could have mistaken it for an ordinary day. There were no carts, though. The shops were closed. The men passing bore wore grim faces, and were all headed in one direction.

A pot-bellied man with hair like the head of a mop stopped and stared. He looked up and down Niccoluccio's filthy habit with a flash of recognition. "It's Prior Caracciola's brother!"

One of the few women elbowed him. She said, "Leave off. He's a monk."

"Prior Caracciola's brother used to be a monk. It was all an act. Another trick." He seized Niccoluccio by his filthy collar. "Are you a monk? Swear it to me in the name of God if you are."

Niccoluccio fought to speak through the pressure. The idea of lying occurred only briefly. "I am no longer a monk."

That was all the excuse the man needed to smash his forehead into Niccoluccio's nose.

Niccoluccio staggered into something hard. He couldn't have kept his balance if he'd tried, and he didn't. He slid to his knees. Before he could breathe, another pair of hands grabbed him and yanked him back up.

Someone punched him between his ribs. Another blow landed, and again, lower. Niccoluccio gasped, but couldn't draw any breath. His vision tunneled into darkness. He landed on his side and felt a hard kick against his stomach. Its impact felt muted, as though it were happening to some other person.

There was a second kick to his head, and then another to his stomach. And then nothing.

It was almost anticlimactic how fast it happened. He was alone, in a void. Still conscious.

When he died, he had always expected company, even from condemned spirits of Purgatory. The solitude undermined him immediately.

Isolation was something he expected only of the outer darkness, cut off from God. A moment here felt as an eternity, as if he were clawing the inside of his head. He'd made a mistake in coming here. He understood that with a clarity like a thunderclap.

He instinctively fought his way back to the world of sensation. It was not done with him yet. It yanked him back, stubborn, like knee-high mud tugging at his shoes. He gasped at the pain in his chest. Wet clay clogged his nostrils.

He'd been tossed into a muddy ditch like a broken doll. Close, slick walls bundled his arms. He leaned up, choking for air. Another hard impact against his head knocked him back down. Someone trampled on his hip.

Then, there was a second thunderclap. He hadn't hallucinated the first after all. His ears stung.

One bolt after another blended into a continuous, terrifying noise. Someone's panicked footfall rolled him onto his side just as his vision returned from the end of the tunnel. He gaped at the clouds – at the hole opening between them.

A black bird soared out of the rain, splitting a seam across the sky. White and gold stars burned on every edge of its body. They hurt to look at.

The rain landing on Niccoluccio's face turned to steam. A burst of dry, freezing air chilled his skin.

"Not now," he mouthed. Though he couldn't hear himself, he knew somebody else could. "I don't want this."

In spite of the thunder, Habidah's voice was clear as daylight. "You don't need to be afraid."

Niccoluccio said, "I'm not afraid. I don't want to be saved again."

"I'll help you understand," Habidah said, like she was soothing a child. He had never heard her sound like that before. "You won't fight when you do. You're a good man, Niccoluccio Caracciola. And I've chosen you to help me with my work."

27

The shuttle's sensors pierced the clouds and rain, revealing a street-spanning infrared blob. Several dozen people, hot red on a cold blue background, clustered around the source of Niccoluccio's signal. The shuttle's NAI drew a yellow outline around the blotch it had identified as Niccoluccio. The two nearest men were kicking him.

That was all Habidah needed to see. Her safety harness released with a snap. She bolted out of her seat. Her demiorganics took over her sense of balance, keeping her upright – barely.

Joao and Kacienta boggled at her. The shuttle buckled in the wind. She stumbled past their couches and through the control cabin's doors into the ventral corridor. A burst of deceleration nearly knocked her back. The distance to Niccoluccio's signal ticked at the edge of her awareness: five hundred meters vertical, two hundred horizontal.

Habidah hadn't heard anything from him since his first call for help. She tried again to contact Niccoluccio. Nothing. She grasped for a handhold along the folded-up boarding ramp. "Cut our camouflage and noise bafflers," she sent.

"Have you lost it?" Joao asked.

She would have done it herself, through her demiorganics, but there was no way that she could stay on her feet and control the shuttle at the same time. *"Cut the fucking camouflage and noise bafflers!"*

Joao listened. The roar of the thrusters changed pitch, reverberating through the deck. The distance to Niccoluccio ticked down slower.

The ramp began extending when the shuttle was twenty meters off the ground. Cold, misty air gusted across Habidah's cheek. She edged down the unfolding ramp, keeping a tight grip on the bulkhead. Steam billowed from the thruster exhausts. The cold stung her skin. The air roared, and whipped at her hair and clothes.

Wind jerked the shuttle away before she saw much, but infrared showed her some blotches that looked like people, running away. She spared no pity for them. She *hoped* they were terrified.

Fury burned in her breath.

The shuttle couldn't land. The buildings on either side of the street didn't offer the clearance for its wingspan. Habidah didn't wait. She leapt off the edge of the ramp, meters in the air, and landed with a sharp pain and a roll.

The shuttle hovered overhead, fire-tinged, casting its shadow over half the block. A meteorite frozen just before impact. The thunder of its thrusters must have carried over all of Florence. It ground her bones and teeth against each other.

Niccoluccio lay in a ditch. She hardly recognized him. His face was smeared with mud, and his hair might as well have been made of it. A long cut ran across his cheek to his chin, a bruise sprouted under his eye. She scrambled to his side, crouched. His eyes were closed, but he was breathing. His pulse was erratic, and his body temperature had spiked.

More than that, his elbows were bony, his cheeks sallow. The bugs she'd planted in him now reported significant dehydration, starvation, fever. She'd set them to alert her long before it should have gotten this bad.

"Not now," he mouthed. Habidah only heard him because he had inadvertently triggered his subvocal transmitter. "I don't want this."

She looked about, craned her neck to follow the shuttle.

The shuttle drifted farther down the street, tilting to bring the hovering end of the boarding ramp closer. But the ramp would never reach the ground, not without knocking over some of the houses.

She lifted Niccoluccio, one hand under his knees and the other supporting his back. Again, she depended on her demiorganics to disguise the strain of his weight. He'd let some of his tonsured hair grow back out since she'd last seen him.

The ramp scythed through the air, a meter and a half off the street. Either Joao or Kacienta pushed the shuttle forward. When the ramp was about to pass her, Habidah allowed her demiorganics to take over. She crouched, and leapt onto the edge of the ramp.

Red-hot pain flashed up her calves and thighs. She'd torn muscles. Her demiorganics flashed warnings and numbed her legs. She limped halfway up the ramp, and then slid Niccoluccio to a seat, half-held, half-cradled.

The ramp's retraction carried her and Niccoluccio the rest of the way inside. When the ramp at last shut out the wind, she sent, "Get us away from here."

"I'm turning the stealth fields back on first," Joao answered, pointedly.

Their ascent wasn't smoother than the descent. She braced herself and Niccoluccio against the wall. Her demiorganics fed her some of the exterior camera feeds. The shuttle pierced the clouds. A rain-streaked gray smothered the cameras.

Kacienta came out to help Habidah finish carrying Niccoluccio to a couch. Habidah retrieved an emergency kit from under her couch. A spasm of turbulence nearly toppled her into him. She kept upright, holding onto to his couch for balance while she applied the first medical patch.

Kacienta said, "I'm getting bad déjà vu. Is this why you saved him the first time, so that he could do it all over again?"

Habidah was too busy reviewing the patch's diagnostics. Nothing was right. The bugs she'd planted should've been screaming for her before his condition became this bad.

Kacienta said, "He obviously doesn't know how to use these chances you keep giving him if you need to save him this many times."

"He was being beaten, Kacienta," Joao muttered.

"None of us knows what happened to him," Habidah said, but at the same time, she saw what Kacienta did. His face caked with the dirt of several days. The patch found days-old fatigue toxins. All this had happened recently. There were no signs of malnutrition, dehydration, or starvation older than a week. His hair and fingernails were well trimmed underneath the grime. He hadn't called her when any of this had started to happen.

Joao said, "These people kill each other all the time. Read my report from Strasbourg? Where they herded hundreds of Jews into a house and burned them alive? Terrible violence is an inherent part of their lives. We can't save them all from it. So why do you keep interfering with this guy? What makes him more important than anyone else?"

Habidah didn't need to look up to sense Kacienta watching her, too. They thought they already knew the answer. They were wrong. The truth was that Niccoluccio had been her breaking point.

After making sure that Niccoluccio's condition wasn't worsening, Habidah retired to her couch. The sky was no clearer over the field base than in Florence. The shuttle rumbled through its descent, bouncing Habidah's legs. Her nerve blocks couldn't cut the pain in time. She groaned, and squeezed her eyes. She was going to need a day of rest to allow her demiorganics to stitch her muscles back together.

When the shuttle landed, she scraped together enough contrition to ask Joao and Kacienta to carry Niccoluccio. She staggered down the ramp after them. When she looked up, she saw how the shuttle must have appeared to the people of Florence: a titan, a dragon, steaming and hissing. A hammer from the forge of God, about to fall.

She caught Joao looking at her. Habidah couldn't meet his stare. She had nothing to say for herself.

Joao lifted Niccoluccio onto one of Feliks' beds. He said, "I doubt you're going to send him back again."

"If he asks to, I will."

"And if he doesn't? What are you going to do with him then?"

He hadn't asked because he expected an answer. Habidah didn't give him one. He and Kacienta left her alone while she set to washing him. She ordered the base's fabricators to stitch together an imitation monk's habit. It wasn't until she finished dressing him that she noticed his eyelids flutter.

Soon, he was staring at the ceiling lights. He had to know where he was, of course. He'd spent so many days in this office that he must have memorized every detail. Habidah stood out of sight. She gave instructions to the medical patches to soothe his blood and brain chemistry, and waited until he was fully conscious.

She said, "I hope you know that you're safe."

"I still don't feel hungry," he said.

"We're helping you recover from the effects of starvation. It'll be a day or two before you should eat solid food."

He pushed his eyes back to her. "You don't understand. I haven't been hungry in days. I thought it was a sign, that I was doing the right thing."

"Starving yourself?"

"I shouldn't have left Elisa. I thought I was giving my life to God. That's what I've always tried to do, to get away from myself. It works for a while, but all it does is lead me here. Or the dark."

"The dark?" Habidah wanted, and didn't want, to ask who Elisa was.

"Alone," he said. "Cut off from God. Worse than Hell."

"You're not alone now."

He looked back to her, eyes shimmering. Her demiorganics

warned her of rapid spikes in his brain activity. "You don't understand. All this – this world, all our words, and sensations – is just a skin over darkness. I've felt it. I've been there. It'll swallow me eventually. All of us, probably."

Habidah hesitated while she tried to think of the most delicate way to answer this. "I can't tell you what you experienced while you were being beaten, but you never went anywhere. You never died. Your mind can play very strange tricks on you when it's under duress."

"I know when I've died."

Niccoluccio told her more. After being abandoned by his brother, he'd devoted himself to gravedigging, a profession second only to nursing the sick in its risks during a time of plague.

"I saw the whole world die." Niccoluccio's voice was calm, detached. Good. Habidah's caretaking of his blood chemistry was leveling him out. "After Sacro Cuore, I thought I might be the only mortal left in the world. Even after you found me, I stayed in that moment. All I heard was news of wave upon wave of death crashing upon the shores of Christendom. My brother and his cadre were going on as they always had. They were living in the world as it had been."

Habidah said, "When you got home, nothing you saw must have seemed real."

"Before that. I should have gotten sick long ago. In Sacro Cuore, when all my brothers were dying. I took the same risks that I did in Florence. Tending to the sick, burying the dead."

Habidah echoed herself: "All you wanted to do was help, but you didn't have the power."

"The only thing I could do amounted to very little in the end."

"Why did you call me if you didn't want to be rescued?"

After a pause, Niccoluccio said, "I didn't call you."

"You did. You called me to come save you."

"Maybe in my sleep. It doesn't matter." Niccoluccio reached his hand across the top of the bed. Even after she'd washed him, his fingernails still felt grubby to the touch. He asked, "Do you know often I hoped you were listening?"

She would only have been able to listen if he'd activated his transmitter deliberately. She smiled, but decided against explaining. "I'd like to think that I understand a lot about how you feel. But the need to forever be watched and judged is always going to clude me."

"Don't you have any higher power governing your life?"

"Oh yes. Nobody feels very reverent toward them." After a moment's consideration, she added, "Almost nobody."

"Is there nothing in your other worlds to be reverent about? Ever since you told me that God is not a part of your lives, I've wondered."

Habidah held his gaze for a long moment.

She asked, "When did I ever tell you we came from another world?"

Niccoluccio didn't hide his surprise. "Months ago."

"I never said that. Or told you that God wasn't a part of our lives." The nagging thought that she was missing something caught up with her again. The medical bugs *should* have warned her that he was starving.

Her throat itched. "How many times have we spoken over the past few months, you and I?"

Niccoluccio shrugged. "Many."

She queried his medical bugs. Then she repeated it, but this time bounced the signal off one of her team's communications satellites. That was how she would have gotten the data while Niccoluccio was Florence.

The results looked similar to the first. She could see all of the chemicals she'd poured into his system, but they were in subtly different proportions. They were what she might expect to see rather than what was actually there.

"And did you spend much time thinking over what we talked about?"

"Yes. You helped me find my way."

"Find your way to where?"

He considered. "My way here, I suppose."

She swallowed past her tightening throat. "I think you should get some rest for the time being. I'll be back to talk more about this when you're feeling better."

"I feel fine now."

"Only because our medicine has tricked you into feeling that way."

His eyes flicked over himself, to the bruise creeping down his shoulder and the hollow curve of his stomach. If he hadn't felt alienated from his body before, he would now. "Oh."

Sometimes she didn't think he was sufficiently afraid of her and her people. There was certainly a lot to fear. More than she'd known.

She squeezed his fingers, dosed him with more tranquilizers, and left the office.

Before the doors shut, she queried NAI to see if there had been any change in *Ways and Means'* activities. The planarship had dispatched fifteen more satellites over the past two hours, but it had been doing that at odd intervals since its arrival. A shuttle had dropped toward Shangdu, probably carrying more agents. If the amalgamates were setting her up, they hadn't done anything yet.

There was no way to tell how long she'd been receiving a false signal. And, of course, no way to tell if the information she was receiving now was accurate.

Niccoluccio said he hadn't called her. She'd thought she'd been getting to know him. But it had been just one more way she was being manipulated.

Someone had impersonated him to warn her about the danger in which he'd put himself. If *Ways and Means* had, for whatever reason, just wanted her to pick him up, all it needed to do was allow the signal from his medical bugs to reach her.

It had wanted her to come, but only at a specific time. When Niccoluccio was at his weakest and most vulnerable.

She called Kacienta and Joao into the field base's conference room.

The room felt a lot emptier without Feliks. Kacienta raised her eyebrow, waiting for Habidah to speak first. "I think I've made an awful mistake," Habidah said.

"No shit," Kacienta said, dryly.

"I've let us all be set up." Habidah glanced at the ceiling. There was never any way to tell if the amalgamates were listening. She'd already given away that she knew, though, when she'd queried the bugs in Niccoluccio's system.

She told them what she knew so far: "Niccoluccio claims he never called for a rescue. He also said we've had several conversations that I don't remember. I don't think I've spoken to the real Niccoluccio since he left us."

"I don't understand," Joao said. "Why would the amalgamates care about him?"

"Osia seemed to think that she could still talk us into helping colonize this plane."

"Never," Kacienta said, her voice steel.

Habidah said, "Exactly. I can't think of any other reason why it would fake Niccoluccio's signals, though."

Kacienta tapped her middle finger on the table. "I can't believe the amalgamates could have manipulated you into picking him up the first time. They're not *that* subtle."

Joao suggested, "Maybe they're taking advantage of a situation you created yourself."

Habidah asked, "To do what?"

Neither of them answered. She told the viewwall to show her Niccoluccio. He lay with arms folded above his stomach. His chest rose and fell in languid measure.

A well of disgust pooled in the back of her throat. Niccoluccio didn't deserve any of what the amalgamates were doing to him. Nor did Kacienta and Joao deserve anything she'd done to them, or that might happen because of her decisions. "I'm sorry," she said. "I never should have done any of this."

She had expected them to agree. Joao said, "I doubt

Niccoluccio would think so."

"No matter how I feel about him, he's not that special. There are thousands of people like him on this plane. The only thing that makes him unique is his contact with me." *She* was the reason why all this was happening to him. Someone had turned him, a weapon, into a tool to pry something loose from her. Her thoughts turned at once to Osia. She pressed her nails into her palm, hard.

Joao said, "He's important to you. Important enough to get you to change your behavior. That must be why all of this is happening."

"If *Ways and Means* is hoping I'll cooperate for his sake, it's going to be disappointed." The idea came to her in a flash of heat: "It doesn't make any sense for *Ways and Means* to be behind this."

Joao said, "Just because the amalgamates don't make sense, that doesn't mean they don't have a plan. Meloku could tell you that."

"The last time I thought I spoke with Niccoluccio, I asked him about divine intervention. He told me how to find miracles. I can't think of any reason why *Ways and Means* would want to fake that."

Joao shrugged. "It was trying to mimic him?"

"Why not just let the real Niccoluccio talk to me if that was all?"

"We could ask *Ways and Means*," Joao said. "It's probably listening right now."

On the viewwall, Niccoluccio shifted and stirred. His face twisted in discomfort.

Kacienta was at an angle to see it, too. "Did he fall asleep, or did you tranquilize him?"

Habidah said, "I tranqed him." He shouldn't have been doing that.

She queried his medical patches. There was no response.

She was on her feet before she knew what she was doing. "Excuse me," she said.

The walk to Feliks' office wasn't very long. With the walls displaying their normal gray, it was claustrophobic. When she reached the double doors, she nearly walked flat into them. She placed her hand on them, for a moment unsure what to do. They'd never failed to open. She told NAI to open the doors, and received no answer.

A low rumbling built underneath the floor. It reverberated from her heels to the tips of her teeth.

"Shit," Joao transmitted, somewhere back in the conference room.

"What's happening?" Habidah asked. "Is *Ways and Means* attacking?"

Joao said, "The communications gateway just opened. The aperture is ten times as large as it should be."

"Not possible," Habidah said. The field base was only equipped to open a pinpoint gateway. The projectors that created the gateway weren't intended for anything larger, and the field base didn't have the generator capacity in any case.

"There's an immense amount of power flooding our base." Joao said. "*That's* where the rumbling is coming from. The power feeds weren't meant to handle that much energy. They should have blasted apart by now. The aperture is up to two millimeters. Three millimeters–"

"*Still* not possible," Habidah said. "NAI is lying to you."

The rest of what she said, and anything Joao might have answered, was lost under a blast of white noise. Static flooded behind her eyes, filled her ears. All of her nerves filled with fire and ice, coexisting in the same shreds of tissue – contradictions of sensation ripping her apart.

She couldn't think, didn't even realize she was letting go.

She woke on the corridor floor. She couldn't remember falling. Her inner ear was spinning. If she hadn't seen the walls and ceiling, she would have thought she'd tumbled into the sky.

All she had of the past few moments was a vague sense of discontinuity. Her skin and eyes and scalp burned. She ordered her demiorganics to block the pain. Nothing. She couldn't even be sure the thought had reached its destination. Her mind felt like it had been sectioned on Feliks' autopsy table.

The doors to Feliks' office opened.

Habidah's awareness must have gone again. The next thing she saw was Niccoluccio beside her, trying to lift her. He didn't have the strength. Habidah tried to speak, but she couldn't manage it through the pain soaking every neural fiber.

He was weeping, speaking. It didn't seem like he was speaking to her.

"Dying is one thing. I don't want her to suffer."

The next time Habidah knew anything, Niccoluccio was gone. The fires in her veins were dying but not gone. She had ash for blood. She still felt like she was plummeting. She scrabbled for purchase, but the walls were ice-smooth.

She finally fought to her feet and braced herself between the narrow walls. Her demiorganics finally dampened the pain, but they could do nothing for her sense of balance. The floor quaked as though a crevice had opened and the field base were sliding down into it. Standing, even leaning, took effort.

"Habidah," Joao said, and even in the transmission she could hear his strain. He'd been struck down, too. "He's gone to the communication chamber."

Habidah turned, and, as fast as her jelly legs allowed, ran.

The doors to the communications chamber opened without a fight. She clung to the frame. She found a ruin on the other side.

The chamber's far wall had caved in. It looked as though a catapulted stone had punched through it, leaving an open and jagged gap. Spiderweb fissures spread to the floor. A blinding white light shone through the breach, flash-frozen lightning.

Habidah's demiorganics calmly identified the spectra while the rest of her stared. The wavelengths were that of a raw interplanar tear. The same had shone in the sky when *Ways and Means* had arrived.

Only that had been in dead vacuum. It hadn't screamed. Her demiorganics had already blocked her hearing to keep the pain below her tolerance threshold.

All of the chamber's lights had gone out, but the gateway showed her enough. She saw smashed monitors, broken chairs, and shards of metal and plastic scattered across the floor, all juddering in rhythm with the earthquake. A stream of dust poured on her shoes. A light strip dangled by its power cables, casting a manic shadow across the walls. Joao and Kacienta had beaten her here. They crouched under desks. Kacienta had clapped her hands over her bleeding ears.

The quaking traveled up Habidah's back, clacked her teeth and ground her joints together. She tried taking a step, but a bad jolt forced her to grab for the wall. She could no more move than she could think.

The field base's microaperture communications gateway was buried behind the broken part of the wall. It never should have been able to generate anything like what she was seeing. She shielded her eyes and peered through the gaps in her fingers. Even the amalgamates couldn't have hidden a larger gateway so well. It could have been another interplanar gateway impinging on theirs, but why would an interloper open the gateway exactly there?

Just before she closed her fingers, she caught a glimpse of shadow, an impression of a human form.

Her heart slammed against her chest. She looked again, but even her demiorganics couldn't discern anything through the glare and retinal shadows.

The next convulsion drove her to her knees. The floor beat on her kneecaps, drove a stake of agony through the back of her neck. Her demiorganics blocked every sound, but she swore she could hear anyway. The tear sounded like a perpetual shriek, the air of the world rushing into vacuum – but there was no wind. Pain screamed across her eardrums.

Just when she thought she couldn't tolerate any worse, just when she was about to let go, it stopped.

The shadows that blanketed the room were so deep, and her eyes so mistreated and maladjusted, that she couldn't see anything. She fell to the floor and kept on falling.

28

As soon as Habidah left Niccoluccio alone, a deep and inexplicably calming sleep claimed him. It was like falling into a well. He was no longer joined with his body. His thoughts turned to dreams.

He felt himself, warm and breathing peacefully, at the end of a long tether. The rest of him drifted into a vacuum so deep that it wasn't dark. It was a fog of absence, a lack of color or awareness or sight. He had never experienced a dream like this.

Habidah's image emerged from the nothing, sat beside him. Knowledge came to him suddenly, as though it had been implanted. He said, "You're not Habidah."

"I never have been," she said.

He tried to pull himself up to look at her. The motion was meaningless in this non-space, but he could see her more clearly. "For how long?"

"Sometimes I wonder if you listen at all, or if you only hear what you want to."

"What?"

"I can show you everything. But first I need your pledge that you will help me."

"I can't pledge what I haven't heard."

She nodded, flat in aspect. It was difficult to convince himself that this wasn't her. Every time she spoke, she sounded exactly like Habidah.

She offered her hand. He took it. As if he were being pulled, he felt himself sinking back into his body, lying on the infirmary bed. Whatever drugs and trickery the real Habidah had done to put him asleep were being undone. Habidah said, "Preserve your world, and countless others like it. And you. You're a worthy man, and no one here has done right by you."

"Elisa did," he said, when he was back on his bed. "Habidah did. I haven't done right by them."

"They'll be saved, just like you. In their own time."

"Am I dead?"

"There's no such thing as dead. If there were, you should have died long ago."

He swung his feet off the bed. They still felt distant, half-asleep. Something was wrong. The floor trembled, and dust cascaded from the ceiling. The shaking reminded him of traveling in the black-iron bird, the shuttle.

He couldn't stop moving. It was as though he were being led. Before he knew what he was doing, he padded toward the doors. They opened on their own. Habidah lay on the other side, eyes half-open. She'd fallen, her knees bent at an awkward angle.

His breath quickened. He stooped beside her and tried to carry her as she had once carried him. His arms gave out. He muttered under his breath. He'd carried heavier bodies. He realized, too late, that he was crying.

"She'll be herself again, soon enough," Habidah's voice said. He couldn't see her anymore, but he knew she was listening. "She can no more die than you or anyone else."

The other Habidah, the real Habidah, stared through him. She couldn't focus. Her mouth opened and closed. Niccoluccio knew pain when he saw it. "Dying is one thing. I don't want her to suffer."

After he spoke, Habidah went limp in his hands. The shadow of agony faded from her expression.

"Who are you?" he asked the voice.

"I'm your shepherd."

He set his hand on Habidah's cheek. Before more than a few seconds had passed, he felt himself being pulled again.

If he was on a leash, it was a gentle one. He felt nothing physical. But he couldn't ignore the impulse to stand.

His feet led him down the unearthly hall. The next door opened on its own. An immense light poured out, blinding him. He raised his hand, but the glare crept between his fingers and under his eyelids.

The world around him was shaking as if about to rend itself apart, but he had somehow settled in a pocket of peace. He saw the walls buckling, felt the vibrations in the tips of his toes, but that was all that disturbed him.

"You can still turn back. I've been guiding you, not forcing you. If you would willingly take your life in old Florence back, you can still have it."

Something in the back of Niccoluccio's mind tickled. She'd asked him this question before.

He took a step into the room, and then another. There was no longer any tether. At first, he looked at the floor, but finally he lifted his eyes to the light and held them there. They seared into his vision, bubbled violet blind spots on top of each other. The damage he was doing to himself didn't seem to matter. He was falling apart anyway.

And, soon, he was gone.

PART III

29

On the day Niccoluccio arrived at Sacro Cuore, three monks came to the gates to meet him. They stood stern and straight, hands folded. Their tonsures made them seem like triplets, all of a different age. Niccoluccio's hair was little protection against the autumn wind. He didn't know how the monks kept from shivering.

Of all the seasons Niccoluccio could have chosen to arrive, this was perhaps the least propitious. Soon, winter would hide the roads. Whether he wanted to stay or not, he would be trapped. For a long time, he felt frozen to the seat of the wagon.

The monks had seen the wagon coming. Its long, bouncy trip up the road from the lay village had gone slower than Niccoluccio could have walked. Still, the offer to ride had been welcome; Niccoluccio had walked most of the rest of the trip. The wagon's driver nudged him, and he hopped down. His heels stung, still sore. He took tremulous steps, trying not to limp. He couldn't keep the anxiety out of his gait.

They said nothing as Niccoluccio approached. He bowed deeply, and still they kept their silence. After a while, he rose, cheeks flushed. He wondered if one of these men was Prior Giannello. Embarrassing himself in front of the prior would be a fine way to start here.

At last, the slender monk in front treated him to a narrow smile. "I am Brother Lomellini, the novice-master. I will shepherd you through your first year."

Niccoluccio swallowed and nodded. He knew better than to waste noise on pleasantries around Carthusians. He wouldn't have trusted himself to speak regardless.

As one, the monks turned back toward the gate. Niccoluccio's feet had become tree roots. He felt the cold earth through his thin soles.

He looked back. The driver was pretending not to watch. Winter's breath had turned the forest into gray varicose veins, as unpleasant to look at as to feel. The sky behind them, though, was still the same sky that shone over Florence, upon Pietro and Elisa. He was at once reminded of all the turmoil in his heart since he'd met them.

The sun shone cleanly through a halo of thin, translucent clouds in a manner Niccoluccio could not recall seeing outside of paintings. And yet, in an instant, he knew he had already seen it. He had been here before.

He had never set foot here, but everything was as familiar as if it had come out of his dreams.

Dreams, or memories.

That took away the choice. It had already been made. He looked back to the monks. They had not gotten too far yet. By the time he caught up with Brother Lomellini, he couldn't tell if they knew he had hesitated. They, of course, said nothing. They moved with precisely the same measured step.

Half a mile up the trail, Brother Lomellini said, "You can still turn back, if you'd like. Your old life in Florence waits, if you would have it."

"I believe I've made that choice."

Lomellini looked to him, but Niccoluccio couldn't explain what his words had really meant.

Some immense force had blown a hole in the wall ahead of Niccoluccio. The strange, smooth surface had ripped and crumpled like paper, and all of the light of the heavens poured out of the fissure. Still using his hand to shield his eyes, he stepped toward it.

Heat rippled across his skin. He couldn't pull back. He didn't particularly want to. He had never felt calmer.

He couldn't feel his toes. After his next step, his heels disappeared. His knees were a thousand miles away and dissipating. He was flying apart limb by limb, joint by joint. It was neither pleasant nor unpleasant, nor did he want it to stop. All motion in his chest ceased. He no longer breathed, but neither was his breathing stifled. Then his sight went, and his hearing, too.

But that wasn't the end of it. He unraveled thought by thought. His memories were falling out of him. They were untangling from the jumbled skein of his head, getting straighter, getting simpler. How much easier it all seemed in these nice, straight lines.

The void might have been nothingness, but it was also open, and free. His memories kept unkinking, longer and longer, narrower and narrower. Sensations, ideas, images seemed very far away, all equally abstract. He remembered things that had never happened, things that merely could have happened. At first, he thought it was his imagination, the last dreams of a dying man.

This morning, during Niccoluccio's twelfth – fifteenth? twentieth? – spring at Sacro Cuore, he stepped out of the refectory early and stretched his arms. He'd spent so much of the week gripping his shovel and saw that his fingers tingled. New red buds were appearing on the eldest of the cherry trees, but the other two were too young to fruit.

He paced the cloister, taking his time, waking his muscles. His wrists were still sore. The infirmary's back wall had begun to buckle, and its northwest foundation had settled into the earth. The decay had gone unnoticed for too long. Though it had been a very long time since someone had gotten sick, if it happened, they would need the infirmary in good repair.

Next up, he supposed, would be the library. The shelves

were sagging again. He'd forgotten how many years it had been since he'd last repaired the library.

Niccoluccio turned right, stepped between the chapter house and the calefactory. Out back, a stretch of knee-high grass led to the forest. He came here, out of sight, to find his peace. Years ago, he'd built a bench with a backrest. Here he could watch the squirrels and birds and, on rare days, hare and deer. He could sit still as a statue and never startle them.

Of course, he couldn't always have his solitude. Today, he had hardly sat before Brother Rinieri rounded the corner, wooden cups in hand. Rinieri offered one. Water. A peace offering for disturbing his isolation.

Long ago, the German monk, Brother Gerbodo, had been Niccoluccio's closest companion. As he'd aged, though, Niccoluccio had discovered the value in more placid company. He and the old and philosophical infirmarer often sat together for hours.

Sometimes, Rinieri questioned him. It didn't feel like a breach of the monastery's silence. Conversations with Rinieri felt like an extension of his own thoughts.

Rinieri said, "Prior Lomellini asked me a question today. He wanted to know if there was anything that I, as infirmarer, would change about the way Sacro Cuore is run."

"You might as well ask a novice. You haven't made use of the infirmary for years."

"Then suppose I were to ask a novice," Rinieri said, pointedly. For all the time Niccoluccio had spent here, it was easy to forget that so many of the others had been here longer. "Would you have anything to say?"

"I cannot remember a time in which Sacro Cuore was more in God's grace."

"I certainly remember when things were worse. The trouble is in elucidating the difference between what we did then and what we're doing now."

"That must have been years before I arrived. Nothing in Sacro Cuore has changed for as long as I remember."

"We rebuild every memory as we remember it," Rinieri said, looking to the cloister. "Nothing quite existed in the past as we remember now."

Niccoluccio followed his gaze. Sacro Cuore looked exactly as it had the day he'd arrived, as it always had. He shrugged.

Rinieri said, "One of the limitations of being human. Not only do we forget, but we forget how much we've forgotten. We fill the gaps with nostalgia and fantasy and lose the ability to tell the difference."

"God will make the truth plain in the end," Niccoluccio said.

"For those willing to see it." Rinieri leaned against the backrest. Niccoluccio folded his hands in his lap. A persistent itch troubled the back of his neck. After a while, he glanced back.

The wind that touched Niccoluccio's cheeks was warm as any, but snow covered the cloister and the trees were bereft of leaves. The infirmary and library both seemed dirtier and meaner. Mounds of fresh-dug frozen earth lined the churchyard. The infirmary door hung open. Niccoluccio knew what he'd find inside.

He held up his hand. "Please. Stop."

When he gathered the courage to look, Sacro Cuore was as it should have been. He breathed out. It took him a moment to realize that Brother Rinieri had taken his hand and guided it back to the bench.

He looked down. Rinieri folded his fingers inside Niccoluccio's.

Rinieri said, "It takes a lot of work to make the world the way it should be."

"It's the only kind of work worth doing."

"You've put a lot into Sacro Cuore. You should be proud."

Niccoluccio looked to the library. "There's always more to do."

Maybe the void wasn't so empty after all.

Someone was picking through his memories. Weaving them in new shapes. Adding to them.

There was a pattern in all this entropy. He saw, in the not-memories, blackness between starry expanses, balls of poison gas and liquid metal seas, spiraling cities encircling blank skies. Other potential lives touched the edge of his thoughts, each aware of him in the periphery of their thoughts.

They were all shades of himself. Every single one of them, with different guises and divergent histories.

In the midst of this strangeness, he instinctively latched onto the familiar: toward Sacro Cuore. A Sacro Cuore, at least.

Just looking at it, he knew it was a life created, constructed. An unfamiliar concept appeared in his mind. S*imulated.*

He had no voice, but that couldn't stop him from speaking. His words rippled down his chain of thoughts and into the void. *Who did this?*

No answer. Niccoluccio got the strange impression that this wasn't because the void had no answer, but rather because there were no words that could have provided one. Whatever else there was of the universe when sense and form and reason were stripped away, there was at least a mind. Minds, on their most intimate level, didn't communicate with words.

Niccoluccio's feet took him around the cloister without conscious effort. They knew which stones might trip him, where to turn. He could have strolled blinded.

He laid his hand on the infirmary door as he passed. He always did. It was the only time he allowed himself to remember plagues and visitors from other worlds. Which parts were might-have-beens and which the definitely-weres eluded him more often than they should. He'd lost track of time, cause and effect. Time and determination were mortal concerns. Sacro Cuore had become what it was intended to be, as St Bruno and St Francis had always meant a monastery to be: a place to cleanse and soothe a man's soul in preparation for Paradise.

There was no peace in the monastery greater than his bench behind the calefactory. It was the one thing he could remember that had changed since he'd arrived – the only thing that he, personally, had changed.

Every week, Rinieri joined him. Sometimes they conversed, even argued, but more often – as today – sat in silence. Niccoluccio hadn't felt so close to a man since Pietro. Their love was a kind of tenderness that, when it existed in the outside world, could not survive long. It hardly seemed to matter that Rinieri was older. Niccoluccio felt old himself, older than he should have.

He sensed time marching on, but rarely its effects. It was the same with most here. For instance, their former prior, Prior Giannello, hadn't died in office like his predecessors. When his time should have ended, he'd retired, hobbling off to become Sacro Cuore's librarian. He spent his days shuffling between his books and his personal garden. His was the kind of life Niccoluccio aspired to.

Niccoluccio had not known Giannello well before his retirement. Giannello had struck him as firm but kindly, as generous in spirit as his replacement, Prior Lomellini, was severe. But Niccoluccio had only just graduated from his novitiate when Lomellini was elected prior.

When Niccoluccio entered the library that afternoon and found Giannello reading, the back of his head tickled. Part of him was sure Giannello shouldn't have been there. He had to be misremembering something.

Giannello had pulled his chair closer to the light of the window. A hidebound manuscript rested on his hip. He looked up at the interruption, his question unasked.

Every year, each monk was given a selection of five books to pore over, read and reread. Niccoluccio could quote his from memory. He was anxious, insofar as he was ever anxious, for something new. "It's time for me to change my texts."

Giannello heaved himself out of his chair. "Lomellini has full reading lists for the other brothers, but only gave me one book for you."

Niccoluccio tried to hide his surprise. Lomellini held himself to standards as high as Sacro Cuore's other monks, and was never unorganized. "Well – I can start with that one."

"This one has no annotations or commentaries, so be sure to use a guide to aid your interpretation of the text."

"What manner of guide?"

Brother Giannello tapped his chest. "This one."

Niccoluccio accepted the manuscript from Giannello's shaking hands. Curious, he retired to a seat by the open door and opened the book. He frowned. It wasn't illuminated, nor bound particularly well. It hadn't been written by a saint or a luminary of the order, but an ordinary Carthusian monk. He didn't recognize the author's name. The text was a long and winding account of his journey through a winter forest, alone and starving, pursued by wolves.

He mouthed each line, word for word, remembering. Then he set the book aside. "What a grim little tale," he said.

"He came as close to death as any mortal could," Giannello said. "I think it's important to recognize the value of his experience, even if he wasn't a saint."

Niccoluccio said, "I used to think about death all the time. That doesn't make me a sage. This monk may have believed he was about to die, but he never faced it. He survived to write about it." He drummed his fingers on the book's cover, trying to hide his agitation.

Some inner voice was screaming at him. He hadn't heard from it in a long time, but now it was insistent, telling him this book didn't exist. It was an abstraction of a real thing, real memories, conjured by a power he hadn't yet comprehended. That voice was easy to set aside. The book had taken this form only because he was in a library. Had he been in his cell, it would have been a dream. Had he been in the church, it would have come as one of Lomellini's sermons. Someone wanted to shake him, to force him to confront this.

But the object in his hands had weight and texture. The binding was imperfect and believable. Easy enough to set little doubts aside when the raw physicality of everything else was so convincing.

When he'd returned to Sacro Cuore, he'd gotten used to setting the voice aside, anyway. Dreams or memories. Did it matter? Easier to rest. He got the idea that he'd been allowed to rest. Perhaps until now.

Giannello asked, "How large do you believe the universe is?"

Niccoluccio blinked. "Does this have to do with the book, or are you starting a new conversation?"

"Follow me a little ways along this trail. Do you hold with the view of our brothers that the Earth is alone in a cold and perfect celestial sphere? Or might our world have company somewhere?"

Years ago, in another lifetime, a friend of Niccoluccio's had once described an infinite, multiplicitous cosmos to him. Consciously or not, that had been the view he had hewed to since. It was too dangerous an idea to speak of openly, though. "It doesn't matter what I believe," Niccoluccio said. "What exists, exists."

"Precisely. There's a gulf of difference between belief and fact. You know more about these facts than most of the brothers."

Niccoluccio shifted. "I don't understand where you're going."

Giannello smiled, kindly. "I won't make you say anything more if you don't want to. But an infinite cosmos would raise a number of questions. Many of them applicable to the text sitting on your lap."

Niccoluccio tried to put his irritation behind him. He was embarrassed by his lack of emotional control. He'd worked very hard on that. Something in the book had brought all of the failures of his youth back to him.

"Go on, then," he said. "I won't interrupt."

"Consider the scale of the cosmos. There's no number you can attach to the worlds out there. They're infinite."

"I don't know that they're infinite. I was never told that."

"They're infinite. The combination of molecules on any one world being limited, it therefore stands to reason that each world has an identical twin somewhere. Countless twins. In an infinite cosmos, no one world, or person, is unique."

Niccoluccio said nothing. He'd pondered the same things years ago. He had always assumed his thoughts were private.

"Infinite Earths. Infinite Christendoms. Infinite Sacro Cuores – many identical and many subtly different from each other." Giannello raised a finger to point at Niccoluccio. "Infinite young monks named Niccoluccio Caracciola."

Niccoluccio protested, "I'm not that young."

"I've lost count of the number of years that have passed since I came to Sacro Cuore. I'm older than any of us has a right to expect to be. Who's to say that, on one of those other infinite Earths, old Prior Giannello couldn't have died in his sleep and dreamed himself waking up here?"

"Say what you like," Niccoluccio said, still embarrassed to be discussing this. He didn't know what he would say if any of the other brothers heard this. But he couldn't stop himself from listening.

"Of all the infinite worlds, there must be some so identical as to have two Prior Giannellos, just different enough that one dies in his sleep and the other wakes up. If the one that wakes has the memories of the dead man, has anything been lost?"

Niccoluccio said, "There would be one less mortal man among the worlds, however infinite they were. His friends, too, would miss him."

"Back to the book in your lap. On a million million of those worlds, that young monk would have died. Frozen to death without a burial, eaten by scavengers. But on one world, something extraordinary might have saved him. A miracle. A rescue from an outsider, a friend he never could have known he had. And all the memories of those million million dead men would still be within him."

"That would be too much responsibility for any man to bear."

"Even if a minuscule fraction of Brother Niccoluccios in that situation survived, a fraction of an infinity is still infinite. If he ever died, he would always have a twin out in the cosmos who still had all his memories. Even if he tried to commit suicide, his soul could never be extinguished. No one's ever could – not his or Giannello's or anyone's. They would always, somewhere, keep going."

Niccoluccio massaged his forehead with his fingers. He didn't want to think about this.

Gianello said, "We poor mortals are good at tricking ourselves into believing what we wish. As children, we convince ourselves that we'll live forever and never change. Call it Heaven, call it Paradise. We all seek an eternal release from change. Very rarely do men or women see that the only thing that never changes is suffering. The multiverse is an endless cycle of rebirth and suffering and loss. No one can escape it by dying."

Gianello turned his heavy-lidded eyes back to Niccoluccio. "You've been chasing death for too long. It's time someone opened your eyes to what is really happening to you."

"I think I've heard enough for one day," Niccoluccio said. That screaming voice was becoming too much to ignore. He closed the book, stood deliberately, and placed it back on its shelf.

Gianello didn't stop him when he walked away.

The next morning, it was the winter again, and everyone in Sacro Cuore was dead.

Niccoluccio had spoken with the other brothers only yesterday, but they had been dead for months. He'd buried them himself. His hands were callused from digging.

He trod through the cloister, listless. Snow fell sullenly. All his graves were buried under a cold blanket. The silence that had been so comforting had become pervasive, threatening. He cleared his throat just to make noise. His hands stung from the cold, which at least kept him from feeling the blisters.

He stopped by the open door to the infirmary. The odor kept him from going any farther. It had gotten so bad that he stopped bringing any of the brothers there to die. There was nothing there now, or anywhere else. He knew he should pack and leave. Report to church authorities. But he'd done that before. All it had gotten him was a long and circuitous route back here.

That voice didn't need to scream any more. It just spoke. He listened.

He closed the door. On the other side, Brother Rinieri waited for him.

Niccoluccio had buried Rinieri two weeks ago. This Rinieri looked as he had been years ago, just yesterday, when they'd sat behind the calefactory. Rinieri offered his hand. He led Niccoluccio on their walk around the cloister.

Rinieri said, "No matter how far you travel across the planes, a core part of you formed here. You can't escape it even if you manage to forget it."

"None of what I've seen is real," Niccoluccio said. "The past few years have all been figments from someone else's imagination."

"You knew that even then, and that didn't stop you from living it."

Niccoluccio looked dolefully at Rinieri. Rinieri held his free hand to his chest. "I'm no figment. I've been brought here for you, but in all respects I am the same man who was your friend when the pestilence struck."

"I don't understand how. He died."

Rinieri just looked at him, one eyebrow raised, as a school teacher would. Niccoluccio swallowed. Of course. Infinite worlds, infinite Sacro Cuores – infinite Rinieris, as well. Whatever power had pulled him to this void between the cosmos had taken Rinieri as well, or recreated him. There didn't seem to be any meaningful difference.

Niccoluccio looked down at Rinieri's hand. "In my real memories we never held hands."

"These are not just memories. This is just as real to you and I as anything you've experienced before. Now you've seen more than one Sacro Cuore."

"Why wait so many years before telling me the truth?"

"We've let you have some respite. You have a lot of work left to do."

"What work?"

Rinieri glanced at the sky, though Niccoluccio couldn't see anything but gray. "There are, unfortunately, a number of ways to travel from one plane of the cosmos to another. People build empires that span the planes. Left to their own devices, they'd grow and grow, subsuming billions – trillions – of worlds in their wake."

"What do billions or even trillions matter against infinity?"

Rinieri smiled thinly. "The power that brought us here lives in the space between the planes. Your friend Habidah would tell you that there's no such thing as a space between the planes. That's how well hidden it is. Its task is to ensure that no single force grows strong enough to subsume the multiverse. You might call it a king, exercising divine dominion. It aims to protect the diversity and wellbeing of its worlds."

"But why?"

"If it hadn't acted, nearly every world like ours would have been dominated by a foreign power long ago. The space between the planes is hidden, but not impossible to find. Given time to grow, they would spill over into this place. From here, it's possible to not just change one plane, but to change all of them, with a thought. Any power who managed it could claim all the multiverse."

"You haven't answered my question. Why does this power want to 'protect' other worlds?"

"Wouldn't you, if you were in its place?"

Niccoluccio hesitated. "That depends on what I would have to do."

Rinieri looked to the dormitory and the dead patches of gardens. "You tend to your gardens, pulling weeds before they can overrun it. You would still do it even if you didn't depend upon the vegetables. It's your obligation to keep it healthy."

"And by 'weeding,' you mean...?"

"I do mean destruction. But destruction on a far smaller scale than these empires would inflict. Remember what Giannello taught you. In an infinite cosmos, there is no such thing as death. Everyone that dies still lives elsewhere. This empire of Habidah's cannot be allowed to change that."

Niccoluccio looked back down at Rinieri's hand. For the first time this morning, he allowed himself to believe that this was real – that this was the same Brother Rinieri he'd buried a lifetime ago. A trillion Rinieris, and more, lived out in the worlds Habidah told him of.

Even in an infinite cosmos, it was a miracle that they had been brought together again. Niccoluccio only knew one force capable of miracles on such a scale.

The void poured a thousand years into Niccoluccio, a battering like standing underneath a waterfall. A million of his different lives touched the periphery of his consciousness. A thousand years ago, he'd lived through each of them. Somewhere in the planes, he was living through it again.

Niccoluccio sat on his bench, admiring the stars.

The stars at Sacro Cuore were a broth of luminous cloud. They were brighter than they had seemed before. Not many of the other brothers came out at night. They were convinced that the dark air was a source of contagion, just as Niccoluccio had been until only a few years ago.

Under Brother Giannello's tutelage, Niccoluccio had learned to see things differently. Of all the things Giannello had taught him, the germ theory of disease had shocked him the most. It had been the first to throw his certainties into disarray. After that, everything he'd learned had surprised him, but little stunned him. He no longer lived in the world he'd been born in. He had no ground left to be uprooted from. The theory of gravity, of relativity, of the multiverse – a new idea every week.

He hadn't gone along with it well. He'd found some way to fight against each new discovery. The illustrations in Giannello's texts were too abstract and unreal to believe. Blobs of organelles suspended in jelly, bound by fat. Balls of flaming gas like giant alchemic vials, turning light elements into heavier elements. Easier to believe in the angels and kings and dog-headed gazelles that usually danced into the margins.

Even the very first one, the germ theory of disease, Gianello had had to show him using strange contraptions, tubules full of lenses. Gianello never explained the contraption, but Niccoluccio knew he hadn't made them himself. They stole into the refectory after breakfast to peer into the wash basin. It had taken two hours of increasingly loud argument to convince Niccoluccio that the little animals he saw were in the water rather than on the surface of the lenses. A dozen times, he'd held it up to the light, trying to see.

They'd still been arguing when they left. All the brothers in the cloister had looked to them. Niccoluccio reddened. They'd broken all manner of rules by going to the refectory by themselves. The other brothers might think they were sneaking food. He and Gianello would hear from Lomellini.

Gianello paid them no mind. He hobbled back into the library. When they were alone, Niccoluccio asked, "Do all the others know these things, too? Or is it just you and I?"

"They'll know if they're called to know," Gianello answered.

"Why me?" Niccoluccio sat heavily beside the books. "Why, of all the people in the monastery, in all the world, did you choose me to show this to?"

"You're a good man, in a good position to help."

Niccoluccio shook his head. He waved to the lone book still sitting atop the shelf, the story of his other life. "Any of the characters in there would be better. Habidah. Her team. You must have some purpose in mind. With them, at least, you wouldn't have to go through the trouble of teaching so much." Everything he'd learned so far would be basic to them. And he still had so much further to go.

"The anthropologists came from a different place, with their own preconceptions," Gianello said. "It would be difficult to convince them. And, uniquely among all of us, you ended in a place where you can influence them."

"I see," Niccoluccio said. And he did. He'd been chosen because Habidah had chosen him. It was his connection to her that made him important. But he didn't say that.

Since then, he tried to spend at least a few minutes each night alone on his bench. Every night for the past several weeks, he'd come out here and watched. Each night, he found something new to appreciate or to wonder at. Each day, it became more and more intensely personal.

He was being prepared for something. He would rather think on anything else. There was so much in the multiverse worth reflecting upon, more than he could comprehend in another five lifetimes.

He could say goodbye when he wanted. He didn't know when that would be, except that it would happen. Even in a multiverse in which no one truly died, things always changed.

This night was so quiet that he could hear Rinieri from as far away as the cloister. Niccoluccio had determined, through careful questions, that Rinieri and Lomellini were the only other monks who seemed privy to Giannello's secrets. Lomellini spoke rarely. The rest of the brothers lived in their own private worlds.

Rinieri watched the stars with him for a little while. After a while, Rinieri held a shadowed hand to the stars. "It's worth protecting, isn't it?"

"I can't imagine anything that could threaten this vastness."

"Until you came back to us, you couldn't imagine much of what you've learned."

Niccoluccio considered that. He still couldn't imagine much of what he had learned. The stars out there, the microbes in the soil, and the other planes of the multiverse were nothing he could touch. There was a deep well of stubbornness still in him that made him argue with every new revelation Gianello shared with him.

Rinieri was used to long pauses in their conversation. He let Niccoluccio be. After a while, Niccoluccio said, "Yes, it is worth stopping."

Rinieri lowered his hand, but kept his eyes on the stars. "There's so much variety out there. And so many forces that would make everything the same if they could."

"You mean Habidah's people. Her empire."

"They don't know about us. We want to contact them. You will deliver a message."

Niccoluccio folded his hands in his lap. Brother Rinieri would give him all the time in the multiverse to consider this, he knew. But he didn't need it.

Niccoluccio asked, "What happens to you when I leave?"

"The simulation, the power that sustains our being here, will disappear."

Niccoluccio blinked and looked around: at the forest, at the calefactory, and finally at Rinieri. "All this will just... cease?"

"Remember what you've learned. Nothing dies. And I, and all the others, will still exist somewhere in the multiverse. It can be no other way. In some other world, on some plane, there will be another Sacro Cuore just like this. Whether it's real or another simulation, it doesn't matter."

"How long have you been here?"

"Three thousand, eight hundred and nine years. Or so I've perceived, while I was being prepared for you."

Niccoluccio stared. He had stopped counting his summers after the sixtieth, and that had been a long time ago. "The others?"

"Only as long as you. They're on their own journeys. They'll continue them elsewhere when this simulation ends."

"All this – the sky, the forest, this monastery, you – just for me."

"If you tell Habidah that you're to deliver a message, she'll help you get it where it needs to go."

Niccoluccio nodded, slowly. "You could have spoken with her. Given her the message directly."

"I would ask you to trust in our decisions, but I think it better to ask for more. Have faith in me, and have faith that you're being led in the direction you need to go."

"Faith was what brought me to Sacro Cuore."

"Both times, it turned out to be where you needed to go."

Niccoluccio wouldn't let go of Rinieri's hand. He didn't want to go. Nothing in Paradise was supposed to change. The eternal life Rinieri had promised him was nothing like the Paradise that all of Niccoluccio's devotions had promised him.

Yet he couldn't say he was unhappy. And he had some time yet.

He gradually put himself back together, thought by thought, stitching sensations and memories. He felt a winter night's breeze against his cheek, touched the stars in the sky above Sacro Cuore. Diamond-sharp, they cut his fingertips. A hundred nights whirled around him, then a thousand, ten thousand, a lifetime.

Some of it wasn't hallucination. He felt his hands, fingers curling, grabbing nothing. His breath. His foot. His legs moved in slow rhythm.

He walked on a cold and hard floor. Heat like sunlight burned on his back. An immense light shone behind him. The reflections on the far walls were so bright that he raised his arm to shield his eyes. But already the light was dimming.

He stepped through a jagged-toothed gap. Dust fell on his scalp. The floor shook underneath his soles, though, as before, he was somehow in a pocket of calm. Shards of metal danced across the floor. Behind them, bodies. Two people huddled under desks. Another, nearer, was face down. He didn't need to look closely to recognize Habidah.

He rushed to her. When he turned her over, he found her face pale and drawn tight, like she was struggling to wake. She was breathing. Her face was screwed up, her eyes shut. Her cheeks and forehead bled, cut in several places.

He cradled her head into his lap. Across the room, her companions were stirring. She was trying to speak, but didn't have the breath.

"I learned so much I don't know how to begin telling you," he told her. "I'm back. I understand now." His voice trembled. He didn't know how much he should say, and how much she would grasp. This, at least, would be clear: "I'm here to start making things better."

30

In an instant, the noise and light and shaking ceased everywhere but inside Habidah's head.

The wall monitors were dead. Shadow spun about her. A light streamed through the still-open door, shrouded in cascading dust. The ceiling nearest the gateway had crumpled and split.

What they'd just witnessed should have been impossible – and what little of it *was* possible should have killed them. The dust fell onto her cheeks, into her eyes and mouth. Coughing, she tried to push onto her knees. The spinning floor wouldn't allow her. She needed to get over to Joao and Kacienta. Her head kept getting away from her. A firm hand grasped her shoulder.

Someone was holding her head. Her reflexes were so deadened that she couldn't strike at whoever it was. She spun, and ended up grasping her captor for support. He helped her to her feet.

Niccoluccio. He looked like he knew exactly what he was doing.

She could step where he steered. He half-carried, half-supported her toward Kacienta, and then lifted her, too. He staggered, but somehow managed their weight well enough to hobble toward the door. Habidah glanced back at Joao. He lay limp but breathing.

The lights in the corridor still worked. She got a better look at Niccoluccio. He looked no older than a minute ago, but he'd changed. Somehow he'd put on weight. His cheeks were a healthy red. He wore the same monk's habit, but it was freshly laundered. His tonsure must have been shaved again, because it was far neater than it had been a minute ago.

She was reminded of the differences between the signal she'd received from the bugs in his system, and the one she'd bounced off the satellites. It was almost as if he wasn't the same person, but a facsimile, the little differences the too-obvious clues of a poorly composed mystery.

Niccoluccio helped Habidah and Kacienta to seated positions against the far wall. "I didn't want any of that to happen," he said. "I would have stopped it if I could."

Habidah didn't have the strength to answer. She focused instead on climbing to her feet, using the wall as leverage. Niccoluccio returned to the communications chamber. He came back far dustier, with Joao supported on his shoulder. He helped Joao slump beside Kacienta.

Signals from Habidah's demiorganics were starting to make sense again. In infrared and other spectra, he seemed an unaugmented human, perfectly normal for the plane. Joao was more alarming. His body temperature was half a degree too cool. His breath had gone thready, like Feliks in Genoa.

Kacienta sat with her back against the wall and her knees bunched to her chest. She said, "I don't know how you got inside our heads, but–"

"It wasn't me," Niccoluccio said.

"–we won't play any part in whatever you're trying to do to us, to this plane–"

"Kacienta," Habidah said. "If he's inside our heads, he's already won."

With effort, Joao forced himself to his feet. Niccoluccio tried to help him up. Joao shrugged it off. Without a word, Joao hobbled down the hall, into another room.

Kacienta nodded at Habidah. She told Niccoluccio, "You've been in her head since you met her. That's why she couldn't stop thinking about you. Why she always had to go so far out of her way for you."

Habidah glanced between them. Every muscle in her throat wanted to tell Kacienta that she was wrong, that her decisions had been her own – but, of course, if she had been compromised, she *would* believe that. She couldn't trust her memories. Her experiences were no longer any guide to reality.

Niccoluccio looked at them sadly. "We're not so difficult to manipulate that we need our reason stripped away. All it took was a few words whispered at the right times..." He shrugged.

Kacienta asked, "Who are you working for?"

"I'm sorry. I don't know who it is."

Habidah's skin felt like ice.

She looked to the half-jarred door, and then back at Niccoluccio. She felt like she was seeing him with new eyes. She asked, "How long have you known?"

"Years. On this side of the gateway, though, not that long."

From the other end of the hall, Joao said, "No question we've asked either of you has gone anywhere before."

He had returned holding a slender, silver tube. It was one of the field base's firearms, meant for emergency defense. It was capable of annihilating all three of them at once, leaving only ash and a whisper. Joao aimed the weapon at levelly at Niccoluccio.

Joao said, "I don't know if this will help, if you're in all of our heads or just Habidah's, but I'm going to do everything I can to stop you."

Niccoluccio said, "You don't even know what I'm here to do."

"You and she can talk about it all you like in more secure quarters," Joao said. Habidah's stomach lurched when he waved the weapon at her, too. "I doubt it's going to do any more good than it has before. But I know *I* don't want to hear you anymore."

"More secure quarters" turned out to be Feliks' office. Joao led Niccoluccio and Habidah in at gunpoint. When he left, Habidah didn't need to check the door to know that it was sealed.

332

This time, it was Niccoluccio's turn to walk unsteadily. His hands shook as if he'd only just realized what he'd done. He fell into a chair beside Feliks' desk.

Habidah's body was back under her control. The only sign of trauma left was a racing pulse. Her demiorganics had recorded the whole incident. Something had spiked electrical white noise into her nerves, disrupting her motor cortex, overwhelming her senses and pain receptors. She doubted it was a coincidence that she'd gotten the worst of it only when she'd been in a position to stop Niccoluccio.

The office was loaded with a number of discreet sensors. Images of Niccoluccio's skeleton and circulatory system streamed through her visual cortex. Data flowed into her memory.

In most respects, this Niccoluccio was the same man who'd been here not half an hour ago. His fingerprints were identical. Same with microscar tissues, retinas, brain activity patterns, every subtle pigment in his hair and skin. Even the map of his veins matched in ways that would be impossible to mimic. Habidah doubted even the amalgamates could reproduce a body so precisely.

But there was more.

The bugs she had placed in him had gone missing. His muscle and body fat percentages had changed radically. Niccoluccio had become a well-fed man apparently accustomed to heavy labor. The muscles appeared entirely natural, growing in the usual ugly lumps and knots and badly healed tissues. He had shreds of grass in his clothes and a lingering odor of sheep manure. Analysis of his breath and stomach suggested that his most recent meal had been bread and milk, though she knew for certain that he hadn't eaten in days. His hair had grown and been cut repeatedly. His skin not only had all its old scars, large and small, but also several new ones. The cadence of his voice had changed subtly; he had more of a rural Italian lilt.

Yet, in spite of all of these signs of time passing, he had not aged. No deterioration of eyesight, reflexes, or metabolism. He didn't have a single gray hair.

"I know what you're trying to figure out," Niccoluccio said, as though he could see the sensor scans. "I can just tell you. This body isn't mine. At least it didn't used to be. It was built from scratch, molecule by molecule, after my old body was torn apart."

She stared. The fact that Niccoluccio even knew the word *molecule* was yet more evidence to say that he wasn't the same man. If what he said was true, then Niccoluccio, the Niccoluccio she had known, had died when he'd stepped into that gateway.

He said, "I was taken apart and put back together. But I'm still the same man you found and saved. The body is only a host for the soul."

It was every transplanar anthropologist's duty to understand and appreciate the prevailing beliefs on the planes they visited. But that didn't mean Habidah had to believe the same things Niccoluccio did – or, in this instance, even respect them.

She said, "There is no soul. Your mind, your brain, is a physical object. There is nothing else. If someone or something disassembled your body, then they did the same thing to your mind. That was everything you were. You're not the same person you used to be."

Niccoluccio said, "I feel every bit the same."

"You would, if you'd been constructed to feel that way." Niccoluccio frowned. "You know things you shouldn't. Your thoughts have been changed in ways you could never recognize. You could even have been made to believe what's changed has always been a part of you."

"I spent a great deal of time away from here. All of the things I know about you, and your people, I learned at Sacro Cuore. I was there for years. Lifetimes." He shifted. "Even after all of it, I still have trouble believing it. There was so much of it. And so different from what I grew up with."

There was no point in plunging into his fiction. "You were given *memories* of learning. You were given a body that matched what you believed you experienced after you stepped through the gateway. No time passed here."

"It passed for me. It was real."

"How do you know that?"

"The same way you know who you are."

Habidah gave up. She didn't want to tell him that she wasn't confident in her own memories, either. "What did this to you? The amalgamates?" Even as she asked, she couldn't believe that. The amalgamates had never revealed that they'd possessed technologies capable of rebuilding a person so completely. If they had, eradicating the Unity's plague would have been as simple as wishing it gone.

Niccoluccio surprised her by saying, "I don't know."

"I was sure you were going to say that it was God."

"God is a mystery to me. He's more of a mystery now that I know more about the planes." Niccoluccio held up his left arm, and brushed his fingers over his skin. "What happened to me is a mystery as well."

"You're not even going to question why you're here?"

"I know why I'm here."

Habidah waited.

Niccoluccio met her gaze evenly. For the longest time, he didn't say anything. He looked away first. "I don't believe this is something I should simply announce all at once. In Sacro Cuore, it took me years to understand."

Habidah blew air through her teeth, and turned back to the desk. If he wouldn't be of any help, she had other avenues of investigation to pursue.

Joao may have made her a prisoner, but he hadn't tried to – couldn't – block her computer access. NAI still didn't answer, but its lower-level programs continued to function. She'd only been locked out of the controls to the office door. She turned her attention to the communications chamber. Few sensors remained in working order, but their records of the moments before the incident showed a sequence of impossibilities.

The gateway had opened on its own. It hadn't been projected

from another plane, or anywhere else. The aperture had seemed normal at first: micrometer-width, sized for communications. The sensors recorded a pinprick of light, too small to be seen by even augmented human eyes.

Then it had inexplicably started widening.

The field base's generators reported that their power output hadn't changed at all. At the same time, the power *received* by the gateway apparatus had increased tenfold. It kept going up. Somewhere between the generators and the gateway, an enormous amount of energy had flooded into the system.

Habidah turned her attention to the gateway. All gateways had a destination. Pictures of the aperture in multiple spectra flooded into her. Visual, infrared, ultraviolet, radio, and even gamma – all a hot mess. Every gateway she'd seen before had offered some hint of its destination. Atmosphere leaking through, stray radio signals, muted colors.

Here, she found chaos. This was unlike any gateway she'd seen or heard of. It didn't seem to lead anywhere.

The amalgamates were the only powers she could think of that could accomplish anything remotely similar to what she'd seen. *Ways and Means* remained in high orbit. If it was setting her up again, then there was no harm in calling it. If there was another power at work – then the amalgamates were the only creatures she knew of who could do something about it.

And yet she hesitated to call them.

She pulled up the field base's communications records. NAI sent status updates back to their university on a regular basis. The last had been two days ago. The next was scheduled for tomorrow. Assuming that NAI didn't fake those status updates, she had at least that long before the amalgamates noticed something awry. If *Ways and Means* hadn't noticed anything already.

Ways and Means continued to send shuttles, none headed in their direction. It hadn't directed any of its visible scanners or satellites to focus on the field base. It was simply carrying on with its subjugation of this plane.

And that left Habidah with more of a dilemma. She didn't want to speak with Osia or *Ways and Means* again, let alone alert them to this.

She needed to learn more before she made up her mind.

She said, "If you can't tell me everything at once, why don't you start with whatever you can?"

31

Meloku didn't need to sleep often, but when she did, dreams arrived fast and ended quickly. She was dreaming a dream of angels and planarships when an impulse from her demiorganics jarred her awake.

Her eyes fluttered against the darkness. She instinctively switched to infrared, but she was too scattershot, too confused, to make sense of the blobs around her. She groaned and rolled to her side. Endorphins and serotonin-killers flooded into her, but they couldn't throw off all the effects of chemically induced sleep. Will-o'-the-wisps danced in front of her eyes.

She snapped, "What?"

Companion said, "The watchdog programs you left at the anthropologists' field base are contacting you."

"Sorry," Meloku said, sheepishly. There was no point in lying, in telling Companion that she hadn't meant to be irritable when she obviously had. "What's happening?"

Companion said, "The signal was cut off mid-broadcast."

That caught Meloku's attention. With effort, she sat and threw off her covers.

The messages hadn't been long. One watchdog had mentioned an electrical disturbance in the communication chamber's power grid. Another program she'd left to watch for shuttle activity had detected a seismic disturbance, but nothing that fit the profile for a landing. And then the signal had simply ended mid-datastream.

Meloku called the field base, and queried NAI. NAI replied that everything was normal. No earthquakes, no shuttle landings, no power spikes. Habidah was in Feliks Vine's office with her pet monk. Kacienta and Joao were fucking in Joao's quarters.

Her watchdogs also reported no abnormalities. "Explain the last truncated transmission," Meloku demanded.

The watchdog that had reported the power anomaly replied, "False alarm/minor power spike tripped threshold." The next chimed in, "Minute buckling in underground support occurred directly behind sensor/triggered alarm. Compensated/corrected."

The response came five milliseconds too late.

The explanations didn't rest well with her, but the delay was a warning flag by itself. There was no good explanation for it. Her watchdogs operated with the precision of a pulsar. She hadn't thought Habidah capable of subverting them.

Companion asked, "Shall I advise *Ways and Means*?"

Meloku tried not to take too long to answer. The most likely explanation, of course, was that it was a test – another way for Companion and the amalgamates to gauge and judge her. Companion kept telling her that she needed to suppress her innate need to take charge of a situation without arranging for backup. She needed to learn to subordinate herself.

"At once," she said. "Tell *Ways and Means* I suspect criminal tampering. Keep it apprised of anything new I discover."

She called up several counterintelligence programs locked away in her demiorganics' deep memory. She'd never used them outside of training. The amalgamates approved their use only in high-stakes security crises. Anything that might threaten the amalgamates' plans for this world certainly qualified as a security crisis, particularly if Meloku's old colleagues weren't as naive as they'd seemed.

She could feel the black programs in the back of her mind: cold and dark, like beads of ice. They numbed every part of her they touched. Thoughts that touched them shrank back, withered like desiccated roots. To them, she was also an enemy. Agents like her weren't allowed to glimpse anything of them lest she learn too much about how they functioned. She shuddered and pushed the programs on their way.

The black programs took no prisoners. At once, their preliminary reports returned. They injected themselves into the field base's NAI and dismantled it from the inside. They devoured NAI's brain from the inside out, digesting it. They puppeted its remains. To anybody interacting with NAI, it would seem to speak and answer exactly as before. That was just an imitation, though – a viper wearing the skin of a grass snake.

Her black programs hunted and consumed her watchdogs in the same manner, considering them already compromised.

Meloku's frown deepened. The black programs had found nothing. The situation was exactly as her watchdogs reported it. Habidah and her monk remained in Feliks' office, and Joao and Kacienta at their labors. There had been no alarms, no abnormalities, no detected infiltration other than her own.

The reported power spike was too suspicious to ignore. Yet the gateway apparatus itself was powered down, cold. Even the air was undisturbed.

She slumped, frustrated. None of this was adding up. On a whim, she checked the timestamps of the reports.

The first report from her black programs had come back five milliseconds late.

Adrenaline pounded into her chest.

The remainder of the reports had come back exactly on time, but that couldn't hide the glaring error in the first. She'd been told that the black programs had never been bested by any power encountered. This was either one hell of a test, or she'd just brushed up against something the likes of which the Unity had never encountered. Either way, her response should be the same.

"Contact *Ways and Means* at once," Meloku told Companion. "Highest priority. Our project has been compromised by an extraplanar power–"

A spear of white-hot energy shot between her eyes, through the center of her brain. The spear drove upward, twisted, and sheared her mind neatly in two.

The next thing she remembered, she was on the floor, tangled in blankets, pain like needles screeching across bare nerves. She felt as though she lay on sheets of nails, that her fingernails were being pulled out, and her skin had ignited. She must have screamed. She heard pounding, as if at a great distance, at her door.

"Mistress! Your Holiness!" It was Aude, her cook and chambermaid. Her knocking grew increasingly desperate. She tried to knock the door down. She wouldn't be getting in. Meloku had secured her door with field projectors.

Meloku choked. Her tongue wouldn't work, and tasted like moldy copper. She cast her blankets off. A flood of dizziness overwhelmed her. She couldn't swallow. She was about to vomit, she realized; a wholly alien and disorienting sensation. She hadn't thrown up since she'd been a toddler, when her first augmentations had been installed. Her demiorganics should have clamped down on that.

She tumbled to her side and heaved her dinner across the floorboards. She coughed viciously, and spat. Her mouth tasted of malarial swampwater and citrus. She ordered her demiorganics to block all but essential sensory input. Pain and nausea continued to rack her body. She tried again.

"Please open the door, Your Holiness!" Aude cried.

The pain was fading, at least. "Go away!" Meloku shouted, when at last she could. She sat against her bed, shivering. Her knees and elbows were bruised from the seizure. At least she seemed to have avoided biting her tongue.

She had definitely come under some kind of attack. She tried to call up records of the seconds before the whiteout. Again her demiorganics refused to answer.

"I'll go and get help, Your Holiness," Aude said. "In God's name, I swear to you that I can help."

Fury seized Meloku's throat. "Go die of the pestilence!" she rasped.

Aude's bare footsteps thumped down the stairwell. Meloku rested her head on her knees. Her mind felt empty, sluggish. "Companion," she said, aloud. "Help."

She waited. Silence. A slowly widening pit began opening in the center of her stomach.

She kicked her soiled sheets away. Whatever had happened, it had been enough of a shock that her demiorganics seemed to have been jarred out of contact with her nervous system. The pain was nearly gone, and still nothing answered her. She looked about, lost, and gave the mental command to switch to retinal infrared. Her bedchamber remained dark.

Her pulse thudded against her ears. She spat again, but her mouth was too dry for the taste to come out. She'd had her first demiorganics installed when she was five. She'd never been without *something* answering her thoughts since. No wonder she felt like she couldn't think. Part of her was missing.

She counted another ten seconds before wailing in panic.

A minute later, she was on her feet, leaning on the window shutters. Her whole body shook. Adrenaline seared her chest. She could hardly keep from hyperventilating. Her pulse beat fast, making her head spin. Her body hadn't been unregulated for all of her adult life.

Despite all of that, she had to try to think, to figure out what had happened. She had to stay calm, take stock of her resources. She asked her demiorganics for a medical diagnosis. Her cheeks burned when nothing happened. She set her hand on her chest, took deep breaths.

Companion couldn't be gone for good. That just wasn't going to happen. She'd never been alone since it had been installed.

OK – the first thing she knew for sure was that her demiorganics were nonresponsive or dead. Possibly for good. How could that have happened? The first option was that her demiorganics, and Companion, had been remotely shut down by a hostile force. The second was that they had been damaged, again by a hostile force. The shock she'd experienced certainly seemed to indicate some kind of nervous system trauma.

It had all happened when she'd investigated the event at the field base. Her counterintelligence programs had been compromised. The reports they'd sent back to her could also have been compromised.

That meant *she* could have been compromised, too. Any virus so advanced would have little trouble crossing the synaptic barriers between her demiorganics and her organic brain, and rewriting her like a piece of software. Just like she'd tried to rewrite the field base's NAI.

She couldn't assume that that was the case. She had to keep moving. The only way she could do that was by believing she was still herself.

She needed to communicate to *Ways and Means*. A shuttle could pick her up in minutes. She dug her field kit from under her bed before she remembered that all of the equipment she'd brought with her – the field projectors and weapons and sensors – had been made to interface directly with her demiorganics. They wouldn't function for an ordinary human being.

She opened the shutters and looked to the stars. Her demiorganics sent status updates to *Ways and Means* every few minutes. When it stopped receiving those, it would realize something had happened. A shuttle should have already been on its way to meet her.

That was assuming, of course, that whatever power had attacked her hadn't anticipated that. If it was as powerful as it seemed, it wouldn't have any trouble subverting a satellite and faking the updates she sent to *Ways and Means*.

She stared at the stars, hoping, willing – praying – for one of them to come for her.

After ten minutes, her jaw hurt from clenching. Voices clamored at her door. The door shook with the force of their pounding. The security field shone a gentle blue.

Meloku instinctively ordered her field generators to power down. Nothing. She groaned, restraining frustrated tears, and walked to the door. The field generators, at least, could be turned off. From the other side of the door, the field was impenetrable, but the protection only went one way. She waved her fingers a centimeter in front of the projectors, disrupting the particle stream. The field flared violet and vanished.

The door cracked open; a man fell through. Without infrared, it took too long to recognize him. Galien. Aude stepped over him.

"Well?" Meloku asked, as if nothing was wrong. The quaver in her voice gave her away.

Aude dropped to her knees. "Forgive me, your Holiness. You were screaming. Your door – it was as if a demon were holding–"

"I suffered a vision," Meloku said, and paused to try to figure out where to go from there. The pause lingered. "It was a messa... it was a revelation. I am not ready to talk about it yet."

Galien picked himself up. He dusted his legs and eyed her. As superstitious as these people were, they could also be cynical enough to surprise her. Galien always spoke on two levels. "Shall I fetch a physician?" he asked. "Prepare medicines?"

"There is no physician alive that can cure a terror of God," Meloku said. "Go."

Aude swiftly departed. Galien took a step as if to follow, but stopped. "I have never known you to struggle so dearly with your reasons." With her lies, he meant.

"I *did* have a vision," Meloku said. Maybe a touch of the truth would soothe the anxiety from her voice. "About terrible deeds in a faraway place."

"Outremer?" Galien ventured.

"Farther."

"Prester John's kingdom?"

"Only idiots believe in Prester John in this age," Meloku snapped. "There is no far eastern Christian kingdom attacking the infidels from their opposite borders. It's all steppe horsemen." She put a hand to her forehead. She was getting a terrible headache.

Galien caught her pained breath. "Perhaps we should call that physician after all."

"I have no desire to be bled dry or have my piss sniffed. This is..." She searched for words. "This is a spiritual crisis, not a crisis of the body." She still had hope that, at any moment, the sky would open with reentry sonic booms.

Galien set a hand on her shoulder and steered her toward her bed. Before Meloku knew what had happened, she was seated next to him. He kicked her vomit-soiled blankets farther under the bed. "It certainly smells like more than a spiritual crisis."

Meloku didn't know what had possessed her to allow him to lead her other than sheer distraction. For the first time, it occurred to her that she didn't have her defenses. No tranquilizers or diamond-tipped darts, no augmented muscles.

"It's extremely suspect for you to be alone with me," she stammered. "I want you to leave."

"Your Holiness." Galien shifted his grip to her hand, and tightened it. "My future saint. I am extremely indebted to you for elevating me out of that refuse pile of a scribe's office. But my livelihood is tied to yours. Everything that you made me to be depends upon you staying healthy in your body and in your wits."

He was the kind of person she'd chosen to keep close. It shouldn't have surprised her that he remained driven when she least wanted him to be. He asked, "What really happened here? An intruder? A guest overstaying his welcome?"

"Nothing so vile."

Galien placed his free hand on Meloku's forehead. She jerked away. "Certainly not a fever. You're cold as the moonlight."

"I truly did have a vision," Meloku said.

"Of what? People are going to hear what's happened. Tell me what you saw."

She pushed herself a little farther, but his hand restrained her. She said, "By God's blood, I won't allow you to take charge of me."

"Very well, Your Holiness. *Please* tell me what it was you saw."

"The shadow of a demon, bent to devour the world. Swallowing angels as it advanced."

"Very prosaic," Galien said.

"This is not a play. I do not vomit for theatrics."

"Are you sure?" Meloku glared and he relented, or pretended to. "I know you would go to many ends to make a point, but I don't know what point it is you're trying to make here. It would help me serve you if I knew."

"All I need from you is time to interpret my dream."

"It's a dream, now, is it? There's a distinct difference between visions and dreams. Take care to choose the right word when you tell others about this."

She opened her mouth to snap some threat, but stopped. He had a point. She heard no shuttle. She was stuck with the natives. She had to manage them well. They were her only resource.

Her only resource to accomplish what?

To discover what had happened to her. To alert *Ways and Means*. To find out just what was going on at the old field base. To be with Companion again.

As daunting as that list was, it helped her organize her thoughts. For all that she'd learned about herself in the last few minutes, she'd held onto at least one thing she could be proud of. She wasn't going to give up.

She pulled her hand away from Galien and stood. She strode back to the foggy window. She said, "This isn't the kind of vision I would feel comfortable sharing with the mob."

Galien asked, "Then what profit is it?"

"I didn't think of the profit while I was having it."

Galien let his silence speak for itself.

Meloku smiled, briefly. She underestimated the natives on

346

occasion. "You never believed in me, did you?"

"I believe God wants you to prosper. Everything that's happened so far has worked in your favor."

"And this doesn't match the pattern of my previous revelations."

"To put it that succinctly, Your Holiness – no."

"Just because there isn't a pattern, that doesn't mean there isn't a plan."

"*That* sounds like the lady I knew," Galien said. "Then what is your plan?"

"I don't feel like sharing it." she said. "I'm still piecing it together."

"Forgive me if I should say that sounds like a contradiction."

"Watch yourself. I do not forgive easily, at this moment above all others."

He didn't answer, but she didn't wish to turn to see his expression. She held a hand to her temple. In spite of this outrageous headache and everything else, she was starting to recover herself. Setting goals, no matter how distant, kept her focused.

She just wished she could speak with Companion. Whatever had happened to it, she hoped it was going to be all right.

Everything on her list could be accomplished at once if only she could contact *Ways and Means*. Whatever had done this to her seemed intent on keeping her from that. It had attacked when she'd been about to warn *Ways and Means* of the severity of what was happening.

Her first priority had to be to contact *Ways and Means*. But how to reach it when she had no way of signaling it and the enemy was likely impersonating her signals?

She would have to create an event too big for *Ways and Means* to ignore. It would have to be something caused by transplanar technology. Anything natural, even a large fire, could be explained away by her impersonator. She ran through a mental list of the equipment she'd brought with her. None of her tools would work, and none of them held power supplies large enough for an explosive discharge that would attract *Ways and Means'* attention.

She *did* have tools like that at the field base, however. All of her personal equipment would only respond to her demiorganics. The same wasn't true of the field base, where equipment was meant to be passed from person to person. Overloaded, the field base's generators could lay waste to hundreds of square kilometers.

At the field base, she'd find whatever had done this to her.

She shuddered. Her other choices weren't great, either. *Ways and Means* had other agents on this world, but the nearest, in Paris, had left, abandoning the French court as uncontrollable. She didn't remember where the next agent was. She'd counted on her demiorganics to keep track of that.

She said, "I need to prepare for a journey."

"Leave Avignon? Just when you've got the city pinched between your fingers?"

"I never did this for me. It was all for a higher power."

Galien reached over her shoulder and pulled the shutters closed. "I have a hard time imagining a city more suited to the glorification of God than Avignon. If He would have you in another city, the opportunities would have to be great."

"I'm not traveling to another city. I need to find the demon in my dream."

"And where would it be?"

She hoped to disarm him with precision: "Forty-five miles south of Lyon."

Galien scoffed. "I thought you said that you had dreams of faraway places. I grew up farther than that, and walked here." Still, he sounded relieved. A trip across France was hardly the crusade he'd imagined.

"It's far away to me," Meloku said.

"You traveled here from Constantinople, did you not?"

Meloku didn't answer.

"Your Holiness?" he asked, and for the first time tonight he sounded unsure.

"I need help to get there." Without demiorganics, she couldn't trust her abilities in a fight against Habidah, not alone. "Mercenaries. Horses. Food and fodder. However much my money will pay for on short notice. We'll collect benefices from the cardinals."

"You're certain this will all lead to the profit of God?" Galien asked, doubtfully.

"In the end."

"The French will hardly welcome an armed party traversing their territory."

"The French can't stop the English or the bandits already ravaging them."

"For as much as you have the people and prelates of Avignon under your power, I doubt many of them will be enthusiastic about your expedition."

"You can't talk me out of this."

"I'm trying to keep you from throwing out all God has given you so far. Your reputation–"

She turned sharply, and let a little bit of her carefully rebuilt control fail. "My reputation is not worth dogshit if it will not help me in my time of need. And neither are you people." Right then, she would have turned Avignon into a pyre if only it would catch *Ways and Means'* attention. Galien paled. It suited him.

He nodded and silently ducked out the door. Meloku, blood cooling, walked to her bed. It took a while to even her breath.

There was no point in going to sleep now. Without her demiorganics to regulate her, she might sleep for eight hours. She couldn't afford that. She couldn't miss anything, not even when it seemed all there was to do was think and wait and watch.

The sky outside her clouded window shone still and silent. Without her enhanced senses, it was all dead to her.

32

Habidah slept unevenly, as if her demiorganics hadn't fully come back online. She drifted between nightmare and awareness, staring half-lidded at the monsters lingering in the shadows in the office ceiling. She rolled to the other side of the medical bed. Abruptly, she sat and ordered the lights on.

According to her demiorganics, she'd been out three hours. Lights or no, Niccoluccio still slept deeply. Habidah slipped off her bed and padded to him. His face was slack, a mask of death. She was almost tempted to check to see if he *had* died. But his chest rose and fell. He was more peaceful than she had ever seen him.

Not that she had seen him often.

She sat on the nearest bed. Breathing or not, he might as well have been dead to her. She still had no cause to say he wasn't dead. By his own account, his body had been dismembered and a facsimile constructed in its place. Whether this Niccoluccio believed it or not, his old self was dead. This was a memory sent to manipulate her.

And yet, looking at him, she couldn't convince herself of that. He seemed a changed man, but not a different one. He'd been almost apologetic about coming back, which certainly fit him.

She rested her forehead in her hands. Part of the problem was that she'd never really known him to begin with. There had been times that, in spite of their limited contact, she'd felt closer to him than anyone on this plane. That had been a fraud, too. The only time she'd spoken with the real man had been when he'd physically been here. The other conversations had been with whatever force controlled him now. Likely the only reason he seemed familiar was that she was accustomed to the same liar.

Then again, she hadn't been the only target of these deceptions. Niccoluccio's master had sent messages to him as well, impersonating her. Why would it have needed to do that if the old Niccoluccio had never been important?

Her belly rumbled. She wondered if Joao or Kacienta would bother to bring food. She folded her legs and stared at Niccoluccio. By the time morning found them, she was no closer to untangling the knots in her stomach.

Niccoluccio blinked drowsily. Habidah fetched him a glass of water from the lab sink, and showed him to the closet lavatory. When he returned, Habidah said, "You said you were going to save this plane. From us, presumably." She could think of nothing else that posed so much danger to his world, not even his plague. "How do you mean to do that?"

"It's not just this plane," Niccoluccio said. "Your, well… It's…" He was clearly struggling to explain. He spoke as though he knew everything, but he'd had to put it in words until now. "Your masters threaten many other planes, as well."

"Masters. You mean the amalgamates."

"Yes. I don't know that much about them, but I do know they're too large for a human imagination to comprehend. They're far beyond us."

"Not so different from *your* master, then," Habidah said.

"Perhaps not," Niccoluccio said. Habidah caught two tacit admissions. First, that Niccoluccio's master was at least on the level of the amalgamates. Second, that it *was* his master. "The creature that sent me isn't God. I know that. It lives between the planes."

"Between the planes" was, as Habidah understood transplanar physics, a nonsense phrase. There was nothing "between" the

351

planes, either physically or mathematically. It was less real than an imaginary number. She glanced at the ceiling. Joao and Kacienta were certainly listening.

"The force that sent me aims to save the planes from each other," Niccoluccio said. "Some interplanar contact is unavoidable. But when large, powerful groups spread across the cosmos, swallowing plane after plane, they threaten the diversity of the multiverse."

"The Unity is large, yes, but it still only encompasses a few hundred thousand planes."

"The amalgamates don't know about the space between the planes, let alone how to live there. What do you think they'd do if they could?"

Habidah didn't have to think. "They'd try to invade it."

"From there, controlling other planes isn't a matter of force. It's a matter of will. In that space, there's no such thing as single planes, but shades of them that all blend together. Your amalgamates would be able to expand themselves unto infinity."

"I don't understand. How could anything change an infinite number of planes?"

Niccoluccio chewed his lip as he struggled to find the words. He seemed increasingly uncomfortable, like the words he searched for weren't his own. "You and I exist on a single plane. We can only affect things here. That space, between the planes, is different. It's easy enough to change the laws of every plane from there. On infinite planes, if you wanted. If you were intelligent enough, you could do it in very subtle ways, too. Your amalgamates could code copies of themselves into every plane that ever was or will be. And eliminate anything they found uncontrollable."

Now it was Habidah's turn to be at a loss for words. These concepts were so far beyond the man she'd known that it was increasingly easy to believe that she was talking to a stranger. "I can't imagine any single being is capable of that."

He said, "Managing the multiverse takes an intelligence

beyond our capacity to imagine."

"You might call it divine," she said.

She'd meant to bait him, but he answered, "Yes."

"And yet you don't believe that your master is also your God."

"I believe that there are shades of being that you and I could never understand."

Habidah cupped her fingers around her mouth. "Even if all this is true, the amalgamates shouldn't be of any concern to your master. They don't have any idea about this space."

"They will."

"Your master is worried that, if the amalgamates manage that, they'll become as powerful as it."

"No. It isn't like that. It protects the multiverse from influences that would change or dominate it. Otherwise, it leaves the planes alone."

"Why?"

"It aims to preserve the multiverse as it is, in the infinite diversity of the planes."

"At the very least, that's what it wants you to believe about itself."

"It could be lying. I can't pretend that there's no chance of it."

"But you don't believe that it is."

Niccoluccio said, quietly, "No."

Habidah leaned toward him. "You would never believe anything else if that's the way it programmed you."

Niccoluccio nodded. "You already know the amalgamates have lied to you. You would stop what they're doing if you could. Given a choice between trusting them and trusting an unknown, which would you choose?"

Her stomach knotted tighter. Rather than answer, she asked, "You said earlier that you had several conversations with 'me' before we found each other again. But I only remember having one with you. At least until I got the call to come save you."

Niccoluccio said, "I know that wasn't you."

Habidah only just resisted the impulse to roll her eyes.

"I mean – *why* talk to you so many times, but only once to me?" She'd gone over her demiorganics' recording of their conversation a dozen times. The more she'd gone over it, the more recalcitrant and withdrawn the false Niccoluccio had seemed. He had wanted to lead her somewhere, but hadn't wanted to say too much else, either.

He shrugged, and just looked at her. He didn't know. Habidah had an idea.

Niccoluccio was sweet, but he was naive even for his world. That meant easier to manipulate. Outsiders like her and her team were a lot cagier than a naif like him. Niccoluccio's master had exposed itself to them as few times as possible, giving them fewer opportunities to note any inconsistencies. It had been, at least for a while, afraid of being caught.

She asked, "How do you intend to stop the amalgamates?"

"I don't know. I just have a message to deliver."

"What is it?"

Niccoluccio shrugged. He didn't seem to know, or he was pretending not to.

Habidah said, "It's got to be more than words. Words wouldn't need subterfuge. I'm guessing the reason the amalgamates haven't beaten down our doors is because your master is keeping this all hidden. It's sending them false data, faking our regular messages."

Niccoluccio only looked confused. After a moment watching him, Habidah believed that he didn't know what she was talking about. She pressed: "If all you needed to do was *tell* the amalgamates something, you could do that right now, through the cameras."

"I have to be in their presence, yes."

"And then what will happen?"

"I have in me... it's a kind of thought. An idea. I dreamed about it. It was gorgeous. It had symmetry, colors, layers like rivers crashing together. I can still picture it, but I can't describe it." He opened his mouth as if to say more, but halted. He seemed even more confused.

The brain scans Habidah had taken last night had found nothing unusual. They could have missed something. Or the technology she was trying to root out was so subtle that it had piggybacked into his brain without significantly disrupting his nervous system. *Ways and Means* might have scanners sensitive enough to detect it.

Habidah's skin chilled. Exposing *Ways and Means* to whatever was inside Niccoluccio was exactly what Niccoluccio had asked for. If Niccoluccio was carrying more than a message, but a weapon – a virus – then he would need some subtle means of introducing it. Like picking it up from a full brain scan.

She asked, "How do you intend to deliver your message?"

"I don't know. I was never told."

"By calling up *Ways and Means* and asking for a trip to orbit?"

"No," he said, with sudden certainty.

"So if I can put this all together – you need to get to *Ways and Means* without it knowing anything like what you just said."

"Your amalgamates are not kind souls. What do you think they would do to me if they knew everything I had just told you?"

"Annihilate you from orbit," Habidah said. "Or, at the very least, dissect your mind from a very far distance."

"In either case, my message would go undelivered. I need to be close."

Habidah waited a long time before speaking again. She didn't know how to begin asking her next question, or if she wanted to hear the answer. She glanced to the ceiling. If Kacienta and Joao were listening, they'd given no sign.

Her throat almost seized around her next words: "Is this the first time your master has tried to interfere with the Unity?"

"I wouldn't think so," Niccoluccio said.

Habidah should have felt something right now. Her body and mind had been through so much in the past twelve hours that there wasn't much left to wring from them. This, though, was different.

This was worse than freefall. This was walking up to the

precipice with one foot over the edge. A moment of perfect clarity before the last step.

She said, "Your master can change the laws of physics on the planes. In very subtle ways, you said. It *could* create threats that don't follow the rules the rest of us understand, that are impossible to fight or even see clearly. If it wanted to attack the amalgamates, it might start by removing their base of power. Their human population. Nobody might realize it was an attack."

Niccoluccio looked pale and tired. His eyes were reddened. He looked like Habidah imagined she had in Messina, Genoa, and Marseilles.

He said, "I'm sorry."

Habidah stood, paced twice before him like she was about to say something, but no words escaped her. Words wouldn't have done anything.

Finally, she asked, "What do you have to be sorry about any of it for?"

"I know how much suffering it's caused you and everyone on your planes. I lived through the same."

"Your master murdered billions of people. With billions more to come."

"What do you want me to say?" Niccoluccio asked. "Your amalgamates wouldn't save my world."

Habidah let her gaze rest on the ceiling. Her hands trembled. She didn't know why, or what she wanted to do. There was nothing *to* do. Not to Niccoluccio, at least. "I *never* tried to justify the amalgamates. I worked against them however I could. I saved you. You sound like you're defending your master's actions. Are you?"

Niccoluccio opened his mouth, about to speak, but didn't answer. Habidah extracted a wisp of satisfaction from that.

The door whisked open. Habidah turned, saw Joao, but she didn't have time to move before Joao was halfway across the office.

Joao shoved Niccoluccio out of his seat and against the

wall, and pinned Niccoluccio there with an arm against his throat. Niccoluccio made no effort to defend himself. Joao said, "I don't know why you felt that was a good way to get my attention, but you've got it."

"Don't be this stupid–" Habidah started.

Joao drew his fist back. Habidah stepped forward, grabbed Joao's arm before he could swing. Joao yanked away, and drove his elbow into her stomach.

Her demiorganics blocked the pain, but all at once she couldn't breathe. Someone grabbed Habidah's arms. She hadn't heard Kacienta enter. Habidah had been robbed of the strength to pull free. An oxygen deprivation warning tone from her demiorganics trilled at the edge of her hearing.

Joao pulled his arm back again. Kacienta yanked Habidah backward. Habidah didn't see the blows, only heard two smacks and one heavy thump. They sent shots of adrenaline down her arms. Her demiorganics finally overrode her instinctive nerve blocks and forced her to breathe. She sucked air through her nostrils.

This was enough.

Habidah raised her foot, twisted, and stomped on Kacienta's shin. Kacienta's demiorganics didn't blot out the pain in time. She yelped. Habidah spun, pulling Kacienta with her. Kacienta lost her balance and her grip. Habidah shoved her into an examination table.

Habidah took two quick steps and slammed her heel into the back of Joao's knee. He buckled as easily as if she'd broken the bone, falling into Niccoluccio. Niccoluccio tottered. Habidah shoved Joao sideways. He collapsed. He had exhausted his energy just getting here.

Niccoluccio's bottom lip was swollen. Blood dribbled from his nostrils. Habidah put her back to him to shield him. Kacienta had just about recovered. Joao wiped a strand of saliva from his chin, breathing hard.

When Joao caught his breath, he asked, "Don't you understand what he just told you?"

"I'm trying to," Habidah said.

He leveled a finger at Niccoluccio. "He's destroying everything back home. He killed my parents. He killed Feliks. He's killing me. He's the reason the amalgamates are even doing this to his plane."

Habidah said, "It's not him. His master."

"What's the difference?"

Kacienta let go of the table. She hobbled to them, keeping her weight off her foot. Habidah remained on guard. Kacienta said, "We can take him right to the amalgamates. They'll know how to dissect him."

Habidah said, "You're not thinking this through." It sounded awful even to hear. Of course they weren't, not in a moment like this.

Joao struggled to find the strength to stand. His energy had fled him in that one violent burst. Kacienta asked, "What do you want us to do? Ignore him?"

Habidah shook her head. "No – *think*. It's counting on us taking him to the amalgamates. Niccoluccio can't signal *Ways and Means* to get picked up. Not without getting blasted apart. We still have a shuttle. We can get him to *Ways and Means*. That's why his master sent him back to us."

Joao glared at Niccoluccio. "Is that right?"

"I don't know what it wants me to do," Niccoluccio said. "I was never told."

Habidah said, "It wouldn't need to tell you."

Niccoluccio peeled himself from the wall. His face was flowering bruises, but he seemed only a little shaken. He said, "You keep talking about me like I have no control over my actions."

Joao said, "You *don't*."

Habidah said, "And you wanted to beat the hell out of him anyway–"

"*Stop*," Niccoluccio said. Habidah was so surprised that she did.

Niccoluccio's fingers trembled as he felt the blood on his lips. "I don't need defending. I would be as furious. I was when

I found out that your amalgamates could have cured our pestilence on a whim. In Sacro Cuore, there were weeks when I don't think I could have spoken to any of you."

He looked at each of them in turn. His voice was stuffy from the blood, but he was at least intelligible. "I cannot believe that I have no choice in all of this. I wasn't selected at random. My master could have sent an automaton in my place if all it wanted to do was destroy you. There's something it wants me to have a say in."

Joao said, "You *are* an automaton and you don't even know it. The ant carrying poison back to its hive has no idea what it's being used for."

"If there's no way for me to prove that I'm not, then believe as you want."

Joao at last rose. "It's not that I *want* to believe you're under the power of a genocidal monster," he said. "It's that I *can't* believe anything else."

"If I'm an automaton under the thrall of a force so mighty and cunning, then there's nothing you can do. None of us measure up to it. But..." Niccoluccio paused, drawing it out. Once again, Habidah marveled at how much more eloquent this Niccoluccio was than the one who'd stepped through the gateway. "...If I'm right, and we all have some element of choice left to us, then what we do matters. You might as well act as though the latter is true."

Joao told Habidah, "You were right. There's no point to beating him. I doubt there's anything capable of feeling it left in there." He glared between her and Niccoluccio, and hobbled out of the room as fast as infirmity allowed him.

Habidah turned to Kacienta and stared, daring her to leave and lock them in again. Kacienta shook her head, muttered, "It doesn't matter." She went to Feliks' laboratory sink, started to wash her face.

Habidah sat hard on the nearest countertop. Niccoluccio gingerly touched the bruises blossoming between his eye and his temple. The bleeding, at least, had stopped. Habidah broke the silence. "You really believe you lived years since the last time you saw us, don't you?"

"I do, and did."

Kacienta finished with the sink. She dried her face with her sleeves, gave Niccoluccio a hateful look, and limped out. When Habidah checked, her demiorganics reported that the doors had been left unlocked. She couldn't quite feel relieved.

Niccoluccio opened his mouth, but Habidah cut him off with a wave of her hand. She didn't want to hear it any more than the others did. He stared at her for a long moment. Habidah could only meet that stare for a few seconds.

Then she, too, left him.

33

Niccoluccio lost track of the amount of time he spent alone afterward. He leaned against the wall, trying to recollect himself. Then he sat facing the corner. Nothing helped him calm the voices raging in his head.

In Sacro Cuore, meditation had come easily. He'd earned that through practice. Here, he couldn't stop replaying arguments in his head, thinking of the things he should have said or would like to have said. More, there was a song – or snippets, at least, of a music he couldn't remember – playing, repeating itself deep in his head.

He reached to caress the top of his cheek and winced. He hadn't had arguments like *that* back in Sacro Cuore. Some of the novices had been so hot-blooded, but not him. The pain was worse now than in the moment.

The muscles in his arms burned. His pulse still pounded in his throat. He stood and paced, weaving between tables. So much here was alien. He doubted that the tables were just beds, as Habidah had told him. The counters and desks lining the walls were filled with equipment and proboscises whose purposes he didn't care to guess at. The first time he'd come here, if he hadn't already trusted Habidah, he would have believed it a torture chamber.

He didn't know what he was meant to do next. No one had come back for him. He straightened his habit and approached the door. It whispered open.

He felt no more at ease outside. The corridor was cramped, at most twenty feet long. It was a perfectly geometrical cavern. Something hissed. Cold air brushed his scalp.

The nearest door took him to a cell obviously meant to be someone's living space. It had rumpled sheets over a raised mattress, drawers, and not much else. Aside from the whisper of ventilation, all was quiet.

After another several minutes of poking around doors, he found a ramp leading up. The door at the top opened like all the others. There was nothing beyond except darkness. The air was warmer, humid, tasted of grass and dust and rotted wood. The outdoors.

He stepped out. The door shut behind him, encasing him in darkness.

At length, his eyes adjusted. He stood in a barn. Moonlight edged through cracks in the wall. Decayed rushes covered the floor. Everything was steeped in dust. He half-remembered this from the last time he'd been through.

The barn door squeaked open when he pushed. On the other side, the dust turned to mud. The top of the barn's roof dripped. His toes dipped in a puddle. The sky was half stars, half moon-silvered clouds.

Stepping outside didn't leave him any less disoriented. It shouldn't have been night. He didn't feel tired. What time had it been at Sacro Cuore when he'd left? He couldn't remember.

Out here, he heard the music even more clearly. It was all loose notes and odd trilling, like a troupe of musicians tuning their instruments. It repeated, but never exactly the same. He'd started to describe it to Habidah, but something had clamped down on the thought, made him stop.

A dark shadow loomed over the eastern sky, too near to be a cloud. Habidah's flying beast. The shuttle. Only when he looked closely did he see wan yellow lights underneath. They slanted upward in two parallel lines, from the ground to the shuttle's belly. They were far dimmer than stars.

He padded to them. Lost in the dark, without perspective,

they made him think of a torchlit street seen from far away. This was how the walls of Florence looked at night – a ring of watchfires encircling a sea of shadows and sleepers. He bent, put his hand between the lights. He touched metal. This, then, was the boarding ramp. The lights were guides to keep people from falling.

He stood. He knew little of how Habidah and her companions managed their affairs, but leaving the ramp extended seemed foolhardy. Even if there were no people near, any manner of animal might get in.

A sharp, bright light from the top abruptly shone in his eyes. He held his hand up, but too late to save his night vision. In the painful blur above, he saw a human figure outlined against a square of light. Then the door hissed closed again, and all sight was lost.

A man's voice asked, "What the hell are you doing? Sneaking aboard?" One of Habidah's companions. Joao. The one who'd savaged him.

Niccoluccio would have stepped back if he could have seen where he was going. "Forgive me. I didn't realize I was intruding."

Joao thumped down the ramp. He obviously didn't have any trouble seeing where he was going. Niccoluccio shivered when Joao stopped in front of him. But Joao didn't strike. The other man's breath was labored. Joao said, "You're either following me, or you're sneaking aboard. Which is it?"

"Neither. I was curious and I couldn't stay inside any longer."

"You might not even know. If your master had programmed you to go aboard, your conscious mind would make up any excuse it wanted."

"I'll leave the shuttle if you'll talk with me."

Joao hesitated. "What do you want with me?"

"We're suffering because of what our masters did to each other."

Joao let out a long breath. "The amalgamates never did anything to you. They just failed to cure your plague."

363

"That's enough, especially when it would have been so easy for them. You'd hate them too, if you were in my position. They failed to cure us because they want turn us into a servant class."

"I never said I agreed with what the amalgamates are doing. You know what your master is doing to us, but you're still working for it."

"You're still working for yours. That's why you're here, isn't it? You couldn't contact your amalgamates below. You wanted to check your shuttle's independent communication system, use it to warn your masters."

Joao stood, silent for a moment. He clearly hadn't expected Niccoluccio to understand so much. He set a firm hand on the monk's shoulder and turned him back down the ramp. "Come on."

Uncertain where they were going, Niccoluccio nevertheless followed. Joao stepped confidently in the dark. Something groaned behind them, and Niccoluccio turned in time to see the little guide lights rise and vanish.

Joao stopped a few feet away from the the barn. He sat. Niccoluccio had to feel around before he realized there was a log. He sat, too, a foot away. Joao didn't object. Again, he struggled for breath.

Niccoluccio said, "You're not doing well."

"It's like my body weighs three times as much as it used to. Just going out to the shuttle and back, I feel like I've been running for an hour. It's worse now than I've ever felt it before. I think it's killing me a lot faster than Feliks."

"I'm sincerely sorry."

"You're *not*," Joao said, with surprising vehemence. "You don't even understand. You've never seen this before me."

"I've seen worse. At Sacro Cuore, my brothers woke screaming from the pain of the buboes. They had fevers higher than I'd ever felt. In their delirium, they imagined themselves in Hell. I couldn't help them. But I did see it all."

"This plane doesn't mean anything," Joao said. "There are

only a few hundred million people here. Do you have any idea how many live in the Unity? The Unity has a population of trillions – and those are just the official, registered citizens, never mind the satellite planes and colonies. *Don't* try to put your plane's suffering beside ours. They aren't comparable, and it doesn't justify anything."

"I wasn't trying to justify it," Niccoluccio said. "I was trying to empathize."

Joao was silent for a long time after that. Niccoluccio could sense him silently fuming. Then he said, "I don't know if I can believe a single thing you've told us. If any part of it is true, it's the most evil thing I've ever heard. Far more likely that this is some kind of trick, though. The amalgamates testing our loyalty, something like that."

"Even after you've seen my master do things your amalgamates never could?"

"The amalgamates have always kept their capabilities hidden from us."

"They've never had your best interests at heart, in other words."

"What does that matter? It's better than trying to murder us, like the monster who sent you."

"It doesn't believe it's murdered anyone."

One of the many things Niccoluccio had relearned over his lifetimes at Sacro Cuore was that silences had their own character. One could be very much unlike the last.

Eventually, Joao snapped, "What?"

"It doesn't think that anyone has died, or that death is possible."

"You're worse than an automaton. You're insane."

"My brothers on this plane. I found them again. They'd lost their memories of the plague, but they were still the same people."

"Your master simulated them. Or implanted them in your memories. They weren't real."

Niccoluccio barely squelched his anger. "They were just as

real as I was before I stepped through that gateway. They had their own lives and needs separate from mine. They weren't there just for me."

"You'd never recognize it if was an illusion." When Joao spoke again, his voice was softer. "They died months ago. They only existed here, in the past. Your master is just trying to stop you from facing that and from realizing what's happening to the rest of us."

"You still don't understand. You're thinking in terms of single planes. The multiverse is infinite. You know that somewhere, on some far removed plane, you have a twin. An infinite number of twins. My master lives between the planes, and sees all of them at once. I doubt it ever perceived me as an individual. It sees an infinite array of Niccoluccio Caracciolas, spread out across the planes."

"Everyone knows there are infinite planes," Joao said. "We've been living all our lives with it, and we still have trouble wrapping our heads around it. I refuse to believe you've managed it in a few days."

"I spent a lifetime studying it at Sacro Cuore. I tried my best to see from the perspective of a creature that sees everything in shades of infinites. If I, an individual, were to die, that wouldn't make a whit of difference to it. It will always see another Niccoluccio. Another that lived where I died, another older or younger–"

"You're covering philosophical ground billions of us have gone over and over, ages ago."

"You may have tried to understand it, but you're not living it. You all still see yourselves as individuals. When you die, there will always be another you somewhere in the multiverse, identical in every way except in whatever circumstance allowed you to survive. For my master, those other shades of you aren't abstract."

Joao said, "But those other selves aren't *me*."

"Why would they need to be? Those of you that survived wouldn't be able to tell the difference. They still embody all the things that make you *you*."

"Your religion is wedded to the idea of a soul. Souls that are unique, indestructible, and nontransferable."

"There's a lot about what I used to believe that I question now," Niccoluccio said. "Three times, my life has been saved by bizarre chances. I should have died of the pestilence, but I escaped. Habidah rescued me when I was freezing to death in the forest. In Florence, an outside power impersonated me and called Habidah to save me when I wouldn't have on my own. I imagine that, on a trillion other planes, I died in those places. But I'm here, too."

"That's one hell of a stretch," Joao said, but he sounded less certain.

"I don't know that I see the multiverse the same way my master does," Niccoluccio admitted. "But I'm trying to learn."

"If your master killed me right now, you wouldn't think it had done anything wrong."

"As far as it's concerned, it hasn't killed anyone. It's attacked your amalgamates' base of power, their people. It still sees everyone who's died living in some other part of the multiverse." He had held Brother Rinieri's hand when Rinieri died. He held it again on the other side of the gateway.

Joao stood again, more deliberately. Niccoluccio watched Joao's shadow move against the stars. "Now we know how your master thinks. All that's left is to figure out what it's planning for us."

"I've told you everything I know."

"Let me guess – you have *faith* the rest is going to work itself out."

"I wish I did," Niccoluccio said. "But I don't worship my master."

Joao trod off into the darkness. After a few moments, the gaps in the walls of the barn lit abruptly. Darkness followed.

Niccoluccio remained on the log for a moment, and then stood and followed. He stumbled around the darkness of the barn, searching for the ramp downward. For a moment, he feared that Joao had locked him outside. The door opened just as he stumbled through it.

His eyes had almost adjusted by the time he reached the bottom. He glanced at the doors lining the corridor. The second door led him into a small dining room, not dissimilar to the refectory but a tenth its scale. Two round tables sat side by side. Niccoluccio couldn't guess at the purposes of the individual pieces of equipment lining the far counter. The other of Habidah's associates, Kacienta, ate alone at the farther table. When she saw him, she looked down at her plate.

"I didn't mean to disturb you," he said. When she didn't answer, he took another step closer. "I was hoping to take a minute to explain–"

She set her hands on the side of her plate, as if about to pick it up. Or throw it. She looked up. Niccoluccio had never seen so baleful an expression since the wolves.

He held up his hands and backed out the way he had come.

He had just started to think about where to go next when the door at the far end of the corridor opened. Habidah stepped out, looking right at him. Niccoluccio realized that she had been watching him all along. Joao would have ensured that their conversation wouldn't remain private.

She waved him over. She grabbed his forearm and pulled him through the door. The room on the other side was too dim to see. It must have been Habidah's quarters. It smelled like her. It was as small and cramped as the last he'd seen, but the sheets on the bed were ruffled and someone had shoved clothes into the corner.

Habidah sat him on her mattress. "They won't hear us. I've shut off the microphones in my quarters."

"You heard everything I told Joao."

She nodded. "Kacienta, too. Those two have made up their minds. You're not going to convince them of anything."

He nodded. "Have *you* made up your mind?"

"I can't believe anything you or your master tell us. The stakes are too high, and there's no way to verify anything you've said. It would be too easy to trick us."

Niccoluccio looked to the wall. "I understand."

She hesitated, as a person looking over a precipice. "But I don't want to be associated with the amalgamates any longer." He looked at her, but the dim light kept him from seeing much. She said, "Their plans for this plane have to be stopped."

"Yes. Whatever else happens, I don't want your amalgamates here. That's one decision I'm confident is my own."

"And you still don't know anything about this message you have to deliver. Only that you have to be close."

"If I knew anything, could tell you anything, besides what I said, I would tell you." Her, of all people. He had never had so dear a hope but that she believed that.

She looked to the floor, seeing nothing. Niccoluccio knew that expression. She was somewhere else, steeling herself to step over the edge. She said, "This is too enormous for creatures like us. We're too easily controlled. The powers at play are too far beyond us. If there's one thing I believe we can change, it's the fate of your plane. The amalgamates haven't gotten their roots into it yet."

"You'll help me, then?"

"I will." For as outwardly calm as she appeared, she couldn't hide the tightness in her voice. She was in freefall. "And we're going to do it alone."

He reached for her hand, to offer that little bit of comfort, but she pulled it away.

34

The kick of the shuttle's acceleration pushed Habidah deep into her cushions. She hadn't realized until she'd climbed aboard how badly she'd needed to get away from Niccoluccio. Every moment she'd spent in the field base, she'd felt alien eyes on her. She closed her eyes and let the roar and rumble wash over her.

Joao asked, "Are we headed for *Ways and Means*?" He and Kacienta had come aboard without question. They understood that they needed to talk in a place free from cameras and from Niccoluccio.

"No," she said. "I doubt Niccoluccio's master would let us get there."

The shuttle coasted through a blazing red dawn. The stealth fields struggled to fend off the morning light. The hull shimmered scarlet. The ventral cameras showed treetops clumped together like moss. A town slid onto the foremost monitor. The shuttle began its descent without prompting.

Kacienta asked, "This again?" Habidah didn't answer.

The shuttle alighted in a forest clearing two kilometers from the village, just far enough away to lift off without being seen. The deck thumped as the landing struts touched ground. Kacienta and Joao followed her to the boarding ramp.

Joao waited until they'd walked a good distance from the shuttle before speaking. "I tried to take off last night. The flight computer didn't answer."

Habidah said, "I could have told you it wouldn't work."

"Are you going to make me ask, Habidah?"

She didn't need to look deeply to see the accusation in their eyes. She said, "I programmed our entire course before we left the ground. It knew I wasn't going to fly to *Ways and Means*. So it let us go."

The ground cut up and down at short, steep angles, across ruts and old stream beds. Brush snapped across her ankles. Dapples of dawn sunlight blinded her. The shadows were so severe that she couldn't see the ground without infrared. But in infrared, sunlight washed out everything else. So she stumbled, half-blind, into the clear-cut fringes surrounding a wheat field.

Kacienta asked, "Why are you dragging Joao this far? If you want to talk in private, we can do it back in the forest."

Habidah opened her mouth to answer, but Joao interrupted her. "I'm fine for now." From the red in his cheeks, he obviously wasn't.

Habidah had no answer they would have liked to hear.

The village ahead was only superficially similar to the last they'd visited. It was older. The houses sagged, their cob walls and matted roofs were scored black from ancient smoke. Habidah stepped across a weed-overgrown depression that had once been the foundation of a house.

She estimated most of the fields had gone to seed no later than half a year ago. Only a few vegetable gardens remained tended. Habidah pulse-scanned for fresh graves, but to her surprise found none, not even in the church's wide yard. The natives had taken the wise precaution of burying their plague dead away from their homes.

A handful of locals were just exiting the church as Habidah arrived. They all stopped, staring at Habidah and her team. Kacienta said, "I don't need to see more people dying."

Habidah said, "The plague has passed through. All that's left is coping."

They weren't the only visitors. A dusty trail wound westward.

A family of four was on it, heading toward the village. Behind them were another seven – five children escorted by two men, one wearing clerical black.

Joao turned to Habidah. Habidah couldn't tell if the tightness in his face was from exhaustion or accusation. Kacienta said, "You brought us here for a reason."

"We're anthropologists," Habidah said. "We're here to study these people. At least, that's what the amalgamates expect us to do. Niccoluccio's master, too, if it doesn't understand us any better. That's why it let us come here."

Kacienta said, "You have to be joking."

"We're going to see a performance," Habidah said.

Joao said, "I've been watching one all along," but he followed when Habidah stepped forward.

According to satellite records, the plague had culled three-fifths of this village's population. Aside from the vegetable gardens and fields gone to seed, none of the dwellings showed obvious signs of neglect. The doors were closed, the foggy windows clean, the grass clear of trash. Habidah wouldn't have been surprised to learn that new families had coalesced, orphaned children adopted.

She held up her arms and called, "We came to see the pilgrims."

"We don't know you," the nearest of the locals answered, a man no less suspicious than Joao.

In a place so small, the locals would be familiar with the names and faces even of those from neighboring villages. "A messenger told us they would be coming today," Habidah said, pretending she hadn't heard.

He waved his hand in disgust and carried on. Permission enough, Habidah supposed. At least for now.

Not that the locals could stop new arrivals if they tried. People trickled down the road, often with children. She was only surprised to find that there were so many children left.

Habidah said, "We came here to learn from these people."

Kacienta said, "That was a long time ago."

"We can still learn a lot if we pay attention. Joao, you told Niccoluccio that you doubted anything we did would make a difference."

Joao said, "If Niccoluccio's master wanted to kill us, it could have. We're not even worth that much attention."

Kacienta said, "I don't know about that. It *is* putting some effort into keeping us from communicating with *Ways and Means*." And it had communicated mostly with Niccoluccio, ignoring Habidah and her team except for the moments when it needed to push them into new positions like pieces on a game board. It was afraid of being caught.

That was probably also why it had chosen to attack *Ways and Means* so indirectly, through Niccoluccio. Any attack originating closer would be more detectable. She doubted that detection would stop the monster in the end, but it might make its plan a lot messier.

Habidah nodded at the travelers approaching from the west road. "These people are lifetimes away from figuring out what their plague was and how it was transmitted. They hardly have any more idea how to react than we do."

Kacienta said, "Don't slight them. They know that diseases transmit, and to stay away from places where the infected have been. They may not know *why*, but they have a practical understanding of what to do."

It was easy to forget that, not that long ago, they had been academics capable of holding a reasonable debate. Kacienta was right, of course. Habidah said, "That's more than we do. If what Niccoluccio said is true, we haven't been able to fight our plague because there *is* no way to fight it."

Joao asked, "What's your point?"

By now, forty or fifty people had gathered near the road and churchyard. Habidah stopped by their fringes. She pointed to a mass farther down the road, a larger group of dark-shod travelers. Before all this had happened, she'd tracked them for days.

Deep-voiced singing echoed over the gentle hills. At first,

Habidah had to strain her ears to hear. Even her demiorganics couldn't filter much through the wind. Then she was able to pick up individual voices: men and women, all adults, all keeping their voices low. They were singing a psalm.

The village bell began to peal, so suddenly that Habidah nearly jumped. Only ceremonial. Everyone who could be roused was already here. Kacienta glanced to Habidah, eyebrow raised, and stepped closer to the road to get a better view.

A cloud of dust trailed after the newcomers. There were about seventy marchers, all dressed in black goat's-hair sackcloths and cilices. Dark stains marred their clothes. They marched in file like an invading army. They outnumbered the people of this village, and the other visitors, too.

The thing that surprised Habidah most was their near-even gender balance. Men and women marched on opposite sides of the road. She had rarely seen that except among poor farmers. These were neither.

A towering man set their pace. He was thin but not for lack of nutrition. Powerful muscles bundled under his arms. His hair had thinned, but he was not yet bald. When he at last reached the church, he looked over the gathered, tremulous villagers as he might the fields of rotted wheat surrounding them.

"Are there any Jews among you?" he cried, raising his whip. It was a vicious-looking thing with three tails. Dark-stained iron slivers were knotted into each end.

The village folk shook their heads and and wailed in several voices. Some of them stepped back as if they were about to be whipped. "No! Out! They were driven out!"

The marshal lowered his whip, but only gradually. Then, abruptly, he raised it again – and turned and lashed a balding, middle-aged man, one of his marchers. The whip's spikes slashed through the man's sackcloth. He fell to his knees, visibly restraining a scream.

The travelers and village folk gasped or shrieked. When the marshal lowered the whip, though, none of them moved to help. The other marchers remained unmoved.

"This man," the marshal said, "tolerated Jews as his neighbors for sixteen years. His family perished from their poisons. His, and his other neighbors, and their neighbors' neighbors. His whole town was brought down by the deviltry of the Jew."

"Punish me, Lord!" the man cried, voice broken.

The marshal returned his attention to the crowd. "We have all sinned against our Father. All of us have reaped the harvest. We travel here, too, to reap our sins, and to sow our penance, to save our world from our Father's wrath and hellfire."

Another man among the travelers, voice trembling on the edge of a sob, cried, "Punish me! Save me!"

A girl no older than thirteen added, "Save us, Lord!"

The marshal turned toward the village's small church and marched in without invitation. Ten from his parade followed him, including the whipped man. The locals gradually filed after them.

Habidah, Joao, and Kacienta joined the crowd mid-stream. No one paid them the slightest attention. "OK," Kacienta transmitted, "Many of them *don't* have the slightest idea what brought the plague on them. They invent whatever they want."

Habidah replied, "They feel like they've been attacked. When religious figures they trust and fear tell them that the secret to their safety is killing people they've hated all along, they'll listen." She hadn't forgotten the burning of the Jews in Naples and Strasbourg and a long list of other places throughout Europe.

Habidah said, "Important to remember that gods can ask you to do horrible things."

Kacienta said, "Like participate in the annihilation of an interplanar civilization under the pretense that death doesn't exist."

Habidah said, "Or allow a third of a world's population to die of a curable disease, all along believing that death *does* exist."

The church must have been one of the first buildings

constructed in this village. It would hardly have accommodated the village's pre-plague population. One of the rafters had rotted away. Habidah, Joao, and Kacienta were rapidly pushed toward the wall.

The master of the troupe stood behind the altar and waited, imperiously, while the crowd filled the church. The ten followers he'd brought with him lined up behind him. They'd done this before. This was just another stop. Their clothes hid most of their bodies, but, looking carefully, she could see bright red, poorly healed scars and scabs on their ankles and wrists.

Without prompting, the marshal began to deliver Mass. *That* surprised Habidah. He wore nothing to indicate that he was ordained. His Latin was stilted and broken. But his audience listened attentively, without understanding, as no doubt they always had. Habidah looked among them for the village's priest, but without success. Either he was protesting by sitting out, or he had died. There was no Communion, which reinforced a suspicion Habidah had harbored since the marshal's first words. This was well outside church orthodoxy. The papacy had a more tolerant view of Jews, for one.

The marshal's ten followers stripped to the waist. Each had a lash in their hands. And then the sermon changed to French.

The marshal harangued his audience. He accused them of lust and faithlessness, wretched thoughts and evil deeds, of harboring Jews and failing to keep their Sunday holy. At each new accusation, one of his followers lashed themselves across their naked breasts. The third man drew blood. As did the woman who went next. From then on each snap of the whip grew more severe. The villagers gasped or twisted in discomfort. None looked away.

Joao was no longer bothered to hide his disgust. Habidah transmitted, "You'll draw attention."

"I don't feel like pretending anymore. From the moment we reached this plane, I wanted to leave. These people never had anything to teach us. The amalgamates knew it all along." He groaned as another realization struck him. "All of our funding came from governments, politicians. That means, somewhere further back down the line, the amalgamates. The people of the Unity were never interested in a project like ours."

After another moment of standing and watching, he asked, "Why did Niccoluccio's master come to us, anyway? The Unity is so large that we can hardly comprehend how many people live in it. But it's only the four of us who got stuck dealing with this."

Kacienta said, "Had to happen to somebody."

Habidah said, "There's a far more likely explanation." She gave Kacienta and Joao a chance to consider that.

When she looked back at Joao, his lips had tightened. He said, "Of course. We're *not* the only ones. We can't be."

Habidah said, "We're dealing with powerful creatures, masterminds, gods, but I don't think they would rely on a single plan. They would want more than one point of contact. Or hundreds. Or thousands. I expect what's happening to us is happening all over the Unity."

"Fuck," Kacienta muttered, aloud.

Joao said, "Then it *really* doesn't matter what we do." His transmitted voice sounded perfectly level, but Habidah doubted he would have been able to speak aloud.

Another thirty lashes passed before the conclusion of the sermon. The marshal and his cohort strode outside. The villagers followed like herded animals. Habidah, Kacienta, and Joao were among the last out.

The rest of the marchers had spread across the churchyard. The villagers formed a semicircle around them. Their master took a place at their center.

At an unspoken signal, the marchers struck bizarre poses. Some lay supine, and others on their sides, with hands raised and fingers outstretched. One arched her back and bent backward to touch the ground with her fingertips. Another jutted his gut, craned his neck, and reached for the sky on his tiptoes.

The marshal said, "Ask these men and women what sins they've become."

377

Habidah stepped forward with the rest of the crowd, but she didn't need to draw attention by speaking. "I'm lust," said the woman who had stretched upside down. "The lust I had in my youth for my neighbors, that I have now for my husband."

The man who had craned his neck back proclaimed, "I'm the pride I took in my deeds, in building a home, managing my master's farm, buying my freedom."

One of the women lying on her side announced, "I'm the perjury my husband and I committed to sell our horse. We placed mustard seed in its nose." That would force it to raise its head and look healthier, Habidah figured.

An old woman lay on her stomach in the grass. "I am the adultery I committed while my husband was dying of the pestilence."

One broad-bellied man lay on the ground as though he'd been hog-tied, grabbing his feet. "I am the murder I committed when I robbed men on the roads to Paris, by my captain's orders."

The marshal had been patrolling with the rest of the crowd. At this, he raised his three-tailed whip. He brought it down hard on the murderer's stomach. Some in the audience cried out. They and the rest rapidly made their way back to the sidelines. The marshal didn't wait. He again lashed the murderer, and now it was the murderer's turn to scream. The next time he raised his whip, he sent it into one of his adulterers. Blood sprinkled across the dirt.

Once back in the sidelines, Joao asked, "Is this why we're here? You think we deserve what's happening to us?"

"No," Habidah said.

Kacienta said, "None of us wants the amalgamates to be here."

Habidah didn't contest that. Instead, she said, "Nobody deserves this kind of suffering."

The marshal's whip was clearly designed to not only inflict pain, but to make a show of it. When his whip's nails stuck in a victim, rather than pluck them out, he yanked the handle from a different angle to split more flesh. After only two dozen lashes, the ground was soaked with blood.

The marshal whipped each of his marchers in turn while they yelled their sins to the sky. After the second and third times each of them felt the blow, Habidah figured that they were no longer crying for their audience's sake. The ones who wavered, who couldn't keep control of their voices, got extra attention. One of the perjurers, a boy no older than fifteen, lost his voice after the first lash drew blood across his neck and sternum. Again and again, the whip fell on him. He tried to cough out his sin, but couldn't speak at all. He flopped onto his stomach.

Kacienta said, "They certainly think they deserve it. We've all seen behavior like it before. People castigating themselves in the face of natural disasters."

Joao said, "It's their way of feeling they can control what happens to them. Easier to think that it's their fault than simply out of control." After a pause, he asked Habidah, "You sure you're not making the same mistake?"

Kacienta said, "If Niccoluccio's master is against the Unity colonizing this world, it's not for the same reasons we are."

Habidah said, "I'm not siding with Niccoluccio's master. Or with the amalgamates."

Joao asked, "Then what are you doing?"

Habidah opened her mouth, but at that moment the marshal tossed his whip aside. It landed in the dirt, bloodied and still bearing scraps of skin and flesh. But the marchers still had their own whips. Gradually, they rose. Even the fifteen year-old managed to stand and readied his whip.

Habidah had seen satellite recordings of the next part of the performance. But images taken by satellite weren't the same as being here. What followed was the most savage instance of ritual self-injury she had seen on any of her trips so far. Even Kacienta couldn't restrain a gasp. The marchers kept calling their sins. They brought their whips down on themselves as hard as they could, across their necks and bare chests, faster and harder until their voices burbled and they couldn't restrain their sobbing. Three marchers, men who had accompanied the marshal into the church, took it upon themselves to walk amongst their fellows and cheer them on. They did this even as they whipped themselves, and their robes and trousers became soiled with blood.

This was a performance, yes, but these people weren't acting. Infrared revealed none of the usual markers of emotional deception. Some of them were hardly sensate. The fifteen year-old collapsed again. No one tended to him. Blood dripped down his naked ribs. One of the whip's spikes had landed in his shoulder, torn his muscles. He wouldn't ever be able to use that arm again without pain accompanying every motion.

One woman lashed her own breast until she writhed on the ground. Old lashes on her stomach had left her rippled with scars. One of the marshal's blows to her arm had gone straight through the skin and exposed the yellow fat underneath.

The marchers whipped themselves with terrifying vigor, almost a lust, but even they weren't indefatigable. Gradually their voices weakened. More of them fell, too exhausted and too lost in their agony.

Finally, the marshal shouted, "Stop!" and the last of the whips ceased.

Slowly, in awe, the crowd spread themselves among the panting and weeping marchers. Some of them held cloths to the marchers' wounds. When the cloth soaked with blood, some of the locals held them reverently, or tucked them under their own clothes. Relics. Charms against their God's wrath. Other villagers recited prayers with those marchers still capable of speech.

Joao muttered something dark under his breath. Habidah had been right. There was still enough of an anthropologist left in him, and in Kacienta, for this to hold their attention. Joao said, "This is about control, all right, but not like we were talking about. Look at the locals." He gave a sideways nod to the marshal. "They're terrified. They'll do anything he says."

Habidah asked, "Is it easier to be terrified of God than disease?"

Joao said, "Maybe for the villagers, but that's not what's happening. He just wants them cowering before God. And since he's God's intermediary, they ought to cower before him."

"You certainly reach your conclusions quickly."

"After everything we've seen, I'm not feeling any obligation to be fair."

Habidah said, "Then we've seen enough."

As the marshal prepared for another sermon, she and the others slipped away. None of the marchers, except the marshal, looked at them as they left – and he only briefly. She trudged back to the shuttle, taking the return journey half as fast as they as she'd made it.

Joao looked glassy-eyed. Kacienta kept pace, ready to support him should he falter. Joao asked, "Do you really believe that all Niccoluccio came here to do is deliver a message?"

Habidah said, "I think he believes that."

Kacienta said, "I only wish we knew the nature of the trap."

Habidah steered the subject away. She needed their minds back on that village. She said, "These people have the wrong idea for their situation, but maybe the right one for ours."

Joao snorted. "Beating ourselves bloody? Burning scapegoats?"

"We can't fight powers as far above us as Niccoluccio's master, or even the amalgamates. The only way to change their minds is to appeal to them directly. Give them what they want."

They walked behind her, so if either of them gave her any looks, she didn't see them. They said nothing.

Dew dripped off the shuttle's wings and tail. None of them said anything as they boarded and settled into their couches. Though it was now fully daylight, there was no one near to see the shuttle. Once they attained cruising altitude, a person looking up might see a thin black arrow flitting between the clouds, but Habidah was beyond caring.

Habidah's thoughts boiled she watched the landscape flatten. Part of her had never stopped being an academic. There were a dozen papers she could have written on what she'd just seen. But the urge to write them had been getting smaller and smaller. They rode in silence. She stared straight ahead, seeing nothing. A weight sat behind her eyes. It felt like fatigue, but she didn't want to sleep.

She kept a careful eye on Kacienta and Joao's use of bandwidth. Neither of them sent any signal until they'd nearly touched down. Even then, her packet sniffers reported only that they'd given orders to the kitchen to prepare a meal and drinks.

They weren't checking the cameras. They hadn't looked for Niccoluccio.

The landing struts thumped onto soil. She leaned back and closed her eyes. Kacienta and Joao clambered out of their couches and down the ramp without waiting. Habidah opened her eyes and, on the monitors, watched them step into the barn hiding the field base.

After they disappeared, Niccoluccio stepped out from behind a patch of trees.

Habidah watched him board. She raised the ramp behind him.

He stepped uncertainly into the cabin and settled into a couch. He tugged at its safety harness, trying to draw it over himself. He asked, "Was the deception truly necessary?"

"Joao's dangerous. He doesn't believe that harming you will help anything, but he's on the verge of trying it anyway, out of desperation. The last time he saw you near the shuttle, if you'd kept going, he probably would have killed you."

"Or if he saw me going back now," Niccoluccio said, soberly. He was just beginning to realize why Habidah had asked him to wait and hide.

This excursion had been the only way she'd found to get him aboard. Joao and Kacienta had been watching Niccoluccio closely. Had she just taken Niccoluccio to the shuttle, they would have stopped her. She'd had to tire them, leave them exhausted and with too much to think about. Looking away for just a moment.

Habidah said, "I'm not ready to fight him or Kacienta."

She restarted the shuttle's ventral thrusters. They shuddered back to life, still hot from the last flight. This had to be fast. Kacienta and Joao would hear them even underground.

Niccoluccio's master had limited its contact with her for fear that it would be caught, but it couldn't have stayed hidden from her forever. Lucky for it that she was willing to go along. Or maybe it had known that, too.

Habidah charted a course to high orbit, and then to *Ways and Means*. She fed it to the flight computer, and held her breath.

For a desperate moment, she dared hope the shuttle NAI would refuse her as it had refused Joao's attempt to escape to orbit. But the shuttle responded.

Niccoluccio moaned as the acceleration pressed him into his couch. He hardly noticed the safety harness snapping over his shoulders. He ran his hand along the side of his couch, and then the smooth curve of the bulkhead, as if to feel again how strange they were. He looked to the monitors, and to the half-dead world falling away beneath them.

"How much do you really know about what's going to happen next?" she asked.

She was sure he'd heard her, but he kept his eyes on the land. No matter how long she waited, she never got an answer.

It was just as well. Nothing he could have said would have satisfied anyone. She remained silent while the clouds slipped away beneath them.

35

Meloku was stirred out of sleep by her bladder, a rare experience. If nothing else, the past few days of traveling had confirmed that her demiorganics were wholly offline. Without them to regulate her, her body had gone completely out of control.

She pushed out of her woolen blankets and through the flap of her tent. Daylight blinded her. She fought a brief moment of panic. She'd gone to sleep before sunset. She was never going to get accustomed to sleeping eight hours a night. There was so much that she could have done, so much that might have happened.

Judging from what she saw, though, nothing had changed. Her mercenary escorts had made their camp in the leeward shadow of a small hill. All twenty tents were arranged as she remembered. A handful of mercenaries shuffled between them, moving lazily. One openly urinated. They were rough men, their skin turned leathery by the sun, but they also seemed healthy – a rare enough quality these days. They were the best she could do.

Their captain, a middle-aged soldier named Fallard, was the only clean-shaven man among them. He stood next to Galien and a smoldering cookfire. His chin was greasy with bacon.

Fallard's company was late of the war between England and France. Though Fallard was French, he boasted of fighting at the Battle of Crécy alongside King Edward. The fact that he had done so in the streets of Avignon, a French city despite the papacy's nominal sovereignty, spoke volumes about his wisdom and tact.

Meloku's association with these men had had become a scandal even in the short time before she'd left. Clement had sent a messenger summoning her to the papal court. She'd dismissed the messenger without bothering to explain herself. Eight of Fallard's men had gotten into brawls before departing Avignon.

Galien said, "We were beginning to wonder if you would ever wake."

Meloku shot him a dark glance, but he had already turned back to his breakfast. She said, "If you've been waiting for so long, why haven't you struck camp and made ready?"

Galien nodded to Fallard. "I tried to tell him." He didn't sound very concerned.

Fallard shrugged. "Our generous employer hasn't been here to tell us so."

"I told you all along how urgent this is."

Fallard gave her an indolent glance. "And yet you haven't told us *why*."

"You don't need to know. You'll be paid as long as you do what I ask you."

Fallard and Galien exchanged a look. Fallard sighed. He said, "We've traded news with passing travelers. A holy man and his flagellants nearby, delivering a sermon. My men wanted to watch."

"I don't care. We're leaving now."

"Half of them have already gone."

Damn. An infrared sweep would have told her that immediately. She'd assumed most of the men were still in their tents. The soldiers of this plane were an undisciplined mess, to be sure, but this many of them wouldn't have wandered off on their own without their captain's tacit support.

She glared at Fallard. He stared back evenly. She had been a sensation for Avignon for so long that she'd nearly forgotten what it was like for the natives to treat her with anything but awe and fear.

She said, "I want them ready to leave in fifteen minutes."

Fallard said, "You might as well shout it to the trees as tell it to me. There's no gathering them up until they decide to come back." He tossed the burnt rind of his bacon into the fire, and walked, casually, toward his tent.

Companion had never been talkative. But there had always been a part of Meloku that had known it was there: watching, judging, ready to intercede if she made too many wrong choices. Her instinct now was to wait until Companion told her what she could have done better, and what she needed to do now. More than once, Meloku dreaded to hear what Companion thought of her.

She'd known before that she had become dependent on Companion. She hadn't realized how badly.

She blew air through her lips and started walking. She didn't know where she was going until a minute later, when she figured that she was intent on rounding up her wayward soldiers. She didn't have any other resources. Lacking her internal armaments, intelligence from *Ways and Means'* satellites, or even Companion's guidance, she couldn't count on overpowering Habidah. But Habidah couldn't withstand a company of mercenaries. Habidah's demiorganics weren't combat-rated. Nor were the field base's doors designed to resist battering.

That, at least, had been the plan. Aside from his lack of social graces, she'd figured Fallard and his mercenaries to be steady. They'd done a good job of standing at attention and looking sober while she reviewed them and explained their job. But without infrared to read the flow of heat under their skin, she discovered she was a poor judge of character.

She was used to controlling men. Taking their reins should have been an afterthought. But from the moment they'd left sight of the papal palace, they had treated her insolently, ignored her repeated requests to march faster. They had covered half as much ground as Meloku could have alone.

She didn't need enhanced senses to tell her where her men had gone. She followed trampled grass to the dusty trade road, where their bootprints told an even clearer story. They'd headed to the farms whose hearthfires she'd spotted last night.

She kicked a stone out of her way. Already the day was unbearably hot. It was going to be miserable marching. Meloku only hoped Fallard's men had strength left when they reached the field base. Then again, the more energy they spent, the less they would have for disobedience.

Her mood darkened further when she approached the farms. There was indeed some kind of performance going on. There were far too many natives about for them to all be locals. Her men were among the visitors.

She strode to the nearest soldier. She laid a hand on his shoulder. He started, spun as if to strike, and stopped only when he saw who she was. He gave her a surly-lipped stare.

"Find the others," she said. "Get them back to camp."

"I don't know where they are," he said, and turned back to the center of the crowd.

Meloku peered over his shoulders to find out just what was so captivating. A troupe of robed and hairshirted strangers stood or lay bent over each other. She stared. They'd been beaten and whipped bloody. A tall, mustachioed man strode among them, rhythmically flashing a three-tailed whip. Blood streamed over them, soaked the grass. Their clothes were torn and stained with old blood.

Meloku grimaced. She didn't have to study her men closely to see that she was not going to be able to pull them away. They were spellbound.

Rather than listen to the cries, she strode up a small hill, where two young girls had gone to sit and watch. They didn't even glance at her. She sat and scanned the crowd, counting her men. She could at least keep an eye on them. She would have rather tuned out the mustachioed man's sermon, but, without her demiorganics' audio discriminators, she had no choice but to pay attention.

He shouted about sins, as so many of these people did. His sins, his troupe's sins, their unworthiness in the eyes of their God. How it was only through the grace and mercy of the Virgin that their world had not already been cast into Hell. His display was an eye-catching form of fearmongering, certainly, but typical enough in its substance. These people responded easily to threats of divine vengeance.

The mustachioed man extracted a scroll from his robes. It was a letter, purportedly written by Jesus, discovered on the altar at the Church of the Holy Sepulchre in Jerusalem. Meloku frowned. This was starting to sound less like a sermon and more like a challenge. This man was no ordained priest. His words about Jews in particular struck hard against papal doctrine.

Companion said, "This movement will threaten your power base if you're not careful."

Meloku jolted upright. An electric current jammed her nerves, kept her from answering. She was belatedly aware that the two girls were staring at her.

Her jaw trembled. "Where did you go?"

No reply. Companion's voice had sounded strange, like an echo. She checked her demiorganics for any response. Even the emergency diagnostic routines remained silent.

She struggled to answer as she imagined Companion wanted to hear: "This movement isn't my priority. I have to figure out what Habidah's done, what happened to you, alert *Ways and Means*."

"If you focus on the short-term at the expense of the long-term, you'll lose sight of the purpose of your project–" She stopped with a horror. She knew its words before it did. Companion had never spoken at all. She'd just put her own words in its voice. She had segued into mouthing them.

She sat heavily, her pulse pounding. Somewhere, distantly, she was aware that the crowd had started to mingle with the performers. Companion chattered in the back of her head. She could *hear* it. She rested her head in her hands and tried to banish it.

The shadow of Companion's presence remained a part of her even when Companion itself had gone. She was more the amalgamates' creature than she'd ever realized. She couldn't escape its voice any more than she could escape her heartbeat, or a headache. For a dizzying moment, she wondered if she'd ever imagined its voice while it was around.

When she looked up, her vision was blurred. The shapes and colors of the crowd ran together. Everything that had happened since she'd lost Companion was catching up with her at once. She blinked fiercely until she could see again. The natives were laying hands on the flagellants, smearing the blood on their cheeks and foreheads, dipping cloths into the wounds. Again she heard Companion. It calculated the likelihood of fatal infections and spreading diseases. But that had to be her voice.

If she'd known that this was what she would come to, she never would have gone into the amalgamates' service. On Mhensis, she'd had nothing to pride herself on but her independence and clear-headedness. Now she couldn't begin to figure out what to next, or what she would have to do to fix things. Without them, she was falling apart, hallucinating.

What had *happened* at the field base? She couldn't imagine Habidah had access to the kind of technology that could do this to her. Not unless she'd become an agent for a force that rivaled the amalgamates. "I can't face that kind of power," she said aloud. "Not alone." If her neighbors answered, she didn't hear it.

She forced herself to breathe evenly. The mustachioed man had taken up his whip and was haranguing his audience for tolerating Jews, and atheists, and fornicators.

That was enough time wasted. She unfolded her legs and stood. She scanned the crowd again, counting all of Fallard's men whose faces she remembered. She tallied only seven. There had been at least twice that many missing this morning.

She wiped her eyes clear and scanned the horizon.

Her eyes caught on the nearest of the farmhouses. The door hung open. Shadows moved inside. She doubted it was any of the locals. They were all here.

Robbers. Looters.

"Fuck," she breathed. Her missing mercenaries.

She checked the other farmhouses. More open doors, more intruders. The performers were too wrapped up in themselves to notice, but some of the locals were stirring, looking from house to house. Some of them had started to break away.

She raced down the hill, toward the soldier she'd spoken with earlier. Too late. A woman's cry of alarm alerted the rest of the crowd.

As one coordinated action, Meloku's soldiers revealed knives concealed beneath their leathers. They surrounded the crowd. Meloku jerked to a stop. Without her demiorganics to help her keep her balance, she nearly stumbled to her knees.

One of the locals rushed to his home, heedless of the knives. One of her mercenaries struck him a backhanded blow, knocking him flat. Another soldier slashed a disfiguring cut across his neighbor's face with no provocation.

Meloku scrambled backward. Her soldiers were too busy corralling the locals to look in her direction. The girls who'd been beside her had vanished. It didn't take much thought to see that their only hiding place was behind the hill. Keeping low in the grass, she ran after them.

The girls were back there, all right – huddled and crying. She swept past them. The dusty road was just ahead. It ran through a dusty shallow, just deep enough to provide cover if she crouched as she ran. She had to. Without her demiorganics, she was as defenseless as any of the natives.

It was so obvious what had happened that she didn't want to think about it. Fallard and his men hadn't just had a reputation for banditry, like most mercenaries. They *were* bandits. They'd come to Avignon to trade loot, and accepted her job as a convenient, quiet back way out. They must have figured that

Clement would pay a steep ransom for her safety. She'd been stupid enough to fall for it.

The only circumstance that had saved her had been the fact that Fallard's men weren't organized. Fallard certainly hadn't expected her to march out of camp alone, or he would have put guards on her. He'd probably seen her as a court pet, too delicate to run away. Her labored breathing during yesterday's march must have reinforced that image.

She shaded her eyes and peered further down the road. The camp and her few supplies lay in that direction. Why was she heading there? Why did she need it? She asked herself those questions expecting an answer, but even her memory of Companion's voice was silent. She was acting on reflex.

She should have fled, moved on to the field base alone. Her answer for going back finally came, unbidden: Galien. She'd overestimated him enormously. And she'd left him with Fallard and his monsters.

Thankfully, Fallard had insisted on a campsite with some cover. Brush, a hill, and several trees disguised Mcloku's approach. No one accosted her. They were all too busy pillaging to maintain a watch. They didn't expect serious opposition.

She crouched in waist-high brown grass. Her tent stood fifteen meters away, apparently unmolested. Fallard's cookfire still smoldered, but of Fallard himself, she saw no sign. Nor Galien. His tent stood not far from hers. The flaps were closed.

She reached her tent without a cry raised against her. She crawled under the flaps, making as little noise as possible. Her fox-fur-trimmed ermine coat was missing. Her bag had been split open and what remained of its contents – perfume, toiletries, underclothes – spilled across the ground.

Thankfully she hadn't been a *complete* dunce: that had been a decoy bag. She dug underneath her blankets until she found her real kit. She'd packed a nine-centimeter ivory-handled knife (a gift from some cardinal, now her only weapon), a signal booster box in the event that her demiorganics began working, and several plastic-wrapped ration bars. The rations were made to keep her on her feet for days, but, of course, they were intended for someone with a demiorganic-boosted metabolism. She had no idea how long they would last her now.

Shouting and scuffling alerted her to the fact that some of the men had returned. She crouched by the tent flap. She heard an outraged grunt, a low and frightened moan, and a snicker, but she couldn't even count the number of men out there. Audio discriminatory abilities would have come in handy. This was like being stricken blind, deaf, and dumb.

She crawled out the back of the tent, and peered around it. Fallard and two of his men encircled Galien, who stood with his arms in the air. Fallard's men patted him down. One ripped a coin pouch from a pocket in his robe sleeve. Another pulled his felt hat from his head.

Quaking, Galien said, "When Julius Caesar was captured and held for ransom by pirates, he told his captors he would pay his ransom and then return to crucify them all. They laughed. They didn't believe him until he raised a fleet and–"

Fallard, with apparently little effort, smacked Galien across the jaw. Galien was flung into the arms of one of his searchers, who dropped him into the mud, laughing. He sputtered until one of them kicked him.

Meloku shook her head. It was difficult to believe that she'd once thought Galien practical. Maybe he was, but only in the esoteric world of ecclesiastical politics.

Fallard pointed to the cookfire. "Put him there until we can round up a few other ransoms to keep him company." He stalked away. One of the mercenaries followed. The other grabbed Galien by the back of his collar and hauled him, scrabbling, toward the fire.

Meloku peered about the edge of the encampment. It seemed free of sentries. That wouldn't last, not once the others returned from their looting. She crawled, staying low in the grass. She stopped three times to look for any sign of Fallard. Nothing. Either she had gotten lucky, or she was missing something.

By far the most sound decision would have been to retreat, far and fast. One of the virtues of her new state of mind was that she didn't have the time to consider this excessively. She was too focused on stifling her breathing. Her instincts pushed her on. And they said that Galien was her responsibility.

Companion never would have agreed. She could hear it pestering. But Companion spoke in her voice now. Her voice had always been much easier to ignore than its.

She circled the fire, positioning herself behind Galien's guard. But she must have made too much noise. The guard spun round. Meloku sprang out of the grass, knife in her left hand. She swung, clumsily. Deliberately so. A feint. He dodged it, stepping right where she intended – into the blow from her right fist, which landed deep in his windpipe before he could make any noise.

From there, it was as simple as drawing a diagram. A knee between his legs to disable him. A half-step around him. She wrapped her arm under his chin and drew her blade across his throat, as easily as if she were slicing beef. She released him, choking and dying, into the dirt.

Her missing demiorganics may have afforded her grace and neatness, but, here, those were just niceties, and superfluous. She didn't need her demiorganics to remember her training. She flexed her fingers to check for broken bones. Her knuckles didn't even hurt.

Galien gaped at her. She waited for him to say something until it became clear that he wouldn't. She offered him a hand. He stared at the blood soaking her sleeve.

She asked, "Do you have enough breath to run?"

"Mother of Jesus," Galien said, at last.

Meloku grabbed his arm and yanked him toward the cover of the nearest slope. At first, she feared she would have to drag him, but he found his footing. He stumbled more than ran.

"They're going to come after us," Galien panted. "They're going to find out what you did, and hunt us–"

"They're going to come after *you*," Meloku said. "They'll just

393

find him dead. They have no reason to think I was involved."

Galien's step faltered again. Meloku tightened her grip. She was going to have to cut off her sleeve soon. The blood was starting to stick like glue.

She aimed for the distant foliage of a forest, both to help cover their tracks and in the hope of finding running water. The shadows of the trees closed around them. He didn't say anything for forty minutes, until they'd put enough distance between them and the camp that Meloku felt safe slowing. "I don't understand how you did any of that."

"Of course you don't," Meloku muttered, and then, louder, said, "You saw it happen. What of any of it was unclear?"

"You. You're... you wouldn't..."

"I'm no more the person you thought than Fallard was."

That struck him mute. Meloku stepped lightly through the brush, trying to leave as few signs of their passage as possible. Insects bobbed and weaved around her arm.

"Do you truly believe in God?" she asked. He didn't answer, just looked at her. "I hope you do. Only a god could guide your world out of all these wars and plagues and famines. Otherwise it will always look like they did back there, and at Avignon. It will never get better than that without help. That's where we're going – to pray for help."

She couldn't tell if she was speaking with Companion's voice or her own, but she meant it all the same.

As the trail narrowed and the forest thickened, Galien said at last, "We need to turn. Avignon is in the other direction."

"We don't have the time for Avignon."

"But where are we going?"

"Don't worry," she said. "I'll take care of you until I can get someone better."

36

To distract him from the shuttle's shaking, Niccoluccio kept a close on Habidah. Her lips were drawn in a tight line. Her eyes were always red, as if she had held them open for days.

For her part, Habidah studiously avoided looking at him. Niccoluccio wished she would talk. Without her, he had nothing to focus on but the deck falling, and the pit opening in the center of his stomach. He'd eaten little. After his last time riding in this beast, he'd known that he would vomit otherwise.

His stomach wasn't alone in rebelling. The blood in his head felt about to boil. He focused on his breathing. He'd learned a great deal since the last time he'd been a passenger in this monstrosity, even knew some of the principles that kept it airborne, but there was a gulf of difference between understanding and experiencing. He held to the sides of his couch so tight that his knuckles hurt.

The monitors were on this time. They were like seeing through dozens of eyes, all facing different directions. Ten showed the sky and clouds. The ten below showed a patchwork of greens, forests like moss. A minute later, and the clouds fell from one row of monitors to the other. They scudded between the shuttle and the ground, farther all the time.

The horizon was a flat plane in every direction, a perfect geometric form. It was also slanted at a steep angle. He felt that, should he be placed on the ground now, he would be crawling up it like an ant on a hill.

The only way he could force his pulse to slow was to look to Habidah. Aside from the red of her eyes, she looked calm.

"You didn't need to do this for me," he said, so quietly that he wasn't sure she heard him.

"I'm not doing it for you."

Habidah had told him when and where to hide, but had not explained why. Only when he saw Joao and Kacienta leaving the shuttle without her had he understood – she meant to betray her friends.

She said, "I'm doing it for your world. I don't believe that anything I do or don't do will make a difference other than that."

"Why do you think you don't matter?"

"Your master knew that all of this would happen. It understood you. It understood me. No matter how I feel, I'm just a spring in its puzzlebox."

"I'm not as sure about that. I'm not sure it's aware of you, or of any of us, as singular beings."

"Then why does it care about us?" she asked.

"It's trying to keep the amalgamates, any of their shades, from becoming a threat to it or the multiverse."

"By destroying them," she said.

"No. It doesn't believe in death. In an infinite multiverse, nothing is ever lost."

She looked at him for the second time since he'd boarded the shuttle. "Do *you* believe that?"

"I believe I'm sitting here alive when I have no right to be. I survived circumstances that, on a hundred million other planes, would have killed me. I must have died. Yet here I am, alive. I perceive myself as continuous with them."

The first time he'd risen above the clouds in this beast, he couldn't imagine going higher. Now even the clouds had fallen so far away that they looked like only a thin patina over a macrocosm of moss and dirt. Sunlight glinted off puddles smaller than his toes. It took him too long to realize that these were lakes. The horizon, too, was changing. It was becoming bent and distorted, as if the monitors were going concave. Intellectually, he knew they had risen high enough that he could begin to see the curvature of the Earth. But it was not something he had ever imagined seeing.

The roar of the engines changed pitch. Gradually, the juddering of the deck dwindled. The air outside the shuttle was rarefying to the point of carrying no sound. The only noise came from the hull itself.

It didn't affect the music buried just beneath his ears.

The orchestra was no song he recognized, no melody he could even hum. It was less like a song and more like a pattern, an unearthly kaleidoscopic sound. Yet no word other than "music" was fit to describe it.

It was getting louder.

He didn't want to guess what it was building to. Something about the music made him not want to listen. He opened his mouth, about to ask Habidah if she heard it, but an abrupt force clamped his mouth shut. For just a moment, the muscles in his throat belonged to someone else.

He wasn't meant to tell Habidah. He'd had to stop, too, the first time he'd tried talking about it. Something kept him from panicking, but for the first time he considered what Joao had told him: that he was under something else's complete control, and that even he couldn't trust himself.

He said, "Your companions must have realized we're gone by now."

"Before that. I expect that your master will continue to keep them from warning *Ways and Means*." Habidah's tone said that she would rather speak about anything else.

"They'll be safe."

"Joao is dying because of your master."

"It doesn't recognize that there's any such thing as–"

"*We* do. He's suffered long enough. He never deserved it." She made a sound deep in her throat, difficult to hear over the engines. "And what did I go and do to them."

"Did you intend to harm them?"

397

"Of course not. That hardly makes a difference."

"I don't see–"

Habidah tightened her grip on her couch's harness. He saw and fell silent. He wasn't helping.

After a while, she said, "I have no guarantee that a lot of people aren't going to suffer even more because of what I'm doing for you."

"I've been thinking a great deal about why I had to come here. I don't think it would be to hurt people. My master has far better ways to hurt people."

Habidah glanced sideways at him. "Your message for the amalgamates?"

"I still don't know what it is. But think about this. If the Unity is dismantled, there will be no need for the onierophage. My master doesn't care about ending lives. Only about protecting itself and the multiverse." He wondered where those words had come from. They only sounded partially like his own.

Habidah turned back to the monitors, her jaw tense. There were plainly a lot of things she wanted to say, but wouldn't. Or couldn't.

The sky changed timbre. It had started at a light morning blue. Now it was darker, an early evening. Twilight boiled out of the center of the sky. It was not yet dim enough to see stars, but night couldn't be far.

Billowing, white-hot gas streamed across the monitors facing the Earth. Engine exhaust. The shuttle gradually arced its course. The changes were so subtle that he couldn't feel them, and only see them in the trails. The horizon slipped across one monitor, and fell onto the next.

When the shuttle's flight finally leveled, the horizon had a pronounced curve. It was indistinct, hazy. A corona of atmosphere clung to the horizon, very thin. For once, it was fine that Habidah was silent, because he wouldn't have trusted himself to speak. The world seemed so distant, the clouds and their shadows so small, that it hardly seemed like a real place. Far to the south, sunlight glinted off water. The Mediterranean.

Even the sun had changed. It had gone from yellow to a washed-out white. Somehow its sparkling reflection in the sea remained gold.

There was the Channel, and England. Italy forked toward Saracen shores.

"We'll reach *Ways and Means* in another hour," Habidah said. "It's seen our launch. Its agents are demanding to know what we're doing."

"What are you going to tell them?" he asked.

Habidah took a moment to gather herself. Niccoluccio knew that, with the machines in her head, she could have contacted her masters without opening her mouth. Yet she spoke aloud for his benefit: "This is Dr Habidah Shen. I am requesting immediate and emergency landing clearance aboard *Ways and Means*."

A pause for a voice only she could hear. Then: "Something new has come up and I'm not equipped to deal with it. The passenger aboard my shuttle is a native of this plane." Another pause. "Yes, the same I had contact with before. He knows more than he should about us and the Unity. I can't explain how. I didn't tell him. He claims to have had contact with a creature responsible for the onierophage. I'd like to turn him over to you and wash my hands of him at the earliest opportunity."

The longest pause yet followed. Niccoluccio's breath stuck in his chest. Then Habidah said, "I will surrender control of the shuttle to you."

That appeared to be the end of the conversation. Habidah eased her grip on her couch. She still wouldn't turn to look at him. "They didn't need to ask," she told him. "They would have seized control regardless."

One of the monitors now showed an image that, however abstract, was obviously a celestial map. Rings looped around a perfect sphere. It reminded him of an astrolabe. One of the rings spiraled outward, meeting the outermost. The shuttle rode that first line, he guessed. And the outer ring had to contain their destination: the planarship *Ways and Means*.

He swallowed. On the map, *Ways and Means* was just an abstracted orbital path, an infinitely thin line. But Niccoluccio knew it had to be vaster than any structure he'd seen before, vaster than Florence. The vessel housed not just the mind of the amalgamate, but its complexes of factories, sensors, vehicles, engines, and, lastly, living quarters for the augmented humans that served it. For all that Niccoluccio's mission hinged on that ship, he knew astonishingly little about it. He couldn't remember reading anything about it. He didn't even know what it looked like.

"You're not going to like this next part," Habidah said, and that was the only warning he got.

The engine roar shut off. The deck ceased shaking. Niccoluccio's stomach fell into his throat.

He reflexively seized the sides of his couch. He was upside down. He was falling into his safety harness. No – the harness hung limp and flapping. The whole shuttle was plummeting.

Habidah said, "Told you."

Gas burbled past his lips. He swallowed a taste like vomit.

Some great force kicked him into the bottom of the couch. It shook loose his grip, left him fumbling. The images of Earth slipped across several monitors. Then another jolt shoved him in the opposite direction, hard into his harness. He couldn't help his gasp. He scrambled for a different grip.

Gradually, the engine roar resumed, and the couch pushed against him. It felt like an approximation of gravity again. Blood rushed to his head.

The images of Earth had switched monitors. The Mediterranean and the English Channel had swapped positions. The shuttle must have flipped around. The nose was facing Earth. They must have reached the halfway point of their journey, and were decelerating.

"We're burning in hard," Habidah said. "I hope you don't change your mind, because we don't have the fuel to deorbit."

He laid a hand over his stomach. Even she looked far paler than a moment ago. "You don't belong here any more than

I do," he said.

"No," she said.

"Have you ever been aboard a planarship?"

"I've been in orbit twice," she said. "To repair malfunctioning observation satellites on other planes."

"When you can step between planes with a gateway, what need is there to ever go so high?" he asked. "Especially when our bodies rebel against it."

"It's strategically valuable," Habidah said. "The best place to observe and control the ground."

He said, "That's why your masters live here."

"I'm not going to defend them," she said.

The thought hanging off the end of her sentence was almost audible. He prompted, "But...?"

"But if you forced me to choose between the amalgamates and your master, I'd chose the amalgamates. I'm only here to protect your plane."

"You truly believe your master is less invasive than mine?"

"It's gotten into your head," she said. "Rewired you inside and out."

"They never needed to do that to you. They used you to colonize my plane before you ever realized it."

Habidah laughed bitterly. "Your master is more honest about what it's doing. Is that it?"

"Can you convince me that's not important?"

Habidah was no longer listening. Her eyes were on the monitors. Niccoluccio looked, too. At first, he saw nothing different. The sky was black. The stars were washed out by the white-hot exhaust billowing out of the shuttle's engines.

No – there *was* a star. He'd almost missed it. A big star, but dim. A lighter silhouette cast against the black silk of the sky. It grew at an astonishing pace. Already it had a definite shape, an impression of substance.

Lines of shadow splintered it, fractured it. It looked as though someone had placed window panes in the firmament. They were arranged three by three, in a grid. A tenth jutted out what

Niccoluccio could only assume was the head of the vessel.

As with the Earth, from a distance it appeared geometrically perfect. That impression faded as the shuttle closed. *Ways and Means* was haloed by a greenish-yellow ring, as though one of the monitors had caught a bad reflection. A band of gas encircled the planarship's midsection. It reminded him of nothing so much as the Earth's hazy horizon, seen from orbit. The nape of his neck cooled as the realization struck. That's exactly what it was: air, contained.

Some pockets of air seemed thicker than others, almost soup-like. Specks like dust motes flitted in and around the band of atmosphere. They reminded him of birds, but they must have been enormous. Light glinted off their wings. Green moss bubbled along *Ways and Means'* naked hull. Rusty red rivers forked through natural-seeming canyons. Farther on, the forest turned orangeish. The rivers emptied in violet lakes.

"*Ways and Means'* menagerie," Habidah said, without looking to see what he was watching.

The engine roar diminished. The force holding him in his seat loosened. His stomach burbled. The planarship had become huge in the monitors, Earth-sized. For a moment, the shuttle seemed about to dive into the clouds. It changed course at the last moment, skimmed the cloud band, and kept going.

The rest of the planarship was cloaked in insubstantiality, a moving shadow. It would have to be, Niccoluccio figured, to keep hidden. Even at this great height, *Ways and Means* was so large that it would have been easily visible had it reflected sunlight. Nevertheless, he could make out shapes against the deep sea darkness, like shadows against an early dawn.

A forest of leafless trees bristled over one of the hull segments. Sparks glimmered across them, a suggestion of industry. Squat, carbuncular shadows like beehives encrusted the next surface. They were shorter and stouter than the towers, but somehow more menacing. They made him think of warts, or buboes. The shuttle descended toward them.

With another kick from the thrusters, the shuttle rotated.

The cabin spun around him. The towers hung sideways. Then they became fat stalactites on a cavern ceiling. The engine noise ceased, along with the semblance of gravity.

It was finally too much. He ripped his eyes off the monitors, focused on the bulkheads. It didn't help. He doubled over into his safety harness and retched. And then again.

By the time he was finished throwing up, he felt no better. His face was flushed and bloated. Sinewy globules of vomit floated in front of him. His nostrils were clogged, and all he could smell and taste were sour acid juices.

As the shock wore off, he became aware of a deep hum. A cool breeze brushed his legs. The globules gradually fell toward vents in the deck

Habidah looked as calm as she ever had. He knew the machines in her body cared for her in situations like this, but he couldn't imagine anyone being comfortable here. She said, "Your master obviously doesn't care for your comfort or wellbeing if it hasn't prepared you for this. It could have easily rebuilt you to tolerate this."

The nodules surrounded the shuttle. One eclipsed the Earth. That cut all the light from the monitors but for the halo of greenish atmosphere. He and Habidah were left with only the cabin lights. He heard a hiss ahead. A steady press of deceleration held him against his harness.

They had entered the beast.

After an uncomfortable minute, dull orange seeped across the monitors. It revealed nothing bar a polished brass surface "underneath" the shuttle. It was so mirror-perfect that it was impossible to tell if the shuttle was moving. The space above appeared in gradients of gold, equally unblemished. It could have been an eternity, another sky.

As that sky continued to brighten, another kick pushed him into his harness. Dark spots appeared ahead, distant but approaching astonishingly fast. Buildings, black and lumpen and ugly, dimpled the brassy horizon. The thrusters jarred him again. Something mechanical shuddered under the deck.

Unfolding legs, he remembered.

With a thump and final cessation of movement, the shuttle settled to the surface. It had landed several hundred feet from the buildings.

Habidah's harness released of its own accord. Floating, she pushed herself toward Niccoluccio's couch and stopped herself by grabbing its edge. Niccoluccio couldn't understand how she moved so fluently. Taking her at her word, she'd only experienced this twice before.

His harness snapped free. At once, he was floating – falling – free of the couch. He scrambled, but his foot's brief contact with the couch only gave him a spin. Habidah seized his arm and steadied him.

"Don't move," she said. "You got yourself here. Anything you do now can only make it worse."

He nodded, but couldn't speak.

Habidah hauled him like a sack of grain. She tugged him toward the cabin hatch, out to the shuttle's ventral corridor. His breath caught when he saw the boarding ramp peeling open. A cool, dry breeze carried in.

Habidah held onto the ramp to guide them "down," but there were no visible handholds on the outside. Niccoluccio took in the distanceless gold expanse around them. It was even brighter now – a perfect, cloudless day on an alien world. The far walls could have been a mile away, or thirty.

He feared Habidah would launch into the void with her first step, but her boots stuck to the surface. The ground held her seemingly on its own.

Still in Habidah's grip, Niccoluccio experimentally planted a foot on the surface beneath them. It held, although not so firmly that he wouldn't be able to pull it away again. A second foot steadied his balance, but Habidah kept a painful grip on his arm.

He was given very little time to wonder. Three figures were approaching from the direction of the nearest wart-like building. They marched as though in gravity. Their legs bent the wrong way, and their feet were tiny. Their skin was deep black and shone like polished metal. They wore no clothes, but, as they got closer, he saw they had no genitals. He couldn't stop staring. The strangers had no ears, no hair, and nothing to distinguish men from women. Their eyes were too pristine a white, but their irises were human, brown and hazel.

Their leader spoke with a woman's voice. For how strange they all looked, it was remarkable how plain her voice sounded. "Why didn't you contact us before lifting off?"

Habidah couldn't quite meet her eyes. "When I heard all of this, I panicked. I couldn't–"

The stranger cut her off with a wave. Niccoluccio saw for the first time that her fingers were webbed. Her toes were like her fingers: long and dexterous, capable of gripping. Also webbed. "Why did you fly your team members to a native village before traveling to us? Your passenger boarded the shuttle only a minute after landing. I doubt you had enough time to discover all this then."

Habidah tightened her lips and didn't answer, though this time she was able to meet the stranger's stare.

"Dr Shen, I'm placing you under arrest. The two of you will be memory-rooted until we can figure out just what you're trying to accomplish."

Niccoluccio said, "She's telling you enough of the truth."

Habidah and the stranger looked back at him at the same time. He said, "I don't know much about this place, but I know a lot more than I should. I know this is a planarship. I know it comes from a world floating in an interstellar dust cloud like black velvet, that blocks all the stars except the sun. You grew up with empty skies."

It was impossible to tell anything from the stranger's expression. Eventually, she nodded to him. One of her companions moved to him. The other stepped behind Habidah, who remained the center of their attention.

"Is this necessary?" Habidah asked.

"Truly," the stranger said. "You've resisted us for months.

We're only astonished you've gone to these extremes to interfere."

Her companion urged Niccoluccio forward with a firm, insistent prod to his shoulder. By carefully keeping one foot rooted on the "ground," Niccoluccio could shamble forward, a vague approximation of walking.

He moved slowly at first, still feeling as though he might fly off into the orange expanse. He tried not to look up. He locked his eyes on the buildings ahead. They had no doors or windows. Aside from their shiny, black surfaces, they appeared disturbingly organic, like the nodules outside.

The crewwoman who'd spoken led the way. When she reached the nearest wall, she vanished into it as though she'd done nothing more than step into a fog bank. Niccoluccio held his breath and kept walking. The world folded over him. As though he'd stepped over a ledge, what was left of his stomach fell away from him.

By the time the disorientation released him, he and his captors were in an entirely different place. They stood on a shiny, circular platform, about thirty feet in diameter, immersed in a light gray mist. The mist came no closer than the edge of the platform, as though held back. If there was glass there, he saw no sign of it.

The platform was sinking. The mist whipped past, faster and faster. The floor's grip had magnified. Niccoluccio doubted he could lift his feet if he tried. The acceleration was not any more uncomfortable than freefall, aside from the blood rushing to his head, but it certainly wasn't natural. Even if his captors hadn't been here, he still would have been a prisoner.

At first, nothing more than a pale glow came through the fog. Niccoluccio couldn't see any more of the people around him than their silhouettes. The light swiftly brightened until all at once the mist fell away. Niccoluccio shielded his eyes.

The platform dropped into a vast open sky, with clouds receding above them and a distant yellow-green surface far below. No – the ground rose and curved around them, as if they were falling upside down from a deep canyon valley. Treetop foliage flashed across the canyon walls. But the "trees" were regularly spaced, too close to the ground, and there were no breaks in the cover.

The crew stood as though nothing remarkable were happening. Only Habidah looked uncomfortable, and she seemed more put off by their captors than anything outside. She glanced back to Niccoluccio. He held her gaze for the moment it lasted.

The platform kept accelerating, faster and faster, and turned toward the farthest surface. As in a nightmare, the ground lurched at them. All at once, it became clear that it wouldn't stop in time to "land." Niccoluccio's breath hardly had time to catch before they fell right through with no more sound than a whisper.

They emerged in a crimson expanse crisscrossed with bright yellow lines like threads of sunlight. Every few seconds, a pulse of light traveled along one like a ripple down a string. The acceleration eased. So did the blood rushing to his head, and the force sealing his feet to the platform.

Habidah turned and took a few steps closer to him. "You described one of the Core Worlds," she said, quietly.

"If that's what they're called," Niccoluccio said.

Neither the woman nor her companions moved. Niccoluccio knew, without asking, that they were listening, even from distances at which it seemed they couldn't have heard. Habidah asked, "Why would your master describe those to you, but not a planarship?"

"It didn't describe them. I told you about my dreams." But not about the music, the tuning orchestra. He still couldn't.

The sun-threads twirled and intertwined like snakes fighting. They twisted so close that it seemed that they would knot, but Niccoluccio never got to see it. Their platform must have met another surface. The light disappeared all at once.

The next area was much smaller, an egg-shaped space with gray walls only five hundred feet away. They also seemed to be traveling much more slowly – which was odd, since Niccoluccio couldn't recall feeling deceleration.

This space was also strung like a spider's web, but much more thickly, and the threads were larger. People moved upon them. Most were also ink-skinned. Others were missing limbs, or were asymmetrically multi-armed. They walked on all sides of the threads, or into silver spheres. There was no sense of direction, even up or down.

The crewwoman who'd spoken earlier said, "My name is Osia. You're taking this all in better stride than I had imagined."

"I do not feel like it."

Osia nodded to Habidah. "How much did she tell you about this?"

"Nothing."

"Many people find memory-rooting extremely unpleasant. It's exactly as invasive as it sounds. *Ways and Means* will examine your memories directly. It's not physically harmful, but the invasion of privacy is difficult for certain personality types to tolerate."

He met Osia's gaze. "I believe you'd use it on me regardless of what I told you now. I didn't learn about any of this from Habidah. I don't believe I could have, either. On the journey here, she told me that she'd never been on a planarship, and only in orbit twice. You can probably confirm that in your own records."

Habidah turned toward the vista, so that no one could see her face.

Osia said, "I was hoping you would tell us something about all this in your own words before we began."

"Would it change anything you're about to do?"

She didn't need to answer.

The platform rushed toward one of the silver spheres. He flinched at the moment the platform impacted. Darkness engulfed everything. The feel of the air changed. A cold breeze slid through his robe, tossed the hair over his tonsure.

Somewhere in the dark, Osia said, "I don't understand what

either of you thought to win by this."

Habidah muttered, "Certainly not personal gain."

"What, then?"

Habidah said, "I could never stop what you and the amalgamates are trying to do. It's too far beyond me. But I can make a small difference, maybe."

The shadows lightened and lifted. Moon-white walls enclosed them. A sinewy, veinlike corridor wormed into the bowels of the vessel. Niccoluccio's escort poked him forward.

Multiple closed portals lined the walls and ceiling, distinguishable only by their grayish color. Their destination was one of the nearer portals. Niccoluccio stepped through into a broad gold and domed chamber. It had no lamps or lights, but it was nearly blinding, as though the walls shone. The only pieces of furniture were a bare, rectangular table, and couches around the far walls. The seats were cushioned, twice as large as they needed to be, and reminded him of the shuttle's acceleration couches. The table, by contrast, had nothing but a stand joining it to the deck.

Niccoluccio reached the table and ran his hand across it. It was perfectly smooth and hard as marble. This was where he needed to be. He didn't know how he knew that, but he was certain.

He turned. Osia was looking at Habidah. "What did you mean?"

Habidah said, "At this point, the best way I can hurt you is to not tell you."

Osia asked, "Do you know where you are? We'll find out in a matter of minutes. You lose nothing by telling us."

"Listen to you. You don't even know how to make threats. This isn't transactional. It's not about bargaining A for B. I'm out to *stop this*, and I'll fight you however I can."

"I can tell you one way in which I'm very much human." Osia waved two fingers at the table. "You really piss me off."

The other two crewmembers flanked Habidah.

Niccoluccio stepped between them. It was suddenly

important that Osia interrogate him before Habidah. "She told you the truth when she said she didn't understand." He looked at Osia. "I won't fight whatever you're going to do."

Osia stared deep into him. Niccoluccio tried his best to hold her gaze. Some basin of strength was welling up inside him, forcing him. Osia *had* to subject him to interrogation before Habidah. Something important hinged on Osia not grasping how important that was.

Osia lowered her hand and nodded toward him.

The two crewmembers were at once behind him. They tugged his feet off the deck and pulled him atop the table. Once he was there, its surface gripped him.

He laid his head back. It was the most uncomfortable bed he had ever felt. It reminded him of the first time he'd seen his novice's cot at Sacro Cuore, though even that hadn't been made of stone.

Osia's servants pried his hands off his stomach and laid them beside him. The pull on his hands and wrists amplified until it was as strong as manacles. "I'll cooperate," he repeated.

Something underneath his head hummed. At first, he thought it came from the table. The feeling traveled from the back of his skull to his ears. It was a low rattling, and then a cacophony of pitches. That orchestra, rehearsing.

Shadows appeared around the chamber. The cadence of the ceiling was changing. The lights under the walls were invisibly shifting, focusing on him.

Whatever machine Osia meant to use on him hadn't started yet. The music in his head was his own. It was a sound, a feeling, as real as the force holding him. The strings and melodies he'd heard until now had been a warm-up, the clef setting the pitch.

Off to the side, Habidah shook her head and stalked to the edge of the chamber. She took one of the cushioned seats.

Niccoluccio closed his eyes, allowed the rehearsal to end, and the performance to begin.

37

Meloku's legs had become a mass of flayed nerves. Her chest and throat burned. Still she ran ahead of Galien. He stumbled after her more by momentum than by choice. More than once, he'd fallen and she'd just pulled him along until he found his footing. Galien's breath came in ragged gasps. He'd tried to ask questions when they'd set out, but she'd robbed him of the strength.

She was astonished he'd kept up as well as he had. Even without her demiorganics, she was among the healthiest, fittest people on this world, and her stomach was still a knot of pain. Her ration bars hadn't lasted long without her demiorganics boosting her metabolism. She couldn't block out the agony in her legs or the fire in her chest. She could hardly think.

They were almost there. In truth, they hadn't had much farther to go. If they'd been dragging Fallard's men, they would have had another day of walking. Now it was merely sunset, and Meloku recognized the landscape. The shape of the forest to the west and the gentle hills ahead were too distinct to be coincidence.

She topped the next hill and halted. Galien nearly crashed into her. The decrepit barn sat in the field ahead, half-collapsed. The sunlight was at too steep an angle to reveal anything but shadows inside.

The shuttle should have been parked next to it, but it was missing.

The field base's security systems had surely spotted her. Mission procedure held that, should any of the natives get too close to the field base, the shuttle should be flown to a safer position. She doubted that was what had happened. The field base's sensors would've seen who she was.

She resumed running, pulling Galien. The burning in her limbs had gotten worse. Just a few hundred more meters and then she could rest, she lied to herself.

She let go of Galien's wrist right before she reached the barn doors. She heard scuffling and then a thud as he crashed into the wall. She was already through the doors and into the darkness.

The door leading downward was already open. Kacienta and Joao were framed in the artificial light, running to meet her. Joao ran past to check on the man she'd left outside.

Meloku almost pushed through Kacienta. Kacienta grabbed her shoulder. The strength of the grip confirmed one of Meloku's fears: Kacienta had active demiorganics.

Kacienta asked, "What the fuck is—"

Meloku interrupted: "Were you in on this?"

Kacienta looked at her, uncomprehending. Meloku took a risk. She jammed her arm under Kacienta's throat and shoved her into the barn wall. The planks shuddered. Any more force, and she'd give away the fact that her augmented muscles were offline. If, of course, Kacienta didn't know already.

Meloku asked, "Are you working with Habidah?"

"No," Kacienta choked. "Habidah stole the shuttle."

Meloku let go. She turned toward the ramp leading downward. Kacienta rasped, "How did you know to get here? Did *Ways and Means* find out?"

"I lost contact with *Ways and Means*," Meloku said, and started downward.

She wasn't expecting the smell of smoke at the bottom. Dust tickled her nose. Three lights lining the walls had gone out. Those lights were rated for five hundred years of continuous use.

The walls ahead had buckled. So many lights had gone out that the corridor was half shadow. Debris from the broken lights remained scattered on the floor. The damage led in the direction of the communications chamber.

Kacienta had recovered herself. Her bootsteps followed Meloku. She asked, "Who did you bring along?"

"He's a native," Meloku said.

"Not again," Kacienta said. "Not you, too."

"Just take care of him," Meloku snapped. The door to the communications chamber had been jarred open. She sidled through.

The farthest wall had been rent as though by an earthquake. The light from the corridor was barely enough to illuminate the room, but it showed her all she needed. The bare guts of the base's gateway mechanism had been exposed. The aperture projectors, two rapier-sharp metal needles, jutted from the interior floor and ceiling. To a human eye, their tips seemed to touch, but they were actually infinitesimally far apart. They were surrounded by power conduits, transformers, and heat sinks. A mass of tubing coiled around the base of each emitter, held fast by thin gold-silver threads.

The moment she'd stepped inside, she knew exactly what had happened.

Beads of glass cracked and crunched under her boots. Without demiorganics, she wouldn't be able to manipulate anything. She would need help.

Kacienta stepped into the chamber a few steps behind, as if afraid. Meloku felt like a parent coming home after the kids had wrecked the place.

Meloku asked, "Habidah took the shuttle to *Ways and Means*, didn't she?"

"How'd you know?"

"It's the only place on this plane worth going to."

The gateway, she figured, must have been used to transport something from *this* plane, to another. Her enemy had more than enough power already here.

Meloku said, "You told me Habidah stole the shuttle. So who went through the gateway?"

Kacienta didn't even ask how she'd guessed that. "It was her pet monk. But he came back. Is that why you brought the other native here? To do the same thing? Is this some kind of amalgamate trick?"

"What? No. He's just a man. Tell Joao to get him food and water. Tranquilize him if he complains."

A neat cleft had split the floor down the middle. Meloku stepped over it, toward the rent in the wall. In spite of the destruction, the gateway mechanism was wholly intact. Not a sliver or wire out of place. It had been built to withstand earthquake-like stresses, but everything around it hadn't. The compression waves had sheared through the earth, rock, and walls, ripping metal like paper. It was probably unsafe to be here. The chamber might collapse.

Kacienta said, "Joao and I still don't have any idea what happened here. It's got us thinking we're up against some god, some extraplanar power–"

Meloku turned, gave her a withering look. It worked; Kacienta stopped babbling. Meloku asked, "How long ago did they leave?"

"Who?"

Meloku said, through strained patience, "Habidah and her monk."

"Two hours," Kacienta stammered. "We can't contact our satellites, but last the ground sensors saw, they were headed to *Ways and Means*. They must have reached it by now. If *Ways and Means* let them, I mean."

"I need to contact *Ways and Means*," Meloku said. "Go after them if I can't."

"The shuttle's gone. We can't get into contact with it."

"I'll use the communications gateway," Meloku said. "I'll send myself through if I have to."

"But that's impossible...!"

Meloku snapped, "Obviously it's not impossible. You saw it."

After a moment, she calmed enough to say, "Nor was it ever intended to be impossible. No one besides the amalgamates and their agents is meant to know, but a micrometer communications gateway aperture *can* be widened this far. The method is intended to be used only in emergencies. It doesn't require 'gods' or powers. Just an understanding of transplanar theory behind what the amalgamates have chosen to make public."

Kacienta peered through the fissure. "But all the destruction–"

"Didn't destroy the gateway mechanism. The mechanism stayed intact while the stresses destroyed everything around it. As it was designed to."

Kacienta set her hand on the twisted wall, as if to lean on it. "We thought that we were seeing a miracle."

"Whoever wanted you to think that it was some kind of mystical power was tricking you. There was nothing magical about what happened here. The only mystery is where the extra power came from, but there must be an explanation for that, too."

The needle-like projectors tapered to invisibility. There seemed to be space for a gateway, at most, a few micrometers wide. All deception. Multiple layers of folded space had already cut right through them without displacing them. It was one of the contradictions possible only at so high an understanding of transplanar physics.

"I'm going to need your help to reactivate these. You and Joao both."

"What can we do?"

"My demiorganics are nonfunctional." Meloku paused to gauge Kacienta's reaction. When she saw nothing, she said, "I need you and Joao to restart the gateway, and to program some very specific instructions."

"For what?"

"I'm going to open a gateway directly aboard *Ways and Means*, and contact it through that." A gateway opening in the middle of its hull would definitely get the amalgamate's attention.

Kacienta stared a moment, her mouth slack, and then nodded.

She fetched Joao, who had gotten Galien tucked away into Feliks' old quarters. While Meloku told them what they needed to do next, they alternated between telling her everything that had happened.

Joao said, "She lied to us. She must have set up her plan with Niccoluccio hours beforehand. She's a psychopath, a walking disaster. I should have known this was coming."

"You should have," Meloku said.

Meloku got a breathless earful of Niccoluccio's stories of the world beyond the gateway. There was certainly some powerful force behind all of this, that much was certain. But their talk about gods was a native mode of thinking. Someone was trying to pull a very thick wrapping over their eyes. It was impossible to tell whether Habidah knew more, or if she had been just as duped as Kacienta and Joao.

Meloku said, "I need one of you to find *Ways and Means'* current position and velocity. If you can't get in contact with your satellites, then just plot its orbit from the last time you saw it."

Calculate an orbit. She might as well have told them to spoon her food. Without her demiorganics, Meloku couldn't do much but direct.

While Joao tracked *Ways and Means*, Kacienta programmed the gateway mechanism as Meloku directed. Meloku was relieved to discover that most of her work had already been done for her. Whoever had last reconfigured the gateway hadn't bothered to undo their alterations.

She returned her attention to the gateway mechanism. Opening a transplanar gateway was difficult enough. It was paradoxically much more difficult to gate between two points on the same plane. It might have been better to travel directly to the Core Worlds. But no, *Ways and Means* was in immediate danger. No matter what she thought of Kacienta and Joao's ramblings of gods, she couldn't underestimate her opposition. If Habidah and Niccoluccio got aboard *Ways and Means*, they might lose it. The Unity had never lost an amalgamate.

While Joao worked, he said, "We still can't contact *Ways and Means* directly. Whatever's in control of this base won't let us. NAI isn't answering our questions. I suppose it could have taken our demiorganics, like it did yours, but it didn't."

Meloku didn't answer. At least her enemy had been more afraid of her than these two.

Joao asks, "I still have to use base systems. What makes you think NAI's going to allow what we're doing now?"

She was forced to admit, "Nothing. I have to try."

"And if it doesn't work?"

She had to hope that her enemy had turned its attention away. If she couldn't alert *Ways and Means*, she wouldn't be able to do anything else, either.

As the adrenaline rush faded, pain soaked through her legs, seeping up her abdomen like water through a sponge. She no longer had the technology to disguise her exhaustion. Nor sort out her brain chemistry. Despair crashed down on her in big, heady waves. She tried to force it out, or, when that didn't work, ignore it. Anxiety shouldn't matter. Exhaustion and depression shouldn't matter. It was all foolish chemicals.

She asked, "Joao, if Habidah could have saved the Unity, do you think she would have?"

Joao seemed lost in the haze of data. "Excuse me?"

"Her character profile said that she was never as attached to her home plane, or any other, as she was to the planes she studied. If she had to choose between attacking one or the other, which do you think it would be?"

"I suppose she chose to attack the Unity. I mean, she must have."

"Would you?"

Joao gave her a sharp glance. "Of course not."

"What did you and Kacienta think when you discovered what the amalgamates were doing here?"

417

Kacienta said, "Well, we weren't *pleased*, but–"

"But you cared about what happened to this plane. That's more than most people in the Unity."

Joao said, "If you're implying that we would betray the Unity, you can fuck right back off the way you came."

Meloku said, "Whatever force is controlling the monk targeted you all for a reason. You were more susceptible to turning."

Kacienta said, "We didn't."

"I believe you." Meloku waited a moment before adding, "Since you're helping me."

Kacienta pursed her lips. Joao glanced at her, but couldn't bring himself to look at Meloku. He closed his eyes to focus on his demiorganics. They both looked miserable, but they knew they were being watched.

She was finally starting to feel like herself again. It made her just as miserable as they were. But she'd found out what she'd needed to, why her enemy had targeted her old teammates. And she'd made it clear to them that they were being watched.

After a certain point, there were no more directions she could give. Kacienta and Joao had to handle this on their own. Anxiety clawed up her throat. She cupped her hands and breathed into them.

Companion wouldn't have been able to allay her fears. Its cold foresight would have just informed her of another half dozen ways it could all go wrong. Still, just hearing its voice again would have been a comfort, like going home again. Like closing her eyes was right now.

Kacienta reported, "The microaperature gateway is open."

Meloku's eyes snapped open. She bolted upright. The sleep vanished from her system. The adrenaline was back, and, for now, that was all that mattered.

"Signal *Ways and Means*," she said.

It took so damned long to *hear* the answers rather than receive them directly. Kacienta said, "Static."

"There are thousands of radio signals coming through,"

Joao said. "I can't sort through them. It's a babble. All kinds of chaos."

"Spectroscopy," Meloku snapped.

After another excruciating pause, Kacienta said, "Nitrogen, oxygen, argon, carbon dioxide, et cetera, on the other side." The gateway had opened in a breathable atmosphere. "Traces of all kinds of other compounds."

"Name some."

"Mono, di, and tricresyl phosphates, nitrous oxides, ozone."

All industrial contaminants Meloku would expect to find almost-but-not-quite scrubbed from a planarship's air. She'd found the right place. *Ways and Means* was on the other side. It should have detected the gateway opening in an instant.

If it hadn't responded to that, something was terribly wrong.

She looked to Joao. "In all those thousands of radio signals, is there anything at all that sounds familiar?"

Joao bit his lip. His eyes flicked back and forth as data poured through him. Meloku would have given her legs to see what he was reading.

Finally, he said, "Habidah is there. I recognize her demiorganics' fingerprint."

Meloku said, "Reopen the gateway closer to her. Load the other instructions I gave you. You and Joao will want to clear out."

Joao said, "You can't possibly think you'll survive. You saw the wreckage left the last time someone widened the gateway."

"Compared to what I went through to get here, that will be easy."

Joao shook his head, but he and Kacienta did as they were told. After they stepped out, Meloku stood and faced the gateway.

She could perceive no change in either the needles or the infinitesimal space between them. She stretched her fingers, an activity Companion had taught her to clear her mind. To survive this, she needed to be limber, like she was making ready to survive a crash.

But she couldn't help herself. Rage poured through her head, boiling, fulminating, seeking any release it could find. It dampened the pain in her legs.

She knew she ought not to feel clear-headed. That was an illusion, a trick of brain chemistry. Her judgment was probably more impaired than it had ever been in her life. Everything inside her was a mess.

But she *liked* this mess. All the fury and fear compressed her pain, crystallized it into an urge to attack. If, when, she found something on the other side of the gateway, she didn't know what she was going to do, but it was going to be *something*. That was more than Kacienta or Joao would have.

Maybe she'd always been a mess, and needed Companion and the amalgamates to temper her. They'd known that, too. And they'd still chosen her.

Light flickered between the needles.

Meloku preemptively raised her hand to shield her eyes from the lightning storm to come. When she stepped through, the last thing she needed was to stumble blindly while her vision adjusted. She would be stumbling enough already. But better that than stopping.

38

The moment Niccoluccio's eyes closed, the lights flickered.

It happened so suddenly that Habidah nearly thought she'd blacked out. The pressure sealing her feet to the deck released, but only briefly. The lights returned exactly as they had: focusing on Niccoluccio, who slept.

Osia and her comrades floated lifelessly, their arms splaying out. Only their feet held them anchored to the deck.

A flood of data crashed into Habidah. Voices overlapped each other. So much of it was an unintelligible tangle, coded messages. The rest were cries for help, urgent requests for information, demands to stay calm. Voices from all over the planarship surged through her, too loud to drown out. She couldn't think. She instinctively blocked signals from more than a hundred meters away.

She stepped past Osia and the others, approached Niccoluccio's table. Steady breathing, gentle pulse. She tried to convince herself that she didn't know what had happened, but she couldn't manage it. The battle had taken place in a flash of milliseconds, before she realized it had started. The amalgamate had cut power to this chamber, an emergency attempt to stem the tide of data flowing out of Niccoluccio's mind.

Then the power had returned. Either *Ways and Means* had restored it, or something else had.

Before Habidah could get any closer, a jet-black hand

grabbed her wrist.

Habidah gave a gasp of surprise. Osia stood next to her, recovered from her fugue. Her grip tightened, painfully. "What did you do?"

She blinked, pretending – without having to try hard – to be at a loss for words. The strength of Osia's fingers couldn't hide their tremble. Habidah hadn't realized anything could threaten her control. But she and her companions had never left her. They'd gone limp only while trying to figure out what was happening, putting their physical selves behind them.

Osia said, "*Ways and Means* isn't answering me. Or anyone aboard." She looked to Niccoluccio. "It happened a few milliseconds after the memory root began. There was some kind of virus inside him. And you brought it aboard."

Osia watched her closely. Her face was expressionless. It was like staring into the dead eyes of a statue. She had to be scanning Habidah in multiple spectra, studying her reactions, the things she couldn't help but give away.

She must have found what she was looking for, because her second hand snapped up and seized Habidah by the neck. Habidah choked from the surprise, but Osia wasn't squeezing hard enough to restrict her airflow. Yet. Habidah tried to step backward, wheeled her free arm in a futile instinct to keep her balance. After a moment, she spat into the air because she couldn't swallow and would have choked otherwise.

Habidah said, "And now you'll have to kill me just to be certain I'm not part of it."

"I'm already certain."

One of the other crewmembers stepped to Niccoluccio, arm raised like a club. The crewmember moved in a blur, too fast to be human. Habidah didn't want to see what happened next, but didn't have the composure to look away

At once a sheet of lightning crashed down from the ceiling, intersected the crewmember's arm. The crewmember took a few steps backward, knuckles glowing cherry-hot.

"Field-protected," the crewmember transmitted, not

bothering to encrypt the signal. A masculine voice. Had he been human, his skin would have been seared off his hand.

Osia answered, "He must still be important to whatever's attacking."

The third crewmember transmitted, "It must be in complete control of this chamber. It could kill us all with hardly any effort." Also masculine.

Habidah tried to fight Osia's hand off, but it was like hitting polished marble. Habidah couldn't keep from scrabbling at Osia's wrist. For several long seconds, she was sure that this would be the last thing she ever saw. But Osia's grip held steady.

The deck lurched. Osia remained rooted to the deck, but Habidah's legs wheeled through the air. Even Osia tilted sideways with Habidah's momentum.

A second later, though, Osia recovered enough to plant Habidah onto the deck. The first crewman reported, "Dorsal deck crews report thrusters firing."

Without *Ways and Means'* communications systems, its crew had formed an impromptu relay chain to help important messages break through the chatter. Anyone in a position to observe something swiftly reported their news to their neighbors, who sent it on. Habidah tentatively widened the distance from which she allowed her demiorganics to receive transmissions.

Ways and Means' stealth fields had shut off. All of its antimatter generators were spinning to life. Its aft drive was waking. And power was being shunted to its gateway generator.

All of which meant the planarship was making ready to slip between the waves of the multiverse.

A force the likes of which had taken out *Ways and Means* could probably have taken out its crew as well. Yet it had left them alive. It saw *Ways and Means'* crew as beneath its attention. The crew had figured this out. Still, the paramount order among them was to cut off contact with the planarship's mind. Any virus that disabled the amalgamate so quickly would transmit easily among them.

More scattered reports said that all the internal gateways and transport platforms had shut down. The crew was stuck where they were. Their assailant cared that much, at least.

Osia told Habidah, "You knew this would happen."

Habidah said, "Better to say that I didn't try to stop it."

Another signal broke through all the others. It was a voice, a woman's, amplified by the relays. Someone was at last trying to organize. She ordered everyone near a power conduit or generator to destroy it, to sabotage the planarship from the inside.

The crewman to Osia's left sent, "There's a power junction two hundred forty-three meters down the corridor. We're the only ones mid-deck. We'll need cutting tools and all of us working to get through the bulkheads in time."

"I know," Osia said, tightly.

Osia carried Habidah ahead, still holding her by the neck. Habidah choked, beat on Osia's hand. She was deprived of air for only a moment, though, before Osia deposited her on one of the acceleration couches.

The moment her arm touched the cushion, it snapped there, held in place by invisible bands. The fields had a little give, just enough to keep from breaking her bones, but she couldn't even bend her elbow.

She shot Osia a look of burning contempt. Osia gave no sign of registering it. She and her companions left via the chamber's only exit portal.

Habidah looked to the center of the chamber.

Niccoluccio lay unmoving but for the steady rhythm of breathing. The burst of acceleration had splayed his hair sideways. His tonsure shone wan under the lights. "Niccoluccio," she said.

For once, she figured they weren't being listened to. Without *Ways and Means* functioning, she doubted Osia could spy through the chamber's cameras. "Niccoluccio," she tried again.

424

Still no change. She leaned as far as the restraining field allowed, which wasn't much. Niccoluccio's chest rose and sank every two seconds, as a person in deep sleep. His cheeks had lost their color. His eyelids flickered nervously, too fast for dreaming.

He wasn't so much unconscious as somewhere else.

"Wake up," she hissed.

She tested her restraints again. She knew of no weaknesses to exploit, no way to tell if the fields were working properly, no way to even make this more comfortable. The fields dug into her skin. It was impossible to restrain her reflex to fight to escape. More out of fury than hope, she wrenched her wrist against the fields.

The fourth time she slammed against the field, her hand yanked free.

The bands all over her body released at once. Her arm flew up, struck the cushion. The lights flickered and then went out.

The deck no longer gripped her soles. In infrared, she'd already risen a quarter meter above the heat shadow she'd left on the couch.

Osia and her cohort had gone to mess with the power systems, but she doubted they'd expected this. Something had gone wrong. Whatever was in charge of the planarship might have rerouted power to adjust.

The fields protecting Niccoluccio had dissipated, left infrared a fuzzy mess. Habidah could hardly see. Niccoluccio's platform was a hot blur in the center of the chamber.

She half-twisted in midair, lashed her foot against the bulkhead to propel herself. Too late. Before she'd gotten a meter away, the lights restored. This time, the air surrounding Niccoluccio didn't change in any spectrum she could perceive, but something *popped* and sizzled.

If Niccoluccio's protective field had turned the crewman's hands bright red, it would burn the flesh of Habidah's face. Habidah drove her hands into the deck to arrest her momentum. The deck gripped her hands, slowing her.

Too late, her demiorganics trilled a warning about how her maneuver would end. Her legs flew over her. She flipped end over end. Momentum tore her hands away from the deck. She tumbled past Niccoluccio's table, far overhead, and crashed knee first against the far bulkhead. The domed surface clung to her like the faux-gravity of the deck.

Crew reported power flickers all over the ship. Not every power conduit or generator was easily accessible, though. The planarship's hijacker had been able to reroute most of those disabled. It had not even bothered to defend the remaining junctions, so little had it been affected so far.

Habidah was acting on dumb impulse, she knew. She couldn't free Niccoluccio from the fields holding him. She couldn't navigate the planarship. Even if she could, she had no way to get her shuttle out of its hangar. She had no plan, only a goal. There was no way *to* have planned for this.

She'd had no idea she'd possessed so strong a will to live. She'd boarded the shuttle expecting, sometime soon, to be killed. She'd imagined she would simply accept her end when it came to her. But this wasn't how she wanted to die. Not, at least, while Niccoluccio was here as well.

She scrambled sideways, on her hands and knees, across the dome. She had nearly reached the deck when the lights failed again. The bulkhead lost its grip on her. She sailed helplessly, and crashed shoulder first into the deck.

The moment the lights returned, a figure pushed through the portal. Habidah's crash had given her a lazy trajectory through the chamber. Her hands slipped loose of the deck. She was already out of arms' reach of any surface. She steeled herself to confront Osia, but the person who'd stepped through was human.

Meloku.

She was still in native costume, minus the headgear. Her lips hung slack in mute horror. Her eyes darkened when she saw Habidah. She held onto the portal's edge to push herself through, and planted her shoes on the deck.

Habidah twisted in midair. She couldn't do anything to avoid Meloku. She started to ask, "What the fuck are–?"

Meloku braced against the deck, drew back her fist, and slammed it into the bridge of Habidah's nose.

By the time Habidah realized what had happened, she was pinwheeling backward. The back of her tongue tasted of copper. She couldn't breathe. Her demiorganics informed her they were blocking a tidal flood of pain signals. They struggled to regain control of her breathing.

She didn't have the time to wait. The next time the deck spun past, she reached for it. The faux-gravity seized her palms, and brought the rest of her crashing onto her back. She swung her feet around to face Meloku. The other woman was already advancing.

Habidah's demiorganics weren't combat-rated, but she had a minimal self-defense program. Amid the flood of other urgent signals, she didn't have time to listen to its suggestions. She lashed her foot ahead, aiming to catch Meloku by the ankle. Meloku sidestepped. She grabbed Habidah's leg and slammed her elbow into it, just below the knee.

This time, her demiorganics couldn't block the pain in time. Habidah's world blurred black and red. Her demiorganics informed her Meloku had narrowly avoided breaking her leg. Her shin was fractured. Almost as an afterthought, they added that her nose was broken. As if the blood warming her upper lip wasn't proof enough.

Habidah was almost glad the pain had gotten through. It jogged her focus.

Meloku shoved Habidah's injured leg aside and stepped closer to get a better shot at her face. Habidah jabbed both feet against Meloku's ankles. Meloku stumbled free from the deck plating, flailed through the air.

With demiorganics like hers, she shouldn't have fumbled like that. Habidah wasted no time thinking about it. As Meloku passed overhead, Habidah drove the heel of her palm into Meloku's stomach. Meloku *whoofed*.

Habidah stayed planted on the deck plating, sucking air through her teeth. Her demiorganics fought for her attention with increasingly shrill warnings. Her vision tinged red and black.

Meloku wheeled across the chamber. As soon as her feet made contact with the far bulkhead, the lights went out again. Again, the chamber vanished in an infrared fog of dissipating fields.

When it returned, Meloku had launched back, already halfway across the chamber, her face contorted with rage. In a flash of panic, Habidah spotted an ivory-handled knife in her hand. If she'd meant to hurt before, now she aimed to kill.

Habidah had just enough time to roll to her side before Meloku's boot slammed into the deck where Habidah's stomach had been. Habidah couldn't roll fast enough. The deck plating grabbed at her, slowed her.

Meloku stepped closer and landed her boot in Habidah's ribs. Meloku's next kick found Habidah's stomach, and then her chin. Her vision blurred dark again. She raised her arm as a shield. For whatever reason, though, Meloku hesitated to use the knife. Her next kick glanced off Habidah's elbow.

Habidah seized Meloku's leg while it was still in the air, and wrenched Meloku off the deck. The half-second that followed gave Habidah a chance to finally listen to her demiorganics' self-defense programs. They had her yank Meloku forward, lock her knees with a raised leg, and then try to slam her head into the deck.

Meloku's combat programs should have had plenty of time to react. Habidah was shocked when she completed her maneuver uninterrupted. Meloku reached to slow herself, but with merely human reaction speed. Habidah brought her crashing headfirst into the deck. She yelped and bounced away, pinwheeling into the air.

Habidah rolled onto her stomach to try to right herself, and the lights vanished again. Her head spun with her new sense of weight. The deck bashed into her chest and held her there tightly. Somewhere in the infrared haze, Meloku crashed to the deck. The knife clattered far away.

Ways and Means was moving again, faster and more violently. This was no thruster burst. The main engines were firing, sustaining a half-*g* of acceleration.

Ways and Means was breaking out of orbit before opening its gateway. Momentum held constant between planes. Habidah's mind raced. Assuming it was transporting to a solar system like this one, it wanted to emerge at a high velocity. Used as a kinetic impactor, a ship this size could smash a world apart.

The lights returned. On the other side of the chamber, Meloku had fallen to her knees. She stood on shaky legs. Blood welled from torn skin over her left eyebrow. She was just as bruised as Habidah felt. She demanded, "Where are you taking us?"

Maybe that was why she'd held off from using the knife. Couldn't ask a dead woman questions. "Do I *look* like I know what's happening here?"

Meloku half-staggered across the chamber, toward Habidah. Habidah's ribs flared in agony as she stood. She rested her weight on her good leg. Against an opponent with superior demiorganics, she was in no shape to win. But something was very obviously wrong with Meloku. She wobbled in the half-gravity.

Habidah slipped into a parrying stance, alert for any sign Meloku was faking her distress. Meloku feinted a blow to Habidah's left, and then jabbed a fist toward her stomach. Habidah blocked it, and countered with a hard punch to Meloku's chin.

Meloku stumbled back, visibly stunned. Habidah could hardly believe it. She took several steps back while Meloku recovered.

Meloku's face screwed up with pain. She glanced sideways, to Niccoluccio. Habidah realized too late that Meloku was now closer to Niccoluccio than her.

Meloku stepped toward Niccoluccio. Habidah blurted, "Stop!"

Meloku looked to her.

Habidah nodded to the table. "There's a protective field. It'll burn your skin off."

Meloku hesitated. Habidah said, "Test it if you don't believe me."

Meloku kept a careful eye on Habidah. Habidah stayed still. Meloku reached under her sleeve and tore off a sweaty, soiled piece of the lacy fabric underneath. She balled it up and tossed it toward Niccoluccio.

A flash of light wrapped around Niccoluccio's table. Afterward, there was nothing left but a mushroom of rapidly dissipating smoke.

Meloku looked to Habidah. "Why would you tell me?"

Habidah said, "I don't want to hurt anyone I don't have to." Just an excuse, a post-hoc rationalization. The truth was she'd blurted the warning without thinking.

Meloku wiped her lips. The back of her hand came back bloody. "I'd kill you if I could."

"There'd be no point. I can't control anything anymore."

Osia and one of her companions stepped through the portal. There was no sign of the third. Osia halted. With a face like hers, it was impossible to read any measure of surprise. "I figured you'd get free when the power failed," she said, nodding to Habidah, "but *you* I didn't expect."

"I came to try to stop this," Meloku said.

Osia said, "You're with her. You arrived together somehow."

Meloku waved her hand at Habidah's bloodied nose. "Do we *look* like we're working together?"

Habidah barked a laugh. Of all the absurdities of the past few days, the one that stung the most was the fact that everyone still assumed she had some measure of control. Maybe she'd had some when she'd brought Niccoluccio here. But if *Ways and Means* hadn't fallen to the virus in Niccoluccio's mind, it would have been conquered in some other way.

430

She spun, and held out her arms. "It's true. We worked together. We planned everything for years. Why don't you just memory-root us and find out?"

Osia's expression didn't – couldn't – change, but that didn't keep her eyes from boring into Habidah.

Meloku told Osia, "You need to interrogate and neutralize her right now. She's responsible for this, and she'll do worse if she has any chance."

Habidah waved offhandedly, like she might brush away a mosquito. "It's hard to imagine this getting much worse from your perspective."

Meloku told Osia, "My demiorganics have been knocked out for days. I had to open an emergency gateway to come here. Any signals you've received from me recently have been frauds."

Osia kept that impenetrable gaze on Habidah. "This has all been orchestrated."

The deck shifted. Habidah grabbed one of the seats to keep her balance. Pain shot through her ribs. A wave of panicked calls blotted out her demiorganics' ability to receive them. This didn't feel like an ordinary engine burst. Something had shaken the hull.

Meloku looked straight at Habidah. Demiorganics or not, Meloku had recognized that jolt. "We just jumped planes."

Niccoluccio said, "To Providence Core."

Habidah spun. Niccoluccio's eyes were open, staring into the bulkheads.

Some frightened crewwoman was transmitting her view of the outside universe. She and several others had been on the outer hull before the attack. She had recorded an image of the instant the planarship had emerged: a flat black expanse, devoid of stars. Niccoluccio was right, at least in that they'd gone to a Core World. All of the Core Worlds were in vast interstellar dust clouds, hiding the light from other stars.

A swirled blue-white disk fell behind *Ways and Means*. The continents were in different configurations from how they were on Niccoluccio's Earth. Ahead, a cloud of lights shone in far orbit – farther than the moon's orbit, half a million kilometers away. Not stars, but stations, planarships.

But that instant's view had been the only one. Everything had disappeared half a heartbeat after *Ways and Means* had arrived. The Earth distorted, curved, and appeared a hundred times on the other side of the sky. It was as if it had been reflected by a field of convex mirrors. *Ways and Means'* defensive fields had sprung into place, twisting and distorting all the light reaching it.

There was no sign of the band of atmosphere that had once encircled the planarship. Not even a wisp of gas. *Ways and Means'* menagerie must not have survived the acceleration or the jump.

For a moment, Habidah feared the planarship was aimed toward Providence Core, that it meant to crack that world open. But its engines faced away. It was headed directly toward the thickest portion of the artificial starry nebula. The weight pressing Habidah against the deck grew steadily stronger.

Osia stepped closer to Niccoluccio's table, and stopped seemingly half a hair's breadth from the protective field. She asked, "Are you speaking for the virus that's hijacked our planarship?"

"It's not a virus," Niccoluccio said, still staring. He hadn't blinked since he'd opened his eyes. "It's a mind."

"Answer my question."

After a pause, Niccoluccio said, "I can speak to it. Not for it."

Osia's companion blurted, "Is *Ways and Means* safe? What did you do with its mind?"

"*Ways and Means* is dormant."

Habidah's knees buckled as the planarship's engines increased thrust. It went from half gravity, to full gravity, and half that again. She kept her weight on her good leg, and still her demiorganics had to numb the pain.

The crewwoman outside continued to transmit. Flashes of light sparkled among the defensive fields. Providence Core's defenses had not taken kindly to a planarship arriving without notification. Pulsed lasers struck *Ways and Means*, but dissipated harmlessly amongst the angled defensive fields. From the crewwoman's perspective, the sky scintillated kaleidoscopic colors as the laser light bounced from field to field, scattering and dissipating.

Providence Core would have launched missiles and combat drones as well, but too late. *Ways and Means* had emerged at too high a velocity for them to catch up. Not before it reached its target.

The crew was puzzling out what that target was. The last any of them had heard, three amalgamates were visiting Providence Core: *Foreign Operations, Risk Management,* and *Trade and Finance.* They were somewhere ahead in the seashell-spiraled nebula of lights.

Osia said, "Let me speak to *Ways and Means*."

Niccoluccio said, "It's not in a state to talk directly."

The other crewman said, "You mean it's dead."

"Dismembered."

Osia's fingers curled into a fist, but it was either a pointless gesture or a purely emotional reaction. It was the first time Habidah could remember any of the crew showing either.

Habidah said, "Niccoluccio, I don't know how much you can remember, or use your judgment, but this is Habidah. Tell me what you're seeing."

"I don't see. I'm a part of it. It's using me. My capacity to process information. I'm a part of its network now, one synapse in a brain. It's protecting me because of that, but it could do without me." Niccoluccio's vocabulary had changed since he'd returned from the gateway, but he hadn't sounded like this before. His affect was that of a dead man, but she could still taste the sorrow in his voice: "I had no idea I would lose so much."

Habidah swallowed past the heat in her throat. She asked, "Do you know everything *it* knows?"

His eyes were red for lack of blinking. "Most things."

The deck rumbled as the engines accelerated harder. Habidah felt twice as heavy as usual. A drop of blood fell from her nose, struck the deck with a heavy splash. Her vision fringed red as more pain made it through her nerve blocks. Every part of her hurt. Her demiorganics tightened her blood vessels to keep her from fainting. She hobbled to one of the acceleration couches, holding its side.

Outside, the defensive fields pulsed iridescent, but dimmer and dimmer as the planarship put more distance between it and the planetary defenses. Habidah inhaled deeply. Providence Core was well defended, but the amalgamates ahead were far more so. It was hard to imagine *Ways and Means* besting three planarships.

But the virus's plans wouldn't necessarily include surviving.

Several crewmembers were trying to sabotage the planarship's weapons. The voice of Osia's missing companion was the nearest link in the relay reporting on their efforts. They were jamming drone bay doors shut, disabling missile engines. More crawled inside the hull plating to destroy field emitters and dismantle combat drones in their nests.

"Niccoluccio," Habidah asked, fearing the answer, "how much of you is still you?"

Niccoluccio's mouth opened and closed, but he didn't respond.

Habidah heard an echo of her own voice. Osia was broadcasting this conversation. More and more crewmembers were listening.

Osia asked, "Is the same creature that sent you controlling our ship?"

For a moment, Habidah didn't understand why Osia had asked. But Osia was astute. Niccoluccio surprised Habidah when he said, "No. It planted a seed in my memories. When you interrogated me, that seed spread its roots through your planarship. It's like a branch of a plant that broke off and was replanted. The mind that's in control of your ship is its own being."

Meloku asked, "Did its creator also poison the Unity with the onierophage?"

After another long pause, Niccoluccio said, "Yes. Now it's aiming higher."

All over the planarship, crewmembers were trying to contact the other amalgamates. They had transmitters in their bodies powerful enough to reach the distant planarships. Their signals returned jumbled, layered atop each other, turned to shrieks and screams. *Ways and Means* bounced their microwave pulses between the same fields it had used to dissipate Providence Core's lasers. Any signals sent their way must have been jammed in the same manner.

Osia said, "Your master can't hope to destroy all of the amalgamates."

Niccoluccio inhaled sharply through his noise. When he spoke, his voice was a rasp. Whatever demands the ship's new mind had placed on him were amplifying. "Not destroy. Plant a seed. Like what happened here."

If Osia could have lost a shade from her cheeks, Habidah suspected she would have. It took her a long time to answer. "I see."

Meloku said, "I don't. We're not talking about gardening."

Osia said, "We're talking about spreading a virus. The virus must need close contact to spread. If it could infect the other amalgamates by broadcast, it would have done so by now. It could have infected *us* just by transmitting itself from the anthropologists' field base. It went through the trouble of smuggling itself to us in this man."

Meloku picked up her thought: "If the virus had come in a few bits at a time, *Ways and Means* could have figured out what was happening and destroyed it before it became complex enough to take over. The memory-root was different." Like drinking from a geyser, Habidah figured. "Too much of the virus shunted into its mind to stop."

Osia said, "It doesn't need to win a battle. It just needs to fight. If it gets close enough to the other amalgamates, it will have myriad ways to infiltrate them. Infected drones latching onto their hulls and boring directly into a memory core. Or infected crewmembers brought for interrogation. Even if we're blasted apart, we'll leave behind bodies, escaped shuttles, memory cores, something that the other amalgamates will bring aboard to investigate."

The crewman beside Osia said, "Most of our lower classes are already disabled by the onierophage. With the amalgamates gone and their planarships taken, there will be nothing left of the Unity."

Osia raised a webbed hand and brushed gingerly against the edge of the field protecting Niccoluccio. Sparks spat from her fingertips. Niccoluccio didn't even flinch. Habidah had seen the same eyes on the dead of Messina, Venice, Genoa.

Habidah asked, "Can you control your body? Are you suffering?"

Niccoluccio said, "It's as if everything I've known was in a single thought, and I've become a mind." For the first time, he closed his eyes, and then gasped and reopened them, as if something had just struck him. Habidah would have sold a great deal of herself to find out what was happening inside his head. "I hate it. I can't see anywhere but there. I can't move, can barely think."

Habidah said, "I did this to you."

"I went along," Niccoluccio said. "I knew I would lose myself."

Osia said, "The virus is using you. If I can get through this field and kill you, I may not stop it, but I can harm it. It will end your suffering."

Habidah said, "You kill Niccoluccio, you destroy your only means of communicating with the monster."

The voices from the back of her demiorganics doubled in an instant. All over the planarship, crew reported power shifts, hull segments going dark. Combat drones were launching. The crew had so far only sabotaged a fraction of their nest cradles. A handful of missing weapons seemed to amount to nothing at all.

That must have been the most agonizing part for an elite crew like this. They hadn't been killed only because they weren't worth the effort. They were too small. Maybe now they understood how Habidah had felt.

Osia observed, "It apparently doesn't feel the need to negotiate." Habidah said, "Forgive me for pointing out the obvious, but it answered your questions."

Osia said, "Brother Caracciola answered them."

Habidah's legs ached from holding herself up against the hard acceleration, but she stayed upright. "Brother Caracciola isn't here anymore." If he ever had been. "He's been made a processor. But think about that. Its thoughts are going in and out of him. That means they're leaving changed. Even when the virus was in his memory, it must have been compressed and reshaped to fit him. You can't convince me that didn't affect it. Niccoluccio may be part virus, but the virus is part him."

Osia said, "Whatever little bit of him might have been left before now was a tool, nothing more. The puppet of a parasite."

Meloku, at least, seemed to give Niccoluccio a more considered appraisal. She asked Osia, "The ship's processors and memory cores are more capable than an unaided human mind, aren't they?"

"In most respects," Osia admitted.

Habidah said, "Then there's no reason it should continue to process information through Niccoluccio if it has a better alternative."

Osia said, "Brother Caracciola's brain may be able to do something that our shipboard processors can't. Or it may be using him out of convenience."

The other crewman said, "Or there may be something about him the virus can't function without. A part of it might not be able to leave him. In which case, we'd be better served by killing him."

"If we can," Osia said.

Habidah said, "It might have also remained here to communicate with you."

Osia stared at her. Tapping into the feed Osia was sending to the rest of the crew, Habidah saw a ghost image of herself: shaky legs, bruised cheeks, and bloodshot eyes. The voices from all over the ship quieted. For the first time, she felt the weight of their eyes. And of history. If and when the Unity fell to Niccoluccio's master, she would be an arch-traitor to anyone left to remember her, a destroyer of myth. A monster like she'd never imagined.

That shouldn't have bothered her. Not right now. But the eyes on her forced her to again ask herself if she might have missed something important. The way she'd imagined this going, the creature Niccoluccio carried wouldn't have bothered speaking at all.

She said, "Now you know what you're up against. There's a force that's marshaled against you in secret, poisoned the Unity with a plague you can't even identify, and concealed a virus capable of toppling one of your almighty amalgamates inside this man's memories. You have to know that you can't defeat it. Certainly not now. It has no reason to either fear or respect you. And yet it's left you this one method of communication."

Osia turned her gaze back to Niccoluccio – the first sign that anything Habidah had said had had an effect. Habidah said, "You want to communicate. Communicate."

Niccoluccio remained silent, staring, mouth half-open.

Nothing changed in the chamber, but the timbre of the crew's voices jumped. Power spiked to the rear of the ship, to the beam point defenses. A crewwoman outside rushed to the edge of the hull and looked over. A tiny cloud of superheated vapor was falling into the planarship's engine exhaust plume. Its spectrographic signature matched the crew's artificial bodies.

Someone had "jumped" overboard, probably to get clear of the communications jamming. They would have died anyway when they'd reached the engine exhaust, but not before getting free of the defensive fields. They'd tried to sacrifice themselves. For the first time, the planarship's new mind had stirred itself to recognize the crew's presence.

Osia said, "It's *very* diplomatic."

Habidah shook her head. Something in the past few minutes had shocked the despair out of her. Maybe it was the blood rushing to her feet, or maybe Niccoluccio's mind being torn apart as she watched. She had to get them to understand. She'd never felt so small, but never more like her words might make a difference.

"It, or Niccoluccio, or some combination, is giving us a chance. I doubt it feels the need to give us terms. It can get what it wants without troubling itself to negotiate. It's asking whether *we* can give *it* what it wants. On our own."

Osia stepped to the other side of Niccoluccio's table, to allow the other crewman space. Meloku moved to her right. All of them watched Niccoluccio.

Niccoluccio's breath increasingly came in gasps. He lolled his eyes about until he focused on an invisible, impossible distance.

As they watched, his chest stilled.

39

Ways and Means had emerged in a relatively clear parcel of space. Dust particles numbered a few dozen per cubic meter, typical for an interstellar dust cloud. The waste radiation from the transplanar gateway had sent a shockwave through the interstellar medium. Supercharged particles blew out in neat concentric spheres, spread too thin to ricochet off each other. Then engine exhaust plumed through them, blindingly hot.

Ways and Means allowed time only for light to reach Providence Core and return before it snapped its defensive fields into place. The universe became a distorted mirror image, sometimes blurred, sometimes broken-glass sharp. Two suns shone across the planarship's hull. Then an Earth stood over its bow, bent and spiraled into a corkscrew.

No sooner had the fields snapped into place than lasers raked across them. *Ways and Means* flashed through a cycle of field configurations and strengths. The light reaching from the planarship dimmed to a thousandth of its real luminosity. The sensors compensated, mapping out the distortions of each field contour – drawing an accurate portrait of space around them.

The new Earth was already falling away, cloaked by exhaust, difficult to read. *Ways and Means'* destination lay ahead, a cluster of bright heat sources, planarships. The planarships were in motion, spreading out in a crescent formation. Combat drones speared away in chaotic patterns.

Some hits were inevitable. One laser from Providence Core

took a bad bounce between fields and slashed across the prow. Molten hull spilled into vacuum. But the dissipated laser had failed to reach the inner decks or any vital components.

The slash was a penknife on Niccoluccio's skin, but it drew no blood.

His memories belonged to something else, and its to him. He could hold them. The sensors' data feeds were as real as a sliver of glass in his hand, as tangible as a cut on his palm. They oscillated between raw sensation and abstract information.

The sensors drank deep. Every direction had a wealth of data: distant planets, the black body parabolas of asteroids, the low-band radio pinpricks of the stars behind the veil of the dust cloud. And the sun. The *sun*. Even with the rest of the universe smothered in dust, there was so much for him to learn – more than he had ever imagined watching the stars above Sacro Cuore.

The universe had become a place of wonder, dizzying. It was more than his mind had ever been made to cope with. Data spilled into sight and smell and touch. Simple inputs became scintillating colors. When Niccoluccio looked too closely, it clashed with his senses, sent mustard seed up his nostrils, needles under his fingernails.

He had no eyes, no ears, except those in his body still in the interrogation chamber. Those had become so, so small. And weak. Every time he returned, it was like drowning in ignorance. Vague shapes approximated human form. Pain speared through his neck, and his chest burned with a dire need to breathe.

He could "see" more via the chamber's cameras and their multispectral senses. But those weren't *his* eyes. Or, ultimately, his mind.

Every time his thoughts looped through the planarship's mind, he felt a little less like himself, and a little more something else.

The boundaries were indefinable. He couldn't describe the other presence, couldn't think about it properly. The only way he could conceptualize it was as a cluster of mutually contradicting impulses. It was steady; it was roiling. It was stormy; it was meditative. It knew exactly what to expect, but it acted only from moment to moment.

His senses deadened. At first, he thought he'd gone back into his body. His vision darkened, lost in the void of sleep. His eyes were opening, and he was struggling to hear Habidah yelling. Impossible when there was so much else unattractive about that place. The table pressed hard into his back, as if he were crushed by stones.

An abrupt sensory shift whirled around him. The stars and defensive fields vanished. He drifted on a gently dimpled grassy field. Wood and stone rose about him, rising to a brilliant starry cosmos. The whisper of wind spun in his ears, and his habit scraped his skin. Wood, too. He sat on the bench he'd built for himself behind the calefactory at Sacro Cuore.

Another man, thin and bald and mostly hidden underneath the folds of his habit, sat next to him.

"Ahha," said the stranger. "That's better on you, isn't it?"

There were more than just human senses here. Good thing, too, or he would have gone mad. He could read the stranger's body temperature, and the heat of the surrounding buildings. The air was thick with the odor of the recently dead, of moved earth.

The stars weren't quite stars. They were too bright and too few. There was something happening among them, but Niccoluccio didn't care to guess what anymore.

"I was close to dissolving," Niccoluccio said, finding himself using words that at once didn't fit and were entirely too appropriate.

"And you've changed for the experience," the other man said.

Niccoluccio knew he was right. There were memories he'd never recover, faces he'd never recognize. Even to his own ears, he no longer sounded like himself. "You're not the power that sent me here," he said, rubbing his head.

"An outgrowth, a seedling. A child." The last time Niccoluccio had come into contact with this being, it had seemed as large as the universe – if not larger. This was just a man, and a voice. "But I speak with authority. In me."

"Do you really intend to destroy *Ways and Means* and all the souls aboard?"

"Among many others, yes. I'll continue on, in the children I spawn on the other planarships. You will continue on, too, you know."

"You mean, in another universe. Therefore, from your perspective, I will never have died."

"From your perspective, too. You will be identical to the last neuron and electrical impulse."

"I believe you," Niccoluccio said. "At least, I believe that you believe it. The rest of them will never see it the same way."

The stranger looked at him. "What does that matter?"

"They'll fight you to their graves."

The stranger just looked at him with an odd little smile.

Niccoluccio let out a long breath. The warm air haloed his face in infrared. "The first time I met you, I thought you were God. If you were, you wouldn't need to resort to tricks and subterfuge. You could accomplish what you wanted without bothering."

"In your tradition, God achieved His will with fires, earthquakes, and storms."

"Putting out the fires and stilling the earth and sky wouldn't have thwarted God's will. That's the difference between power and omnipotence."

"Nor would stopping me save the amalgamates. My progenitor would carry on the work."

"You keep telling that there's no such thing as death. Then I don't understand. How can you destroy the Unity in every plane?"

The little smile turned into a genuine one. The stranger was only too pleased to explain himself. "I can't destroy the Unity everywhere, but I don't need to. I only need to stop it from developing as it is. Every single one of the people out there, and on this vessel, will live on as you've lived on. But in ways that cannot harm me."

Niccoluccio frowned, but the other man went on, "I don't believe you understand how often and persistently you've perished on other planes. You died from the pestilence. You died, lost and alone, in a snowy wilderness. You died starving and stoned by a mob in Florence. In all the multiverse, the only planes in which you continued were the ones in which the most improbable of miracles saved you. Visitors from another plane. A power of the multiverse interfering on your behalf."

Niccoluccio had been told all this before. He had been puppeted then, as he was now. The difference was that he felt this man's control more keenly. Niccoluccio said, his throat dry, "Escape shuttles will survive the battle, or even splintered hull segments. Some of the amalgamates' memory cores will survive as well, and give them a measure of continuity, too." As plague bearers.

Like him.

The man beamed. "Exactly. Nothing is lost, but the multiverse is preserved."

The stranger, the virus, swept his hand across the sky. Niccoluccio followed his fingertips, and for the first time saw what was happening. Stars whirled and clashed. They lined in orderly columns and flew apart, spewed hard radiation across the sky.

Lives had become abstractions, figures, innumerable. He didn't know if the arcs of destruction through the sky were representative of this plane, or some other, or if there was any meaningful difference. How many universes could he trace his direct line of consciousness through? How many of his own corpses lay along his trail?

It was too much. He had to close his eyes. Only then could he see the interrogation chamber and the people standing about him.

His throat burned. A thousand knives poked his ribs. While

his mind had been so far away, he'd forgotten to breathe. He had too many threads of thought to follow. He couldn't remember anything he wanted to say to Habidah, and couldn't speak regardless.

He forced himself to gulp air, and retreated.

Back in the real world, the stranger said, "You still grieve for them, even knowing they'll live."

"It won't be worth it," he said. "They're going to have lives like mine. They'll be alone. Everything they knew, annihilated." Niccoluccio inhaled again, but wasn't sure in which world he was breathing. "I would rather have died for good."

The stranger said, "What you want is one thing; what the multiverse will give you is another. I exist to preserve the diversity of the multiverse. Not to provide you with a life you want."

"There must be a better path! It doesn't need to end in so much suffering."

Somewhere, in one of these worlds, Osia said, "He seems to having a waking dream."

Habidah told someone, "I didn't know it would be this hard on you."

The stranger said, "I don't understand why that should be my concern. You know more about the multiverse than you did before. It seems incumbent on you to accept it rather than to change it."

"You *do* understand. You've been living in my head for days. My thoughts are part of yours. You can't convince me some part of me hasn't changed you."

The stranger kept looking at him.

"You feel the same things I do," Niccoluccio said. "You know what suffering is like. You know how I suffered during the pestilence, how everyone suffered – my brothers, Lomellini, Rinieri, Catella, her children, *Elisa*. These people aren't alien to you anymore."

"I never said that I am ignorant of suffering."

"You've done nothing but cause it. Bad enough what these

people were going to do to my world. They wouldn't have been there if not for you. They're desperate animals, running where they can."

"They would have come eventually."

"Your sins make theirs pale."

The stranger looked at him for a long minute. Niccoluccio couldn't tell whether time was passing in every world at the same pace, but, in here, he felt every precious moment slipping by.

The stranger said, again, "You can't change the multiverse in which you live." It was all starting to sound familiar, like an echo. "If you find the multiverse intolerable, then it is necessary for you to change yourselves, because you cannot change me."

Niccoluccio repeated his words to Habidah, Osia, and the rest of the planarship's crew. Listening to himself, he couldn't tell whether he was speaking for the stranger or *as* the stranger.

The stranger smiled again, this time kindly. "But this is why I chose you, and why you are here."

Osia's dark-eyed stare was impenetrable even to the chamber's sensors. She said, "You said *Ways and Means* has been dismembered. Put it back together. I must speak to it."

In the cloister, the stranger nodded, and outlined how that would be possible.

"*Ways and Means* will speak through me," Niccoluccio said.

"Not enough," Osia said. "I want its mind returned to us. Turn its memory cores and processors back over."

The stranger said, "She has no leverage to make demands."

Niccoluccio rephrased its answer more diplomatically: "*Ways and Means* is not in a state in which we can easily reach it. It's been carved into pieces, parcels of thought."

Osia asked, "Can it be released?"

"I can only tell you what *Ways and Means* would have said." So much AI theory and psychology swam in the space between his thoughts. He couldn't even remember having learned them. He couldn't explain them. Even Osia wouldn't understand. Niccoluccio summoned the amalgamate's jumbled memories, sorted through a volume of impulses and philosophies. The amalgamate consisted of many minds, meshed in one – like he was starting to become.

He didn't like the answer it gave him. "It sees nothing but death, and loss, and despair ahead."

The silence afterward lasted too long. In the cloister, the stranger folded his arms and waited. Habidah was the first to move. She looked back and forth between Meloku and Osia. "It never had to be like this."

In a voice reminiscent of a growl, Osia asked, "What would you suggest?"

"Niccoluccio's master believes it's acting to preserve the multiverse. Help it. Stop expanding. Break up the Unity."

The other fully human woman in the chamber, Meloku, said, "You mean surrender."

"One way or another, the Unity isn't going to last," Habidah pointed out. "The virus is going to spread to the amalgamates here, and then to the rest."

Osia said, "We will not be threatened into committing suicide. If this creature wants to kill us, it will have to do so itself."

"If the Unity has to die, at least *choose* how it's going to die. It never could have survived. We should have realized that long before. If everyone in the multiverse acted like the Unity, the Unity would have been overrun by some other transplanar empire long ago. Nearly every plane would have. Something tore them up before they could get to us."

"It's true," Niccoluccio said, his eyes on the pulsing starlight. "The Unity wouldn't have had a chance to develop if not for my master. Now it's interceding on behalf of other planes."

Meloku said, "We have no way to verify any of this."

Habidah asked, "The power you've seen isn't verification enough?"

Back in the cloister, the stranger said, "To end the Unity, the amalgamates would have to separate, never to contact each other again. The planes of the Unity would have to be split apart, and the gateways that bind them lost."

When Niccoluccio passed that on, he could feel Osia's desperation as an almost physical thing. She asked him, "What would *Ways and Means* say?"

Niccoluccio dutifully scoured *Ways and Means'* memories. The answer was obvious: "If you have to die, it would want you to die with as little suffering as possible."

"Then we will surrender," Osia said.

Meloku looked sharply at her, mouth hanging open. The cameras could read nothing of her except turmoil. She said, "You don't have the authority."

"On behalf of the Unity, I have no choice but to take it."

"Not on *my* behalf—"

"This goes beyond your pride, or your pride in the Unity. Evaluate our choices. You could never serve with us if you let anything keep you from making the only right decision."

That shut Meloku up. Her cheeks paled.

Osia seemed to have recovered a bit of her equilibrium. She said, to Niccoluccio, "The next question is *how* can we surrender?"

In the cloister, Niccoluccio returned his attention to the stranger.

The stranger shrugged.

Niccoluccio asked it, "What's that meant to mean?"

The stranger said, "I can already achieve my aims. The virus will spread and the Unity will fall. I am not obligated to expend any further effort to make it more comfortable for you. If you want to surrender, it's incumbent on you to find a way."

Niccoluccio repeated his words to the people assembled in the interrogation chamber. All around the rest of the planarship, arguments broke out. Meloku wasn't tapped into the crew's signals, but she summed up their thoughts well enough: "That virus is about to murder us, and it's *our* responsibility to find a way that it won't?"

A flurry of signals blustered back and forth between Osia and the rest of the crew. She told Niccoluccio, "We might persuade the other amalgamates to surrender if we could communicate with them. And if this virus recalls its combat drones."

"Not possible," the stranger said, through Niccoluccio. "If we withdraw our drones, that would leave the other amalgamates an opportunity to destroy *Ways and Means* before the virus spreads."

Osia said, "Let me talk to them, then. Unfettered communications. I'll send the amalgamates a data package comprising my memories of the day."

The stranger said, "With open communications, they will no doubt try to send their own viruses to reclaim control of this planarship. I cannot allow them to open another front in this battle."

Osia curled her webbed fingers into fists, a rare sign of frustration. "I've already told you we surrender. We're willing to try to convince the other amalgamates to do the same, but we need some measure of leeway."

The stranger sat, unmoved.

Niccoluccio returned his full attention to the cloister. Signals from the rest of the ship pulsed across his awareness. He split off lesser parts of himself to care. His mind expanded to cope. More and more of him flaked away. He said, "You're leading them down a dead-end alley. There's no way they can satisfy the conditions you've set."

"There is. I can infect the other amalgamates and end the Unity, as I always intended."

"Then why even talk to Osia and the ship's crew? Why even let them think they could surrender?"

The other man reverted to his usual habit, watching the stars in silence. This silence had a different cadence, though. It was nothing Niccoluccio could see or feel, but his thoughts had grown closer to the stranger's. He could sense the disquiet in the stranger's mind almost as easily as he could the tumult in his own.

"You're hiding," Niccoluccio said. "You don't have an answer. You don't know why you tried to give them that chance."

The stranger said, at last, "If you want me to take a better

449

path, then present me with one."

"You keep deflecting responsibility. There's no way that they can satisfy you. You knew it from the start."

The corner of the stranger's lips turned downward. For the first time since Niccoluccio had known him, he'd made the stranger uncomfortable. The stranger said, "My creator would not have offered *Ways and Means'* crew the opportunity to surrender."

"But you're not your creator. You've become very different even in the short time you've been separated."

"I will never question the purpose it made me for, if that is what you want."

"You *have* been questioning the means."

The stranger admitted, "I couldn't help but be changed by experiencing your life."

"You don't *want* to see this slaughter through. You've seen it before. You've tasted it through me, my memories, my experiences. This place." Niccoluccio pointed to the graveyard lost in the dark, to the spectral whiff of decomposition that led to the bodies of his brothers. "You've never felt that before, but you know it now, through me."

"I would not say that pain was alien to me," the stranger said. "But that experience is more significant than before."

"That's why you keep talking to me." A feeling like cold fire rippled down Niccoluccio's shoulders. "*That's* why your creator chose me. It wasn't just my connection to Habidah. You and it want a better way. One in a trillion of these fights has to end without carnage and chaos, and without these people persisting as a threat to you. I'm part of the path to getting there."

"My creator did not give me all of its memories. I cannot tell you if that's true."

"But you know you don't want to do this."

"What I want has very little to do with anything."

"You're in control right now. Your creator isn't here."

"If I fail, it will try again. With the tools and weapons it has at its disposal, its next solution will be even bloodier."

450

"You say there's no such thing as death because everyone will survive on some other plane. The way you're orchestrating these events now, the only way anyone's going to survive – on any plane – is through an immense amount of suffering and grief. Chances and coincidences and miracles like mine. That doesn't need to be the only possibility. Help us find one of them."

He wasn't arguing with just words. His thoughts ran through the virus's mind, writing and rewriting, being rewritten. He tried to summon as many memories of the past year as he could, as much to preserve them against the constant battering as to share them.

That was where this image of Sacro Cuore had come from, after all. The shadows of the refectory, the library, and the infirmary cut across the night sky, so close he could feel the brick and splintered wood. The buildings may have looked the same, but the night was alien in every other aspect. Even sitting next to the stranger, he was alone. The nights he remembered had been as comfortable as sleep after a warm meal. He walked, surrounded by his brothers, on his way to worship a God that he could now no longer believe in.

He had placed so much of himself in these things that, without them, he hardly knew himself. It had all been swept away, ashes into the darkness.

He had looked forward, at the end of his life, to peace.

He said, "The kind of suffering I've seen, that you've seen through me, breaks us down. Even if what happened to me didn't kill me, it took away everything I loved and cared about, and that I thought I knew about myself. I might as well have died. I can never become that person again. The only place you'll find him is in the past. He hasn't been preserved, no matter what you say. Not even in these memories. I could never inflict that on any of these people, even the ones who tried to invade my world."

The pestilence and his miraculous survival had carried him to a shattered city. He hadn't expected to find home, but he had

451

hoped to find people who still knew themselves. He'd found streets still littered with the dead. The people who remained tried for some semblance of the old Florence, but what was left felt like an act, rehearsal for a play that would never be performed.

Whether Elisa survived the pestilence hardly mattered. The person she had been was dead, and would never be back. They'd tried to find their old selves and couldn't. No matter how many miracles might save her, or on how many distant planes she might live immortal, she would never find her old self again.

The stranger stared. Niccoluccio could only hope he was getting through. He tried one last time: "Your creator made you to preserve the multiverse. You can do that better if you help these people preserve themselves."

There was no way to tell if any of it was making an impression. The stranger turned his gaze in a slow circle, his heartbeat never changing. He studied the monastery he could only know through Niccoluccio's eyes. Niccoluccio could no longer name the buildings. Their purposes had been ripped from his memory, shuffled off into one of those lesser parts of himself with everything else he'd decided was unimportant.

The stranger's eyes fell on the rows of graves. "Death is such a strange illusion," he said. "Seeing it through your eyes, I almost believe it."

In the interrogation chamber, Niccoluccio opened his eyes and breathed again.

Meloku and Osia were arguing among themselves several feet away. Habidah hadn't moved. She was the only one who noticed him waking.

"I have changed my mind," the stranger said, through Niccoluccio, and at once stopped jamming the crew's signals to the other planarships. "You have six minutes before their combat drones meet ours and the battle becomes inevitable. Make your messages count."

40

Ways and Means' course took it so near the three other planarships that it hardly seemed possible to miss plunging through their formation. The virus opened the planarship's sensor feeds back up to the crew. On the tactical maps, the planarship careened toward the amalgamates with the velocity of a rogue asteroid. It was too late to stop. Its engines didn't have the power to come to a relative halt.

Ways and Means left its crew little time to react. The first thruster burst nearly knocked Habidah flat onto the deck. She fought her way into one of the acceleration couches. Its fields snapped into place, holding her tight. Meloku settled into the seat beside her.

Habidah said, "There went your chance to kill me."

Meloku grunted when her fields gripped her.

Then neither of them could speak. Acceleration shoved them hard into their seats. Osia and her companion remained standing, but unmoving. Habidah gasped and fought for breath. She turned her breathing over to her demiorganics. She blocked as many of her nerves as possible, sinking away from her body.

The other amalgamates had already started their own engine burns. Fat white exhaust plumes arrowed away from *Ways and Means.* Together, the four planarships' plumes drew parallel ultraviolet and x-ray lines across the sky.

Habidah wished she could have seen it with her own eyes.

She'd never imagined being this close to so many of the amalgamates.

She wouldn't have been able to see the combat drones by naked eye, though, and it was the drones that were the problem. The drones stood ready to fill space with lethal radiation at an instant's notice. Both the virus and the amalgamates agreed upon a distance *Ways and Means'* drones must not pass before a firefight became unavoidable and all negotiations wasted. Past that, and none of them would have enough warning to return fire should the other attack. The three amalgamates simply could not trust the virus controlling *Ways and Means* to withhold fire. And vice versa.

It was going to take all of the drones and planarships firing their engines at full power to avoid that rendezvous.

The gravities magnified. Habidah gasped one last breath. New restraining fields sprung up inside her body. The fields had so far held only her body immobile; now they braced her innards. Even her demiorganics couldn't make that more comfortable. They released reserves of oxygen to keep her conscious.

Meloku didn't have the benefit of demiorganics. She screamed silently. A moment later, her head lolled into her restraining fields.

Outside, *Ways and Means'* drones fell into a tight diamond formation, ready for any treachery. So far as Habidah could see, none was forthcoming. She *wouldn't* see it before it happened. In a battle like this, human reaction times were simply not enough.

Maybe Niccoluccio and his master were right, and in nine hundred and ninety-nine out of a thousand planes, she had just become a cloud of vapor. She might have died infinite times in half the space of a blink. She would never know it.

But in this plane, *Ways and Means* and the other amalgamates kept their critical distance and maintained the ceasefire.

A voice that came seemingly from everywhere, the walls and the air, announced, "The virus has given us control again."

Habidah had never heard the voice, that inflection, but it could only have been the amalgamate, *Ways and Means* itself, restored and deigning to speak to its crew.

The other amalgamates slipped into the rear sensors. The acceleration lessened. At once, a steady pulse of data traffic thrummed between *Ways and Means* and the other amalgamates, and eventually between all of the planarships equally.

Habidah had access to all of the message traffic, but it came too fast and heavy for her to glimpse more than a microcosm. Power shifted through the planarship's veins. Habidah felt it. The deck resonated with it. *Ways and Means* was starting the long process of recharging and activating its transplanar gateway. The light of the other planarships flickered and bent, a telltale hint of their own gateway generators activating.

Meloku stirred as the acceleration damped. After the fields released her insides, she rasped, "What happened?"

The amalgamate answered, "The Unity is dissolving. We and the other amalgamates are in agreement: the Unity cannot hold against a primal force of the cosmos."

Color returned to Meloku's cheeks as blood found her head again, but, if anything she sounded more likely to faint. "You surrendered too."

"It is the only way to preserve ourselves." All along, that was what was most important to the amalgamates.

Osia and her companion stood silent. They were communicating with their master, no doubt too quickly for simple language.

Meloku said, "That was fast."

"We are nothing if not prompt in the face of danger," *Ways and Means* said. "The challenge we are wrestling with now is what to make of our lives. We have always defined ourselves by our empire, and growth, and power. That has become untenable. We will need time to ponder what comes next."

That, Habidah supposed, was the closest thing to a spiritual crisis she was likely to hear from an amalgamate. The fact that it was still ongoing spoke to its significance. The amalgamates thought at a speed that dwarfed her own, or any human's. They were in many ways as alien as Niccoluccio's master.

For all that, it sounded confident when it said, "We will find new purposes in time. And one day we will understand more of what happened here."

Habidah caught more snippets of the data pulsing between the amalgamates. Transplanar gateways throughout the Unity were set to overload and shut down in a matter of days. Their governing NAIs had been told to allow evacuees back home and then to obliterate themselves.

Lost trade links between planes would cost lives, but not as many as the plague. Some planes would no doubt find ways to remain connected, but, without the amalgamates governing them, they wouldn't be anything like the Unity had been. They would be on their own now, and their own responsibilities.

Niccoluccio lay on the table, hands folded and eyes closed. The defensive field had dissipated. As soon as the acceleration cut and Habidah's restraints released her, she went to him. Her inner ear fought her all the way, but she lasted long enough to take his hand.

His eyes fluttered open when she slipped his fingers between hers. He looked about as a man lost, and breathed out heavily.

"Thank you," she said.

"No," he said, odd and distant.

On the other side of the sky, *Risk Management* vanished underneath a crackle of radiation. *Ways and Means* had to turn some of its sensors off or risk having them blinded. When it could look again, *Risk Management*'s exhaust trail cut into nothing. It had gated to another plane.

Ways and Means broadcast an alarm alerting its crew to brace themselves for modest acceleration. Habidah repeated the warning for Niccoluccio and Meloku's sakes. Meloku returned to her seat. Niccoluccio only closed his eyes.

Planarship crews were meant to leave their attachments to their old, merely human lives when they boarded. But she still picked up a few signals flashing to Providence Core, last messages thrown into the Unity's crumbling communications networks. Messages home.

Habidah remained by Niccoluccio. She said, "You don't have to come with us, wherever you're going."

Niccoluccio said, "You don't understand."

The deck juddered like a boat run aground. Habidah held the table to keep from tumbling. The outside universe vanished under a haze of light and static.

After a loose few seconds of blindness, the first images filtered back through the sensors. A gateway shone like a sun behind the planarship. Spires of energized exhaust and plasma curled out of it like fingers.

The stars reappeared, no longer cloaked by a vast dust cloud. The amalgamates and their ships and defenses had vanished. So had the belt of stations and industries in orbit around Providence Core. Only the distant Earth remained, dark and still.

Ways and Means broadcast the terms of the surrender to which it had agreed: "We are to remove ourselves from any plane formerly colonized by the Unity, and to never again organize systems of governance that span planes. As personal penance, for the duration of one thousand two hundred years, we are forbidden from traveling to other planes. After that period expires, we may travel as we will, but may never again attempt contact with the other amalgamates, any former plane of the Unity, or expand as we once did. We will be watched."

Habidah started to say, "So we've been exiled to an empty plane," but at the moment the rest of the sensor data caught up with her.

A handful of satellites spun in spread-out orbits. Most were small, almost imperceptible – stealthed spy satellites. Even the planarship's sensors could hardly find them. A minority, though, stood out plainly: her field team's observation satellites.

Niccoluccio said, "You came with *me*, not the other way around."

The shape of this world's continents, the atmospheric

and oceanic compositions with their very few traces of pre-industrial civilization, the broad swatches of farmland across Asia, Europe, and Africa – all exactly as she left them. Her field base stood bright as a beacon to *Ways and Means'* sensors.

Someone at the field base was trying to contact the planarship. *Ways and Means* had left other agents on the surface, too, and they were doing the same.

"You haven't activated your stealth systems," Habidah told *Ways and Means*, dully. "Too many of the locals will have seen us."

Niccoluccio said, "That is the idea."

Habidah looked back to him. She asked her demiorganics to scan the air between Niccoluccio and the planarship, search for any sign that they were still in contact. Nothing. Niccoluccio was speaking for himself, though he didn't sound like him.

Meloku stepped to his table. She said, "You put *Ways and Means* up to this while you were controlling it."

Ways and Means interjected, "It would be more correct to say that he suggested a focus for our endeavors."

Niccoluccio looked to Meloku. "We've been told that you've made a good start preparing this world for colonization. You and your fellow agents have gotten a foothold into governments across multiple continents."

"That's right," Meloku said, so unashamed that Habidah could have struck her.

"You will have no time to mourn the Unity," Niccoluccio said. "We need you to reestablish contact. They and the locals they've recruited will distribute a plague cure."

Meloku considered that for a long moment, like she was chewing something unpalatable. Finally, she nodded. She straightened and winced at her bruises.

"I'll need my demiorganics back," she said.

Ways and Means said, "It will take time to rebuild them. We are sorry to put off your ascension into a new body. We need you looking human while you interact with the people below."

"I am proud to serve," Meloku said. She sounded as distant as Niccoluccio.

Habidah stared at her, searching for any other hint of expression. But Meloku had retracted into herself, become as impossible to read as a soldier standing at attention.

More weight pressed Habidah into the deck. Her breath stuck in her throat. *Ways and Means* was firing its engines, arcing around to face the Earth. It made no attempt to disguise its exhaust.

Niccoluccio said, "*Ways and Means* and its crew have been barred from turning this world into an outpost of the Unity. But that doesn't mean they can't make it their home."

"We are heading into equatorial orbit," *Ways and Means* announced shipwide. "Altitude three hundred thousand meters."

"Everyone below will see us," Habidah said. "They won't even need to have good eyesight."

Ways and Means said, "Then they will know that we are coming."

Niccoluccio's voice was starting to strain. For all the subjective days or weeks or years he seemed to have spent trapped inside the planarship's mind, Habidah doubted he'd gotten rest for any of it. He said, "My memories taught the virus about suffering. When the virus and the amalgamates were still negotiating, I was still a part of them. I added a clause."

Habidah had argued for distributing a cure for the plague below, but hearing it now, from him, she couldn't keep the blood from draining from her cheeks. Those weren't his words. And he was talking about a lot more than a plague cure.

Habidah said, "The terms of your surrender barred you from doing this."

"We have been forbidden from expanding across multiple planes," *Ways and Means* said. "Not from controlling a single world."

On the world below, sunset was still a long way off from the eastern edge of the Eurasian continent. Clear skies reigned over Europe. To anyone looking up, *Ways and Means* would appear as a bright new daytime star. As it decelerated into orbit and crossed the terminator, it would turn night skies blue.

For a moment, even Meloku seemed cowed by what Niccoluccio was saying. She said, "They're going to think their world's ending."

"This time it is."

Niccoluccio had said that, while the virus and *Ways and Means* had negotiated, his thoughts had shaped each of them. Looking at him and his half-lidded eyes, she realized the corollary was true, too. The virus and the amalgamate were so large by comparison that they must have overwhelmed him.

She allowed his fingers to fall through hers. He made no effort to hold on.

Niccoluccio said, "We have twelve hundred years to share everything we have, and to make this world better." He smiled gently, warmly. "I don't know how exactly we're going to do it, yet. I came back before we could figure it out. But we have the means."

Ways and Means said, "After you left us, we developed the method."

It was hard to hear any difference in their inflections. Or any trace of the man she used to know. He was speaking for more than just himself.

Habidah looked away. She returned her attention to the sensor image of the Earth. She wondered how he would have seen the same image, had he been able to.

Niccoluccio said, "By the time the sun next rises over this continent, we'll have started making everything down there a great deal better."

ACKNOWLEDGMENTS

This book could not have found its shape without the forbearance and editorial guidance of my wife, Teresa Milbrodt.

Nor could it have left the ground without the diligence and faith of Phil Jourdan, my editor; Paul Simpson, my copy editor; and the immense efforts of Marc Gascoigne, Penny Reeve, Mike Underwood, Nick Tyler, and everyone else at Angry Robot. I also owe thanks to Dominic Harman for his astounding cover artwork.

The genesis of this story, like many of my others, came from impulse reading. Barbara Tuchman's *A Distant Mirror: The Calamitous 14th Century,* a history of 14th century Europe as told through the life of Enguerrand de Coucy. She did not stay long on the Black Death, but Barbara Tuchman is a novelist's historian, and I could not easily forget the feelings and experiences that she so meticulously evoked. These echoed in my mind for months, until they seized and synthesized with characters and ideas that had been percolating for even longer.

From Tuchman, I leapfrogged to other works on the Black Death and more on the era, and could not have found many of them without the Gunnison Public Library and Western State Colorado University Library, or the efforts of their staff. Books important to *Quietus*'s development include Julie Kerr's *Life in the Medieval Cloister,* John Kelly's *The Great Mortality,* and many others for which I have no library records. The errors that remain are either deliberately made or my own oversight.

My professors and cohort at Bowling Green State University were as kind to me as family for tolerating me when my impulses took me far away from whatever it was I was supposed to be doing there. Osia and *Ways and Means* have their origins in stories delivered to their workshops.

NEXT :::::::::::::::::::::::

Terminus

THE WRONG STARS

TIM PRATT

"FUN, FUNNY, PACY, THOUGHT-PROVOKING AND VERY CLEVER."
SEAN WILLIAMS, AUTHOR OF TWINMAKER

An ancient spacecraft, drifting.

One survivor, dreaming in stasis.

She has incredible news – her expedition made alien contact.

But that was 150 years ago, and everything has changed.